Gingerly, Polly lifte[...] [...]
erlet, inserting herself [...] it and the feather
mattress. She lay motionless, holding herself away
from the large male body beside her as she tried to
decide what to do next. Neglectfully, her planning
had not taken her any further than this moment. Perhaps she should not do anything, simply wait and see
what happened when her bedfellow awoke. Besides,
it was wonderfully soft and warm in this enclosing
darkness. Her body seemed to be sinking, heavy as
lead, into the welcoming arms of oblivion.

Nicholas became aware of something warm pressing into the small of his back. The sensation seemed
to twine so inexplicably with the rich sensuousness
of his dream that when he moved his hand to identify
the object, and found the bare, silken curve of Polly's
hip, he was not unduly surprised. Until reality exploded.

"Lord of hell!" He yanked aside the bed curtain so
that the pale light of the risen moon could offer
some illumination. The golden eyelashes swept upward. Shock leapt from the deep hazel pools as Polly
stared in utter bemusement into the sleepy, furious
face hanging over hers. Then she remembered where
she was and why. It clearly behooved her to do
something. Instinctively she reached a hand up to
touch his lips, her own mouth curving in a warm
smile of invitation. . . .

Also by Jane Feather:

Vice

Vanity

Violet

Valentine

Velvet

Vixen

Virtue

And coming soon:

The Diamond Slipper

VENUS

JANE FEATHER

Bantam Books

New York   Toronto   London   Sydney   Auckland

VENUS

A Bantam Book / published by arrangement with the author
Originally published under the title *Heart's Folly* by
Avon Books / September 1988
Bantam paperback edition / June 1996

All rights reserved.
Copyright © 1988 by Jane Feather.
Cover art copyright © 1996 by George Bush.
No part of this book may be reproduced or transmitted in any form or by
any means, electronic or mechanical, including photocopying, recording, or
by any information storage and retrieval system, without permission in
writing from the publisher.
For information address: Bantam Books.

If you purchased this book without a cover you should be aware that this
book is stolen property. It was reported as "unsold and destroyed" to the
publisher and neither the author nor the publisher has received any payment
for this "stripped book."

ISBN 0-553-93767-7

Published simultaneously in the United States and Canada

Bantam Books are published by Bantam Books, a division of Bantam Doubleday
Dell Publishing Group, Inc. Its trademark, consisting of the words "Bantam
Books" and the portrayal of a rooster, is Registered in U.S. Patent and
Trademark Office and in other countries. Marca Registrada. Bantam Books,
1540 Broadway, New York, New York 10036.

PRINTED IN THE UNITED STATES OF AMERICA

OPM   0   9   8   7   6   5   4   3   2   1

VENUS

Chapter 1

Nicholas, Lord Kincaid, was in a morose mood—a state of mind not alleviated by his present surroundings. The Dog tavern was situated in a narrow, fetid alley off Botolph Lane and seemed to be frequented solely by oarsmen, scullers, and wherrymen—foulmouthed and deep in drink for the most part.

It was a Wednesday night, in the year of our Lord 1664, and beyond the door the late December fog swirled around the London streets, hung like a miasma over the River Thames running sluggishly a few yards down Botolph Lane. Kincaid could not blame the watermen for neglecting their work on such a night; customers needing passage along the river would be few and far between, and even the most knowledgeable ferryman would be afeard of losing his way in the impenetrable gloom. It was presumably that same murk that had prevented De Winter from making this secure if inhospitable rendezvous.

The sea coal fire in the hearth belched greasy, noxious smoke, and Nicholas coughed in disgust. This smoke that poured from chimneys throughout the city added its own heavy canopy to nature's fog; but when there was a dearth of wood, and fire was a necessity, the townsfolk burnt what was available and affordable.

The smoke haze cleared, and his lordship's watering eyes suddenly focused in incredulous astonishment. A vision had materialized in the dim, dirty, low-ceilinged room. He peered into his tankard of mulled white wine. He'd been drinking liberally enough in an effort to ward off both bodily chills and spiritual depression, but surely not sufficient to create devastating phantoms out of this thin, murky air.

He looked up again. The specter had a definitely corporeal form. It moved toward him, a laden tray balanced easily on a flat palm held high above the throng. Hair like honey, he thought—rich, dark honey flowing over faultless shoulders, straying across the creamy swell of her bosom rising unconfined from the tawdry scrap of lace at the neck of her gown. Exquisite breasts, their beauty not a whit diminished by the garish dress she wore—a costume that was deliberately designed to flaunt every one of her manifold attractions. A grubby petticoat showed beneath the hem of her scarlet skirt, hitched up to reveal the curve of knee and calf, the promise of thigh. The rough clogs could not hide the slenderness of her ankle, the narrow length of her foot.

Nicholas allowed his mesmerized gaze to drift upward again, to take in the wondrous line of her neck, the curve of her upraised arm, finally to rest in stupefaction upon her countenance. A perfect oval, ivory caressed with rose, a wide brow and straight, slim nose, arched eyebrows over glowing hazel eyes whose slight slant was somehow matched by the uptilted corners of a beautifully drawn mouth, the full lower lip promising a depth of sensuality that sent shivers down his spine.

Lord of hell! *What* was such a jewel doing in this malodorous hole amongst louts and river rats? Even as he opened his mouth to articulate the thought, the vision smiled—a comehither smile that rendered him momentarily breathless. Her arm brushed his sleeve as she passed his table, threading her way through the crowd toward the long plank table in the middle of the room. The noisy group of drinkers greeted her arrival with loud ribaldry and straying hands as she bent to place the tray on the table before handing out the foaming wooden tankards.

Nicholas watched the display with a grimace of distaste. The girl was only receiving the usual treatment meted out to tavern wenches; normally he would hardly have noticed; she was dressed to invite it, after all. But the sight of dirty, raw-boned hands groping beneath her petticoats, pawing at that matchless bosom, turned his stomach. And across the small distance that separated them, he could sense the girl's unmistakable revulsion.

Polly fought the usual battle for control, forcing herself to keep still under the pinches and pats, to master the urge to kick and spit and claw as her skin crept with disgust. She must smile and toss her head coquettishly and answer lewdness with its kind, or Josh would swing his studded belt with customary vigor. She could feel the gentleman's eyes on her; somehow that added another dimension to the normal misery, as if a witness to this degrading business could possibly make it worse, she thought bitterly.

"Polly! Get over 'ere, you idle trollop!" The tavern keeper's bellow seemed to shiver the rafters, blasting through the cheery, liquor-fed cacophony of raised voices and laughter. It gave the girl an opportunity to make her escape. She grabbed up the now empty tray and turned to push her way back to the ale-stained counter at the rear of the room. The gentleman was still looking at her with unnerving intensity. Polly tossed her head and smiled at him again, just in case Josh had his eyes on her and might accuse her of neglecting the chance to coax an extra coin or two out of a clearly well-to-do customer.

Josh drained his tankard of porter, wiping his mouth with the back of his hand. His little bloodshot eyes bore a look of satisfaction. He hadn't missed the gentleman's fascination with the wench. It was a look he'd seen on many a young gentleman's face when their eyes fell upon her. Josh could understand it well enough. Lust stirred his own loins with painful urgency whenever he thought of her, thought of her sleeping in the little cupboard under the stairs, her smock caught up . . . Odd's breath! If Prue wasn't such a sour-faced prig, he'd have had the girl long before now! It wasn't as if she was *his* blood kin.

This remembered frustration brought a vicious twist to his mouth, an obscene glint in his eye as Polly came up to him. If he couldn't enjoy those charms for himself, he'd make damn sure they were put to good use. "Get to your aunt in the kitchen and tell her to prepare another tankard of the mulled white wine," he directed. "Prepare it *special,* under-stand!" Polly did understand and felt the familiar dread creep up her spine at the thought of the loathsome task ahead of her. "You give it to the gentleman and make sure 'e drinks it afore ye take 'im abovestairs. He'll 'ave a fat purse, I'll be bound, to say nothing of them stones on his fingers." The obscene leer intensified. "Just you make the right promises, girl, and get 'im on the bed."

"Not again, Josh," Polly heard herself plead, although she knew it was unwise. " 'Tis the second time this sennight."

The back of his hand flashed, catching her across the side of the head. She bit back a cry, rubbing her ringing ear as she stumbled 'round the counter and into the kitchen, where an amazon of a woman with fleshy forearms and gnarled, liver-spotted hands was presiding over bubbling cauldrons. The hot, damp atmosphere was filled with heady fumes, coils of steam wreathing to coat the smoke-blackened beams on the low ceiling. The woman looked shrewdly at the girl, detecting the film of tears in the hazel eyes.

"You angered yer uncle again?"

"He's not my uncle," Polly spat, taking a tankard from a hook in the wall.

"You watch yourself, my girl. If it wasn't for 'im, ye'd 'ave no bed and no food in your belly," Prue declared. "Looked after you, 'e 'as, just as if you was one of his own kin. Instead of a Newgate brat," she added in an undertone.

Polly heard it nevertheless, but she had heard it so many times in her seventeen years that it had lost the power to hurt, if, indeed, it had ever had any. "Josh wants a special," she said listlessly. "In mulled white wine." She handed Prue the tankard.

Her aunt nodded. "The gentleman in the corner, I suppose. Thought 'e was waitin' for someone at first, but if he's on 'is own, 'tis safe enough." She dipped a ladle into one of the aromatic cauldrons and filled the tankard, then began to add spices from an array of little ceramic pots. Polly watched. One of those jars held a powder that was far from innocuous, and as her aunt, in stained apron and grimy cap, mixed and stirred the malevolent draft, to Polly's suddenly fanciful eyes, the bubbling, steamy room came to resemble a witch's kitchen.

Moisture beaded her forehead, and she bent her head to wipe her face with her own far-from-clean apron. There had to be a world beyond these walls; there had to be a way to achieve the ambition that danced, glittering with promise, before her mind's eye during the long reaches of the night. One day she would act upon a very different stage, play a very different role from the one assigned to her in this sordid, circumscribed existence, where the exigencies of poverty were the only determinants, and the hangman's noose the only feared outcome. All she needed was a patron, some rich gentleman who could be persuaded of her talent and would introduce her to the people who managed the theatres. The trouble was that gentlemen with fat purses and possible influence in high places did not often frequent the Dog tavern, and when they did, as with the present prospective victim, Josh had another fate in store for them, one that effectively precluded their offering any assistance to Polly.

She took the tankard from her aunt and returned to the taproom. She was now required to persuade the gentleman into the bedchamber abovestairs, where, thanks to Prue's potion, he would be rendered unconscious to await the thieving ministrations of Josh and his cronies. What happened to him after that was no concern of hers. Her task completed, she would be packed off to seek her pallet beneath the stairs, closing her ears to the thumps and creaks, the muttered imprecations, the scuffings and shufflings in the passage.

Polly looked across the crowded taproom, trying to decide what approach would be best with this particular gentleman. Mostly the gulls were so boorish, so repulsive with their lewd suggestions, insulting in the way they handled her as if she were meat on the butcher's stall, that a delicate approach would be wasted. This gentleman seemed of a different order. He was a large man, certainly, with broad, powerful shoulders and thighs barely contained by his velvet coat and breeches. But the impression was of muscle rather than fat, and the sword at his hip was of plain design, instrument rather than ornament. In a fair fight, Polly decided, he would be a better than even match for Josh and his bully boys.

He wore his own hair, curling richly to his shoulders, the candlelight catching auburn glints, and his eyes were a clear emerald green. She remembered the way they had been fixed upon her earlier, how he had witnessed the way she had been pawed by the revelers at the center table, and a ripple of self-directed disgust ran through her at the impression she would have given him. He was not to know it had all been pretense, necessary if she was to keep on the right side of Josh. Why should she imagine that he, so demonstrably a gentleman, would find anything appealing in the advances of a tavern whore? But then, she didn't have to play the part of a tavern slut, did she? She could be anything she chose as long as she achieved the desired end.

Her chin went up. She would surprise the gull with this performance—intriguing him with the speech and manners of a gentlewoman, even while she made the whore's offer.

Nicholas watched her come toward him. He had kept his seat with the greatest of difficulty earlier when that bullet-headed brute had struck her. Such a spectacle would not normally have interested him in the slightest—a man was entitled to keep order in his own establishment, and if the girl was not his daughter, she was certainly in his employ, as much subject to his authority. But there was something utterly repellent about the idea of such a man holding mastery over that beauteous creature—as repellent as had been the groping hands of the tavern's customers.

"Will you take another tankard of mulled wine, sir?"

Her voice was amazingly sweet, carrying none of the harshness he had expected. The vowels were softly rounded, each word carefully articulated, her speech wildly at odds with the tawdry vulgarity of her dress; but not with the perfection of face and form. She placed the fresh tankard at his elbow. "May I bear you company, sir?" That come-hither smile drew him like a lodestone, and he half rose from his seat as he gestured in invitation to the bench beside him.

"I should be honored." Both the words and the gesture were out of keeping when a man was simply accepting the company of a tavern wench who, it was to be presumed, was as much harlot as serving maid. Nicholas was aware of the absurdity of his courtesy, just as he was aware of the dirt beneath her fingernails, the grubbiness of her dress and apron, her uncombed hair, and the chapped skin of her hands. Yet none of these things seemed to matter, transcended as they were by her amazing beauty, and by her own manner, which seemed to deny such disadvantages utterly. Nicholas Kincaid felt himself bewitched.

"Will you not drink with me?" he asked, smiling. "I hate to drink alone." He put sixpence on the table.

Polly picked up the coin. "My thanks, sir." She went to the counter and drew herself a mug of ale. Josh's sharp eyes had not missed the flash of the coin, and he snapped his fingers imperatively. She handed over the sixpence without protest, although her spirit rebelled. Sometimes she was able to secrete a few coins if they were slipped to her in the throng, but it was a rare occurrence, and her chances of amassing sufficient funds to enable her to make an escape from this hellhole without assistance were minuscule. But such gloomy thoughts were not appropriate to the part she was playing at present.

Polly returned to the gentleman, sitting down close beside him, her eyes glowing with invitation over the rim of her tankard while she waited for him to fondle the breasts pressed so temptingly against his velvet-suited arm, to put a hand on her knee, pushing up her skirt to reach the softness of bared flesh. These preliminaries were not usually long acoming; then the suggestion that they should continue matters abovestairs would follow naturally.

What a crying waste of such perfection, thought Nicholas, drinking deeply of his mulled wine, wondering through his enchantment if he dared risk accepting the invitation. Young though she was, disease was the inevitable concomitant of this life that she led, and he had no wish for a case of the pox. She moved sinuously against him, her fingers whispering across his thigh as her wonderful, sensuous mouth hovered too close to his own for refusal. He yielded with a tiny sigh, his arm encircling her, enclosing the peerless body that melted instantly into his embrace, her lips parting sweetly for his kiss. There was no further question of resisting temptation.

"If you've a mind for a little privacy, sir, we could repair to a chamber abovestairs," the temptress whispered, a delicate blush mantling the ivory complexion as if she were overcome with embarrassment at her temerity in making such an improper suggestion.

Baggage! Nicholas thought, a flash of amusement bringing him back to earth for a moment. A consummate little whore who would play at the innocent maiden! And did so with great skill, he was obliged to admit as a small hand found its way into his with a tentative squeeze. Such pretense of sweet innocence and modesty yielding under pressure added another dimension of entrancement, he found—no ordinary whore, this one; not in face, form, speech, or manner.

Polly glanced covertly into his tankard as she stood up, her fingers twining tightly around his. It was not quite empty, but he had surely taken sufficient for Josh's purposes. Prue laced with a heavy hand.

Nicholas's head buzzed, and he wondered uneasily if he could be overgone with wine. The taproom seemed very hot suddenly, the innkeeper's raddled face, rearing up in front of him, was fuzzed at the edges. But the girl held his hand fast as she led him toward a narrow staircase at the rear of the room, so he shook his head as if to dispel the fuzziness and concentrated on keeping his footing on the stairs.

Polly unlatched the door of the single chamber on the tiny landing. "In here, if you please, sir," she murmured in dulcet tones, curtsying for all the world as if she were ushering him into some palatial apartment. He walked past her into a mean, ill-furnished room, where a tiny fire smoldered sullenly in the grate and the wind whistled through the cracks in the poorly fitting casement. The coverlet on the bed was crumpled and stained; something scurried under a lopsided dresser propped against the far wall. His head swam, and he decided abruptly that he did not feel strong enough for whatever games he had contracted to play in this unsavory place, however desirable his prospective playmate. He reached into his pocket for his purse. She was entitled to payment.

Then his hand stilled; his entire body became motionless as she began to unlace her bodice in a strangely matter-of-fact fashion. In a gesture devoid of artifice, she opened the front of her smock beneath, revealing the full, creamy swell of her breasts, rose-crowned and proudly upstanding. Nicholas sat down on the lumpy flock mattress on the narrow bed. The ropes creaked in protest beneath his weight. His eyelids were inordinately heavy, yet he could not take his gaze off her as the tawdry red dress fell to the floor, to be joined by the grimy petticoat.

Polly stood still, wondering desperately what to do next. She had never been obliged to remove her smock before. The gulls had always lapsed into unconsciousness before she had slipped off her petticoat, yet this one remained awake, and was clearly waiting for the disrobing to be complete. She looked anxiously into his eyes for the dilation and cloudiness that would indicate the potion was about to take effect. The eyes remained fixed upon her; clearly she had no choice. Her hands moved to slide the opened smock off her shoulders.

Nick found himself slightly breathless as she slipped slowly out of the thin garment to stand naked in the cold, dirty chamber. The contrast between their surroundings and that flawless body, glowing opalescent in the flickering light from the oil lamp, was beyond contemplation.

"Come over here." The soft command seemed to shriek in the silence. Polly swallowed, taking a tentative step toward the bed. The room spun suddenly around Nicholas; with a dreadful flash of apprehension he realized that things were not as they should be. Even as she drew close, this amazing creature seemed to flicker and fade before his eyes. "In the name of God!" he exploded, rubbing his eyes in the vain hope that his vision would clear. "What have you done to me?"

To Polly's mingled relief and dismay, he tumbled onto the bedstead. She stepped cautiously over to the bed, looking down at the inert figure. Her task as lure was completed; she should now dress and go back to the taproom, leaving the rest to Josh. What would they do to him? They would not kill him, surely? But she knew that they would. Left alive, he would bring the Watch down on them, and they would all end up at the end of a rope—herself included.

She bit her lip, thinking of the wise man's prayer: Give me not poverty, lest I steal. But she had been dealt poverty in this world of scant justice, and permitting regrets or the voice of conscience was a luxury she did not have. A roar of laughter from the taproom below set the oak boards shivering beneath her feet. It was a timely reminder. Josh would be waiting for her, and if she didn't reappear, he would come in search. Her eyes drifted to the bulge in the gentleman's doublet where he kept his purse. Josh would not miss a guinea. He could not know how much the purse had contained.

Stealthily, she bent over the still figure, her fingers sliding inside the pocket of the velvet doublet.

"So that's your game! *Thieving doxy!*"

The world seemed to tilt; then Polly found herself flat on her back on the bed, staring wide-eyed with shock into a pair of dazed but unmistakably livid emerald eyes.

"You take your payment before rendering the service, is

that it?" His body was heavy on hers, one hand holding her wrists above her head, the other gripping her jaw with a determined force that was not consonant with the drinking of one of Prue's specials.

"You are supposed to be asleep," she gasped with mistaken, ingenuous candor.

"And God help me, I deserve to be!" he muttered. "Of all the dupes! To be taken in by such a trick in a place like this." Nicholas did not know why the feel of those probing fingers had penetrated his torpor, but he did know that he must fight the continuing creeping insensibility with his last ounce of strength—both mental and physical. Anger was a powerful aid as he examined that beautiful, deceitful countenance, the enormous glowing eyes leading him into a green-brown land of promise, the sensual mouth slightly parted over perfect white teeth. The soft body moved beneath him, bringing the image of her nakedness to vibrant life. Lust was also a powerful force, particularly when combined with fury. "This time you provide the service *before* payment," he said, bringing his mouth to hers.

Polly writhed and twisted beneath a ravaging assault; the buttons of his coat bit into her softness; the velvet seemed to rasp against her skin. And threading through her panic was the infinitely terrifying thought that Josh and his cronies would arrive at any minute, would find her naked . . . would find their victim in possession of his senses . . . She did not know which thought was the more hideous. She had not waited for the gentleman to finish his mulled wine, and to that extent she was responsible for the failure of the plan. But Prue must have miscalculated, also.

"Please!" She fought free of his mouth. "You do not understand."

"Understand!" Laughter cracked in sharp derision. "I understand that I am buying what you promised to sell."

"But I did not promise . . ." Polly's voice faded as she realized how pointless and unconvincing was her defense. She had always known that one day her luck would run out; one day she would not be able to protect herself; one day would come the unvanquishable assault on a maidenhead that she had so far managed to preserve against all the odds, knowing that its possession was the only thing that set her apart from the ranks of dull-eyed slatterns who peopled her world. Lost virginity led to a swollen belly, to the pox, to the hopeless, self-perpetuating cycle of rape and childbirth, broken only by the grave. Once she had started upon that road, there would be no turning back, no possibility of theatres and stages and applauding audiences—no possibility of a future.

But if the time had come, then perhaps it was better at the hands of this man, who might have some delicacy, than for a few pennies with one of the hardhanded, foul-mouthed customers belowstairs. Her struggles ceased. "Do not hurt me," she whispered.

Nicholas stared down at her. "Hurt you! Why should you imagine I would do such a thing?"

Two large tears rolled hotly down her cheeks. "It hurts to breach the maidenhead, does it not?" Her voice was small, her face set.

Nicholas took a deep breath, struggling with the sense of unreality that seemed to have transcended the physical confusion brought about by whatever had been slipped into his drink. Since when was a tavern whore in possession of her maidenhead? "You would have me believe you are a maid?" he demanded incredulously, releasing his hold. He got off the bed and stood looking down at her as she lay sprawled on the coverlet. She seemed to be quite unconcerned at her nakedness, almost as if she had forgotten it, he thought, trying to shake his head clear of bewilderment.

Polly nodded, sitting up. "I am only supposed to bring the gentlemen up here," she explained. "They always fall asleep before they can—"

"And then you rob them?" he interrupted harshly, seeing nothing to contradict in her statement. It was extraordinary to think that she had preserved her innocence throughout this fraud, but not an impossible feat in the circumstances she had described and he had experienced.

"Not I," she corrected, as if it could possibly make any difference to her degree of guilt. "Josh and his friends."

"And then what happens?" He began to pace the small chamber in an effort to keep the fog at bay. The girl did not reply. He swung 'round on her. *"And then what happens?"*

She shook her head, eyes wide with appeal. "I do not know."

"Liar!" He caught her chin, forcing her to meet his eyes. "You are a liar, a thief, an accomplice to murder." And all that malefice was contained in a form so beautiful that it almost defied belief. He turned from her in disgust.

"No, you cannot go downstairs." The urgent whisper arrested him as he put his hand on the latch. "They will not let you out of here alive." Polly jumped from the bed, catching his arm. "There is a cupboard on the landing. If you hide there until they come up, then you can slip down the stairs when they come in here."

"You expect me to hide from a pack of river rats?" he exclaimed, drawing his sword in one easy movement.

"There are six of them," she said. "You may be brave as a lion, but against such odds—" She shrugged and turned from him, bending to pick up her smock from the floor.

Her buttocks and thighs were bruise-tinged, the deep purple of fresh contusions overlaying the yellow of old hurts. Nicholas saw again the vicious Josh, his great red hands raised against her, the obscene glint in his little eyes. The anger ran from him. What right had he to judge this girl for whom violence was an inextricable part of daily living? She did only what she was compelled to do, and life was cheap in these back slums.

"And what will happen to you?" he asked quietly. "I doubt you could take another beating so soon after the last."

Polly flushed. She had forgotten about the welts. Hastily, she pulled on her smock. "He only does it 'cause he wants to do the other." Amazingly, an imp of mischief danced suddenly in her eyes. "But Prue won't let him. Says she's not about to share her husband with a chit of a girl she's brought up from babyhood, and she'll cut it off if he tries anything with me." A tiny chuckle escaped her, despite the desperation of the moment. "She would, too. She's bigger than he is."

Nicholas could feel his own mouth curving in response. She did have the most infectious smile, even when, as now, it was one of pure mischief, with none of the come-hither quality of before. But then, that particular smile had been intended to deceive; this variety appeared to be without artifice.

Heavy footsteps sounded on the stairs, and all desire to laugh fled. Polly went as white as milk as Nicholas, sword drawn, whirled to face the door. The door was flung back on its hinges to reveal Josh and five burly men ranged behind him, all armed with cudgels.

Why would they need cudgels if their intended victim was supposed to be unconscious? Nicholas wondered with dispassion, moving backward to give himself maneuvering space. They'd probably enjoy bludgeoning him to death before dropping him in the river, he reflected, still dispassionate.

"Get out of here, girl," rasped Josh. "I'll deal with you later." He advanced on Kincaid, the others fanning out behind him in the small chamber. Nicholas wouldn't have a chance. His sword flashed, catching Josh's arm as he raised the cudgel. Blood dripped from the cut; the tavern keeper roared like an enraged bull, bringing the cudgel down with full force. Nicholas jumped aside, and the club just missed shattering his arm; but he was almost against the wall now. There would be nowhere to jump the next time.

A sudden blast of freezing air filled the room, setting the sullen coals in the hearth to hiss and smoke. Someone had opened the casement at his back. "Quickly!" Polly's anguished cry from behind told him who to thank for that piece of quick thinking. He relinquished all vainglorious thoughts of fighting to the death to preserve the honor of the Kincaids. There'd be no honor in the demise that awaited him here, beaten to a pulp like a rabbit in a harvested field. He leapt backward onto the broad stone sill, keeping his assailants momentarily at bay with rapid thrust and parry of his sword, desperation lending him both speed and strength. Then he consigned himself to the air, jumping backward into the unknown.

He landed with a jarring thump. But he had landed on earth, not stone, and for that he could be grateful. The cold air, combined with the tension and excitement of the last few minutes, cleared his head miraculously. He blinked, trying to accustom himself to the darkness. The men would know how to find him, and since he didn't know where he was, he could not know how to remove himself from this insalubrious neighborhood.

"Catch me!" a now familiar voice called in a desperate plea. He looked up to see Polly in her white smock poised on the sill. A hand reached to seize her waist; with a wild shriek she kicked herself free before tumbling, unbalanced, from the window. Nicholas managed to break her fall, although she knocked him to the ground again, and he wasted desperate seconds trying to disentangle himself from her flailing limbs, swirling hair, and the folds of her smock.

The sounds of confused bellowing from above ceased abruptly. "Quick," Polly said. "They are coming downstairs." She grabbed his hand, tugging him into the shadowy darkness, away from the lamplight of the window. "This way."

Nicholas opened his mouth to protest, then closed it again. So he was going to run through the streets of London on a foggy, freezing December night in the company of a barefoot tavern wench wearing nothing but her smock! It seemed a fitting enough conclusion to such an evening.

Chapter 2

~~~~~~~~~~~~~~~~~~~~~~~~

Nicholas had no idea where Polly was guiding him, but she was fleet of foot, showing no hesitation about their direction, so he followed where she led and saved his breath for running. The sounds of pursuit, at first alarmingly loud behind them, finally faded; the racing figure beside him turned yet another corner onto another narrow alley and came to a fast-breathing halt under an archway.

"They'll not find us now." Her breath came on a sob; she shivered as the heat engendered by movement abated and the freezing air whipped her smock against her body.

"God's good grace!" her companion exploded softly. "Are you crazed, girl? To come out like that!"

"Had I stayed for my clothes, I would not have come out at all," was the tart rejoinder. "And had I not done so, they would have caught you easily. There is only one way out of that garden, and ye'd never have found it in the dark." She hopped from one foot to the other. The mud in the alley was frozen in hard ridges, and her feet were rapidly becoming numb.

"Just what do you intend doing now?" demanded Nicholas, shrugging out of his coat. "Put this on."

"Coming with you." Polly went on to inform him blithely of the part he was to play in her life. The idea had hit her with the blast of cold air from the opened casement, complete and perfect—the opportunity she had sometimes despaired of being given. It would require a little cooperation, of course, but surely he would be happy to take what she could offer in exchange. Men were not in general indifferent to her charms—an interest that so far had been nothing but a burden, but in this instance could be put to good use. Wrapping the coat around her shoulders, she stroked the sleeve, wonderingly. "I've never worn velvet before."

"What do you mean, you're coming with me?" He looked at her uneasily.

"Well, I can't go back, can I?" she pointed out with impeccable logic. "Josh'll kill me . . . if Prue doesn't first." Her dance on the frozen mud became more vigorous. "Besides, I saved your life, so now you can be my . . . my . . ." She searched for the right word, then found it. "Protector," she finished triumphantly. "Or do I mean patron? Actors have patrons, don't they? But I suppose, if I am to be your mistress, then you would also be my protector. Anyway, either will do."

"Either will *not* do!" Nicholas, unable to make head or tail of this assured statement, stared at the prancing figure swathed in velvet. "May I remind you that it was you who made the saving of my life necessary in the first place?"

"Ah," Polly bit her lip. "I suppose that is true. But what am I to do? I cannot become an actor without a patron. I have been waiting for one forever. And now you have turned up so fortuitously—" A violent sneeze brought an end to this confusing recitation, returning Nicholas to his senses. She was going to freeze to death if he left her here, if she had not already contracted an inflammation of the lungs. He didn't want her death on his conscience—time enough when they found shelter to decide what to do with her.

"Where are we?" He peered into the murk, but could see nothing familiar.

"Near Gracechurch Street," was the prompt reply. "Cornhill's up that-a-way." She pointed ahead. "We'll mayhap find a hackney there. If there's a jarvey

willing to ply his trade on this filthy night." He glanced
down at her bare feet. "Can you walk that far?"

Polly shrugged. "Have to, won't I?" She began to run up
the lane—an extraordinary figure in underdress and a gentleman's coat, that honey hair streaming in the wind. He'd
be lucky to find a jarvey willing to take such a motley creature, Nicholas reflected gloomily. She looked as if she'd escaped from Bedlam! Mind you, he was beginning to feel as if
he had done so. He set off at a brisk walk in her wake.

There were few people abroad to witness the strange pair,
but Nicholas, alert for footpads, kept his hand on his sword
hilt and his eyes peeled for a sight of the Watch, unsure how
he would explain matters should he be challenged. They
reached Cornhill, where Polly stopped. She dashed a hand
across her eyes—a gesture that did not escape Nicholas,
coming up beside her. It was too dark to see the extent of
her distress, but her posture had lost its previous jauntiness.
He looked anxiously up the street. Not even the lantern of a
linkboy showed through the fog.

"Lord of hell! You could at least have brought your
shoes!" The irritable mutter produced a gulping sound from
his companion, but he was too worried about her physical
state to care overmuch about wounded sensibilities. Then
the sound of hooves pierced the dark. Nicholas stepped into
the street. A coach lantern wavered, its light a will-o'-the-
wisp in the fog-dark. He ran toward the vehicle, praying that
it was a public hackney so that he would not be obliged to
throw himself on the mercy of some late-night traveler, who
would be justifiably suspicious of an apparently benighted
gentleman and a half-clad female.

"Wha' y'want, then, foin sir?" The muffled figure on the
box swayed, his words slurred. "Foul night to be abroad."
He raised a bottle to his lips and drank deeply, hiccuping.

"Your services," said Nicholas briskly, pulling open the
coach door. He turned to yell for Polly before the jarvey
could whip up his horses and take off without them, but she
was right beside him. He bundled her inside. "A guinea for
you if you can take us to Charing Cross, man."

"Ah'm for me bed," the coachman protested in spite of the promised largess. "Wrong direction."

Nicholas put his foot on the step to the box and sprang nimbly up. "Either you drive us, or *I* do!" The menace was so clear in both voice and stance that the jarvey, muttering ferociously, turned his horses.

Polly sat in the pitch darkness of the frowsty interior, where the smell of onions and unwashed bodies mingled in a noxious bouquet with stale beer and fusty leather. She chafed her sore, frozen feet as the carriage swayed and jolted over the cobbles under the direction of its inebriated driver. There was a time when the vehicle lurched violently, and she fell onto the floor. An enraged yell came from the box, followed by a significant thump. She struggled back onto the seat, pulling aside the scrap of leather curtain that shielded the unglazed aperture serving as window.

"Sir?" Her voice quavered as she craned her neck to peer up at the box. "Is everything all right?"

"That rather depends upon how you define all right." His voice drifted down through the darkness. "Our friend here has finally succumbed to persuasion to yield up the reins."

There was something infinitely reassuring about the dry tone, and Polly withdrew her head, wondering what form the persuasion had taken. At least the motion was rather less erratic now, but the pain in her feet, as sensation returned, brought tears to her eyes. Secure in her isolated darkness, she made no attempt to stop them, and they rolled down her cheeks as the events of the evening took their inevitable toll.

Nicholas accorded the motionless figure of the jarvey, slumped on the box beside him, a brief glance now and again as he turned the horses from Fleet Street onto the Strand. It had required little more than a tap to render him unconscious, and he would be well paid for the indignity once Lord Kincaid had attained the comfort and security of home.

Home was a large house in a quiet street off Charing Cross. Like its fellows on the street, the windows were in darkness at this hour of the night, although a lantern burned,

hanging from an iron hook set into the stone pillar beside
the door. Margaret would have been abed these past two
hours, Nicholas knew, which, perhaps in the circumstances,
was all to the good. He did not feel like explaining his unorthodox companion to his straight-laced sister-in-law, or indeed, to anyone at this juncture. Springing off the box, he
opened the carriage door.

"Are you still in there?"

"I cannot imagine where else I would be." It was a brave
attempt at a light response, but tears were heavy in her voice.
"Where are we?"

"At my house," he replied, holding the door. "Come."

Polly stepped out of the carriage, forgetting her sore feet
for the moment in her fascinated contemplation of her surroundings. This was not the London she knew, which was a
city of plaster and lath buildings on narrow, crooked streets,
the gables protruding so far over the lower floors that they
formed a roof across the lanes. Here, the light from the lantern showed her a broad, paved thoroughfare and a mansion
of warm brick and white stone. Polly did not think she had
ever seen so many windows in one building. The gentleman
must be a very important man, as well as a rich one, to have
a house with so many glazed windows. Her luck had certainly turned. On one thing she was resolved—this opportunity was not going to slip through her fingers. She was going
to stick closer than his shadow to this influential gentleman
until he had helped her to achieve her goal.

Nicholas missed the speculative, determined look she gave
him; he was too occupied with the insensible jarvey, who
seemed to have lapsed into stertorous sleep and was like to
freeze if left to sleep off his intoxication. A night standing
still on the street would not do the horses much good, either. At last he managed to get some sense out of the man,
although he appeared to have no recollection of the past
hour or of what had led him so far from his usual beat. He
pocketed the two guineas Nicholas, troubled by conscience,
gave him, clicked his tongue at his horses, then slumped
back against the seat as the carriage moved off. Trusting that

the beasts would know their own way home, Nicholas turned back to his other, rather more bothersome, responsibility.

She stood huddled in his coat, her face white and tear-streaked—a fact that did not appear to mar her beauty in the least, Nicholas thought distractedly; it simply aroused in him an overpowering desire to take her in his arms. She was rubbing one bare foot alternately against the other leg in a futile effort to reduce their exposure to the frozen ground. Nicholas swung her into his arms, telling himself that it was simply the practical solution to her problem.

"Oh!" Polly said in surprise. It was not at all an unpleasant sensation for one who had never before been offered a helping hand in the seventeen years of her existence. "Am I not heavy?"

"Not excessively," replied her bearer with credible insouciance. "Sound the knocker."

Polly grasped the heavy brass door knocker, banging it vigorously. The sound of bolts scraping followed almost immediately, and the door swung open at the hand of a young footboy whose sleep-filled eyes and crumpled livery bore witness to his inability to stay alert while waiting up for his master's return.

"You may go to bed, Tom," Nicholas said, walking straight past him, ignoring the startled stare at the bundle in his arms.

"Yes, m'lord," the lad muttered as Nicholas strode to the stairs.

"Are you a lord?" his burden asked, realizing with a slight shock that despite the intimacies they had shared, she did not know his name. If he was, indeed, a nobleman, then he would be even better placed to help her than she had hoped.

"As it happens. Nicholas, Lord Kincaid, at your service." She chuckled at the absurdity of this dry formula of introduction, and he looked down at her, recognizing that same infectious smile that had so entranced him earlier. He had intended sending her up to the attics to find a bed with the servants, but they would all be asleep, the place in darkness, and she was still chilled to the bone, not in a fit condition to explain herself to strangers—even if a reasonable explanation could be found. With a half shrug, he entered his own chamber, where a fire glowed in the hearth and the soft light of wax tapers in a many-branched candlestick offered a welcoming light.

Polly gazed, awestruck, at the luxury of the huge feather bed with its embroidered hangings and carved bedposts. "The walls are painted!" she exclaimed as he set her on her feet. She ran across the smooth, waxed oak floor to examine the scenes and designs delicately worked in blue and gilt on the wooden paneling. "How pretty." Suddenly the image of her straw pallet in the airless cubbyhole beneath the stairs at the Dog tavern rose vivid in her mind. How could there be such contrasts in the same city? The delight and excitement in her novel surroundings withered, and the cold, miserable exhaustion she had felt in the carriage returned.

Nicholas saw the shiver and the quick turn of her head as if she would hide something from him. He went over to the bed, bending to pull a truckle bed from beneath. "You may sleep here tonight. Margaret will know what to do with you in the morning."

At that she swung round. "Who is Margaret?"

"The lady of the house," he responded.

"Your . . . your wife."

"My brother's widow. She keeps house for me."

Polly wondered why the information should be such balm. "I do not wish her to do anything with me in the morning," she informed him. "With you as my patron, I will be introduced to Master Killigrew at the king's playhouse, and he will see what a good actor I am." She sat on the truckle bed, massaging her feet. "Then, if you do not wish to continue being my patron, once I am established I will find someone else. It is usually so, is it not?"

Nicholas felt his jaw drop. It was not as if the plan was extraordinary. Since the king had decreed three years ago that only women should play female parts in the theatre, the young and attractive, talented and not so talented, had chosen the stage as offering the shortest path to a noble husband or a wealthy keeper. There were men aplenty, both rich and noble, eager to pay whatever was required, not excluding marriage, for the attentions of the most desirable of these frail creatures. Nicholas was in little doubt, also, that one look at this ravishing girl, once she had acquired a measure of polish, and Thomas Killigrew, who managed the king's company, would not care whether she was accomplished or not—and neither would the audience. Indeed, it was not inconceivable that if she played her cards aptly, this erstwhile tavern wench from Botolph's Wharf could find her way, via some nobleman's bed, into the intimate circles of the court of King Charles.

And then the idea hit him—brilliant in its simplicity. What if she could be steered into one particular circle—into Buckingham's circle, to be precise—where she would hear certain things, things that she could be encouraged to divulge to Nick's own faction? Could they possibly make an unwitting spy out of this exquisite vision who had materialized so serendipitously out of the fetid fogs of the back slums? A frown buckled his forehead. He would need to tread very carefully. She would have to be groomed for the part and maneuvered in the right directions. He would put it to De Winter and the others, but in the meantime she could not be permitted to move prematurely.

"It is possible that we may be of service to each other," he said carefully. "However, if you wish for my assistance, you must agree to put yourself in my hands. You may have to do things that you do not care to, at first, but you must promise to trust me, and do as I bid."

Polly looked puzzled. "I do not understand why there should be difficulties. You have only to introduce me to Master Killigrew in the morning. I will do the rest myself."

"No," he said, firmly and decisively. "It is not as simple as that." His eyes narrowed as he saw that beautiful, sensuous mouth harden. "Do you know your letters?"

A tinge of color touched the high cheekbones. She shook

her head, dropping her eyes to her lap. "Books and teachers have not come my way, sir."

"Hardly surprising," he replied matter-of-factly. Learning was an unusual accomplishment for most women, and unheard of for either sex in the world where she had dwelt hitherto. "But how can you expect to become an actor if you cannot read a part?"

"I have a good memory," she said a little truculently. "If someone reads the lines to me, I will remember them."

"And you imagine that someone is going to be prepared to devote that amount of time to an inexperienced slip of a wench?" He allowed a faint note of derision to creep into his voice and saw her flush deepen.

"Then I will teach myself. If you will lend me a book, I am sure I will be able to learn." The note of confidence rang true, and Nicholas wondered if this was another of the actor's tricks, or if she genuinely believed it.

"It will be quicker and easier if you have a tutor," he pointed out mildly. "I will undertake the task in exchange for your agreement to abide by my decisions." It would also give him the opportunity to assess the quickness of her wit, he reflected. If she was as intelligent as he suspected, the task ahead of them, in all its manifestations, would be greatly facilitated.

"What is it that you wish me to do for you in return?" Polly asked with slightly unnerving directness. "You said we would be of service to each other." Slipping his coat from her shoulders, she stood up and began to open her smock. Her fingers shook slightly, but he had seen her naked already, so any embarrassment was surely ridiculous. "Do you wish to lie with me now?" This was the exchange she had expected—her virtue for his patronage. And she would count her fiercely protected innocence well lost, the currency that would buy her access to ambition.

Nicholas knew that he did want her—very much. And that if she removed her smock again, revealing that peerless body, he would be lost. Circumstances had intervened the last time, but there would be no disturbances in his own house, his own bed, and the task he had assigned himself was sufficiently complicated without added entanglements. "No, I do not for the moment," he denied, his voice a trifle thick. "I think you should get into your own bed quickly." He wrenched his eyes away from the temptation of her breasts and walked over to a low table where reposed a decanter of brandy.

"Do you not find me desirable?" She sounded surprised, and a little disconsolate. "It is not the case, in general."

He whirled on her. It was a mistake since she now stood quite naked, glowing and perfect in the lamplight. "You said you were a maid?" he rasped.

Slowly she nodded, the honeyed river of her hair pouring over her shoulders. "I am, but many men have wished . . . have tried—" Her shoulders lifted in an expressive movement. "Prue stood my friend in that, else I'd have succumbed to rape long since. When I have taken the gulls abovestairs, they have always fallen asleep almost straightway."

Gulls! Nicholas winced at the appropriate term. He had been gull enough to fall for that beauty and the accomplished performance. He tried to look at her dispassionately as she stood before him and found that he could not. He tried to find anger, but there was none. This exquisite creature, who talked so matter-of-factly about her narrow escape from rapine brutality, had been sufficiently bruised and battered by life's ferocity.

It was an effort, but he managed to turn back to the brandy decanter. He filled two glasses. "Put on your smock and get into bed." He waited with averted back until a rustle and a creak indicated that he had been obeyed, then he turned and brought one of the glasses over to the truckle bed. "This will warm you."

Polly took the glass of Venetian crystal; never before had she handled anything so delicate or so precious.

"Where did you learn to speak as you do?" Nicholas asked casually. It was a question that had puzzled him, but he also hoped that a change of topic would deflect the awkward intensity that had sprung up between them.

Polly sipped her brandy, a thoughtful frown creasing her brow. "Speak like 'ow? Oi speaks awrigh', dun Oi?"

Nicholas laughed, and she smiled mischievously over the lip of her glass. "You are an impertinent jade, Polly. Answer my question."

"Prue used to be in service with a parson in the country. Long time ago, before she married Josh. They let her keep me with her, although I was too young to work. No one really noticed me much. I used to hide in the corners and listen to the gentry talking. Then I'd practice to make the same sounds." She chuckled. "I'd make the folk in the kitchen laugh when I mimicked the master and mistress, and then I'd get an apple tart or something, so I learned to do it all the time. The family, and any visitors . . . I'd just listen for a bit, then I'd have it perfect." Her shoulders lifted in a tiny shrug. "Then, of course, Prue had to go and wed Josh. We came back to London, and no one thought it at all funny that I could speak like that—quite the opposite. It used to make Josh madder than a cornered fox. So I stopped."

A perfectly simple explanation, Nick thought, seeing in his mind's eye a lonely little girl of whom no one took any notice, slipping in and out of shadows, listening and observing, performing party tricks for attention and an apple tart. It was not a happy picture. "Prue is your kin?"

"My aunt." Polly drained her glass, holding it out to him. Her eyes closed, and she swayed a little. "I seem to be falling asleep." She slid down the bed, drawing the covers up to her chin. "I was born in Newgate. They were going to hang my mother, but she pleaded her belly, so she was sentenced to transportation instead. Prue took me as soon as I was born, and my mother was sent to the colonies."

There was silence, broken only by the hiss and pop of the fire. Kincaid replaced the Venetian glasses on the tray. It seemed an eon since he had walked into the Dog tavern for his rendezvous with Richard De Winter. It would be dawn in another hour; before then he had to concoct an explana-

tion for the presence in his chamber of this ravishing Newgate brat—an explanation that would satisfy Margaret, who
ruled her household with a now unfashionable Puritan's severity.

The Lady Margaret first heard of the night's strange doings
from her maid, when she brought her mistress her morning
draft of chocolate. "A wench?" she demanded, sitting up in
bed and straightening her nightcap. "Lord Kincaid brought a
wench to the house?"

"So young Tom says, m'lady." Susan bobbed a curtsy, her
demure expression hiding the inner excitement. There
would be a mighty explosion over this, and the entire household was waiting with bated breath. The master did not
share his sister-in-law's Puritan inclinations, and indeed, was
known to mind his lust and his pleasure with the best at the
court at Whitehall Palace. But he had some consideration for
the Lady Margaret and, in general, kept those activities of
which she would disapprove out of the house. Although
undisputed master of the house and all within it, he had been
hitherto content to leave the management entirely in his
sister-in-law's hands, as long as a fair table was kept and
matters ran in decent order so that he need never be afraid
for the hospitality he would offer his guests.

Margaret sipped her chocolate, torn between the desire to
hear all that the maid had to tell her and the knowledge that
listening to servants' gossip was bad for household discipline.
"And where is the girl now?" she asked, with an assumption
of casualness.

There was an instant's silence as Susan bent to poke the
fire. "No one's seen her, m'lady." She hesitated, then continued boldly, "But Tom says that his lordship carried her
into his bedchamber." Susan kept her back to the bed, afraid
that if there was an explosion of wrath, she might receive the
overspill. Her statement could be considered insolent in its
forwardness, and Lady Margaret corrected insolence with a
supple hazel stick.

"I will rise," announced her ladyship, sending Susan bustling to the armoire.

Since it would never occur to Lady Margaret to show herself outside her chamber in even the most respectable undress, it was an hour later before she deemed herself ready. Her graying hair, free of curl, was confined beneath a lace coif. A wide lace collar adorned the kirtle of black saye that she wore beneath a sober gray silk day gown. Not a touch of color lightened the Puritan severity; the unimpeachable lace was her only decoration.

Eyes followed her measured progress down the corridor to her brother-in-law's chamber, but the owners kept themselves well hidden in doorways, or apparently busy with some domestic task that had brought them into the upper regions of the house. The house itself seemed to hold its breath as her ladyship rapped sharply on the oaken door.

This imperative demand for entrance brought Polly awake in the same instant that Nicholas pushed aside the bed curtains, irritably bidding the knocker enter. As his sister-in-law rustled in, his eyes fell on the occupant of the truckle bed; memory returned. He groaned inwardly. Margaret's eyes held the fanatical light of battle, and he had fallen asleep before he had time to concoct either explanation or a plan of action.

"I did not believe it possible," Margaret said, an extended forefinger shaking in accusation, her eyes blazing with righteous fury. "That you would bring a whore into this house—"

"I am no whore!" Polly protested indignantly before she had time to consider whether a discreet silence might be wiser. "You do not have the right—"

"Quiet!" thundered Nicholas, pressing a hand to his temples. The effects of mulled white wine, whatever potion had been intended to render him unconscious, and too little sleep were now combined to produce an appallingly dry mouth and a splitting headache. "Before you accuse, sister, you might wait for an explanation. You do not see the girl in my bed, do you?"

Margaret turned her full attention to the occupant of the truckle bed. Her mouth opened on a slight gasp. The girl's beauty was undiminished by her tumbled hair, sleep-filled eyes, and clearly indignant expression. Such beauty, in Margaret's opinion, could only be the devil's gift, sent to lead the unwary into temptation. The wench was bold-eyed, too, meeting Margaret's scrutiny, unflinching. It was not a reaction to which that lady was accustomed. Lowered eyes were the rule in her household when meeting the inspection of the mistress. She was dirty, too; her smock begrimed, black beneath her fingernails, her hair bedraggled, dark with dirt.

The Lady Margaret made rapid assessment, concluding that whether the girl be trull or no, her brother-in-law had not enjoyed her favors—not yet, at least. He tended to the fastidious.

"She's but a child, Margaret," Nicholas said in soothing accents, gauging his sister's reaction with a degree of accuracy. "An orphan. I found her last night in some danger of her life, through no fault of her own, and bethought me that you said Bridget was in need of a kitchen maid. You would not be so uncharitable as to deny her houseroom." It was a shrewd stroke. The Puritan, while she could be narrow and hard, could not permit herself to be thought uncharitable, although the charity she would offer would not necessarily be of a kind that suited the recipient.

"But I do not wish to be a kitchen maid," Polly expostulated. "I wish an introduction to—"

"Do you remember what we agreed?" Nicholas interrupted swiftly. If Margaret got wind of Polly's theatrical ambitions, she would cast her into outer darkness without compunction. The theatre was the devil's breeding ground!

Polly thought of being able to read and write, of a world far away from taverns and the grasping hands of drunkards, from Josh's belt and the obscene leer in his eye. She thought of the now-broken circle of her allotted destiny, and she kept silent.

"How is she called?" Margaret asked, directing the question at Nicholas.

"Polly," he answered. "What is your surname, Polly?"

Polly shrugged. "Same as Prue's was before she married Josh, I suppose. Don't know my father's name," she added. "Prue didn't know either."

Nicholas winced as the pounding in his head reached a new pitch, unaided by this still uninformative if artless recital. "And what was Prue's name before she married?"

"Wyat," Polly said. "But I've no need of it."

"Of course you have need of it," declared the Lady Margaret. "No decent girl goes around unnamed."

"But I am a bastard," Polly pointed out, with devastating effect.

"You are insolent!" Margaret glared in ice-tipped fury, and Polly looked at Nicholas in sudden alarm. She was accustomed to bearing the brunt of Josh's anger, and Prue's on many occasion, but this lady seemed much more formidable than either of them.

"She but speaks the truth," Nicholas said swiftly. "It is innocence, not insolence, sister."

There was a tense silence while Margaret, lips compressed, continued to fix Polly with a baleful eye. Then, to Polly's heartfelt relief, she turned back to her brother. "Where are her clothes?"

Nicholas scratched his head; he had been expecting this question, but no satisfactory answer had yet come to mind. "There is the difficulty, sister. She has none but her smock."

Margaret looked astounded. "How should that be?"

"It is a little difficult to explain, and I do not care to do so at present." Kincaid opted for the assumption of authority—the master of the house who chose not to be troubled by certain matters. "Send one of the girls to the Exchange to purchase necessities for her. I will bear the cost myself; it need not come out of your household purse. In payment for her services as kitchen maid, she will receive three pounds a year and her keep." A hard look at Polly ensured her continued silence.

Margaret was not happy, but she could not gainsay the orders of her brother-in-law. Her own authority was dependent upon his, for a man was master in his own house. It was a sore shame that Nicholas, unlike his late-lamented older brother, seemed to care little for the sober and devout regime that she and her late husband had fashioned for their household during the days of the Lord Protector. But Nicholas, his brother's heir, had been Baron Kincaid for the last three years, and his widowed sister-in-law was dependent upon him for house and home. Not that he was ever ungenerous in spirit or fact, but Margaret wished for the past, when he was still leading the life of a younger son, seeking what advancement he could at the court, where he was so manifestly at home. Now, with such a one at its head, what had been *her* household was becoming infused with the dangerous ways of that same loose and licentious court.

Such thoughts were acid and wormwood, as usual. She turned to the cause of all this trouble. "Come," she said shortly to Polly. "It is not decent for you to be in here." She went to the door, calling for Susan, who appeared, wide-eyed, almost before her name had been spoken. "Take her down to the kitchen." Margaret pushed Polly through the door with a grimace of distaste. "I will come down and see what is to be done with her in a minute."

"Sister!" Nicholas spoke with sudden briskness as he got out of bed, drawing a furred nightgown over his shirt. "One thing more." He walked to the window and drew back the heavy curtains, examining the gray day with a slight frown. "I know you do not believe in sparing the rod, Margaret, and while I would not in general interfere in your running of this household, which you do impeccably, in this instance you will stay your arm. If you find fault in her, bring it to my attention. Is it clear?"

Margaret's lips tightened. She was not accustomed to being spoken to in such a manner. "And is she not to be subject to my authority, then, brother? I cannot have, in my household, one who is excused faults for which others are punished."

"You will bring such faults as there may be to *my* attention," he repeated with gentle emphasis. "I do not imagine such a slight diversion from the usual will disturb the immaculate order of the house. Your hand on the reins is too secure, my dear sister."

"And do you find fault in that?" She spoke stiffly through compressed lips, her backbone rigid as a steel rod.

"I think you are on occasion a little severe," he said with a sigh. His head was worsening by the minute, and he could not find the energy to speak with his usual circumspection. Margaret had been left to his charge by his brother's last wish, and he would honor that commitment in more than letter, for all that he despised the narrow rigidity of the Puritan. He had discoursed endlessly with Edward on the possibility of a happy medium between a life governed to the last degree by the rules of divinity and sobriety and one where there were no rules except those of excess. But Edward had been a learned Puritan, one with whom it was possible to discourse. His wife, unfortunately, saw only dogma, and Nick, for love of his dead brother, was obliged to keep the peace with the dogmatist. However, on this occasion, if Margaret's sensibilities were wounded by the truth, it could not be helped. He would not subject Polly to the Puritan's severity, certain as he was that that somewhat mischievous personality with its talent for improvisation would be sure to offend without intent within a very short space of time. However, he reflected with a slight smile, if that brute Josh had not managed to beat the spirit out of her, it was unlikely that Margaret would succeed.

The enigmatic smile did nothing to improve matters with his sister-in-law. "You are entitled to your opinion, brother," she said with harsh dignity. "I must, of course, be glad to have my faults pointed out to me. You may rest assured that I shall reflect upon what you have said." She turned on her heel, and left his chamber, closing the door with a gentleness that contained more reproach than the most violent slam.

Nicholas winced, pulling the bell for his footboy. Somehow he was going to have to weave a path through this tangle, and he had best start by discussing last night's inspira-

tion with De Winter. He had failed to make the rendezvous
at the Dog last night, but he would be found at court this
morning, where there would be opportunity for a brief
word, a new rendezvous. Buckingham's suspicious eye had
not yet fallen upon them, and for as long as they continued
to play the gay courtiers with nothing on their minds but the
pleasures of lust and dalliance, it would not do so.

If all went according to plan, the duke's eye would eventually fall upon the most ravishing actor yet to grace the
king's theatre on Drury Lane. And that actor would then
have another part to play.

Chapter 3

When Lord Kincaid finally left his bedchamber, he was feeling somewhat less fragile, although his hands had proved inordinately clumsy when it came to the tying of his cravat—a sartorial activity that had consequently taken him a full half hour to complete, and had left the chamber floor littered with the crumpled evidence of his failures. His eyes were heavy, but no fault could be found with the cream silk waistcoat revealed through the slashed turquoise doublet, or his brocade coat, embroidered in silver, the wide sleeves turned up to reveal the lace cuffs of his shirt. His gloves were embroidered, his shoes buckled with silver, and his lordship had every reason to be satisfied with an appearance that would come under the informed and critical scrutiny of all those who attended the court of King Charles that morning.

He descended the staircase and paused in the hall, taking a pinch of snuff from the little onyx box that he then dropped back into the wide pocket of his coat while he pondered the question of whether the uncertain weather precluded his walking to Whitehall. The air would do him good, but his garments would not take kindly to rain. A loud caterwauling broke into this not unimportant debate.

"Gawd, sir, whatever's that!" Young Tom, who had hastened to open the great front door for his master, jumped as if he had been burned, and the door banged shut again.

"It sounds remarkably like a scalded cat," observed Kincaid, frowning deeply. The wailing, which seemed to originate from the back regions of the house, increased in volume. It was not at all the sort of sound one expected to hear in a gentleman's household, and Nicholas was soon in little doubt as to who was making it. But why? It was clearly incumbent upon him to find out.

His lordship did not in general frequent the working areas of the house, so his arrival in the kitchen caused gasps of alarm from the group there assembled. As far as he could judge, everyone, from the boot boy to the cook, was present, witnessing a scene presided over by a grim-faced Lady Margaret, swathed in a large white apron. Polly, wailing piteously, was seated on a low stool before the range whilst her ladyship, mouth set in an unyielding line, was pulling a steel comb through the tangled mass of honey-colored hair.

"Lord of hell!" exclaimed his lordship. "Polly, stop bellowing for a minute; I cannot hear myself think." The noise ceased with a suspicious immediacy, although the combing continued. "What is going on, pray?"

"I'll not have her bringing lice into the house," declared her ladyship tightly. "Her head is crawling with them."

"It hurts!" Polly protested with a vigorous sniff. Matters were not proceeding at all according to her chosen plan, and at this point, she rather thought that life at the Dog tavern had a certain appeal.

"Then it must be cut off," announced Margaret with ill-concealed satisfaction. "It is the devil's vanity anyway."

"No," Nicholas said. "Devil's vanity or no, sister, it is not to be cut. Why do you not send her to the hothouse? She may be bathed there and her hair washed."

"Bath!" Polly stared at him in horror. He could not surely expect her to immerse her entire body in hot water. "All of me? No, I will not. It is dangerous." Infinitely more dangerous than life at the Dog tavern!

"It will not kill you," Nicholas said with an effort at patience. "Have you never bathed before?"

Polly shook her head. Prue washed her hair for her when it became too itchy, and she occasionally took a damp rag to her body, but she could never really see the point; a little dirt hurt no one.

"This is hardly an appropriate matter for you, brother," Lady Margaret said. "You may safely leave it in my hands."

Polly instantly began to wail again, the soft, sensuous mouth quivering pitiably, her eyes fixed on Kincaid so that he thought he would drown in their liquescent green-brown depths. There was no resisting that appeal even though he was convinced that her distress was in some degree feigned.

"Stop that noise," he said softly. "You are not going to be hurt. I will take you myself."

"Brother! You cannot do such a thing." Margaret, in her outrage, forgot the unseemliness of a brangle with her brother in front of the servants.

"May I not?" He lifted an incredulous eyebrow. "I think I may be the judge of that, Margaret." He turned to Susan. "You will accompany us. We shall stop at the Exchange for clothes on our way. You will know what to purchase that will be appropriate, and then you may assist Polly in the bathhouse."

Susan cast an anxious look at her mistress, uncertain whether obedience to the master's commands would be construed as disobedience to the mistress. But Margaret knew when she was defeated, just as she knew that further protest would simply make her look ridiculous.

"If you wish to burden yourself with such a task, brother, far be it from me to object. Susan will know what clothes I consider suitable for a girl in that position." Casting Polly a look of loathing, she swept out of the kitchen.

"Tom, have the carriage brought around," Nicholas instructed the footboy. "Susan, find a cloak or some such to cover that smock; and some pattens for her feet." He also left the kitchen, well aware that his intervention had done Polly no good with Margaret, but confusingly unsure what else he

could have done. It should have been simple enough to leave
women's work to the women, but when Polly had looked at
him in that manner, he had become as putty. Now, instead
of spending his morning at Whitehall in the leisured pursuits
of a courtier, he was going to drive around the city with two
maidservants, buying stuff gowns and petticoats, and encouraging one recalcitrant, lice-infested wench into the hothouse!

"Lord love us!" Susan ejaculated, once the kitchen was
returned to the sole use of its accustomed occupants. She
regarded Polly with awed interest. "What you done for 'is
lordship, then? 'E never goes against her ladyship, never."
She nudged Polly with a salacious grin. "Given 'im a bit o'
the other, 'ave ya? Aren't ye the lucky one, takin' 'is fancy
like that!"

Polly frowned, thinking of last night and his refusal of the
offer of her body. "I don't think I have taken his fancy," she
replied honestly, not a whit put out by the girl's manner or a
conclusion that she could see would be the only reasonable
one. She was perfectly at home in the kitchen; which, in all
its essentials, except for the extraordinary degree of cleanliness, resembled her usual haunts, and perfectly at ease with
Lord Kincaid's servants for much the same reasons. "I did
save his life, though," she confided, her frown clearing at
this happy truth. Just in time, she stopped herself from continuing blithely that in exchange he had promised to help
her with her life's ambition. It would take a much less astute
mind than Polly's to have missed the significance of Lady
Margaret's dress and bearing and pronouncements on the
devil's vanities. She was in the house of a Puritan.

She had scrambled into adulthood in a land ruled by the
Lord Protector, where all forms of entertainment and gaiety
were forbidden as the devil's work. Color and adornment in
dress were held sinful vanities, punishable by stocks and pil-
lory. Only in the last five years, since Charles II had been
brought triumphantly from exile, had the Puritan rule lost its
sway. Indeed, the pendulum had swung to the opposite ex-
treme, and there was little extravagance in dress or behavior

that was now considered impermissible. It was a matter of
some interest, she reflected, that his lordship, whose dress
and bearing bore ample witness to his allegiance to the
courtly norms, should share houseroom with such a stickler
for the sober and divine. But then, kin had claims upon kin,
and not since the reign of Henry VIII had there been anything unusual in two members of the same family holding
opposing views on the manner in which the worship of God
should be conducted. The present rule of the land was much
more tolerant of differences in religious conviction and life-
style than the Lord Protector's.

Polly dismissed the matter as being of little importance
and turned her attention to the immediate issue—that of a
visit to the hothouse. The gentleman—she still could not
think of him in any other way—had told her last night that
she would be required to do certain things that she would
not wish to do, but that it was all part of some plan that
would enable her to achieve her object. If immersing herself
in hot water would draw her closer to her goal, then she
supposed she would have to submit. At least she would do so
in friendly company.

" 'Ow d'ye save his life, then?" asked Susan, rummaging
in a cupboard. " 'Ere, these'll do you." She handed her a
pair of wooden pattens. "Ye'd best borrow Bridget's cloak,
for I'll have need of mine."

"Carriage is 'ere!" Tom appeared breathless in the door.
" 'Is lordship's coolin' 'is heels abovestairs, and bids ye both
come straightway."

Polly smiled her thanks as she took the cloak of coarse
homespun handed her by the cook. The smile, did she but
know it, did much to reconcile Bridget to the loan of such a
precious garment.

"We must make haste." Susan pranced in the doorway, in
her anxiety and excitement quite forgetting that she had not
received an answer to her question.

Nicholas, while he was resigned to the task ahead, was also
regretting his impulse until Polly appeared, wrapped in the
ample folds of the cook's cloak. She turned the full sun of

that glorious countenance upon him and smiled—a smile that carried a hint of shyness behind its gratitude. He ceased to regret the impulse, accepting that it had been as inevitable as the sunrise. Clean, groomed, not at a disadvantage, who would she not entrance? He would welcome De Winter's second opinion, and such an opinion would only be hastened by the speedy performance of the business in hand.

"Come." He gestured to the open front door, where the carriage waited, set his plumed hat upon his head, and followed the pair. "Susan, you may ride upon the box."

Susan climbed up to sit beside the coachman, very much wishing that she could have exchanged a glance with Polly. The sedate Kincaid household had achieved a most lively addition, one who was like to create a fair number of sparks if she continued to bask in the favor of my lord and the disfavor of my lady.

"The Royal Exchange," Kincaid instructed the coachman, before climbing into the carriage behind Polly, who took her seat, patting the leather squabs with an appreciative hand. This carriage was a far cry from the hackney of the previous evening.

"It is a most elegant coach, sir," she said politely. Her gaze ran approvingly over his attire as he sat opposite her, adroitly swinging his sword to one side so that it would not catch between his legs. "And you are a most proper gentleman, my lord."

Nicholas's lips twitched, but he accepted the compliment with a gracious bow of his head.

"You were not quite so magnificent last night," Polly continued, as if apologizing for not having complimented her companion earlier.

"One dresses rather differently when one is intending to visit the court from when one is frequenting a wharfside tavern," he explained solemnly.

"I imagine so," agreed Polly, frowning. "But I do not understand why you would wish to frequent a wharfside tavern when you can go to court or . . . or even to the playhouse."

"Have you ever been to the play?" Nicholas asked curiously, hoping to take her mind off her question.

Her eyes glowed as she shook her head. "Not to a real playhouse, no; but Twelfth Night four years ago, a troupe of strolling players came to the Dog tavern and put on an entertainment to pay for their cakes and ale. It was wonderful!" The glow deepened as she seemed to be looking into another world. "The costumes and the dancing. They let me take part a little and said I had some talent." She shot him an almost defiant look as if daring him to contradict her. "They would have taken me with them, only Josh overheard me asking; so I got his belt instead." She shrugged, cheerfully insouciant. "But I am going to be a good actor."

"That would not surprise me in the least," he said mildly, and Polly looked instantly gratified. "I have witnessed a fair number of your performances since last evening."

There was something in his tone that took a little of the gilt from the statement, but the carriage at this point came to a halt, and Polly, pulling aside the leather curtain, gazed upon the riotous bustle of the Royal Exchange, where stall keepers jostled for custom, calling out their wares to prospective shoppers, maids and mistresses, gentlemen and loungers, who picked over the merchandise and haggled over the prices.

Polly had her hand on the door latch, ready to leap to the ground, when his lordship spoke with soft determination behind her. "Nay, you must stay in the carriage. You cannot possibly show yourself in public in such undress."

Her face fell ludicrously, all the glow and sparkle fading from those great eyes. "But I have never before seen such a place. I will pull the cloak around me—"

"Nay!" he repeated, sharply this time. "It is freezing outside. You exposed yourself to the elements sufficiently last evening." Stepping past her, he sprang lightly to the ground, where Susan already stood in attendance. He closed the carriage door firmly, then, although he knew it to be a mistake, glanced upward. Polly looked at him through the window, as pathetic as any prisoner, as appealing as a drooping violet after a rainstorm. Kincaid sighed. "If you promise not to set the hothouse on its heels with your wailing, we will stop here on the way back, and you may explore to your heart's content."

The violet lifted its head to the sun, unfurling its radiance. Her mouth curved in that devastating smile as she propped her elbows on the edge of the window and settled down to observe the scene from shelter. Kincaid, completely bewitched, shook his head helplessly.

"Come, Susan, let us deal with this matter without delay." He strode off with the maidservant in tow.

When they returned within half an hour, Susan was lost behind the number of packages heaped in her arms. But when the coachman relieved her of her burdens, thus revealing her face, her expression was one of shock. When the mistress shopped, particularly for her servants, every item was subject to careful consideration, a weighing up of necessity against cost. The materials were all to be sturdy and hard-wearing, coarse and without frills or furbelows, and only the strictest necessities were purchased. His lordship, while bearing in mind that a servant in his sister-in-law's house must be clad only in the most sober, modest garments, had bought a petticoat and smock of the finest Holland, a kirtle of warm, fine wool, and a plain dark gown of a mixture of wool and silk. There was a thick serge cloak with a fur-trimmed hood, and a pair of leather gloves. Two pairs of woolen hose, a pair of leather pumps, and a pair of cork-soled pantofles to wear over the pumps in inclement weather completed a wardrobe that would enrage Lady Margaret by a quality and scope that was most definitely unsuited to the status of a kitchen maid.

"Lor!" murmured Susan, climbing back on the box. "There'll be fireworks when the mistress sees that lot." She regaled the fascinated coachman with a full account of the purchases as they bowled along to the hothouse.

Their arrival at this building caused Polly to assume the mien of one about to ascend the scaffold. She stepped hesitantly out of the coach into the courtyard and stood still, clinging to the door handle. The vehicle, bearing the Kincaid arms upon its panels, brought the establishment's proprietor hustling across the cobbles, calling over his shoulder to have one of the privy chambers prepared for his lordship. When informed that his customer was not, on this occasion, to be his lordship, but, instead, the tumbled, begrimed girl at his lordship's side, he rapidly revised these instructions. The common baths in the female wing would do perfectly well. Only the gentry were entitled to privacy.

He was required to revise his plans yet again when he received his lordship's orders, and a more than generous payment. There was to be privacy, a limitless supply of hot water, plentiful towels, whatever assistance was requested for however long the ablutions should take.

The proprietor glanced at the wench again, deciding that it was going to be a long and tedious task. Why was his lordship concerning himself with the cleanliness of this street drab? Then the girl looked up at him, and he understood why. God's grace! But where had he found such a pearl? She was in sore need of cleaning up, though, even if one was not particularly fastidious.

"It shall be exactly as you say, my lord," he murmured, bowing low, rubbing his hands together. "My wife will attend to the girl personally."

"Good. The wench there will help also." Kincaid gestured toward Susan. "I will return in two hours. That should be sufficient."

"Two hours!" Polly squawked. "I cannot spend two hours in water. I will dissolve."

"Do you wish to learn to read and write?" His lordship fixed her with a gimlet eye. "And do all the other things we discussed?"

Polly put her chin up and turned resolutely toward the hothouse. " 'Tis not so very unpleasant," Susan reassured her, trotting along beside her. "We all comes every four weeks, even the mistress. Can't abide dirt, she can't. Says it aids the devil's work. An' lice!" Susan's hands flew up in a gesture of exaggerated horror. "If 'is lordship hadn't stopped 'er this morning, she'd have cut all your 'air off, she would. Did it to little Milly only last month. Right down to the scalp."

That prospect was sufficiently hideous to grant Polly a degree of resignation to the alternative offered her. The proprietor's lady was a large, cheerful woman whose experienced eye immediately took in the full gravity of the task ahead. She grimly rolled up her sleeves and added more hot water to the tub.

Kincaid spent the next two hours in a neighboring coffeehouse, looking through the latest *Oxford Gazette*. The news was as disturbing as ever. Public dissatisfaction with the king and his court was becoming daily more clamorous; the periodicals and tabloids to be found in the coffeehouses all contained tales of the wild doings of his cronies, of how the king was ruled by his mistress, Lady Castlemaine, of the ascendancy of the Duke of Buckingham. There was frank and fearful speculation that the king would make his bastard son, the Duke of Monmouth, legitimate, thus creating him heir to the throne in place of the king's brother, the Duke of York.

For some reason, the king did not seem to see the danger he was in. He ignored the advice of all but those who encouraged him to assert his divine right to absolute power, as his father had done before him. The land had risen against his father's autocracy, and they would do the same again if given just cause. The legitimizing of the Duke of Monmouth and the setting aside of the rightful heir would be seen as just cause. The House of Commons would never ratify such a move, and if the king attempted to force them to do so, he would meet his father's fate. As he would if he continued with a reckless expenditure that was bankrupting the nation. The English people had tasted their own power, and they would not again accept being milked to pay for the king's pleasures and whims.

Nicholas frowned, tapping a manicured finger on the table. Charles II needed wise counselors, not those who were interested only in their own political advancement and per-

sonal power. Unfortunately, the young king had not been
taught to distinguish the true from the false and, having
spent his youth in impoverished exile, had not been bred to
kingship.

Kincaid and De Winter led a small faction pledged to
circumvent the influence of those who would lead the king
astray, the Duke of Buckingham in particular. The king was
a man of whim, choosing and abandoning favorites as the
mood took him. If something could be discovered to Buckingham's discredit, then his star would fall. In addition, it
might be possible to forestall the worst of the king's errors if
they could keep one step ahead, were able to anticipate, so
that, if necessary, the full force of opinion from the opposing
members of the House of Lords could be brought to bear on
the king before he approached the Commons with unpopu-
lar demands. If the Lords made its voice heard loudly
enough, King Charles might listen.

This two-pronged attack depended entirely on having access to Buckingham's inner circle, to the plots and plans he
would weave with Sir Thomas Clifford and my Lords Ashley, Arlington, and Lauderdale. De Winter's manservant had
been recruited, initially. He had left De Winter's service to
become employed as lackey in Buckingham's household, but
not even the substantial sums he received for any piece of
information had been able to compensate him for his terror
at the prospect of discovery. It became obvious to his real
employers that fear was making him unreliable, and one slip
on his part would mean the end for all of them. Spying on
the king's favorite would be tantamount to spying upon the
king—treason, which ended on the block.

The manservant had been retired on a healthy pension,
well away from London, and another spy was needed. Why
not a beautiful young actor? One who would so manifestly
appeal to Buckingham's notoriously lusting eye? A mistress
would have access to all those private conclaves, and if she
did not know she was spying, the danger of discovery would
be reduced. Careful priming beforehand, and skillful ques-

tioning later, should elicit the information from her without her being aware of it.

It was tricky, but it could work. It was certainly the best opportunity they had had in some time. Lord Kincaid consulted the watch hanging at his waist, saw that two hours had passed since he had abandoned his prospective spy to her watery fate, and returned to the hothouse. He found himself most eager to see what transformation soap and water had wrought. He was not disappointed.

"You must have been even dirtier than I thought," he managed to say, once he had recovered from the sight of Polly's now unhindered beauty. Her hair, clean and burnished, was an even richer color than he had realized, and her complexion, free of the dirt that had been embedded in the skin, was a clear, translucent ivory. Only her eyes were unchanged, except that in their now-polished setting they shone even more luminous than before. He could make an informed guess, aided by memory, of the condition of the rest of her, now concealed beneath the modest neatness of her unimpeachable garments. Once her bruises had healed, there would not be a blemish to mar the perfection. The thought brought an uncomfortable constriction in his loins; he turned brusquely toward the coach.

"Come, it is time we went home. I have wasted the greater part of my morning already."

Polly, torn between resentment at his callously matter-of-fact manner and pleasure in the combined sensations of cleanliness and the feel of fine linen against her skin, followed him a little crossly. "But you promised that we might stop again at the Exchange." She gathered up her skirts with unconscious elegance to mount gracefully into the coach.

Now, where had she learned to do that? Nicholas wondered. It was as if she had been born and bred to the gracious management of skirts and petticoats. "I will let you and Susan off at the Exchange. You may walk home afterward."

"Oh, but please, my lord. My lady . . ." Susan stammered, leaning over the side of the box in her anxiety.

"I will make it all right with her ladyship," Nicholas

promised, accepting that he was going to have an unpleasant scene on his hands when Margaret discovered that he had blithely given her maid a holiday.

Polly's excitement when she was finally permitted to set foot in the magic world of commerce was so innocently, childishly at odds with that mature beauty that Kincaid was hard-pressed to keep a straight face. Bethinking himself that wandering around stalls lacked something essential if one was not in a position to purchase, he handed her a sovereign.

" 'Tis hardly riches," he said, laughing, as she looked at him, dumbfounded. "But you might see some trifle that takes your eye." He was aware that Susan was also staring. "To hell and the devil," he muttered. Why should a generous impulse have such an effect?

He knew perfectly well why, of course. One did not hand out sovereigns to servant wenches except in payment for services rendered—services, in general, of a certain kind. It would not do for Margaret to draw such a conclusion. Nothing would prevail upon her to share houseroom with one she would call whore. There seemed only one solution. He handed Susan the sovereign's mate, with the injunction to enjoy themselves but to ensure that they were home for dinner. Then he gave the coachman instructions to drive to Whitehall, and left two blissfully happy girls, with untold riches burning a hole in their pockets, to enjoy a brief holiday.

The Long Gallery at Whitehall was thronged. It was here that gossip was created and exchanged, factions developed and broken, reputations made and ruined. His eye sought for the tall, slender figure of Richard De Winter, Viscount Enderby. Nick's oldest friend, the man with whom he had shared the brutal hells of their boyhood years at Westminster School, was lounging beside one of the long windows overlooking the bowling green, his indolent posture belying the taut power and decision that Nick knew so well. An elaborate periwig fell to his brocade shoulders; diamond buttons on his coat sleeves winked in the light from the window. His eyelids drooped slightly, concealing the razor sharpness of the gray eyes beneath. A lace-edged handkerchief fluttered from his beringed fingers, and a burst of laughter rose from the admiring group of ladies clustered around him. De Winter was a wit with a notoriously sharp tongue, and no scruples as to where and to whom he directed that sharpness. He was feared by many, but no one would show it, any more than they would fail to listen when he pronounced.

Nicholas strolled over to the group, pausing to acknowledge greetings, exchange a word of news, a light remark. He learned that again the king had not left his privy chamber this morning, where he was closeted with the Duke of Buckingham and two other favorites, my Lords Bristol and Ashley. Increasingly, His Majesty was cutting himself off from the conversation and opinions of the majority of the court.

"Why, Nick, my dear fellow, how goes the world with you?" De Winter hailed him.

"Indifferent well, Richard," replied Nicholas airily, bowing with great ceremony to the ladies, his plumed hat sweeping the floor. "I fear I caught cold last night."

De Winter's eyes narrowed almost imperceptibly. "Indeed, I am sorry to hear it, but 'twas a foul night. I was kept withindoors, myself, by some unexpected visitors."

"A fortunate occurrence," Kincaid said with a degree of dryness. "I should have been glad to have been so prevented from making my own journey."

"Lord De Winter has been telling us the most outrageous story," a lady in orange taffeta informed Nicholas with a trilling laugh. "It is said that during a ball at Lord Lindsey's last week, a babe was born in the middle of the coranto. The infant was caught in a handkerchief, but no one knows who is the mother, no lady acknowledging the child, and everyone continuing with the dance."

"Ah," said Nicholas thoughtfully. "But I understand that my Lady Fawcett has since been confined to her bed."

"Nick, you have outdone me!" cried De Winter. "I must retreat in shame." With a sweeping bow, he removed himself from the circle, leaving Nicholas to entertain the ladies with further scurrilous tales before he, too, made his excuses and sauntered along the matted gallery to take the stairs to the Privy Garden.

De Winter was waiting for him at the King Street Gate, at the far end of the garden. "My apologies for last night," he said without preamble. "You had difficulties?"

" 'Tis a long story, Richard." Nick told the tale as they walked toward the Strand, then proceeded to expound his proposition to his rapt companion. "When you see her, you will see what I mean," he finished. "Such extraordinary beauty. Never have I seen its like."

De Winter looked at his friend, wondering if perhaps something had addled his senses. "Is she, indeed, a maid? It seems unlikely, my friend, although I would not doubt your word."

"I have no empirical evidence," Nick said with a slight shrug. "But I would stake my honor upon it. She is quite the most unusual wench."

"Desirable enough for Buckingham? He has more interest in flesh and blood than in the fey."

Nicholas gave a short laugh. "Desirable enough, Richard! I know not how to keep my own hands from her at times. And she is most definitely of this world."

"And Killigrew will take to her?"

"When she is groomed," Nick said with absolute certainty.

"And you can rely upon her cooperation?"

"Her only desire is to tread the boards," Nicholas said. "And I am convinced she has no small talent. Indeed, I am often hard-pressed to tell the performance from the genuine emotion."

"But with such a creature—a Newgate brat who has grown from the slums—you will not be able to trust in her loyalty. It will be given to the highest bidder. For that reason, you may be able to encourage her into Buckingham's bed—there are few higher—but how can you be sure she will remain sufficiently attached to you to enable you to milk her of any information? It will have to be done very casually if she is not to suspect. It seems to me, my friend, that that predicates a certain intimacy." His eyebrows lifted. "Should she begin to suspect the truth, she may well see financial advantage in playing turncoat. Then we will both lose our heads."

Nicholas was silent for a minute. He did not resent this hard catechism. Richard spoke only the truth, and the stakes would be of the highest. Finally he said, "If I may bind her to me . . ."

"She will remain loyal," De Winter finished on a low whistle. "Will you bind her with the chains of gratitude or of love, my friend?"

Nicholas shrugged. "Of the first, certainly. Of the second . . ." He smiled. "We will wait and see. I find I have a powerful desire for her, Richard, one I would consummate; but I must kindle her own first. She is still an innocent in matters of passion, in spite of her background." He paused thoughtfully, then said, "Maybe because of it. Passion and desire are not necessarily synonymous with lust, and she is certainly familiar with the latter in its ugliest manifestations. But we will leave that in abeyance. While she remains beneath my roof, she remains virgin. She must be taught certain things, and in the teaching I will forge some chains."

Richard De Winter nodded, and kept silent. He found himself with a great desire to make the acquaintance of Mistress Polly Wyat.

Chapter 4

Lady Margaret, who had been waiting with barely suppressed impatience for her brother-in-law's return, found herself balked of the opportunity to vent her anger by the presence of his companion. She was obliged to smile and curtsy as she greeted Lord De Winter, pressed a glass of sack upon him, and sent word to the kitchen to lay another place at the dinner table.

"I understand from John Coachman, brother, that you gave Susan and Polly leave to visit the Exchange," she said, finally unable to contain herself, although she was careful to couch the statement in soft tones, accompanied by a smile. It was a smile that did not reach her eyes, but then, Lady Margaret's smiles rarely did. "They have not yet returned, and the kitchen is hard-pressed to manage without them." She plied her needle on her tambour frame with an air of great consideration, continuing casually, "I cannot help feeling, brother, that the granting of holidays should be in the purview of the mistress of the house. A man cannot expect to know when a servant can ill be spared."

"Possibly not," agreed Nick equably. "Pray accept my apologies if my indulgence has caused you trouble. However, the kitchen cannot be missing Polly's services too greatly, since they have not yet had the benefit of them. But they should both be at work shortly. I gave order that they return by dinnertime." He smiled blandly. "May I fill your glass, Richard?"

"My thanks." De Winter schooled his expression with admirable effort and offered the Lady Margaret a comment on the weather. Topics of conversation considered suitable by the Puritan were hard to come by since court gossip, politics, and fashion were all tarred with the devil's brush. Religion, sacred music, and the weather were acceptable, but tended to be unabsorbing subjects.

A slight tap on the door relieved the awkward silence. Lady Margaret bade the knocker enter, and Polly, demure in apron and cap, appeared. "Dinner is served, my lady."

Richard De Winter struggled to capture his breath. Never had he beheld such a beauty. Aware of his gaze, Polly returned the look with a frank appraisal of her own, then she smiled and curtsied prettily, looking up at him in a way that one could only call provocative, through the luxuriant, curling forest of her eyelashes.

It was Lady Margaret's turn to gasp at such an immodest display. She was still trying to recover from the effects of her instant, automatic assessment of Polly's clothing. Her brother must have spent a small fortune on garments that no lady would object to having on her back. The effect of such a creature, dressed in such a fashion, on the discipline and smooth running of her household could only be catastrophic. And she had been forbidden to mend the girl's manners. She glared her outrage at her brother, who seemed not to notice anything untoward in the wench's deportment.

In fact, Nick was satisfied by De Winter's reaction and amused by Polly's response. She had learned the art of responding to such a reaction in the taproom of the Dog tavern, as he well knew, but there was nothing lewd or vulgar about her present demeanor—coquettish, certainly, but there was no harm in that. Indeed, it was an essential if she was to succeed in the life she had chosen.

Ignoring his sister's glare, he said, "After dinner, Polly, I would like you to come to my parlor. You shall have your first lesson."

Polly's eyes glowed with pleasure, and there was none of the coquette about her this time as she curtsied again. "Thank you, my lord."

"What lesson?" demanded Margaret. "The girl cannot be spared from her duties again today." She rounded on Polly, who still stood smiling in the doorway. "Have you nothing better to do, girl, than stand idling here?"

Polly, catching Nicholas's warning glance, bit back the retort springing so easily to her lips. She knew she had a powerful enemy in the Lady Margaret, but she also knew that Lord Kincaid was an even more powerful friend. He would protect her from injustice, she was certain, having put her in this position in the first place. Although why he should have done that still escaped her. She did not think that, in general, patrons, or even protectors, kept their protégées as kitchen maids. They set them up in lodgings of their own, where they could learn things like reading and writing and cleanliness without interference.

She beat a rapid retreat from the drawing room. Of course, it was true that her adopted patron/protector had so far required from her none of the expected services of the protégée. He behaved simply as if he was accepting an obligation which he had the right to discharge as he saw fit. If he would make her his mistress, then surely matters would be conducted differently? Perhaps he required more encouragement. Mayhap, now that she was clean, he would find her more appealing.

"What lesson?" repeated Margaret, sweeping past her brother into the dining room. "I do think, Lord De Winter, that my brother is suffering some disorder of the mind. He finds an orphaned slut upon the streets, and proceeds to treat her as if she were his own kin." A little unconvincing laugh was intended to make a joke of the public criticism, but it failed lamentably.

"I have promised to teach the girl her letters," Nick said, in the same equable tone he had employed throughout. "She has a quick mind, and I see no reason why she should not attempt to better herself if she is able."

"But what will the rest of the household think if such decided preference is accorded one of their number? It is not decent to encourage the lower orders to step beyond their station." Margaret passed a dish of stewed carp to her guest, her mouth small and pursed. "She is a brass-faced wench, overbold and with the deportment of a wanton. She stands in need of a round curbing, which it is to be hoped you will supply, since it appears that I may not."

Nicholas exchanged a look with De Winter. His old friend was well accustomed to Margaret's shrewishness, but she was overreaching herself this afternoon. "Perhaps you would save your scolding for when we are private, sister," he said sharply. "I feel sure that our guest must find it tedious."

Lady Margaret blushed fiercely. De Winter stepped into the breach with a deft compliment on the lavish and elegant table, but none of the three was sorry when the meal was over and her ladyship withdrew, leaving the gentlemen to their wine and tobacco.

"Well?" asked Nick. "What think you?"

"That you have a peck of trouble upon your hands," chuckled De Winter. "Your sister-in-law will not give the beauty houseroom for long. She will ply her shrew's tongue until you are forced to remove the girl."

"You think I am no match for Margaret?" A mobile eyebrow lifted quizzically as Nick set a taper to his long clay pipe.

"No man is match for a scold, my friend," laughed De Winter. "And to speak truth, I cannot find it in my heart to blame your sister in this instance. Never have I seen such a paragon. She is not designed for the humble role, and she most assuredly lacks a Puritan's demeanor."

Nick chuckled in his turn. "Heaven forfend. She would not suit our purposes if she possessed such a thing." His eyes narrowed, his laughter ceased. "Think you that she will serve our purpose?"

"Whether she has talent for the stage or not, Tom Killigrew will not be able to resist her." De Winter spoke thoughtfully. "She would decorate any production. And I grant you that she could well catch Buckingham's eye. In which case, she will be in his bed in no time. I do not know a woman who has yet refused what he would offer." He shrugged. "So long as she also stays close to you, I see no reason why your plan should not work. But as we said before, it is for you to make certain of her loyalty. If Buckingham buys her favors, you will have a high price to meet."

"Such cynicism!" murmured Nick with a slight smile, although he knew his friend spoke only the truth. The Duke of Buckingham, with his immense wealth and influence, could offer a wench in search of fame and fortune a great deal more than could Lord Kincaid. "There are other currencies than mere money and position." He rose in leisurely fashion. "Like love and gratitude, my friend, as we said before. Now let us see whether her wits match her beauty."

The two men went into Kincaid's private parlor. Richard reposed himself on a fine leather chair beside the fire while Nick perused his shelves for an appropriate book for a beginning reader. "Perhaps we should start with the Bible," he said with a smile. "It might reconcile Margaret." He pulled the bell rope beside the hearth, then opened the calf-bound book upon the table.

"Yes, my lord." It was Susan who answered the bell, her sparkling eyes and eager smile ample evidence of her memories of the morning.

"Send Polly to me," his lordship instructed, raising his head from the book.

Susan hesitated. "M'lady, sir, has set her to cleaning the silver," she said.

Lord Kincaid frowned. "Well, she can surely finish it at some other time."

"Yes, m'lord." Susan bobbed a curtsy, and retreated.

"A peck of trouble," mused Richard, tapping his teeth with a fingernail. "How's she to explain the uncleaned silver?"

"Are you trying to tell me, my friend, that this scheme is not going to work?"

"I fear you may have to go about it differently," was the reply.

Polly, on receiving the summons, had no scruples about abandoning her task. The amount of silver in the Kincaid household was daunting, to say the least, when one was expected to polish it. She entered Lord Kincaid's parlor impetuously and without ceremony, well aware that the Lady Margaret was about her business in the stillroom abovestairs. "If I had wished to be a kitchen maid, sir, I could have remained at the Dog tavern. At least," she added with scrupulous fairness, "I could have done so if Prue's potion had worked."

"But just think what a fate that would have condemned me to," protested his lordship. "Bludgeoned to death, and my body thrown into the Thames."

A roguish smile tugged at the corners of her mouth. "Indeed, I would not have wished that. But why can I not meet Master Killigrew, and then learn to read? Or I could sell oranges. I would much prefer it to cleaning silver."

"Orange girls do not just sell oranges," Nick pointed out. "Do they, De Winter?"

Polly noticed the other occupant of the parlor for the first time. She looked askance at Kincaid. "Lord De Winter knows your history and your ambition, Polly," he told her. "It is always useful to have friends."

"Indeed, it is," Richard spoke up. "Particularly in the theatre. But Nick is right, you know. If you wish to sell oranges as a means of introduction to the stage, you will be expected to offer your customers more personal services after the performance. You will not else make a living. If you are setting your sights on loftier patrons when you become an actor, you will not want to have sullied yourself with the gentlemen from the pit."

"I had not thought of that," Polly said with a sigh. "And now I am so clean and unsullied, 'twould be a pity to spoil it." Her eyes, mischievously inviting, sought Nick's, hoping for some responsive spark.

"Aye, it would," he said, disappointingly matter-of-fact, even as he wondered uneasily what lay behind that enchanting look. It was not one he'd seen before; it was neither the blatant come-hither invitation of the tavern wench nor the artlessly impish smile of Polly being herself. "I am certainly not prepared to endure a repetition of this morning's fuss to get you clean again." He offered the remark partly in jest, and partly in the hopes that it would cause Polly to change her expression to one a little less beguiling. It did.

"Then I suppose I had best polish silver." Polly pulled a comical face that drew an involuntary smile from both men. "How long will it take for me to learn my letters?"

"That depends on how quick your wits, and how hard you are prepared to work," Nick said. "Come, let us start." He sat down at the table, gesturing to the stool beside his elbow chair.

With her toe, Polly edged the stool closer to Nick's chair so that when she sat down, his knees were very close to hers. Nonchalantly, she rested her own elbow on the arm of his chair, smiling up at him with an expression of alert eagerness.

Nick drew in his breath sharply. Unless he much mistook the matter, young Polly was playing coquette with him, for some doubtless dubious reasons of her own. He took her arm and placed it firmly in her lap, observing coolly, "You will not learn to read from my face, Polly. The book is on the table." He tapped the open page with a forefinger.

She didn't seem very adept at issuing invitations, Polly thought with a disconsolate flash. It was a novel situation for her, of course, having never before found herself in the position of wanting to invite masculine attentions; more often than not she was struggling to escape them. There seemed to be a great many things she had to learn in this new life. She turned her attention to the jumble of hieroglyphics on the opened page, her frown deepening as she struggled to follow the pointing finger, concentrating on the quiet, patient voice.

At the close of an hour, it was very clear to both gentlemen that they had an apt pupil upon their hands. Nick glanced over the bent, honeyed head at Richard, who nodded, then sat up, the languid posture vanishing under a decisive air that Nick recognized well. "Polly, what do you know of the court?"

Richard's question took her quite by surprise. It also struck her as a rather stupid one. What could she possibly know of the court? She looked up from the paper where she was painfully copying the letters of the alphabet from Nick's original. "We didn't see too much of the court in Botolph Lane," she said, her dimples peeping. "For some reason, the king didn't frequent the Dog tavern."

There was a short silence. Nick bent to the fire, lighting a taper to kindle his pipe. He regarded her gravely through a fragrant, curling wisp of smoke. "That was a fine piece of impertinence, you rag-mannered brat. You're going to have to learn more than your letters if you wish to take your place in the world you have chosen. And one thing you must learn is that overt rudeness is inexcusable. You will *never ever* hear anyone offering the least apparent discourtesy, however much they might feel it warranted. You will hear elaborate compliments that mean nothing. You will hear insults conveyed by soft words and smiles. You will hear gossip spread and reputations destroyed by a seeming kind word, but *never* will you hear an impolite observation. If you transgress that rule, you might as well return to the Dog tavern, because there will be no place for you in the theatre or at court."

Polly nibbled her lip. "It does not sound very pleasant."

"It isn't," Richard said. "But one becomes accustomed to it. Now, I accept that you could not possibly have any firsthand knowledge of court life; that was not, as it happens, the point of my question. However, I would like you to tell me what, if anything, you have heard about the way the court is managed. Do you know the names of any of the king's counselors, for instance?"

Polly frowned. "I beg your pardon if I was impolite. I did not mean to be, but it seemed a silly question. I see now that it wasn't." She looked intent and anxious at the two men with an expression of heartrending penitence.

"There is no need for such a tragic mien," Nick said with a slight smile. "You are pardoned, and I trust you will remember the lesson in the future. Now, why do you not answer Richard's question?"

Polly thought, playing with the quill pen between her fingers. "Sometimes there was talk in the tavern; occasionally there would be a traveler, or a merchant . . . They would complain of the taxes . . . The king spending a lot of money . . ." She looked up for confirmation.

Richard nodded. "Anything else you remember?"

"Some quarrel with the Dutch," Polly said. "There is talk that there will be another war, and it will be very expensive and there'll be more taxes. But the king wants it, although I do not know exactly why." Her frown deepened as she concentrated on snatches of conversations that she had heard while serving in the tavern. "One of the king's counselors is against it, though. I cannot remember his name." Absently, she stuck the ink-stained end of the quill into her mouth, then removed it with a grimace, touching her fingertip to her tongue to see if much ink had found its way into her mouth. "The chancellor!" she declared in triumph. "He is against a war."

"Aye, Clarendon," Richard said. "You know how to keep your ears open, it would seem."

"There was talk of the king's mistresses, too," Polly went on. "He seems to have a great many of them, but there are two in particular. I do not recall their names."

"Lady Castlemaine and Frances Stewart," supplied Nick. "What was said of them?"

"Oh, that the king spends too much time minding his lust and his pleasures, and the government is chargeable for his pleasures, and things were managed better under a commonwealth," she declared fluently. "The talk was always along those lines. I do not think people are very happy with things as they are."

Richard smiled softly, exchanging another satisfied nod with Nick. Untutored she may be, but Mistress Wyat clearly had a lively mind, and a sense of the wider world. She could be schooled for their purposes.

"I think perhaps you should return to the silver," Nick said, glancing to the mantel, where the clock of black mahogany, its base set in silver, showed four o'clock. "Take the book, paper, and quill with you. You may practice when your duties are over, and I will correct what you have done tomorrow."

Polly gathered the book to her breast—a convulsive gesture that caused both gentlemen to experience a ludicrous flash of envy for the inanimate object. "Do you think I will learn enough in a week to be introduced to Master Killigrew?" The hazel eyes were wide and candid in their appeal, her tongue peeping anxiously from between her lips. That matchless bosom rose and fell with the urgency of her words. "Lady Margaret does not care for me in the least, and I do not think I can remain here for very long."

"You need not be afeard of Lady Margaret," Nicholas said quietly. "She holds no jurisdiction over you. You are answerable only to me."

Polly looked as if she did not quite believe this; that lower lip trembled slightly. Then she sighed bravely and left the room, the set of her head and shoulders radiating courageous determination.

"What a masterly performance!" breathed De Winter, rising to his feet.

"In what way?" Nick frowned. His friend laughed.

"My dear Nick, I'll lay odds that she has only to appeal to you just once more in that manner, and you will do whatever she wishes!"

Nick allowed a rueful smile to touch his lips. "The devil's in it, Richard, but I fear you are right. Yet it will not do to present her to Killigrew until she has acquired a little more polish, and until then I must keep her under my eye. I cannot imagine what she would get up to if I set her up in lodgings somewhere, unsupervised, before she is ready to start her acting career. She is not accustomed to idleness or freedom; just think what the sudden acquisition of both might lead to. She will be quite safe here, under Margaret's Puritan supervision, while we teach her what she must know." He shook his head in a slightly defeated fashion. "But, indeed, at times I doubt my ability to resist her blandishments. Are you not also bewitched?"

De Winter drew on his lace-edged gloves. "She has not set out to bewitch *me*, Nick." On this undeniable truth, he left his friend to his reflections.

Polly had ample time while working her way through the mountain of silver to plot her campaign. True, she had received a few setbacks this afternoon, but Lord Kincaid *must* be persuaded to take her into his bed. After that he could not deny her the protection he would afford a mistress, and would remove her from this miserable place so that he could enjoy her without obstruction. One could not summon one's mistress for an afternoon of pleasure if she was scrubbing cooking pots, she thought with a vicious rub at a chafing dish. She would have to live under some man's protection until she had proved her worth as an actor and could command a living wage. Polly could see absolutely no reason why Nicholas, Lord Kincaid, should not be that man. Indeed, she could think of a great many reasons why he should be; the fact that the prospect sent prickly shivers of anticipation up her spine seemed to be one of the most convincing. Lord Kincaid was a most proper gentleman.

She lay that evening on her cot in the attic, listening to the soft snores from Susan beside her, the rather heavier ones from Bridget in the corner. It was still early, and if she had been in her old life, the evening's work would have barely begun; but Lady Margaret kept early hours, and after supper and lengthy prayers, the household had been dismissed to their beds. They would rise at four o'clock, long before

dawn, Susan had told her, tumbling onto her bed with a
groan of relief, so she had best take what rest she could.
Tomorrow was the monthly wash day, when all the linen in
the house must be scrubbed, dried, and ironed. It was a
dreadful day, Susan moaned, and they must be up betimes to
set the water to boiling against the start of the great wash.

It was not a prospect that afforded Polly any pleasure.
Indeed, this passion for cleanliness struck her as a great nuisance. It was not that she found her present wholesome condition at all distasteful—quite the opposite; it was wonderful
not to itch—but such an early rising would rather interfere
with her plan for the night. His lordship had left the house in
the late afternoon, telling young Tom that he might go to his
bed in the little closet off the hall, and that he would be
required only to admit his master to the house on his return.
Unfortunately, no word had been said as to the hour of that
return. It was always possible that a man who would not be
required to rise before dawn might well not seek his bed
until that hour.

There was little point in speculation. Cautiously, Polly
climbed out of bed, gathering up the precious book, paper,
and quill. They would give her some occupation while she
waited. Certainly there was little scope for performing her
learning task if she did not find light and seclusion somewhere. The tallow candle in the attic had been blown out
within minutes of the servants seeking their beds, whether in
the interests of economy or rest, Polly was unsure.

She crept out of the attic, pausing on the landing. The air
was filled with the snores and grunts emanating from the
opposite attic, where slept the menservants. It was very dark,
with no moonshine from the small round window in the
eaves, and she trod carefully, once stubbing her toe on an
uneven floorboard, only just managing to control her pained
yelp.

The main landing was lit faintly from the lantern burning
in the hall below against the master's return. Polly slipped
into the bedchamber with the painted walls and its bright
fire and candlelight. She closed the door softly behind her,

shivering. It was a cold night, and her smock was thin. The
fire invited, and she stretched on her belly before it, paper
and quill in hand, the book open at the passage she was to
copy. But it proved tedious work, even for one with her
enthusiasm, and her eyes grew tired as the light flickered and
threw great shadows on the walls.

When Nicholas, Lord Kincaid, walked into his bedchamber as the Watch were calling the midnight hour, he found
Polly asleep over her copybook, her rich honey hair flowing
over the curve of arm and shoulder, her cheek delicately
flushed with sleep and the lingering warmth of the fire. The
fine cotton of her smock clung to the curves of her curled
body, the pink and pearly tones of her skin barely masked by
the garment.

He stood looking down at her for a moment until the
unbidden onrush of desire had ebbed somewhat. There was
such an air of innocence about her, collapsed in sleep over
her studying, that he acquitted her of deliberate intent to
entrap. He knew the hours Margaret required her servants to
keep, just as he knew her frugality. It seemed reasonable
enough that Polly should have come into the only room
where light and fire were to be found after the imposed
bedtime.

He bent over her, inhaling the scents of the hothouse—
soap and rose water and clean linen. There was something
immensely appealing about her bare feet, he thought distractedly. They peeped from the hem of her smock, the soles
bearing scratches from last night's journeying, the arches
high and narrow; the straight, dainty little toes, their nails cut
neatly now, gleaming opalescent in their dirt-free condition.
God's grace! But he must take a grip upon himself!

"Polly!" He spoke softly, touching the curve of her shoulder, feeling her skin warm beneath the cotton, the soft
roundness . . . "Polly!" He spoke with sharp urgency as if
only thus could he keep desire at bay. She stirred, moaned a
little, but her eyes remained tight shut, her breathing regular,
her body utterly relaxed. Even if he managed to wake her,

how was he to get her back upstairs without rousing the entire household?

With a familiar sense of resignation, Nick got to his feet and pulled the truckle bed from beneath his own. Margaret must make of it what she would. Polly rolled into his arms as he lifted her, but he would have sworn she was still fast asleep; her eyelashes had not fluttered, her breathing had not changed, her body had simply adapted itself to a new circumstance—a circumstance which meant that her breasts were now pressed, soft and warm, against his shirtfront.

Grimly, he bent to lay her on the truckle bed, drawing the coverlet securely over her form. Without volition, his fingers moved to pluck a strand of hair from where it had fallen over her eyes, then his lips followed his fingers, lightly brushing her cheek.

Polly did not know why she knew that she must keep to her pretense of sleep during this feathering caress, but instinct directed the part she played, and she had learned to trust the actor's instincts. It was difficult not to respond, though, to keep her hands from finding their way around his neck, her lips from returning the loving touch.

Nick straightened reluctantly, moving the candlestick so that the light should not shine upon her. He undressed quietly and climbed onto the high feather bed, blowing out the last candle before drawing the bed curtains.

Polly lay in the darkness, hardly daring to breathe as she listened for some indication that her companion now slept. But it seemed a very long time before the tossings and turnings ceased, and the bed ropes stopped creaking under his restless movements. After a judicious period, she slipped from her cot, tiptoeing to the head of the big bed, listening to his breathing. It was deep and even. With a swift movement she discarded her smock and, with the utmost caution, moved aside the bed curtain just enough to let her through. Gingerly, she lifted a corner of the quilted coverlet, inserting herself between it and the feather mattress. Never before had she lain upon a feather bed, and she was taken quite by surprise as the mattress seemed to swallow her when she sank into its depths.

Recovering from her surprise, Polly lay motionless, holding herself away from the large male body beside her as she tried to decide what to do next. Neglectfully, her planning had not taken her any further than this moment. Perhaps she should not do anything, simply wait and see what happened when her bedfellow awoke, which he surely would when he discovered that he no longer slept alone. Besides, it was wonderfully warm and soft in this enclosing darkness. Her body seemed to be sinking, heavy as lead, into the welcoming arms of oblivion.

Nicholas became aware of something warm and soft pressing into the small of his back. The sensation seemed to twine so inextricably with the rich sensuousness of his dream that when he moved his hand to identify the object, and found the bare, silken curve of Polly's hip, he was not unduly surprised. Until reality exploded.

"Lord of hell!" He yanked aside the bed curtain so that the pale light of the reluctantly risen moon could offer some illumination. The golden eyelashes swept upward. Shock leapt from the deep hazel pools as Polly stared in utter bemusement into the sleepy, furious face hanging over hers. Then she remembered where she was and why. It clearly behooved her to do something. Instinctively she reached a hand up to touch his lips, her own mouth curving in a warm smile of invitation. On this occasion, her instinct was gravely at fault.

It was the smile he had seen in the Dog tavern—a come-hither smile full of sensuous promise. Nick jerked his head away from her touch as if he had been burned. That Polly was not the one who aroused him—at least, not to desire. "What in the devil's name do you think you are doing?" When she had moved her arm, the cover had fallen back, leaving her breasts exposed in the moonshine, their crowns hardened under the cold air. With a violent exclamation, he flung himself from the bed, yanked the cover off her, and hauled her to her feet.

Polly, completely bewildered, stood blinking at him, shivering as the cold fingered her bed-warmed skin. "I do not understand," she quavered. "Why should you be so angry? I wish only to give myself to you. I am quite clean now, so you will not catch anything."

"God's grace!" If he looked into those eyes, he would be lost. Was this ingenuousness feigned? It was easier to believe that it was—anger was an effective substitute for lust. "If you were to forget the tricks of a common whore, and learn a little delicacy, the offer might have some appeal," he said, each word coldly calculated to hurt. "If I want a whore, I will find one." He picked up her smock from the floor. "Put this on and get back upstairs. And don't you ever come in here without an invitation again." He turned away from her abruptly so that he did not have to watch her face dissolving with hurt and confusion, and climbed back into bed, twitching the curtain closed.

Polly, numbed in mind and body, replaced her smock and crept out of the room, shutting the door gently behind her.

Hearing the click of the latch, Nick allowed the violent flow of oaths to pour forth unhindered. He had told Richard that he would kindle passion in Polly before allowing himself to consummate his own desire. There would be no chains of love forged in the simple satisfaction of his need, and he was not fool enough to mistake Polly's offer of her body for anything but the pragmatic bargain it was. Although exactly what she wanted in exchange at this point, he did not know. But when he took her, it would not be the tavern wench with the come-hither smile he intended to initiate. It would be Polly in all her beauty and innocence, with that infectious smile and mischievous wit. And she would want his lovemaking for its own sake, not for what it could buy her. Until that time he would manage both himself and her.

But he ached for her, could still feel her warmth in the bed, the imprint of her body against his, could still see her standing naked in the moonglow. He lay staring into the shadows of the bed curtains. It was going to be a very long night.

Polly claimed her cot for what seemed only minutes before a great bell clanged through the house. Her companions in the attic came awake with groans and imprecations. Bridget lit the candle, and they dressed in its chilly light, fingers fumbling in the cold. Polly's silence went unremarked in the general complaining mutters, and once in the kitchen, there was too much to do for conversation.

The interminable morning wore on. The kitchen resembled a furnace, steam from the bubbling cauldrons thickening the air so that one could barely see across the room. The smell of soap and heating irons was entrapped in Polly's nostrils. After her almost sleepless night, she seemed to have lost touch with physical reality, moving in a trance, bumping against tables and stools, once nearly dropping a heavy kettle of boiling water. After that, Bridget set her to scrubbing sheets in a tub, and there she stayed all morning, out of harm's way, kneeling on the hard flagstones, scrubbing until her hands were crimson and wrinkled.

After the noon dinner, there was ironing, folding, mending. Polly moved like a somnambulist. Not even in the worst days at the Dog tavern had she felt so exhausted. She fell asleep during evening prayers, only Susan's swift nudge saving her from Lady Margaret's wrath. That night she slept like one dead, and not even her mortification could penetrate her stupor.

It was there the next morning, however, in hard-etched memory, and she prayed that her duties would keep her again in the kitchen, that she would not be obliged to face him, see the contempt in the emerald eyes.

Nicholas waited for her to come for her lesson in his parlor after dinner. He had not expected her the previous day, not after such a recent confrontation. But he had had neither sight nor sound of her since that ghastly debacle, and it occurred to him, with a sudden flash of alarm, that maybe she had left. She had nowhere to go, but she had proved herself resourceful. He pulled the bell rope and paced restlessly.

It was young Tom who appeared. "You want me, m'lord?"

"No. Polly, as it happens. Is she in the house?"

"She was at dinnertime, m'lord," responded the boy with a cheerful grin. "Shall I fetch 'er for ye?"

"If you would be so kind," said his lordship, dryly.

Polly heard the summons and tried desperately to think of an excuse. She had the cellar to sweep, the pots to scrub . . .

" 'E's waitin' for ye," Tom stated as she hesitated. "In 'is parlor."

"Oh, very well." There seemed no help for it. Polly wiped her hands on her apron and went into the hall. This time she knocked on the parlor door.

"Come in." Nick looked up from the Bible he had again opened on the table and smiled at her. There was no response as she stood in the doorway, looking at her feet. "Why did you not come for your lesson?" he asked.

She still did not look at him. "I did not think you would wish me to."

He sighed. "Why would I not, Polly?"

"Common whores do not learn to read."

"Come inside and shut the door!" He waited until she had obeyed before saying more softly, "I know I was harsh, Polly, but you caught me at some considerable disadvantage. You must understand that I cannot avail myself of what you would offer while you remain under this roof, as a member of my household. Not only would it mortally offend Lady Margaret's principles, and I will not insult her, but it would also make your position with the other servants quite untenable."

"I understand that," Polly said, raising her eyes from the floor. "It is perfectly obvious. That is why I thought that if you lay with me, then I would have to go and live somewhere else."

"Conniving baggage!" Nick expostulated with soft ferocity. "So that was what you had in mind! I knew there had to be some ulterior motive."

To his unutterable dismay, tears welled in the glowing hazel eyes, welled and fell slowly, pouring soundlessly down her cheeks as she stood and looked at him, making no attempt to wipe them away.

"Oh, no, moppet, do not weep," he exclaimed, moving from behind the table, taking her in his arms. "I did not mean to be unkind, sweetheart." The tears stopped as abruptly as if he had closed a tap on an ale barrel. Nicholas stared down at the ravishing, tear-wet countenance. Suspicion grew, became certainty. Crocodile tears, if ever he had seen them. "God's grace," he muttered. "What web have I woven for myself?"

Chapter 5

The fire crackled, and the branched candelabra threw bright illumination on the table, catching the rich tones in the head bent over the big Bible. Her tongue peeped from between her lips, when they were not moving silently, making out the words on the page. It was most amazingly wonderful, Polly thought, how in a mere four weeks a confusing jumble of symbols could fall into a sensible pattern, unlocking a whole world.

"They did seem to do a deal of begatting," she commented, raising her head to look at her companion.

Nick, sitting at his ease beside the fire, chuckled. "You have come across one of those passages, have you? They can continue for pages. Why do you not find another chapter?" He watched her over the rim of his wineglass as she turned the fine paper with delicate fingers. It remained a source of continual amazement to him that such a fine-boned, dainty creature should have emerged from that coarse and brutal environment. Everything she did, she did with a natural grace.

"I cannot make this word out." She frowned deeply, saying with some annoyance, "The letters do not make sense."

He came to stand behind her, looking at the recalcitrant

collection of letters indicated by a slim but ink-stained fore-finger. "The *g-h* is silent, moppet."

"Oh . . . Nigh!" Enlightenment brought heart-stop-ping radiance to the face now upturned to his. "But how very awkward to have letters that don't mean anything."

"Isn't it," he agreed, pressing a fingertip on the end of her nose in one of the casually affectionate gestures that were now so natural for him to administer and for Polly to receive. "I gather you left the house without leave this afternoon." An eyebrow lifted quizzically as he returned to his seat.

Polly did not immediately respond, and he did not press her, concentrating on the business of setting a taper to his clay pipe. "So she told you," Polly said finally, folding her hands on the table in front of her.

"She did." Nick drew on his pipe, narrowing his eyes against the curl of smoke. The list of Polly's infractions pre-sented to him by his rigidly furious sister-in-law grew daily longer and increasingly tedious. "Could you perhaps see your way to telling me the occasion for it?"

A smile flickered at the corners of her mouth at this exag-geratedly polite request. "Had I asked for leave, it would not have been granted," she replied unarguably. "Then I would have been obliged to add disobedience to my offenses."

"It is there already," he commented dryly. "But pray tell me where you went." He threw her a shrewd look. "Unless you hold secrets?"

A tinge of pink showed against her cheekbone. "There is no secret. I had a great desire to visit Drury Lane, to see the king's playhouse, mayhap also—" She paused, then shrugged, seeming to make up her mind. "I thought, per-haps, to see Master Killigrew, to bring myself to his notice."

"You thought, in short, to take matters into your own hands, matters that we had agreed were best left in mine." Nicholas spoke harshly, knowing that he must nip this impa-tient independence in the bud. "Perhaps you will tell me what I have done to earn your mistrust. Am I not fulfilling my side of the bargain? Permit me to tell you that you do not appear to be overly scrupulous in fulfilling yours."

Large tears welled in Polly's eyes, falling down her cheeks to splash onto the table in front of her. "No!" Nick exclaimed, pushing back his chair with abrupt violence. "If those tears do not cease instantly, I shall ensure that they have cause to be genuine! You forget that I am become quite familiar with your tricks."

"It is a very useful accomplishment," said Polly, aggrieved, wiping her cheeks with the back of her hand.

"Doubtless." He resumed his seat, then yielded to his curiosity, although he had no desire to offer encouragement for her more dubious feats. "Just how do you achieve it?"

"I think sad thoughts," she told him. "You were scolding me in that horrid way, and it was all for nothing, anyway, since the playhouse was closed up and I did not see anyone—and I am most dreadfully hungry," she finished on a plaintive note.

"Why ever should you be hungry?" Nick took the scent of his wine, frowning at her.

"For the reason that I have had no supper and am to have no breakfast," she said tartly. "You do not entirely keep your promises, sir. I understood that Lady Margaret was to have no jurisdiction over me. My stomach tells me otherwise."

Nick let his breath out in a low whistle. "Why did you not tell me of this straightway?"

"To have told you of the punishment, I would have had to tell you of the offense," she said candidly. "If you did not know of it, I had thought it best kept to myself."

"With some wisdom." He could not help smiling, recognizing the familiar pattern. She would exasperate him with her impatience and vociferous complaints about her present mode of existence, but then that enchanting ingenuousness disarmed him every time. "However, I am done scolding, so why do you not repair to the kitchen and fetch yourself some supper? Bring it back here."

"And theft will be added to my crimes," Polly declared, although she was halfway across the parlor. She paused with her hand on the door latch. "I suppose, in such an instance, Lady Margaret could turn me out of doors with good cause." Her voice was hopeful, her eyes speculative. "Then we would *have* to find an alternative arrangement."

"Yes. Newgate," said Lord Kincaid amiably. "You will end your days where you began them."

Polly, always one to accept defeat gracefully, dropped a mock curtsy of acknowledgment, her eyes mischievous.

"Get you gone," Nick said. "Or perhaps you are no longer hungry?" The query ensured her instant departure.

Chuckling, Nick bent to mend the fire. Was she ready? His amusement died as he pondered the question, staring into the flames where the fresh log blazed. She was certainly ready for an introduction to Killigrew. In the last weeks she had proved herself an apt and indefatigable pupil at anything she could be convinced was necessary to the achievement of her ambition. The rough edges had been remarkably easy to smooth, aided by her innate talent for imitation and remarkably sharp powers of observation.

He had told De Winter that in the teaching of her he would forge some chains, and he had done so. But was she ready for those other links that would bind her to him? Was she ready to accept the logical conclusion of the easy, trusting affection that he had fostered between them in the last month? He had sworn that when he made her his mistress, she would not feel she was entering into a bargain, would come to him out of her own passion. But he had been too busy either teaching her or refereeing between Margaret and her troublesome kitchen maid to spend much time on the gentle art of awakening the power of desire in that peerless breast. Perhaps it was time to bring the masquerade to a close and turn his attention to the forging of those other, stronger chains.

The door opened to admit Polly, bearing a platter laden with bread, cheese, and a hefty wedge of pigeon pie. She whisked herself into the parlor, glancing guiltily over her shoulder as she closed the door. "There was no one in the kitchen, so I was able to take whatever pleased me," she confided, coming quite unselfconsciously to sit on the floor before the fire, where he still knelt. She broke into the bread

with eager fingers, laughing up at him. "There was fat mutton and watery broth for supper." Her nose wrinkled. "I
have done well, I think."

Nicholas regarded her platter with a degree of astonishment. Obviously she had not exaggerated her hunger. "If
you really intend to consume such a quantity, you had best
have something to help it down." He got up and went over
to the side table to pour wine.

Polly accepted the glass with a smile of thanks and took a
hearty bite of bread and cheese. "I have forgotten. Is it a
marquis who comes after a duke?"

"Do not talk with your mouth full, moppet," he reproved
automatically, sitting in the elbow chair beside the fire.
"Aye, 'tis a duke, a marquis, an earl, a viscount, a baron."

Polly conscientiously swallowed her mouthful. "And you
are a baron, and Lord De Winter is a viscount."

"Correct," he said with a smile. "Humble members of the
peerage. Can you remember who is secretary of state?"

Polly took a sip of wine. "The Earl of Arlington." She
became aware of his hand playing in her hair and, without
undue thought, shuffled backward until she was leaning
against his knees. "And the Earl of Arlington and the Earl of
Clarendon are at outs, and the king prefers Arlington to
Clarendon . . . I have it right, I think." She bit into the
wedge of pigeon pie, savoring it with great concentration.

Nick allowed his fingers to drift over the nape of her
neck, beneath the luxuriant fall of honeyed hair. Her neck
bent responsively beneath the caress, and he smiled in quiet
satisfaction, scribbling a fingernail into the delicate groove at
the base of her scalp.

"Tell me some more about Master Killigrew and Sir William Davenant," Polly demanded. "If Master Killigrew man-
ages the king's company and Sir William the Duke of York's
company, then they must be some sort of rivals?" Suddenly,
without knowing why she did, unless it had something to do
with the strange, prickly warmth spreading through her
body, emanating from those wonderfully busy fingers on her

neck, she looked over her shoulder at him, and suffered a slight shock. "Why are you smiling in that manner?"

"In what manner?" he asked softly.

Polly frowned in strange confusion. There was a glow in the emerald eyes, an intensity to his expression that set up a tingling response in her own. "It is a little hard to describe. I do not think anyone has ever smiled at me like that before."

"Mayhap no one has seen before what I see now," he said, moving a thumb beneath her chin to tilt her face as he brushed a pastry crumb from her lips with his forefinger and bent his head to bring his mouth to hers.

Polly had endured the assault of many a kiss over the last few years, on one occasion even from this man who was now so gently, so sweetly taking her mouth with his own, the tip of his tongue tantalizing her closed lips, the sensitive corners, so that the warmth bathed her like liquid sunshine and her toes curled in delight.

Very slowly, he raised his head, smiling down at the flushed surprised beauty of her. Then the hammering of the door knocker shattered the moment of quiet in which a wealth of meaning lay as yet unsaid but on the verge of articulation.

Nick got to his feet with an exclamation. Apart from the inopportune nature of such an interruption, it was late for passing visitors and the house had been locked up an hour since; he was coatless, wore only doublet and hose as befitted a man beside his own hearth; his sword was abovestairs. He stood listening as the knocker sounded again. Such an imperative nighttime summons could have fell intent at a time when one could never be certain who one's friends were, when lies and whispers abounded, conspiracies thrived, and a man could find himself in the Tower on a single word of an enemy who had the king's ear.

"Hell and the devil, boy, what kept you?" a loud voice, unfamiliar to Polly, boomed from the hall as young Tom finally managed to draw the bolts on the door.

Nicholas smiled and relaxed, saying easily, "Charles can never be convinced that he is not on a parade ground."

"Is your master at home, lad?" It was Richard's voice this time. "Be good enough to tell him that he has visitors. Sir Peter Appleby, Major Conway, and myself."

"I had better go abovestairs," Polly said, unsure whether her dismay at the prospect had more to do with the abrupt cessation of that wonderful new activity to which Nick had just introduced her, or to abandoning her unfinished pigeon pie.

Nicholas shook his head. "Nay, I would have you stay. You may demonstrate the fruits of my labors of the last weeks." He strode to the parlor door, flinging it wide. "Richard, Charles, Peter, you are well come indeed. Come you in and feel the fire. There's wine here. But Tom shall fetch you ale if ye'd prefer."

"Ale, forsooth," boomed the major's parade ground voice. "Lord, but I'm as dry as lenten pease."

Three men, wrapped in thick cloaks, strode into the parlor, bringing a waft of the cold January night with them in their wind-reddened cheeks and tossed hat plumes.

Polly, unsure what Nick meant by a demonstration of the fruits of his labors, had got to her feet and now stood to one side of the fire, neat and demure in her gray kirtle with its lace collar, hands clasped in front of her.

"Why, good even, Polly," greeted Richard, smiling.

"Good even, Lord De Winter." She curtsied gracefully, remembering what Nick had told her of the correct depth to be accorded different social ranks. It was not a kitchen maid's bob, but the carefully executed obeisance of a young lady.

Nicholas smiled. "Polly, allow me to make known to you Sir Peter Appleby and Major Charles Conway. Gentlemen . . . Mistress Polly Wyat."

Now Polly realized what he had meant about the fruits of his labor. He had introduced her to his friends as if she were not his kitchen maid, and clearly she was expected to play the part designated, as he had coached her. "I bid you welcome, gentlemen." She offered another beautifully executed curtsy, this one meeting with responding bows. "May I pour you wine, Sir Peter? Lord De Winter?" Smiling graciously, she moved to the side table. "Tom will bring ale for Major Conway directly."

She was playing hostess as if she were born and bred to it, Richard observed, exchanging an appreciative smile with Nick. Polly, busy with her guests' cloaks and the pouring of wine, did not notice that the cheery bonhomie of the major, and the more restrained courtesies of Sir Peter, concealed a sharp observation that took in every facet of her face, form, and deportment.

Cloaks doffed, refreshment in hand, the visitors took chairs. Polly wondered if it would be appropriate for her to finish her supper, still on the tray before the fire.

Nick, seeing her speculative gaze fixed on the pigeon pie, couldn't help chuckling. "I am certain no one will mind if you finish your supper, Polly."

"Indeed not, mistress. Desolated to have interrupted you," boomed the major. "Shockin' time to pay a call, I know, but we were passin' the door and just thought to see if Nick was by his fireside. Pray forgive us."

Polly murmured some suitable response and wondered whether to resume her position on the floor. The only available seat was a stool by the table, away from the fire and the circle of visitors. Ladies probably did not sit on the floor when consuming pigeon pie, but it was quite clear to everyone from the tray's present position that that was where she *had* been sitting. She glanced at Nick, who had relit his pipe and was seated in his chair watching her cogitations with huge amusement.

He gave her a small nod, pointing to the floor at his feet. Relieved, she settled down, leaning naturally against his knees, and resumed her interrupted meal while the conversation went on over her head. It was clearly a familiar subject for the four men, she reflected, since they began talking with no preliminaries.

"It seems inconceivable that the Commons will vote such a monstrous sum, even to finance a war," commented Richard. "Two and half millions! It is quite unprecedented."

"Aye, but a commercial war with the Dutch could bring

in rich booty," replied Sir Peter. "Expectations are high, even though Admiral Allin's attack on their merchant fleet at Cádiz was disappointing."

"Will the king ask the Commons for such a sum?" Polly put her empty platter on the tray and prepared to enter the discussion. "It would mean they would have to raise taxes, would it not?"

"It would," concurred Nick, "which will do little to improve His Majesty's popularity in the country."

"A fact which His Grace of Buckingham and the others of the Cabal steadfastly refuse to admit," declared the major.

Polly knew now that the Cabal was composed of Clifford, Ashley, Buckingham, Arlington, and Lauderdale. They were referred to as the Cabal for the obvious reason that their initials formed the word.

" 'Tis to be hoped Clarendon will have a steadying influence," mused Richard.

"If he's not impeached first!" The major spoke with a surge of energy. "Since Bristol's last attempt to oust him, he has been riding an uneasy mount. 'Tis imperative we discover—" He stopped suddenly, his gaze resting for a moment on Polly's face, upturned toward him, alive with interest. "Well." He cleared his throat. "Enough of such gloom. I've a mind for a rubber of whist. 'Tis a devilish good game—become all the rage in the queen's drawing room."

"I will fetch the cards," Polly offered with alacrity.

"Nay, moppet, I will fetch them." Nick forestalled her. "Get you to bed now."

"But I am not in the least awearied," Polly protested. "I would watch your play."

"You will be tired enough in the morning," he told her.

"I would not be if I did not have to rise—" She stopped. Nick's expression was not encouraging. Kitchen maids did not argue with their masters, and neither was this public protest in the least ladylike. She appeared to have forgotten her lines in both parts.

"Bid us good night," Nicholas instructed softly. "In proper fashion."

"I give you good night, my lord." Polly curtsied to him, then went scrupulously around the room bidding each one farewell with another courteous salute, although her face and voice were expressionless. She left the parlor, trailing an aura of hurt disappointment.

Richard chuckled as the door closed behind her. "You certainly have your hands full, Nick."

"Aye." Nick grinned. "But I'd not have it otherwise. What think you, gentlemen?" He raised an eyebrow at Sir Peter and the major.

"Amazing beauty. You did not exaggerate, Richard," Sir Peter said. "We had hoped our unexpected visit would afford us a glimpse, I confess. Where does she come from, Nick?"

Nick puffed on his pipe and shook his head. "That is the one secret I shall keep, Peter. It lies between Polly and myself." Richard knew, of course, but the confidence was as safe with him as if he had never heard it. "D'ye think she will captivate Buckingham?" Nick asked.

"And anyone else she chooses," declared Major Conway, taking snuff. "My apologies for slipping like that earlier. I realize she mustn't have an inkling that we've an intention to do more than bewail the king's foolishness and the Cabal's manipulation."

"No harm was done," Nick said easily. "You recovered readily enough. But your visit was timely." In one sense, at least, he amended with a rueful inner smile. "I wished you to see her and judge for yourselves before I took the next step." He looked around at the gravely attentive group. "If everyone is agreed, I think the time has come to begin to put the plan into action."

"You will move her out of here?"

"As soon as I can find suitable lodgings, Richard."

"And you will make her your mistress?" The major spoke matter-of-factly. "Before bringing her to Killigrew's notice, presumably?"

"That is my intention," Nick responded in like fashion.

"To bind her securely with the chains of love," murmured

Richard, casting a shrewd look at him. "Those of gratitude seem well in place."

"They will be when I remove her from Margaret's supervision," Nick said with an indulgent chuckle. "She is not inclined to thank me for her present situation, for all that she relishes her instruction." He sipped his wine. "Do you have any suggestions about lodgings?"

"Not Covent Garden," pronounced Richard. "You want no taint of the harlot attached to her. To be under your protection is one thing, but to inhabit the Grand Seraglio will not do."

"Indeed, not," agreed Sir Peter. "But Drury Lane might serve. It has decent houses and respectable landlords for all its proximity to Covent Garden."

"Aye, and 'tis close to the theatre," put in the major. "She'll not be conspicuous there."

"And you may come and go as you please without drawing undue attention." Richard smiled. "There is so much hustle and bustle on the lane, the houses so well occupied by the busy and the popular. It is always difficult to remember whose house one saw a person enter." The smile faded. "That could be to all our advantages later, when we wish to glean unobtrusively what she has to offer for harvest."

Nicholas simply nodded. "I will look for a suitable lodging run by a fitting landlady on the morrow. D'ye care to bear me company on the business, Richard?"

"Gladly. Now, how about that rubber of whist?"

"You are early from bed, brother," Margaret greeted Kincaid the following morning as he crossed the hall, dressed for riding in buckskin breeches and high boots, a camelot cloak with gold buttons slung across his shoulders.

"I have some business to transact," Nick said easily. "Where is Polly this morning?"

Lady Margaret's lips thinned, as they always did at the mention of the girl and the consonant inevitable reminder that in this instance she did not hold the reins. Apart from anything else, she did not understand what her brother-in-law was about. The wench did not share his bed—of that Margaret was convinced—but whenever he was in the house, the girl was at his side, and the voices and laughter coming from Kincaid's parlor corroded her soul like acid. She was convinced that he never so much as took the wench to task for the faults of which his sister-in-law kept him so religiously apprised.

"I trust she has not made another escape?" Nick queried with a dry smile when Margaret did not immediately answer his original question.

Margaret said frigidly, "As far as I am aware, brother, the girl is in the kitchen. The chapman is here."

"Make sure she is in the house when I return." Nick walked to the door. "I shall be dining with friends, but will be back by midafternoon." He contemplated telling his sister-in-law that she would soon be rid of the thorn in her side, then decided against it. He had no idea how soon he would find suitable lodgings for Polly, and there was no point stirring things up prematurely.

The scene in the kitchen at this point was one unlikely to please the lady of the house, there being for once little evidence of sober industry. Big Rob, the peddler, was paying his quarterly visit, and the contents of his pack—lace and pins and thread, combs and gaudy trinkets—were spread upon the table while the household crowded about like swarming bees, Polly as eager as the rest. The chapman's visits were always a high point in any household. Even the Dog tavern had been enlivened by them.

Big Rob was a mountain of a man, as his name implied. Bright eyes like raisins in a currant bun gleamed as he flirted with the chattering Susan, who bridled and blushed but showed no disinclination for the play, not even for the smacking kiss he gave her as he went on his way.

"Shame on you, Sue," Bridget scolded half-seriously. "You go on like that and ye'll end with a swollen belly."

Susan giggled and her plump face pinkened. " 'Tis only a

bit o' fun. There's little enough of it around 'ere. I'll be careful, never ye fear. I'm no brazen hussy of Covent Garden breeding. No man's goin' to 'ave 'is way with me, less'n 'e can offer me a ring."

Bridget clucked her approval, and Polly buried her head in the pantry, reflecting that these two probably would not draw any distinction between an actor in search of a noble protector and the Covent Garden prostitutes so scathingly described by Sue. It was not a comfortable thought.

But then she thought of those moments in Lord Kincaid's parlor last evening, before his visitors had arrived. If she closed her eyes, she could feel again the press of his lips, gentle yet so very much more than friendly, upon hers. What had it meant? What did it mean when he looked at her in that certain way? When his eyes took on that deep glow that seemed to penetrate to her very essence? And what did it mean when she felt this strange, hot confusion when he touched her with those caressing strokes of his finger, or looked at her as if he was seeing something of which she was unaware. Then, at other times, he was just briskly instructive, short with her when she moaned and complained about having to stay in this house, demanding, though always patient, in the tasks he would have her master. The contradictions must mean something. He had promised to teach her what she would need to know to impress Master Killigrew and to take her place in her chosen world. He was certainly fulfilling that promise. Surely he must want something in exchange? Indeed, he had said at the beginning that they might be of service to each other. But in what way? He had made it painfully clear that he was not interested in her offers of the only thing she could imagine she had to offer. He could have had her maidenhead at any time he chose outside this house. It was a conundrum.

Lady Margaret sailed into the kitchen at this point, effectively dampening the general exuberance left by Big Rob's visit. An hour's idleness had been granted but must now be paid for.

Polly, sent after dinner to polish the brass on the door knocker, and to scrub and hone the front step, shivered in the winter air, deciding that the lady of the house had assigned her this unfriendly task with some deliberation. It was not a day for outdoor work. The sky was leaden, threatening snow, and the wind flogged around the street corner, its rawness penetrating her cloak. The stone of the step was hard and icy beneath her knees. The holystone she was using to scour the step slipped from her numb fingers, and she cursed crossly.

"What in the devil's name do you do out here?" Nick's voice came from behind her, sharp with exasperation. He was astride a raking, long-tailed chestnut gelding.

"Nothing that pleases me," Polly snapped, all memory of kisses and softness vanished under an annoyance and misery now focused on the one who, at this moment, seemed entirely responsible for her present wretched occupation. "Or did you imagine that such a task was by my own choice?" Still kneeling, she twisted to glare up at him, resplendent and warm in his camelot cloak with its gold buttons, and his plumed beaver hat. She rubbed her bare hands together and blew on them, noting his gold-embroidered gloves.

Nick sighed. "In with you; you are like to catch your death of cold."

"But my task is not completed," she pointed out with an acid tongue. "The knocker is yet tarnished."

"Then it must remain so, I fear." Nick ignored her tone. "Go inside straightway! Wait for me in my parlor. I shall be in as soon as I have taken Sulayman to the stables. Then I have some news for you that may not come amiss."

He rode off to the stables situated in the lane behind the house, leaving Polly staring after him. He had sounded vexed, but she knew it was not with her for all that he had ordered her inside in the tone he used for kitchen maids. But that look had been lurking in his eyes again, the one he had had last night, just before he kissed her.

Polly shivered under a frigid blast of wind, suddenly de-

ciding that she could not care in the least about Nicholas,
Lord Kincaid, and his conundrums. She had had as much as
she could endure of the Lady Margaret's household, and so
she would tell him. And this time, he *would* listen! Picking
up the bucket of cold, scummy water, the brush and holystone, she marched into the house, kicking the door shut
behind her.

"You cannot have completed the task in such a short
time." Lady Margaret emerged from the drawing room at
the violent bang of the door. "How dare you slam the door
in that manner!" An angry flush stained her cheeks, and she
spoke through compressed lips.

"Go to hell!" Polly muttered, stomping across the hall
with her burdens.

"*What* did you say?" Unable to believe her ears, the Puritan stared in slack-mouthed outrage.

Polly was cold and stiff, and at the end of her tether
with confusion and vexation. "It seems to me that you
would have a better chance of hindering the devil's work
if you were to go and join him," she said, slowly and carefully.

"Why you insolent little whore!" Margaret hissed, her
eyes blazing with all the fury of the violated fanatic, her body
shaking as she stepped, hand upraised, toward Polly.

Without thought, Polly hurled the bucket of cold, dirty
water at the Lady Margaret's feet.

Nick stepped into the hall just as the water hit the flagstones with a squelching slap, to slurp around the Puritan's
ankles, soaking her shoes and the hem of her petticoat and
gown. The tableau was for a second frozen as Lady Margaret
stared down in disbelief, stunned by such an inconceivable
happening, and Polly, hazel eyes still ablaze with fury, stood
motionless, uncertain what to do next.

"Oh, Polly, you shrew!" Nick exclaimed, laughter lamentably quivering in his voice at this amazing spectacle.

"She was going to strike me," Polly said fiercely.

"I wonder why," Nick murmured, striding rapidly across

the hall as Lady Margaret returned to her senses with a
scream of rage.

"Out of this house!" She took another step toward Polly
and slipped in a puddle. Nick's arm shot out just in time,
yanking the enraged woman against him the instant she was
about to fall in an undignified heap to the floor.

" 'Tis all right, Margaret," he said soothingly. "Why do
you not go to your chamber and change your dress and
shoes? Susan can clear up this mess."

Margaret stared at him, an almost feral look in her eyes.
"Never, ever have I been subjected to—"

"No," he said, still soothing. "Of course you have not,
and you shall not be again. I will deal with this, now."

"There is nothing to deal with!" Polly's voice shook, but
it was clear and strong. "I am leaving." She marched toward
the door.

Nick caught her with his free arm, thus finding himself in
the ludicrous position of having both warring parties in his
hands. Laughter was threatening to overwhelm him and required every last ounce of self-control to keep submerged.
"Yes, you are leaving, Polly," he said. "But for the moment
you will go into my parlor and wait for me."

"Why? There is nothing to stay for." Her chin went up,
but the hazel eyes were overbright, sheened with tears she
would not shed.

Nick spoke gently, realizing that she had as yet no reason
to see the funny side of the situation. "As it happens, there
is. Just go, moppet, please." Feeling some of the rigidity
leave her, he released her.

Polly regarded him for a second. Then she turned and
walked into his parlor, closing the door behind her.

"She's to be turned off without a character," Margaret
said, trembling with outrage. "This instant!"

"Go to your chamber and change your dress," Nick said
evenly. "You need concern yourself about her no longer.
Shall I send Susan up to help you, or should she clean up this
mess?"

The need to make a domestic decision of even that small

nature seemed to restore Margaret to some measure of herself. "I will manage, thank you, brother. Do get that . . . that *creature* off the premises."

"With pleasure," Nick murmured to her retreating back. A gleam in his eye, he turned toward the parlor and Polly.

Chapter 6

"In the name of grace, whatever caused that imbroglio?"
He closed the door of the parlor and stood leaning
against it, regarding Polly's still figure with laughing eyes.
Amusement bubbled in his voice, no longer needing to be
kept hidden.

"I told her to go to the devil," Polly mumbled, still somewhat shocked at the suddenness of her impulse. "And she
raised her hand to me . . . so . . . so I threw the water."
She looked across at him uneasily. "I did not throw it *at* her,
exactly. Just toward her feet."

Nick's shoulders were shaking, and her unease vanished
under a resurgence of indignation. "It is not funny, my lord.
I cannot imagine why you should find it so!"

"Oh, but it is, sweetheart. It was the most richly comic
sight to which I have ever been treated! Margaret, standing
ankle-deep in dirty water, with that look of unutterable disbelief on her face . . ." Laughter finally got the better of
him, and he gave himself up to its enjoyment.

Polly stared at him as if he had taken leave of his senses.
What had just happened meant that she could not spend
another minute under this roof, and he did not seem to be in
the least concerned. "Oh, stop it!" she cried finally. "I will
not have you laughing at me!" Her foot stamped in vigorous

punctuation, and when he showed no sign of a return to
sobriety, she flew across the room, her fists pummeling his
chest in frustrated rage, the pure flame of anger shimmering
in the green-brown depths of her eyes.

"Nay, peace, little shrew!" he exclaimed, catching her
hands and pinning them behind her. "I was not laughing at
you, I was laughing at what you did." He smiled down at her
flushed, wrathful expression where that lovely soft mouth
quivered and confusion stood out in her eyes. "Of course, it
was quite inexcusable, and I should not find it in the least
amusing, but I cannot seem to help myself."

"I have to leave this house," Polly said, conscious of how
close they were, so close that with her every panting gasp,
her breasts seemed about to brush against his chest. Her
heart was already racing with the aftermath of her indignant
attack, and this proximity, the warm imprisonment of her
hands in his, the deep glow flickering in his eyes, were doing
nothing to help her catch her elusive breath. "I have to
leave," she repeated, her voice barely audible as she struggled
to grasp some strand of reality.

Nick shifted his hold on her wrists, taking them both in
one hand, then bringing his now-freed hand 'round to catch
her chin. With infinite slowness, he lowered his head to kiss
her mouth as he had done last evening, lingering and tender,
until the sunshine spread through her again, and the blood
danced in her veins.

"Aye," he said softly. "You must leave here, my flower.
But not as a consequence of that tantrum."

"Why, then?" Her voice sounded cracked and not at all
like her own. He still held her, and the imprint of his lips
upon hers seemed indelible.

"You know why," he said, his eyes a burning probe that
struck deep within her, questing and finding the truth for
them both.

Yes, she did know why. If, as now seemed clear, he would
take her to his bed, he would not do it in this house. "But
why now?" Still the puzzle remained. "Why would you wait
for so long? I have been willing, but you said you did not—"

"I said I did not want a part of the exchange you had in mind," he interrupted quietly. "I wished to wait until you felt what you feel now." He brushed a wisp of hair off her forehead. "Do you understand me?"

The bewildering contradictions seemed to be making a pattern; the conundrum offered its solution. Polly swallowed. "I do not quite understand why such a thing should be important to you, sir."

"Do you not? Then you have much to learn about the ways of loving, sweetheart." He smiled, but there was a gravity in his intent gaze that held her spellbound. "I would have that which no man has yet taken . . ." A finger moved to trace the long, sensuous line of her lower lip. The tip of her tongue darted, dampening his finger in a gesture that was as artless as it was enticing. He drew a long, slow breath, losing himself in the glowing hazel pools as he lifted a strand of hair from her bosom, twisting it absently around his finger. "But I would have you render it joyfully, and in free spirit." He watched her, saw the contemplation of his words lead to comprehension. "Well, moppet?" he prompted softly. "How do you answer me?"

It was this that he had been promising with those caresses and the deep, glowing intensity of his gaze; this that she had been wanting with a powerful, but until now indefinable, longing. Polly found she could not answer him. Words stuck in her throat, and she looked helplessly into that searching but smiling countenance. She noticed the way his wayward red-gold eyebrows flew upward at the edges, the curl of his eyelashes, the blue flames simmering in the emerald depths of his eyes.

"I will have your answer," he said, low but insistent. "Will you render me what I ask, joyfully and in free spirit?"

Polly moistened her lips, swallowed in an effort to lubricate her parched throat. He would have her declare this desire that she had not recognized until this moment. He was not asking her simply to agree to yield her body in payment for his assistance. It was not a whore he wanted, bought and paid for, but a lover. That illumination loosened her tongue, set the blood to resume its customary speed and course through her veins.

"Joyfully and in free spirit," she returned without a quaver.

"Ahhh." It was a long-drawn-out sound of quiet satisfaction. His lips hovered above hers, and Polly waited breathlessly. But with a laugh he straightened, letting the strand of hair he held drop back to her breast. "Perhaps not. I am of a mind to sharpen the appetite with a little procrastination." Polly's pout of disappointment brought the laughter dancing again in his eyes. Releasing his warm grasp of her wrists, he went to pull the bell rope by the hearth.

Young Tom appeared, breathless in his haste to answer the summons, his eyes darting with fascinated speculation at Polly. The entire household was buzzing with the story of the enormity of Polly's behavior—behavior that could not conceivably go unpunished. Lady Margaret might even call the constable, Bridget said. Assault on the mistress, it had been. The master would surely have to take my lady's part this time. But as far as Tom could see, Polly showed no ill effects from having been closeted with his lordship for above a half hour. Indeed, far from being red-eyed with weeping, she was smiling.

"Send a message to the stables, Tom," Kincaid instructed the lad. "I want the carriage brought 'round in twenty minutes."

"Yes, m'lord." Tom backed to the door, his eyes still on Polly. She dropped one eyelid in an unmistakable wink, and his gaze widened in amazement.

"I do not think Tom expected to find me in one piece," she observed with a chuckle as the door closed.

Nick, opening the little drawer in his desk where he kept his strongbox, looked up and observed, " 'Twas fortunate I was here. Nothing I have said in the past would have prevented Margaret's laying her stick across your shoulders with unbridled venom, I fear."

"I would not have done it had you not been here," Polly replied. "I am not such a fool as to court danger."

Nick unlocked the box, turning his attention to the contents. Maybe she would not knowingly court danger, but he was conspiring to expose her to the possibility of a threat much greater than any posed by Margaret and her hazel stick—the penalty for conspiring to bring about the downfall of one of the most powerful men in the land. If she was discovered, she would pay that penalty whether she had been spying wittingly or no. But he would not allow the conspirator's concerns to intrude on those of the lover—not at this juncture. He drew out a purse of golden guineas, dropping it into his coat pocket. When a man contemplated a night's absence from his home, it was well to be prepared.

"Run abovestairs, moppet, and pack up your belongings," he instructed. "The carriage will be here shortly."

"We go to find lodgings?" Polly asked, glancing out of the window, where snowflakes drifted, breaking loose from the leaden sky. " 'Tis snowing."

"The lodgings are found." Nick's eyes followed hers. "We'll be snug and warm before that becomes serious."

"But when were they found?" Bewilderment crept up on her again. "I thought you had only just decided—"

"Did you now?" His smile was teasing. "Then you were mistaken, my love. Now, begone and collect your things. I do not wish to delay overlong."

Polly, devoutly hoping that she would not come face-to-face with the Lady Margaret, left the parlor. The hall was empty, and despite her knowledge of his lordship's protection and her own new status, she could not prevent herself from scurrying like a field mouse up the stairs and into the privacy of the servant's attics.

She had little enough to gather up: just the clothes that Kincaid had bought her at the Royal Exchange, a comb and a few ribbons she had bought for herself on the same day with the sovereign, and a piece of lace that she had bought from Big Rob that morning with her last remaining pennies. She was wrapping her worldly goods into a bundle when the door creaked open. She swung 'round nervously, but it was Sue who crept in.

"Y'are going to be all right, Polly?" she asked in a hesitant whisper. " 'Tis said that her la'ship is turning you off without a character. What will ye do?"

"I can tell you, Sue, I want no truck with any of Lady Margaret's characters," Polly declared, sitting upon the bed with a mischievous smile. "Think how tedious 'twould be to be of a character to suit the Puritan."

"Oh, Polly, y'are awful. Ye shouldn't say such things. 'Tis so disrespectful!" gasped Sue, her hand over her mouth, although her eyes danced responsively.

" 'Twas not exactly respectful to throw a bucket of dirty water at her," Polly said airily. "Oh, you should have seen her face, Sue!" She went into a peal of laughter. "But I cannot tell you what I am going to do because you will be shocked." This morning's discussion about brazen hussies of Covent Garden breeding was not easily forgotten. For all that Polly knew that matters were not to be so conducted, she knew that Sue and her like would not draw the fine distinctions when it came to carnal pleasures enjoyed without the sanction of a wedding ring.

She herself was possessed of a feeling that she could not name—part excitement, part apprehension. Since that December night, she had been hovering on the edge of a wondrous unknown. On the surface she had gone about the tedious work of a maidservant, enlivened by the time she spent with Lord Kincaid. Beneath this apparently ordinary exterior existence had seethed a secret life of hidden desires, of unspoken promises, of visions of expanded horizons and dreams come true.

Now that secret life was to become the exterior life. Now she was about to break free truly, to leave behind her all that was dreary, brutal, exploitative—in short, all that had informed her practical existence until this afternoon. And the excitement was charged with the apprehension of what had only hitherto been known as dream and in imagination. Tonight she would lay her head upon some strange pillow, and she would have crossed into this new life through a physical experience that she longed for even as she feared it.

"Oh, Polly, I'm afeard for ye," Sue said. "Without a decent place and a character, ye'll be sent to Bridewell as a vagrant. They'll whip ye at the cart's tail. If ye steal—"

" 'Twill be Newgate and the common hangman," Polly finished for her. "Those are not in my destiny, Sue. Have no fear of that. But I cannot tell you what is." She put her arms around her friend's plump body and hugged her. "You watch out for yourself with Big Rob and his like! Somewhere there's a husband for you, and he'll take you away from this miserable place."

"I wish I could go with ye," Sue said dismally. "If'n y'are really going to be all right."

"I am, but I must go alone." She turned back to her cot, where lay her bundle, pathetically small in this dim, drear chamber that exemplified every dim, drear aspect of the life she was leaving.

"Oh, Sue," she said suddenly, tears starting in her eyes, "I wish you could come." She hugged her fiercely once more, gathered up her bundle, and flew down the narrow wooden stairs to the landing. There she paused to compose herself before descending the main staircase with the deliberate grace of any young lady of breeding.

But there was one more trial in wait for her. In the stone-flagged hallway stood Lady Margaret, in clean gown and shoes, every inch of her radiating malevolence and outrage. Instead of throwing this abominable slut out into the snow to sink, as she surely would without references or money, into the mire of criminal vagrancy, her brother-in-law was actually taking the creature under his protection, was actually going to escort her from the house in his own carriage!

Beside her, his expression studiously neutral, stood Kincaid.

"You would set up such a one as your whore?" Lady Margaret spoke with cold loathing, spite glistening in her eyes. "I had thought you more fastidious, brother."

Polly quivered, the color draining from her face. Nick moved beside her. "Say nothing," he insisted in clear tones. "That is no accusation for *you* to answer."

"I will answer—"

"For once you will do as you are bid!" Nick, recognizing that he must take charge of this ugliness without a moment's delay, made no attempt to moderate the harshness of the command. Polly bit her lip, falling silent in sudden confusion. It was as if she were being attacked on all sides.

"I daresay you will find life with your brother in Leicester infinitely more to your taste, Margaret," Nicholas was saying with deceptive sweetness, even as he gripped the back of Polly's neck with firm fingers that imparted reassurance as they demanded her silence. "I shall, of course, be desolated at your departure, but I do understand how one of your tastes and principles would find my roof quite unsuitable." He knew as well as did Margaret that her brother, an impoverished country divine, father of a hopeful family, could not possibly offer his sister a permanent home.

Margaret's realization that she had overstepped the line was painfully revealed on her face. She looked, Polly thought with glee, rather like a landed fish. For an instant, the temptation to take advantage of her enemy's discomfiture with a well-aimed thrust offered powerful vengeance for all the injustices and unkindnesses of the last weeks. Then came the thought that to do so could only show her in an ill light, would be a demonstration of the kind of behavior one would expect from a tavern-bred slut, would simply confirm Margaret's accusation. It was one thing to defend oneself from physical attack with whatever means came to hand, quite another to kick an enemy who was already down.

"I will await you in the carriage, sir," she said, her tone one of lofty dignity. She gathered up her skirts, moving in stately fashion to the door, which was instantly opened by the fascinated Tom. The lad followed her to open the door of the coach, to let down the footstep.

"My thanks," Polly said, as condescending as any duchess. But sadly, mischief got the better of her. "Old trout! She is well served," she whispered, grinning at Tom as she settled herself on the seat. He snorted with laughter, leaning in to exchange a further confidence, and then jumped backward as Lord Kincaid came down the steps. His lordship regarded the footboy's suffused countenance, then looked sharply into the carriage. Polly's eyes were brimming with deviltry.

Kincaid climbed into the coach, told Tom that he might go to his bed when he pleased, then sat back in the darkness as the boy closed the door on them. Whatever exchange had taken place between those two, Polly had quite clearly recovered herself, he reflected with an inner chuckle. That had been a most impressive display for one in such an ambivalent position.

Polly glanced sideways at her companion, but could see nothing of his expression. "You are not vexed, are you, sir?"

"Vexed!" he exclaimed. "With *you*? God's grace, no!"

"Then may I ask where we are going, my lord?"

He could hear the mischief in the dulcet tone, and recognized that Mistress Polly was more than restored. "To Drury Lane," he informed her, slipping an arm around her shoulders. "And I think it is time that you practiced using my name. There are times when 'sir' and 'my lord' are appropriate, and times when they are not. The latter time has arrived."

"Oh," Polly said a few minutes later, absorbing the demonstration of this fact with apparent interest. "When you do that, I should call you Nicholas, is it so?" That same dulcet tone, laced with wickedness, set his nerve endings tingling with the most delicious anticipation. Unless he much mistook the case, this young woman was eventually going to prove herself an inventive and playful lover.

"When I do that, and a great many other things," he declared, drawing her back into his embrace.

Chapter 7

The coach and four came to a halt. A strange surge, part terror, part exultation, shuddered through Polly's slender frame. Nick, feeling it, tightened his hold for an instant before leaning forward to swing open the door. The snow swirled thickly now, caught white and effervescent in the yellow light of the lantern held up by the coachman. Nick jumped out, disdaining the footstep, and reached up to catch Polly by the waist, swinging her down beside him.

"I'll not be needing ye again this night," he said to John Coachman. "Get you and the cattle to shelter as soon as may be."

The coachman looked worriedly at the sky. "Has the smell of a blizzard, m'lord."

"Aye. Well, be off without delay. You've not far to go." He turned to Polly, who was squinting through the snow at her surroundings, her head and shoulders coated with white flakes. "In with you, before you become a pillar of ice." He put an arm around her waist, urging her to a door set into a timbered, whitewashed wall. The door swung open before he could knock.

"I was wonderin' whether ye'd make it in such foul weather," a cheery voice declared. "Fire's bright, and there's a good supper waitin' abovestairs."

Polly stepped into a small, square hall and found herself the object of scrutiny from a pair of bright black eyes set into a ruddy-complexioned, well-lined face. The scrutiny was interested but far from unfriendly. "This be the young lady, then, m'lord?"

"Mistress Polly Wyat," Nicholas said formally. "My love, this is Goodwife Benson. She will be looking after you."

Polly had never been looked after by anyone, except by Prue, way back at the dawn of memory, and even then not with any enthusiasm. She looked blank, searching for an appropriate response. The kindly eyes twinkled as if in understanding.

"Come along a' me, m'dear. I'll show ye the apartment m'lord 'as taken for ye." The plump body turned and bustled up a narrow flight of stairs. "Two nice chambers," she called over her shoulder. "Clean as a new pin, they be. No vermin in my 'ouse."

They reached a minute landing, where the goodwife unlatched a solid oak door, pushing it open with a flourish. A neat, paneled parlor was revealed under sloping eaves. A fire sizzled on a stone hearth, and a linen-covered seat ran beneath the low mullioned window. The furniture was plain but highly polished, the hangings and coverings crisply clean and bright. A round table was set with platters, pewter cups, knives, and skewers; the aroma of roasting meat wafted up the stairs.

"And 'ere's your bedchamber." Goodwife Benson opened a door in the far wall. Here was a room dominated by a big four-poster with a carved oak tester and rose-red curtains. There was a paneled tiring table with a branched candlestick and a crystal mirror above it, the whole warmed by the cheerful blaze of yet another fire.

Polly was speechless. She was to have two rooms to herself! And such rooms! Her eyes flew to Nicholas, standing behind her, watching her with the enigmatic smile she had come to expect, even though she frequently did not know why he should have it.

"It's to be 'oped all's to your satisfaction, mistress," the goodwife said when Polly remained silent.

"Oh . . . yes . . . p-please . . . th-thank you . . . indeed, it is," stuttered Polly.

"Then I'll see to your supper," the woman said comfortably. "Ye'll be sharp-set, I'll be bound."

"Indeed we are," Nicholas said when it became clear that Polly had once again lapsed into muteness. Goodwife Benson bustled out, and he snapped his fingers in front of the bewitched Polly. "Wake up."

Her eyes focused, and she saw he was laughing at her. "Am I to live here alone?" she managed to ask, still unable to grasp the idea of so much space for one person.

"I'm hoping I may be a frequent visitor," he said quizzically, unfastening the clasp of her cloak.

"Y-yes, of course, sir," replied Polly, hearing how absurdly polite and formal she sounded, unable to blame Nick for the ready laughter brimming in the emerald eyes. "Shall . . . shall you be staying tonight?"

"Well now." He pulled pensively at his chin, "If I were issued an invitation, I just might be induced to accept it. It being such a dreadful night, you understand? Blizzard threatening . . ."

Her lips twitched. Peeping up at him through her lashes, she swept him a deep curtsy, sinking to her heel, one toe delicately pointed. "I do beg you will take shelter in my humble abode, my lord. I should never rest easy if I thought you were out in such a storm."

"I shall be eternally grateful, madame." A magnificent leg returned her salutation, and Polly, assailed by giggles, lost her balance and collapsed with an undignified thump on the floor. Nick picked her up. "What a lamentable performance," he chided. "I thought I had taught you to execute a curtsy with more decorum." Drawing her into his embrace, he pushed up her chin, consuming that ravishing countenance with his gaze, feeling her pliancy under his hands, seeing the image of her body in the eye of memory.

"I want you." The naked hunger in his eyes and voice

sent laughter scuttling to the four corners of the bedchamber. Then the sound of footsteps next door, the smells of roasting mutton, Goodwife Benson's cheery summons to table, broke into the charmed circle. "Anticipation must again whet the appetite," he said with a rueful smile. "And you will be the better for your supper. Lovemaking on an empty belly leaves something to be desired." He ushered her into the parlor, where a roast of mutton steamed enticingly upon the sideboard and a platter of oysters sat upon the table, ready opened, glistening pearly gray in the candlelight.

He held her chair for her, unfolded a linen napkin on her lap, poured wine into her cup, then took his place opposite. For all the ease of their past companionship it was the first time that she had sat at table in his company. There had never been any question before but that matters between them would be conducted on the terms of tutor and pupil, master and servant. Now Polly felt unaccountably nervous, as if these present attentions were awarded mistakenly and should have had some other recipient than a Newgate brat of unknown parentage. Then she remembered that she was an actor, that she could be whomsoever she pleased. She raised her glass in salutation, her eyelashes fluttering, lips curving delicately.

Nick, absorbing the full impact of this breathtaking performance, was in little doubt as to its cause. He raised his own glass. "Masterly," he approved. "You know well how to adapt to unfamiliar circumstances. It is a talent that will stand you in good stead in the next weeks."

Polly sucked an oyster from its craggy shell. The intensity had quite gone out of the occasion. His lordship was speaking in the easy tones he habitually employed, as if those words of passion had not been spoken with such urgency such a short time before. It ensured that she was able to devote her full attention to her supper; under the benign influence of good food, good wine, warmth, and undemanding companionship, all apprehension left her.

Nicholas noted her gradual relaxation with satisfaction. He was far from such a state himself, although his companion could not possibly guess from his manner at the effort he was exerting to keep his ardor under bridle. It was of the utmost importance to him that the true initiation of this exquisite creature should bear no relation to the brutalities she had endured in the past. He remembered only too clearly her piteous plea that he not hurt her that first evening, when, with the resignation of the accustomed victim, she had ceased her struggles, surrendering herself to whatever new yet inevitable horror awaited her. Tonight she would experience only gentleness as he led her along the sweet paths of pleasure. There would be time enough later for the glorious rough and tumble of lust's urgencies.

He selected a Katharine pear from the fruit bowl. It was a fruit beloved of King Charles and his queen; one, it was to be assumed, never before tasted by the girl who should, if all went according to plan, shortly find herself moving in those exalted circles. He peeled the fruit, quartered it neatly, and laid it upon her plate, remembering pragmatically that he had not yet educated her palate for that role, and must do so. The reminder, for some reason, cast a bleak shadow. It was the second time the concerns of the conspirator had intruded in such unwelcome fashion when he wished only to think of a loving seduction.

"My thanks." She smiled with a hint of shyness as she took the offering. "Seldom have I enjoyed such a supper."

"That was my intention," he replied softly, rising and coming 'round the table.

She turned in her chair to look up at him as he came to stand beside her. "Is it time?"

The forthright question took him completely aback, until he realized that it was only what he should have expected. Seduction rituals would be quite unknown to this maid, whose depths of experience were on the one hand vast, and on the other pathetically spare. "Finish your pear," he said, beginning to unpin her hair.

The heavy, honeyed mass tumbled about her shoulders, and he amused himself by running his fingers through its richness, gathering it at the nape of her neck, twisting it into

a thick knot as he bent his head to brush his lips over the
fragile column thus revealed. Polly shivered deliciously and
found the sensation incompatible with the stolid consumption of fruit. She laid the pear back on the platter, allowing
her head to bend beneath the pressure of his mouth, the firm
smoothing of his tongue in the groove of her neck.

He cupped the rounded edges of her shoulders, slid his
hands forward to mold the shape of her breasts beneath her
gown, rubbing gently with his thumbs until he felt the hardening as her nipples rose to press against the fine wool of her
kirtle. Polly gave a startled gasp and moved her hands instinctively to cover his, whether to keep them at work or to
push them aside was not clear to herself or to Nick.

"Come." He pulled her chair out from the table, drew
her to her feet, turning her to face him. "There are things I
would show you." The pure fire of passion flamed behind
the bright green gaze, but his mouth was soft, his hands
gentle as he cupped her face and kissed her. Her eyes remained riveted on the face so close to hers, as if only thus
could she be certain of missing no nuance of feeling. The
mouth against hers curved, and his fingertips brushed her
eyelids closed before moving beneath the fall of hair to trace
the perfect outline of her ears. Her body tautened beneath
the caress, and his little fingers, in instant response, moved
enticingly within the shell-like contours as his tongue ran
over her lips, demanding entrance. Her lips parted for him,
her tongue joining in a tentative dance with his.

Slowly he raised his head, licked the tip of her nose, a
salute that brought the hazel eyes wide open in surprise. "Do
not look so astonished, moppet," he said on a husky murmur. "Before very much longer, I shall taste every morsel of
your sweetness, drain the last honeyed drop from your
body."

Polly did not know what the words meant, knew only that
the soft promise brought pinpricks of fire darting across the
entire surface of her skin, a liquid fulness in her loins, a
weakness in her belly. She shivered against him, and her

hands moved to her bodice. "Should I take off my clothes now?"

Nick took her hands, holding them away from her body. She was so ingenuously matter-of-fact. He smiled, shaking his head.

"Not this time, my flower. That is a pleasure I wish to take for myself, and in the taking would give to you."

He appeared to be talking in riddles, Polly thought, but they were riddles whose solution seemed redolent with promise, so she made no demur as he led her into the bedchamber, closing the parlor door behind them with a definitive click. He drew her over to the fire and set the tapestry screen between its heat and the window, shielding the flame from the snow-laden drafts fingering their way through every crack between frame and glass. He moved the candlesticks from the tiring table, placing them at either end of the mantel, so that they threw their soft light onto the hearth, where Polly stood tremulous, watching these preparations, wondering what they presaged.

"Now." He took off his coat of green broadcloth, and the close-fitting doublet of ivory satin. He came toward her with a lithe, springing step, the gleam in his eyes and the luster of his auburn head caught by the mingled golden glows of fire and candle. "Now we may begin."

The bodice of her kirtle came unlaced. Polly found herself looking down at his deft fingers as they flew at their work, the square emerald on his left hand, the intricate gold signet ring on his right, winking in the light. He slipped the open bodice off her shoulders, stroking her upper arms as he did so before moving his hands again to her breasts, hidden now by only the fine cotton of her smock. Her breath was coming too fast to catch, and she could feel her skin misting with a light sweat that had nothing to do with the heat of the fire. He stretched the material taut over the soft hillocks so that the pink and pearl of her skin showed against the white, and the deep rose of her nipples stood out, sharply peaked. Polly felt more naked than she had ever felt, even when she had stood before him completely unclothed.

With the same deftness, he unhooked her smock. It followed the path of her kirtle to cluster at her waist, baring her upper body for the touch of his eyes and fingers. She could feel the fire's heat now, and the heat that was spreading from her belly, moistening the deep recess of her body, melting her joints and sinews. He held her breasts, one in each palm, as he kissed her again, but this time with greater demand, his fingers lifting her nipples as his tongue probed the velvet cavern of her mouth. Then his hands moved to grasp her waist, his head bent to take their place on her breasts. Polly whimpered with an inexpressible delight as his teeth nibbled their rosy crowns, his lips tugged, setting up a chain of sensations in her belly and between her thighs so that she moaned again and moved between the hands spanning the indentation of her waist.

His tongue dipped into her bosom's cleft, then trailed upward, painting fire in the hollow of her throat as her head fell back, offering the soft vulnerability. Her own hands gripped his upper arms, fingers curling against the cambric of his shirt, feeling the heat of his skin, the hard ridge of muscle. She found that the material prevented the contact that she now desired, her fingers, hasty, fumbling in their eagerness, tugged at the buttons of his shirt until they flew apart and she was able to push it aside, her breasts now pressing against his bare chest.

Nick inhaled sharply at this independence. He had not expected it, had expected her to remain passive as he aroused her, obedient to his orchestration for this first time, at least. It was a most welcome surprise. He drew back to look down at her. Her eyes were heavy and languorous, her skin damp and flushed with excitement, those peerless breasts proudly outthrust, grazing his chest.

Holding her gaze, he moved to untangle the wadded material at her waist, loosening her kirtle so that it fell to her ankles. The top of her smock hung over the waistband of her petticoat, and it required the attention of eyes as well as hands to unfasten the latter. He pushed both garments off her hips, his hands sliding, lingering over the curves thus revealed. Polly quivered as the heat of the fire licked her bared skin, and passion's flame flared in the emerald eyes riveted to her body, clad now only in her stockings and garters and leather pumps. He dropped to his knees to unfasten her garters and roll down her stockings, lifted each foot in turn as he eased them into nakedness.

Still kneeling, he ran his hands up the straight, clean length of leg to hold her hips as he kissed her belly. She jumped against him, and his grip tightened, holding her steady for the nuzzling caress of his mouth, for his dipping tongue exploring the tight bud of her navel. Convulsively, her fingers twisted in the long auburn curls that fell over his shoulders, whispered against the skin of her abdomen. But when his fingers moved, parting the soft, golden fleece at the apex of her thighs, slipping into the moist, secret furrow, she started with a small cry of protest, pulling on his head.

He looked up, seeing the panicky flutter in those huge eyes, the quiver of her soft mouth. Slowly he rose to his feet. "You must trust me," he said, and there was quiet, calculated reproof in his voice. "I will bring you only pleasure, I swear it."

She hung her head in sudden embarrassment, but Nick caught her chin, forcing her to meet his eye. "Do you believe that I will not hurt you?" She nodded, knowing it to be the truth. "And do you believe that there is no shame in what is about to happen? None for you and none for me?"

There could be none, Polly thought; not when such wonder filled her at his touch, when she felt such a powerful wanting; not when his eyes held such a tenderness, softening his own wanting—a hungry longing that she could read as clearly as her own.

"No shame," she said, and reached a hand to touch his lips. He lifted her then, carrying her to the bed, holding her strongly against one upraised knee as he pulled back the coverlet before laying her down upon the cambric sheet. He leaned over her, his arms braced on either side of her body, and licked the tip of her nose again so that she wriggled deliciously. The tip of his tongue explored her face, moist-

ening her eyelids, her cheeks, tantalizing, sweetly playful at
the corners of her mouth, nuzzling into the deep cleft of her
chin. The hard bulge of his awakened manhood pressed
against her thigh, and when he drew her hand down, guiding it to feel the power throbbing against the constraint of his
breeches, she made no resistance, but her eyes widened at
the thought of that power entering the narrow, unviolated
portal to her body.

Nick stood up to remove his hose and breeches, and Polly
gazed upon the shaft, springing erect from the curly nest at
the base of his concave belly. "Stand up," he instructed
softly, reaching a hand to help her as she got off the bed.
"Hold me. You will not be frightened when you are acquainted with me in this way." Again he guided her hand as
she stood in front of him. She enclosed the pulsing root in
her hand, feeling it hard yet pliant, the blood throbbing in
the ridged veins against her palm. With her other hand, she
touched the dark, flat buttons of his nipples, and Nick threw
his head back on an exhalation of pleasure; his eyes closed as
she continued to stroke him, tentatively at first, then with
increasing confidence as she saw his pleasure and learned her
own. His hands moved 'round to her buttocks, cradling the
firm roundness as he drew her against him, so that his manhood pulsed strongly against her belly. He held her like that,
until she leaned into him of her own accord, her legs parting
in a natural movement indicative of the readiness of desire.

"Lie on the bed now," he whispered, easing her backward, turning her so that she lay again looking up at him, no
awkwardness now, just unvarnished need in her eyes. "If I
am not to hurt you," he said, stretching himself beside her,
"I must learn something of you." He moved aside a heavy
swatch of hair that concealed her breast, taking her nipple
between his lips again as he stroked, long and languorously,
down her length, feeling her relaxation under the almost
hypnotic caress. This time her thighs parted for his probing
fingers, which opened her gently, entered her to seek and
find what he sought. Her hips arched involuntarily at this
invasion. Her body tightened against the alien presence, but

he gentled her with a soft word against her mouth, and proceeded inexorably to bring her to the edge of delight with the skillful play of his fingers.

Polly felt the curling spiral tighten in her belly; her hips lifted and moved, responding to the rhythm of the presence within. Her head moved restlessly on the coverlet; hot blood surged through her veins, and that part of her body she had thought of as peculiarly her own responded to another's possession. With an incoherent cry, she took her release in the only way possible, the muscles of thigh and buttocks tightening around his hand as the juices of arousal flowed sweet and her body opened in joy.

Nick swung himself across her supine body, stopping her mouth with his own as he guided his surging flesh within the still-pulsating gate. He knew now how deeply lodged was her maidenhead, and, with one determined thrust, plunged to her core. Her eyes opened, wide with shock, but in the aftermath of climax her muscles were capable of no resistance and the moment passed, to be remembered only as the briefest spark of an irrelevant pain.

She looked up at him as he hung over her, raking her face for knowledge as he moved himself within, slow and easy now until she picked up the rhythm. She smiled suddenly. It was such a wonderful smile, so expressive of surprise and delight, that he laughed joyously.

"I did not think it possible for you to be more beautiful," he said with soft wonder. "But never have I seen such glorious radiance. I will take you now into a world outside this one, if you will give yourself into my charge."

"Gladly," she returned, her eyes locking with his as he took them both to the outermost edge of bliss, to hover in a timeless, sensate universe until the ultimate could no longer be held at bay, and they slipped over the edge, into the beyond.

Polly came back to a sense of the world around her very slowly. She opened her eyes to find Nick, propped on one elbow, smiling down at her. He brushed a lock of hair from her forehead and kissed her. "It appears that you are an apt pupil in everything, moppet."

"I do not think," Polly said consideringly, "that I could have done otherwise than I did, sir. Matters seemed to take care of themselves." Her eyes twinkled roguishly. "For which I must thank you, I suspect."

"You may thank me by using my name. I have asked you to do so once already this day." His fingers traced the curve of her mouth.

"I have a lamentable memory, Nicholas." She sucked his finger into her mouth, curling her tongue, tasting the slight saltiness.

"Then you had best set about improving it," he retorted, running his free hand down her body in a leisurely caress, smoothing over the fine turn of a hip, one long damask-toned thigh, cupping the curve of her knee. She had the most beautiful knees; but then, it would be ridiculous for such perfection to be marred, even by something as insignificant as a knee, Nick reflected dreamily. Her body shifted in lazy response to the caress, and a bright smear of blood showed on her inner thigh.

Nick got off the bed, crossing to the tiring table, where ewer and basin stood. The water that he poured into the basin was tepid, but the fact that it had once been warmed bore witness to the care of Goodwife Benson. He dipped a towel in the basin, then came back to the bed, where Polly still lay, watching him. "Let me make you a little more comfortable," he said softly, sitting down beside her. She stretched, catlike, as he drew the damp cloth down her body, freshening the sweat-slick skin, parting her thighs to cleanse her of the bright blood of innocence and the residue of passion.

It was the most sweetly tender intimacy, and Polly quite suddenly felt tears welling behind her eyes. They were not tears of sorrow or of joy, but of amazement at such an unexpected ministration so lovingly offered. She had been touched in many ways in her seventeen years, but rarely with gentleness, and never before in this cherishing manner, and the tears rolled unbidden down her cheeks.

"Do not weep, flower," Nick said in distress, not understanding why she should produce this reaction when a bare instant before she had been all teasing, sensual mischief.

"I cannot seem to stop," she sobbed.

Nicholas thought of the dramatic manner in which her life had been transformed in the last few hours, of the suddenness of the change, and he ceased to question. He stood up, going into the parlor, returning with a cup of wine. "Sleep is your best medicine, sweetheart. Drink this first." She swallowed obediently, choked, and managed a misty smile.

"I am not in general a watering pot."

"Not unless it will serve some nefarious purpose," he agreed with a twinkle, pulling the heavy quilt up to her chin before going over to mend the fire, building it high so that it would warm them through the night.

Polly, snug and sleepy, watched him, marveling at the elegance of his movements, an elegance not at all impaired by his nakedness. Indeed, without his clothes, the power of that broad, muscled frame, wide shoulders, narrow waist, slim hips, was there to be viewed in all its inimitable glory.

"You are most beautiful, my Lord Kincaid," she murmured as he trod over to the bed, bearing the single candle that he had left alight.

"You are too kind, madame," he said, placing the candle on the bed table and bowing. Chuckling at the absurd contrast of the stately salutation and his bare skin, she pulled aside the quilt in invitation. Nick blew out the candle and slid in beside her, drawing the bed curtain against drafts and the fire's illumination. Her hand moved in sleepy exploration. He smiled in the dark, catching her wrist. "You will be better served after sleep, sweetheart."

"Oh," Polly said on a distant note of disappointment. "Then I hope it will soon be morning." She rolled into his embrace and was instantly deeply asleep.

Chapter 8

"I cannot help feeling that you are neglecting your duties, my dear Barbara." George Villiers, the second Duke of Buckingham, took snuff with a delicate twist of his wrist, and arched an ironic eyebrow at his cousin, my Lady Castlemaine. "His Majesty has an air greatly disconsolate. Was he, perhaps, impervious to your usual forms of consolation last night?"

The king's mistress shrugged plump white shoulders, the gesture lifting her breasts clear of her décolletage to reveal the nipples. "He had set his heart upon flying his new hawk this morning." She gestured to the long, snow-encrusted windows of the Privy Gallery looking over the Pebble Court at Whitehall Palace. "It is hardly possible in such weather, and you know how he detests being thwarted."

"Then it is surely incumbent upon us to suggest some diversion," Buckingham mused, flicking at his satin sleeve with his lace-edged handkerchief. "There is no knowing what he may decide to do when he is allowed to brood."

"Or whose company he may choose to favor," said Lady Castlemaine, with a shrewd, knowing look at her cousin. "He seems uncommon pleased with Clarendon this morning. They were closeted in his Privy chamber for upwards of an hour. Methinks the lord chancellor is returning to grace."

A laugh, tinged with malice, accompanied the suggestion that she knew would arouse Buckingham to supreme irritation.

The greater part of the duke's energies these days was expended in the discrediting of the chancellor to the king—a task hindered by the facts that Clarendon's daughter was married to the Duke of York, His Majesty's brother, and that Clarendon had been Charles II's most trusted counselor throughout his exile and in the years since his restoration. But the king was coming to apostatize the old man as a bore, a dull dog who would put a bridle on His Majesty's pleasure seeking; one who was forever demanding that he turn his mind to the business of governing, and the placation of Parliament if he was to secure further revenue from them. King Charles did not consider it his task to placate the Commons in order to be provided with the money he required to pursue his pleasures. The granting of such funds was Parliament's duty.

"My dear cousin," said Buckingham deliberately, "it is no more in your interests than 'tis in mine to advance the chancellor's cause. You would be better employed in joining forces with me than in amusing yourself at my expense." Almost indolently, he reached out a hand, catching her wrist, shaking back the fall of lace that had obscured a diamond bracelet. The stones caught the light from the chandelier. They were exceptionally fine stones in a most intricate setting, and His Grace made great play of examining them. "An expensive trinket, madame," he drawled, pointing his meaning with an arched eyebrow. "A present from your husband, no doubt?" He dropped her wrist abruptly, and his eyes, cold and hard, met hers. "Take heed whom you make your enemy, my lady. I will govern the king, and when I do I will remember my friends *and* my foes." With a neat toss of his head to throw back the heavy fall of his peruke so that it should not obscure his face, His Grace bowed deeply.

The irony in the salutation after such a declaration would not have been missed by one much less perspicacious than Lady Castlemaine. She curtsied with matching depth. "I, too, can be a powerful friend, my lord duke. Much can be contrived in the privacy of the bed curtains."

"Exactly so." Buckingham smiled. "Which is why I would have you remain there, Barbara." The smile touching only his lips widened. "We understand each other, I trust?"

"Perfectly." Lady Castlemaine fluttered her fan. She watched him walk over to where the king sat, surrounded by an anxious court, all clearly racking their brains for some solution to His Majesty's ennui. A deep frown drew the thick royal eyebrows together; slender, beringed fingers drummed on the carved oak arm of his chair; a red-heeled, ribbon-adorned shoe tapped an impatient rhythm. The duke bowed and said something that Lady Castlemaine could not hear, but the result was a deep roar of laughter from the king, followed by admiring ripples in imitation from the surrounding circle.

Her ladyship's fingers combed restlessly through her hair, drawing it across her shoulders. Earlier she had tried, but failed, to do what Buckingham had so signally succeeded in achieving—the return of the king's good humor. It was a lesson she had best take to heart. His grace would soon be the most powerful man in the land, and there was no saying whether his influence could reach as far as his majesty's bedchamber, could prove threatening to the mistress of that bedchamber. But it was not worth putting to the test. The Countess of Castlemaine, all smiles, went over to join the laughing circle around the king.

"Nicholas . . . Nick! Oh, wake up, do!" Polly tugged at his shoulder. "It is the most amazing thing. You must come and see!"

Nicholas for a moment did not know where he was as the importunate voice and hand penetrated his deep slumber. Then memory returned. He rolled onto his back, blinking sleepily. The bed curtains were drawn back, but the light in the chamber was dim and gray. "You are awake betimes, Polly."

She pulled a mischievous face. "I have become accustomed to early rising in your sister's household, sir. Lying long abed encourages the devil's work." Her voice was an uncanny imitation of Margaret's, and he burst into laughter.

"Come back to bed. You will catch cold."

"Nay . . . Come and see!" She threw the quilt off him, seizing his hand.

Groaning, Nick obeyed the summons, staggering to his feet. He was not accustomed to leaving his bed until the morning was fairly well advanced, and the sight of Polly, prancing eagerly in her bare skin, was one to encourage a long lie-in, as was the cold air on his own uncovered flesh. "Put on your smock, moppet. You will freeze to death," he protested, reaching for his shirt.

"Oh, 'tis only cold in here because the fire had gone down," she said impatiently. " 'Tis not cold in the parlor." Pulling him behind her, she danced into the other room, where he noted that the fire was newly kindled, last night's supper dishes removed, and the table laid for breakfast. Goodwife Benson was clearly an efficient landlady.

"Look!" Polly gestured dramatically to the window. "We are in a snow house."

Nicholas whistled, crossing over to what had once been a window. It was completely blanked out by snow.

"Could the snow have fallen so deeply that it reached the upper story?" demanded Polly. "Shall we open it and see?"

"If you wish to fill the chamber with snow, by all means do so," Nick said equably. Polly looked so crestfallen as she realized the absurdity of a suggestion made in the throes of excitement that he chuckled. "One would think that you have never seen the stuff before."

"I have always loved it," she told him. "It covers up all the grime and the refuse, and you can pretend for a little bit that it will never come back—that the world will always be fresh and sparkling and white." She shrugged. " 'Tis fanciful, I know. The white cover becomes fouled, then it melts and the filth is still there, only even worse." A metaphor for life, she had so often thought. There would be moments when hope was high, when the idea of radical change seemed not impossibly chimeric, then reality would intrude, made even more vicious by its destruction of dreams. But this time, the white transmuting cover would not become sullied and melt. It could not, because this time she had been given control over her destiny. The prize was there to be seized if she was capable of doing so.

Nick frowned, wondering why the radiance should have been so abruptly wiped from her face. But the bleakness vanished almost as quickly as it had appeared, and she offered him that heart-stopping smile again.

"Mayhap we will be snowbound."

Nicholas returned the smile. "I can think of worse fates, but I had best get dressed and investigate downstairs." He went into the bedchamber to pull on shirt and breeches. Polly followed, scrambling into her smock.

"I wish to investigate, also," she said in reply to his raised eyebrow. "May I not?"

"I had rather you climbed back into bed and awaited my return. I do not intend to be many minutes; then we have some unfinished business to attend to. I seem to recall that you were rather anxious for the onset of morning. Or do you find the prospect of snow so all-absorbing that you will be unable to concentrate on anything else?"

Polly removed her smock and climbed back into bed. "But if you are a very long time, I shall come to find you."

"I can safely promise you that I shall not be," he said, rendered strangely dizzy by the sight to which he had just been treated. Polly's back view as she had clambered up onto the high feather mattress had set up in an inventive and play-ful mind an utterly dazzling series of images and possibilities. Finding themselves snowbound could, indeed, prove decid-edly entertaining.

"I fear you must be having most improper thoughts, my lord," Polly said demurely, peeping at him over the quilt, which she was holding up to her nose. His own gaze lowered without volition to follow the direction of hers. "I do not think you should go and visit Goodwife Benson just yet,"

she continued. "Not until you have . . . have, well . . .
subsided, if you see what I mean." The hazel eyes were
alight with mischief; her tongue peeked from between her
lips.

"I fear you are right," declared his lordship, calmly pushing off his breeches. He reached for the quilt and twitched it
out of her hold, flinging it back.

"But the fire had gone out!" Polly yelped as the cold air
hit her now-rewarmed flesh.

"The price of impudence," he told her cheerfully. "But
you will not be complaining of the cold soon. Turn over."

When Goodwife Benson knocked on the bedchamber
door an hour later, Polly had discovered that there was a
variety of novel ways of increasing the body's temperature.
Nicholas bade their landlady enter and propped himself on
the pillows to smile a greeting as the round figure bustled in.

"Ye'll be needing the fire newly rekindled in 'ere," said
the goodwife, setting a bucket of coal in the hearth. "Will ye
be wantin' my man to trim ye, m'lord?" She wiped her
hands on her apron. "Right handy 'e is with a razor. Been a
gentleman's gentleman, sir."

Nick rubbed a hand over his unshaven chin. "I'd be glad
of his services, goodwife. It's kind in him to offer."

The woman beamed. " 'Tis nothin', m'lord. But ye'll not
be venturin' forth today. Snow's still falling."

Polly sat up at this, observing hopefully, "Mayhap you
will not be able to open the door."

"Like as not." The goodwife's smile broadened. It was
clear to Nick that she was as amused as he was by the contrast between Polly's ingenuousness and that extraordinary
sensual, tumbled beauty. "But my man and the boy'll take a
shovel to it, soon as may be." She turned back to the fire,
busying herself with coals and kindling until a cheerful blaze
filled the hearth. "There now. I'll fetch you up hot water
and send my man to ye, m'lord. Will the young lady require
help with 'er dressin'?"

Polly looked startled. "No . . . no, thank you." The
goodwife inclined her head, bobbed a little curtsy, and bus-

tled out. "Why should she imagine I would need help with my dressing?" Polly slid out of bed.

"Ladies generally do," replied my lord with that enigmatic little smile. His words had the effect he had expected. She stood stock-still and stared.

"I do not think Newgate-born bastards, bred in a tavern, warrant such a title," she said carefully.

"But a lord's mistress might," he suggested. "We have not discussed what background you must assume, but you should perhaps consider this now. When you are introduced to Thomas Killigrew you will not wish to present him with . . . with . . ." He felt for words before deciding that Polly's had been both sufficiently descriptive and accurate. "A Newgate-born bastard. While actors are welcomed at court, such a history as yours is unlikely to be received with equanimity. And you know you must earn the king's approbation if you are to join his company."

Polly moved closer to the fire's warmth as she considered this. She turned herself slowly, like a roast on a spit, maintaining an even warmth on her bare skin. As always, she appeared sublimely unconscious of her nakedness. Such ease with one's body was, Nicholas reflected, a considerable asset in one who would tread the boards. He watched her cogitations in silent amusement for a moment.

"We have spent some considerable time and effort in the last month ensuring that your deportment and accomplishments are consistent with a respectable background," he reminded her eventually. "One that will not come amiss at court."

"I had not fully realized the complexity of this," Polly said slowly. "I realized that Master Killigrew must decide that I have some skill, but I had not thought as far ahead as coming to His Majesty's notice."

"If Killigrew agrees to take you on, he will present you in one of his productions," Nick told her. "He will invite the king to attend the theatre and will recommend you to his notice. The rest will be up to you, for you know that the members of the king's company are servants of His Majesty;

they wear the king's livery and receive their pay from the royal purse. With the Duke of York's company, the same applies, except that they are servants of His Grace. King Charles must decide for himself that he wishes you in his service."

"Oh." Polly found the idea of having to appeal in person to His Majesty, King Charles II, utterly daunting.

Nick read her mind with little difficulty. "I should not be overly anxious, sweetheart. The king is most susceptible to all aspects of female beauty, and you possess them all—lavishly." He chuckled as she blushed. Could she possibly be unaware of it? "If you have even a minimal talent for the stage, you need have no fears."

"I have more than minimal talent," she declared, indicating that her modesty was not all-encompassing.

"I do not doubt it," Kincaid agreed smoothly. "But you would be well advised to conceal the circumstances of your birth and upbringing if you wish to frequent the court."

"But not all actors have genteel antecedents," Polly objected. "I know they do not because the daughter of the butcher on Tower Street became an orange girl at the Duke of York's theatre, and then found a protector and became an actor."

"If you wish to be a mediocre actor, never emerging from the back ranks, then your origins may be as humble as you please," Kincaid said briskly. "But I had thought you intended to star. Star actors become courtiers, or they do not star."

"Perhaps I should be a woman of mystery," Polly said, a gleam in her eye. "With a deep and dark past. Will that serve, d'ye think?" She twirled, showing him her back, kissed pink by the fire's heat.

"Done to a turn," murmured Nick, sliding to the floor. A sharp rap at the door gave him pause. He sighed, reaching for his shirt. "One minute," he called. "I expect that this is Goodman Benson come to trim me. I will join him in the parlor. Do you dress yourself, now, and come out when you are decent."

Polly dressed rapidly, putting on over her kirtle the
daygown that Kincaid had bought for her in the Royal Exchange. It was not an article of clothing worn by kitchen
maids—kirtle, cap, and apron being considered quite sufficient—so she had only put it on when specifically instructed
by Nicholas to do so. Clearly it was incumbent upon her in
present circumstances to wear it. She combed her hair free of
the tangles created by the night and morning's activities. Her
pins, she remembered, were in the parlor, where Nick had
left them last night, so she was obliged to leave her hair to
hang loose over the neat lace collar of her kirtle.

The scene that she found in the parlor was one unfamiliar
to her. The men she had known hitherto tended to the
unkempt and bearded. Nicholas was seated before the fire, a
large towel wrapped around his shoulders, his face lost behind a lather mask, while a thin, birdlike man, presumably
Goodman Benson, razor in hand, was engaged in drawing a
series of swaths through the lather. Polly stood watching,
fascinated and amused at the thought of this delicate, ascetic-
looking man belonging to the rotund and bustling Goodwife
Benson.

"There you are, my lord." Benson spoke in reverential
accents as he wiped his lordship's face with a dampened
towel before standing back to survey his handiwork with a
critical eye. "A little work with the comb, my lord, and I
venture to say that ye'd be fit to attend court." Suiting action
to words, he plied a comb vigorously to my lord's long,
flowing locks, while Polly, nibbling on a slice of barley bread
liberally buttered, continued to watch. If one's morning toilet was customarily this rigorous and extended, it was no
wonder one did not appear belowstairs until the morning
was far advanced.

The task was eventually completed to Benson's satisfaction. "I'd be happy to furnish your linen, my lord, seein' as
how, on account of the snow, ye'll be short of anything
clean."

"Very true," said his lordship. "I'd be most grateful."

"I've a good velvet gown, if yer lordship would be so

condescending," offered Goodman Benson. It was an offer that was accepted with alacrity, and the erstwhile gentleman's gentleman hurried off, beaming, to fetch the required garment.

"I think you have just made him the happiest man in London," observed Polly, turning back to the table to hack at the pink, glistening ham. "Will you permit him to dress you, also? Fastening one's own buttons must be dreadfully tedious work."

"Don't talk with your mouth full. I have told you before; it is both ill bred and inelegant," was Kincaid's affable response to this sweetly uttered piece of provocation.

Benson returned before Polly could marshal her wits for a further attack, and his lordship was shortly arrayed in a velvet gown, which, judging by its size, was not the property of the goodman. The latter took away all my lord's garments, including his shoes, with the statement that the buckles could do with shining.

"Do you shift your linen *every* day?" Polly asked in genuine astonishment.

Nicholas took his seat at the breakfast table. "It is customary. Sit down, now. 'Tis most ill mannered to eat standing up." He poured ale into a pewter tankard, drinking deeply, before slicing bread and bacon for himself.

"I have never known it to be customary," declared his companion, sitting opposite him. "And 'tis not ill mannered to eat standing up if you do not have the time to sit down."

"But you do have the time," he reminded. "And will continue to have; just as you will find yourself amongst people with whom it is customary to shift their linen regularly, if not on a daily basis."

"That is a little difficult if one has only one petticoat and smock," pointed out Polly, helping herself liberally to a dish of anchovies and olives.

"That will be remedied as soon as the snow has cleared sufficiently for a shopping expedition. Until it does, we should perhaps use our enforced seclusion to continue your studies. I must teach you a few of the French words that are in frequent use. They must come easily to your tongue."

"That sounds somewhat tedious," Polly said with a comical grimace. "I can think of many more amusing ways to while away the time. Can you not?"

"Without question," he agreed, managing to conceal the fact that he had quite failed in an attempt to react imperviously to the frankly wanton invitation in the hazel eyes. "And if you wish to abandon your ambition of an introduction to Master Killigrew, then I see no reason why we should bother with such tedious activities."

Polly lowered her eyes to her plate. She had been outmaneuvered in that mischievous little play, and it clearly behooved her to sharpen her wits if she wished to indulge in such amusements in future.

Kincaid grinned. Her thought processes were transparently easy to divine. She looked up, caught the grin, and burst into laughter. "It is odious in you to gloat so! I have not had as much practice as you have in the art of conversational exchanges."

"Oh, was that what that was?" he murmured. "I had thought it more in the nature of a ham-fisted attempt to score unnecessary points on the subject of my sartorial habits—a subject, I might add, on which you are not equipped to expatiate."

"I do not know what that means," Polly declared. "But I collect it is in the nature of a snub."

"Correct," he agreed gravely, then found himself obliged to engage in spirited defense as she hurled herself upon him with an indignation not entirely feigned. "That is *not* an acceptable way of expressing annoyance," he gasped, once he had managed to get sufficient grip upon her to allow him to draw breath. He held her firmly on his knee, her legs trapped between his, her wrists clipped in the small of her back, his other hand twisted in the honeyed mane tumbling over her shoulders. "One does not give physical expression to anger, you rag-mannered brat; at least, not in court circles. One uses one's tongue and one's wits to best effect."

"Well, as you have just pointed out, I am not very good at that," she retorted with an experimental wriggle that achieved nothing.

"You do not appear signally successful at this, either," laughed Nick. "Cry peace!" He tugged on her hair, bringing her face round and down to his. The fight left her rapidly as he invaded her mouth, continuing to hold her head fast until she returned the kiss with the eagerness that so delighted him, the soft body melding, pliant and welcoming, with his.

"But I am more successful at this, am I not, my lord?" she whispered, her tongue swooping in tantalizing darts against his eyelids as she moved her body on his lap to considerable effect.

"Without question," he groaned, hardening beneath her.

"And I learn very quickly, do I not?" Her tongue dipped into his ear, probing the whorls and contours with devastating thoroughness.

"Indubitably." Nick groaned again. Sliding his hands beneath her, he lifted her, pulling up her skirt and petticoat. "There, now sit down again," he whispered urgently, twitching aside his gown, turning her so that she sat astride his lap.

"Oh," Polly said, realizing what was happening when her bare thighs met his. "Is it possible like this?"

"Can you think of any reason why it should not be?" He smiled and guided her opened body onto the impaling shaft.

"No, none at all," breathed Polly, taking him within herself . . . And then, much later, in accents of wonder and awe, "Not a reason in the world!"

It was two days later before the self-enclosed world of the lovers was breached. There had been no snow for ten hours, and the front door was freed of obstruction. Polly tumbled outside with all the vigor and eagerness of a cabined kitten set free, exclaiming as always at the wonderland where the filth of the streets, the soil of the kennels, the ordure-ridden straw of the cobbles, was vanished under a pristine carpet. Nicholas followed her, laughing at the enthusiasm that plunged her headlong into a drift. Other folk appeared on the lane, blinking in the snow's dazzle, calling jovial greetings. One or two snowballs were thrown—a sport that instantly appealed to Polly. She was engaged in a merry battle with a couple of stable lads, her newfound dignity cast to the four winds, when Richard De Winter appeared, astride a powerful beast who clearly made up in strength what he lacked in elegance as he highstepped his way through the drifts.

Lord De Winter was privileged to witness the moment when his old friend, habitué of the court of King Charles, received, full in the face, a snowball thrown by a laughing girl who pranced, taunting, in the snow, neatly evading all missiles directed at her. Nick, with a roar, descended upon the dancing sprite, retribution clearly in mind, and Polly, squealing, took to her heels, her cloak flying out behind.

"Oh, what a joyous sight it is to see children at play," mocked Richard.

Kincaid ceased his pursuit at the sound of the familiar voice and turned, laughing, brushing snow from his face and coat. "Why, Richard, you are well come, indeed. And intrepidly so. The streets are passable?" A snowball flew through the air, struck De Winter's mount squarely on the neck. The horse threw up his head with an annoyed whinny, and both men swung round on the culprit.

"I beg your pardon," Polly said, one hand pressed to her lips, eyes wide in apology. "It . . . it seemed to leave my hand of its own accord." She plowed through the snow toward them. "Lord De Winter, I bid you good day." She reached up a hand, smiling with genuine warmth. Her hood fell back, offering him an unhindered view of that radiant countenance framed in a braided coronet, glinting richly gold under the sun's glow. "Pray grant me absolution, sir. I had not quite realized that playtime was over."

"There is nothing to absolve," he responded cheerfully,

swinging from his mount. "Think you that one of your play-fellows could be persuaded to have a care for my horse?"

Nicholas beckoned one of the lads, and the animal was handed over. "Polly, see if the goodwife has the makings of a punch bowl, will you?"

"Why, yes, my lord. Certainly, my lord. Will there be anything else, my lord?" Polly curtsied in the snow, gather-ing up a handful as she rose. She patted it thoughtfully be-tween her hands, smiling benignly.

De Winter, with a punctilious care, straightened the lace edging to his glove. Nicholas said, "Mistress Wyat, would you be so good as to request Goodwife Benson to supply me with the makings of a punch bowl? I should be forever in your debt." Polly tossed the snowball from hand to hand, debating.

"It is always wise to recognize when one has won a point," De Winter said softly. "Even in sport."

Polly cast him a sharp glance, met smiling gray eyes, and chuckled, tossing the snowball to the ground. "You give good counsel, sir. Come within and warm yourself. I will see what can be coaxed from our hosts." She disappeared in the direction of the kitchen and the Bensons' apartments, and Nicholas ushered his friend to the parlor abovestairs.

"Some considerable transformation," remarked Richard, stepping over to the fire.

Nicholas did not assume that he was referring to Kincaid's new surroundings. He nodded. "She shows great ease at adapting. I do not think that Killigrew will find anything amiss."

"And the chains . . . ?" Richard took snuff, discreetly avoiding his companion's eye.

"Are in place." Kincaid strolled to the window, looking down at the lively scene in the street. Was it possible for those chains to become mutual bonds? He had intended to lead an innocent along the paths of love, to kindle passion in her and teach her the infinite joys of fulfilling that passion. Thus would he forge the chains of love that would ensure her loyalty. For himself, he had intended to consummate a desire he had felt since he had first laid eyes upon her. He had consummated that desire, and looked forward with intense pleasure to its continued satisfaction. But something was getting in the way of his clear thinking. It was Polly herself—that candid, mischievous, loving elf who seemed to be weaving chains of her own.

"Ye'll forgive a somewhat personal remark, Nick, but she'll be of little value to Killigrew, or to us, with a swollen belly." De Winter surveyed his friend's rigid back, remembering the play he had interrupted in the lane. It had a quality that had little place in the formalized relationship of keeper and mistress.

Nick turned slowly, offering a rueful smile. "You may rest assured that at the expense of a slight diminution in pleasure, I am taking the precaution that will prevent such a happenstance."

De Winter simply nodded. "I am come from the court, where I have been immured these last two days whilst you have been disporting yourself. It would appear that Lady Castlemaine and Buckingham are become fast confidants."

"That is hardly good tidings, my friend." Nicholas tossed another log onto the fire. "Had they been pulling against each other, the evil influence of each upon the king would be rendered less harmful. Together . . ." He shrugged.

"They will encourage him to incalculable foolishness," continued De Winter. "If they support Monmouth's legitimacy, and persuade the king to set himself up against Parliament, they will bring the country to the brink of another civil war. The people will not stand for it, Nick."

"I am aware of it."

"And you are still minded to avail yourself of any opportunities Mistress Wyat might afford for circumventing the duke?" De Winter spoke casually. "You are in a better position now to assess how skillful she might be in attracting and keeping Buckingham's attention."

"You may rest assured that she lacks none of those attributes that will appeal to Buckingham," Nick said, in a voice as dry as fallen leaves. Sensual, passionate, uninhibited . . .

What man could resist her? Why the devil was the thought so distasteful?

"So when do you intend effecting the introduction to Killigrew?"

"I see no reason to delay," Nick said. "Once she has a new wardrobe, one more suitable for an aspiring actor. What she has left to learn, she will learn rapidly enough under Tom's instruction."

The door opened at this point, and Goodwife Benson came energetically into the chamber, carrying a tray laden with brandy, hot water, lemons, and spices. She was followed by Polly, bearing a large punch bowl and ladle. "Is it a brandy punch ye'll be wantin', my lord? I've rum, if ye'd prefer it."

"Thank you, but brandy will serve admirably," Nick assured her, moving to take the heavy bowl and ladle from Polly. "If you'd set the tray beside the fire . . ." The woman did so, cast a critical eye around the room to ascertain that all was in order, before bobbing a curtsy and hastening out, her stuff gown swishing with the vigor of her stride.

Polly settled herself on a three-legged stool before the fire and drew the punch bowl toward her. "I was taught to mix a tolerable punch," she informed the two men with a serene smile, reaching for the brandy.

Nick regarded her quizzically. "I am not sure that is entirely wise. The last time I had drink of your mixing—"

"That is unjust!" protested Polly. "As it happens, the drink to which I assume you are referring was not of *my* mixing."

Nick smiled at her. "I spoke in jest, moppet."

"Aye, I am aware." Pushing the bowl aside with an impatient gesture, she came to put her arms around his neck, placing her mouth firmly on his. "And I would forgive you even if 'twere not a jest."

"This is not going to get the punch mixed," observed Richard pensively, kneeling on the hearth to set about the task himself.

"No, you are right." Nick pulled Polly's arms from

around his neck. "Neither is it a practice to be conducted in public, I fear. Pleasant though it is for the recipient."

"I do not understand what you mean." Polly looked hurt. "I wished only to kiss you."

De Winter turned a choke of laughter into a cough and sprinkled nutmeg onto the contents of the punch bowl.

"Will you explain, Richard, or shall I?" Nick asked.

"You. I have my hands full with the punch," replied his friend.

"Sit down, Polly . . . No, not on my knee!" Nick put her firmly back on the stool she had abandoned. "Now, listen to me very carefully. 'Tis a lesson I have not yet imparted."

Polly, looking more than a little rebellious, kept her seat on the stool, folding her hands in her lap. "I do not think this is a lesson I am going to want to learn," she muttered suspiciously.

"Probably not," Nick responded, as equable as always. "But it is a vital one nevertheless." He stood up, reached for his clay pipe and the pouch of tobacco on the mantel, and began to fill the bowl as he talked. "I have told you that any overt discourtesy will put you beyond the social pale. The same applies to public displays of emotion of *any* description. Cool friendship is acceptable, but that is as far as you may go." He bent to light a taper in the fire, then set it to the pipe.

"I may not speak lovingly to you, or touch you, or—"

"No, you may not!" Nick broke in in vigorous confirmation. "In public, you will treat me with a careless indifference, as I will treat you—"

"Nay!" Polly jumped up, horrified at such an image. "I could not do such a thing, and if you treat me with a . . . with a careless indifference, I shall go home."

"Then you will never again be invited to show your face at court," Richard said coming to his friend's aid. "While it will be common knowledge that you live under Nick's protection, you will become an object of disgust if you parade your emotions."

"Why?"

Nick shrugged. "It is not done, sweetheart. That is the only answer I can give you. If you would achieve acceptance in that world, then you must abide by the rules."

De Winter tasted the concoction in the punch bowl with a critical frown before remarking casually, "Should you break the rules in such a fashion, you will make Nick a jestingstock, as well as yourself. 'Twould hardly be a convincing demonstration of affection." He ladled the drink into three pewter goblets. "The very reverse, I would have said."

Polly buried her nose in the fragrant steam curling from the goblet. She came from a world where every facet of emotional life was lived on the surface and in front of all eyes. Kisses, blows, endearments, and curses were administered whenever and wherever the need or desire arose. There was no privacy in the fetid, teeming lanes and houses of the city slums, and concealing emotion was a concept quite alien to her.

Nick watched her over the lip of his own goblet, guessing at her thoughts, just as he knew what Richard was thinking. Not only would she jeopardize her own position at court in such an instance, but she would also destroy all possibility of their own plan's coming to fruition.

As if echoing his thoughts, Richard spoke again. "As an actor, Polly, it will be not in your interests to imply that you have eyes only for Lord Kincaid. You will receive many other offers, which you may or may not choose to accept; but if you wish to further your ambition, then you will not wish to give the impression of one who has lost her heart and cannot be approached. There are those who might offer you marriage." His eyebrows lifted. "You would not be the first female actor to marry into the nobility."

Polly struggled to master the stab of dismay at these words. She could not imagine wishing for a protector other than the one she had. But then, it was always possible that Lord Kincaid would weary of her. Why would he not? She had said that first night, when he had put her into the truckle bed in his room and she had first propounded her plan, that once she was established under his aegis, if he no longer wished to be her protector, then she would be able to find another one. It was the way these matters were conducted, as she had always known.

The idea of marriage was so far beyond her sights, whatever De Winter might say, that she did not trouble to dwell upon the notion. Even if the world was not to know she was a Newgate-born, tavern-bred bastard, *she* would always know.

She raised her head, smiling, and neither of her companions had an inkling of the effort it cost her. "It is just possible, my lord, that I may be successful enough at my profession to support myself. In which case, I would have no need of a husband and may take only those lovers who appeal to me."

"Let us drink to such an admirable goal," De Winter said easily, raising his glass, exchanging a quick glance with Nick, who merely quirked an eyebrow.

Nick drank the toast, wrestling with his own quite unjustified resentment. Without so much as a word to himself, De Winter had appropriated the task of planting in Polly's head the seeds of her future role. It was a task that Nick thought should lie at his own door, but De Winter was behaving as if Polly were common property.

In a sense she was, he admitted grimly to himself—inasmuch as she was the tool the faction would employ in their conspiracy against Buckingham, she belonged to the group. Clearly, it behooved him to keep his eye on the ultimate goal and concentrate on germinating the seeds planted by De Winter. Becoming sidetracked by emotion would serve no purpose and could, indeed, endanger the lives of them all.

Chapter 9

"I will not be long absent, sweetheart," Nicholas said, lifting a honeyed lock from where it lay across her breast. "I must return home to discover how matters are progressing with Margaret, and to find clean raiment. It has been three days since I was last seen alive by anyone but Richard, yourself, and the good Bensons."

Polly reached up a finger to trace the line of the fine-drawn mouth. "You did send the Bensons' lad with a message, so Margaret will not be afeard for you." She smiled ruefully. "But I know it must come to an end, for all that I would it did not have to."

"I also." He bent to kiss her, tasting that sweetness that had become so wondrously familiar. "But think not of an ending, only of a beginning." Reluctantly, he pushed aside the bedcover, swinging his legs to the floor. "When I return I will take you shopping. You may harry the mercers like a plague in Egypt and set an army of sempstresses to work, for without a more alluring wardrobe, my flower, you will be ill equipped to face the world of your choosing."

Polly sat up, hugging her knees. Mercers and sempstresses conjured up a most heady image, one that she could not immediately grasp in all its magnificence. Mercers meant the buying of taffeta and velvet, damask and satin; embroidered

petticoats, lace collars and ruffs; girdles and gloves and hose.
"I think you should begone, sir, in order that you may return the sooner."

Nicholas gave a shout of laughter to see such joyful calculation in those green-brown eyes. The Newgate-born, tavern-bred bastard was looking upon Elysian fields. "Petticoats
of sarcenet," he enticed gleefully. "Nightgowns of wool and
velvet; a gown for every kirtle—"

"Oh, begone, do!" begged Polly. "In your absence, I will
make some drawings of the gowns I would wish made."

That pulled him up short. "You know what you would
like?"

"But of course," she said simply. "If there is paper and
quill and inkhorn, I will show you." A smile touched her
lips. "It is easier to draw than to write, my lord."

"It requires less learning, perhaps," he said doubtfully,
wondering how she could possibly know enough about the
elegancies of a lady's dress to have a sufficiently clear picture
of her wants to present to a sempstress.

"I learned much when I was under your sister's roof," she
explained, grasping with little difficulty the reason for his
hesitancy. "And yet more when I could steal away for an
hour or so to watch the gentlewomen walking in the Strand.
And also the not-so-gentlewomen." An up-from-under look
glimmering with mischief accompanied this addendum.
"Since I belong to the realm of the latter, it may prove to
have been a not unhelpful observation. Their finery appeared unexceptionable. But then, my tastes are but uninformed."

"Somehow, I doubt that," murmured his lordship. "I suspect that there is very little of importance about which you
are truly uninformed."

"Oh, my lord, but I must protest. You do me too much
honor," she simpered with the most grating titter, batting
her eyelashes vigorously. "I feel sure you exaggerate."

Nick tucked his shirt into the waistband of his breeches.
"Probably," he agreed, giving provocation its own again.
"But you must learn to accept compliments without ques-

tioning, regardless of their sincerity." He fastened his doublet, shrugged into his coat, and adjusted the ruffs at his shirt sleeves. "I am heartily sick of these garments. I do not imagine I shall ever wish to wear them again."

Polly regarded him through narrowed eyes. "I cannot imagine what possible point there could be in paying compliments that are insincere."

"Oh, on occasion a very fine point can be made," he informed her. "It is possible to make a compliment sound like an insult, my love. As you will learn."

" 'Tis not an art I have the least interest in learning." Polly thumped back on the pillows, pulling the quilt up to her nose.

"In that case," declared Nick cheerfully, "there seems little point in a shopping expedition."

"Why do you always have the last word?" Polly wailed, sitting up again.

Nick could not help laughing. "Do not think to score against me, moppet. I have had many more years of experience than you, and my wits are fine-honed."

"But I may hone mine on your steel," she suggested, making an admirably speedy recovery. "I know full well how keen and upstanding that steel can be." Her eyes, gleaming suggestively, invested a seemingly innocent statement with a wealth of innuendo.

Kincaid whistled in soft appreciation. That look, that tone, employed when she delivered some of the deliciously wicked lines penned by the most popular playwrights, would bring the house down. "I predict a great career for you, Mistress Wyat. If someone does not wring your neck first." Crossing to the bed, he lifted her chin to plant a hard kiss on her mouth. "I must dine at home with Margaret, but I will return this afternoon, and we will visit the Exchange."

Polly pouted. "I do not care to dine alone."

"Then you must do without your dinner today," was the callous response. Kincaid was not about to be fooled by an aggrieved pout more suited to an overindulged damsel of society's upper echelons than to this hard-schooled wench, for whom an adequate dinner must at times have been the summit of the day's ambition.

A smile flickered at the corners of her mouth as she accepted this further defeat without protest. "I think I shall go for a walk. I presume there is no one here of whom I must ask leave?" A hint of challenge lurked in her voice.

Nicholas shook his head. "You know full well that you are the mistress here. But I would have you take a care. The streets are not entirely safe."

"You forget perhaps that I am of the streets," Polly reminded. "I know well how to have a care."

Nick frowned. "You no longer look as if you are of the streets," he said. "Your present dress does not fit that part. Walking alone, you could well present an attractive prize to one on the lookout for such spoils."

"Then it is possible that they might be surprised," she countered. "I can employ the language and manners of the gutters as well as any, my lord, should the need arise."

"I cannot imagine why I thought you could not," said Kincaid, shaking his head in mock wonderment. "However, notwithstanding, I repeat: have a care."

"Yes, my Lord Kincaid," she responded meekly, folding her hands, giving him a look of anxious innocence. "I will do just as you say."

Nick paused, knowing he must go, yet utterly seduced by her mischief, and the sensual promise in the glowing eyes. But if he postponed his departure, he would not leave today, and there was a world beyond these four walls, commitments he had made and must honor. "Until this afternoon," he said, turning away from her disappointment before he yielded.

Polly heard the parlor door click on his departure, and sighed. There had been a moment when she had thought he would stay, and the idyll would have lasted one more day. But since it was not to be, she would be wise to make the best of things. It was time to test this new life that had been gifted to her. She was mistress of her own lodgings, answerable to no one, free to go wheresoever she pleased. A day where there were no tasks to perform, no orders to obey, stretched before her; and the world outside awaited.

She dressed rapidly, putting her pantofles over her pumps to protect them from the slushy streets, wrapped herself in her thick cloak, and hurried down the stairs.

"What time will ye like to have dinner served, mistress?" Goodwife Benson came out of the kitchen as Polly reached the hall.

The question took Polly aback. It was not a matter on which she was accustomed to being consulted, and in the last three days Nicholas had naturally been the one deferred to in such subjects. "Whenever it is convenient," she said.

Goodwife Benson looked at her shrewdly. "It is for you to say when it will be convenient, m'dear."

Polly nibbled her lip. "At noon, perhaps?"

"At noon," agreed the goodwife. "I've a fine pullet for ye, well dressed though I say so myself." She turned back to the kitchen, saying over her shoulder, "Mind how you go, now. The ways are mighty treacherous after the snow."

"I will," promised Polly, in a warm glow at a caring attention hitherto unknown to her.

It did not take many minutes to convince her that walking was not a comfortable mode of progression in present conditions. Where the snow had melted, it rushed down the kennels, carrying filth with it to spill over onto the cobbles, leaving them thick with malodorous slime. Out of the sun, the snow remained in blackened and unsavory drifts, blocking the paths. There were few people on foot, and those there were were frequently bespattered by the mud and muck flung up from heedless horses' hooves and disdainful carriage wheels. But she pressed on doggedly, determined to attain her goal of the Theatre Royal. This time she had no ulterior motive except to look upon the king's playhouse and indulge in the daydreams that were now so close to fulfillment.

It was a short walk along Drury Lane. Just as she reached her destination, a coach, arms emblazoned upon its panels, swept past her to come to a dramatic halt at the theatre steps. A clod of mud flying up from the wheels landed on Polly's arm, splattering her liberally. In a fury, she assailed the coachman, who was in the act of climbing down from his box, castigating him roundly on his careless driving. Since she chose to do this in language with which the coachman would be familiar, it was not surprising that he should enter the argument in spirited fashion.

"God's good grace! What is going on!" An elegant voice preceded its owner's head, appearing in the carriage window.

"You have a most discourteous coachman, sir," Polly said, switching her accent to one more suitable for discourse with so manifest a gentleman. "He drives his carriage in such a manner that no one is safe on the same street with him, and then has the impertinence to blame his victim!"

George Villiers, Duke of Buckingham, was bereft of words for a moment as he took in the ravishing beauty before him. Never had he beheld such a diamond. Indignation glittered in a pair of magnificent eyes—like forest pools, he thought—flushed a perfect complexion with a delicate pink, stood out in every line of a matchless form. At the same time, he noticed that she was well, if modestly, dressed, and she spoke with a lady's breeding. Except that if it had been she berating his coachman, then she knew well how to assume a different accent.

"Your pardon, madame," he managed, swinging open the carriage door, springing lightly to the ground. He bowed. "I pray you will permit me to make amends. If you would direct me to your lodging, I will convey you there myself."

Polly curtsied automatically as she examined the gentleman covertly. He was most magnificent, with three curling ostrich plumes to his hat, dyed red to match his wine-red velvet coat and breeches, a full-bottomed periwig upon his head, diamonds upon his fingers and on the buckles of his shoes. She raised her eyes to his face as she swam upward, and suffered a slight shock. It was not a pleasant face, although the expression was one of studied amiability—hard eyes under heavy, drooping lids; a thin mouth, with more than a hint of cruelty to it, beneath a long, pointed nose that reminded her of a hawk's beak. It was the face of a cynic and a dissolute, and the examination to which she was being subjected was frankly calculating. Polly quite suddenly wished she were well away from his vicinity.

"There is no need, sir," she replied. "I live but a short distance and would prefer to walk."

"Oh, but you cannot do so," he protested. "Allow me to present myself. George Villiers at your service, madame."

The name meant nothing to Polly, who had never heard the Duke of Buckingham referred to by his family name. She responded with a polite murmur and another curtsy before turning abruptly, walking off down the street.

Buckingham stood motionless, his eyes riveted on the figure until she turned the corner from Drury Lane onto Long Acre. If she lived but a short distance from here, it should not be impossible to discover her address and identity. Such rare beauty would not go unremarked in the taverns and shops. He beckoned to his footboy.

Polly, finding unaccountably that all desire to continue her walk was vanished, returned home by way of Bow Street. The enticing aroma of roasting fowl and a mug of buttered ale before the crackling luxury of her own fireside offered some measure of compensation, and she was sitting before the fire, wriggling her toes in its warmth, feeling completely in charity with the world, when she heard De Winter's voice in the hall belowstairs.

Jumping up, she went to the parlor door, appearing on the small landing as his lordship mounted the stairs. "Why, sir, are you come to visit? Nicholas is gone to his house."

"Then may I be permitted the conceit of thinking you might be glad of my company?" He smiled, bowing as he reached the landing.

" 'Tis no conceit, sir, but the truth." She gestured to the parlor. "Pray come in and let me pour you wine."

"Y'are a most accomplished hostess, Mistress Wyat," Richard said, smiling, as she took his hat and cloak.

Polly hesitated, then said, "If you would care to join me for dinner, my lord, I would be very happy to have your company. Goodwife Benson has gone to some trouble to dress a fine pullet."

"Prettily said!" Laughing, he flicked her cheek with a careless finger. "I should be delighted. The prospect of the goodwife's pullet quite sets my mouth to watering!"

Thus it was that when Nicholas came hotfoot up the stairs into his mistress's apartments, he found a cozy scene. The two diners were quite clearly upon the easiest of terms, and Nick was surprised by a most unjustified pang of what he could only recognize as jealousy. He knew that Richard would under no circumstances set up a flirtation with another man's protégée, and even more vital, he knew that Richard would never lose sight of the greater goal. De Winter was a dedicated politician, committed to his country's well-being; no personal whim would be permitted to intrude upon that commitment. Polly Wyat was necessary to the furtherance of that cause.

Nevertheless, the ripple of Polly's laughter, the provocative flash of her eyes as she responded to a sally, the flush of enjoyment painting her cheeks, twisted a malevolent skewer in his gut.

"Oh, you are well come, Nicholas!" Polly sprang from her chair, running to greet him, standing on tiptoe to kiss him. "How is Lady Margaret?" An imp of mischief danced across her face before she schooled both expression and posture to those of a devout sobriety. "She has not, I trust, found too much to aid the devil's work in the past days?"

"Minx!" declared Nicholas with some satisfaction, finding his moment of unease now fled into the realm of irrelevancy. "You have been amusing yourself, I see."

"Oh, famously," she agreed, pulling him over to the fire. "Lord De Winter is a most entertaining companion." She poured wine for the newcomer. "He has been telling me about fox hunting. I should like to learn to ride a horse."

"Then so you shall," promised Nick, taking the proffered goblet with a smile of thanks. "When the weather improves."

"Oh, I should tell you: I had a most strange encounter this

morning," Polly said thoughtfully, remembering for the first time the man in wine-red velvet. A little shiver prickled her spine, but she could not really imagine why. There had been nothing sinister in his manner or words.

"Yes?" Nick prompted. "A strange encounter with whom?"

"It was outside the playhouse. His carriage splashed me!" The statement was underpinned with remembered resentment. "I was having a fight with his coachman . . ."

"You were what?" interrupted Nick at this somewhat horrifying image.

"Well, I was telling him exactly what I thought of him," Polly elucidated. "And in no uncertain terms, when this gentleman climbed out of the carriage."

"He might well," murmured Nick, picturing the scene. "I might have shown a degree of interest myself if my coachman was engaged on my time in a verbal brawl with a foul-mouthed wench."

"If he had driven with a little more consideration, he would not have smothered me with mud!" Polly retorted tartly. "Is one not entitled to object in such a circumstance?"

"There are ways . . . and ways . . . of doing so," Nick said, carefully circumspect. "So what did the gentleman say when he had climbed out of the carriage to find himself confronted by your outrage?"

Polly frowned. "He was most apologetic and desired to drive me home. He was most insistent." She shrugged. "Maybe that is not in itself strange, but there was something about the way he looked at me."

Nicholas felt himself stiffen. He could well imagine how the unknown would have looked at Polly—with unbridled lust. He had seen it often enough; but then, so had Polly, and she usually had little difficulty dealing with it. So what had disturbed her particularly this time? "You did not accept his offer?" It was a rhetorical question.

"I think that had I not been so close to home, I might have found it difficult to gainsay him," Polly said frankly, putting her finger at last on what had so disturbed her. The gentleman had given the impression of one who possessed both the power and the inclination to take for himself what was not freely rendered.

"I told you to have a care," Nick said quietly.

"But this was not one of those of whom I was supposed to be careful," Polly pointed out. "There were arms emblazoned on the panels of his coach. He was no footpad or street rogue. I would not have been afeard of such as they."

"You did not discover his name?" De Winter put in.

"Yes . . . he offered an introduction in a most proper manner. I did not return the courtesy but walked away. I imagine he must have thought me sadly lacking in manners."

"If you were accosted, I do not think you were obliged to be mannerly." Nick offered reassurance.

"But you could say that it was I who did the accosting," Polly said with ruthless candor, this matter of manners seeming suddenly to assume an inordinate importance.

De Winter prompted again. "What name did he give you?"

"Oh, yes . . . Villiers," she said, still frowning. "George Villiers. I think that was it."

"Buckingham!" Nick's eyes met De Winter's over the honey-hued head, and read the warning. He mastered the mixed emotions of surprise, anger, and unease. "Well, it appears that you made the acquaintance of His Grace, the Duke of Buckingham, moppet." Tipping her off his knee, he stood up, sauntering over to the table to refill his goblet. "You will undoubtedly meet him again when you become one of the king's company. Indeed, you may well perform in one of his plays. He is considered an accomplished playwright."

"I did not care for him," Polly informed them bluntly. "I had liefer not meet him again."

"Oh, you are being fanciful," Nick said with a feigned easiness. "He has the king's ear, my dear, and is a most important gentleman. You should be flattered rather than alarmed to have caught his eye."

"I had somehow formed the impression that he is no friend of yours?" Polly gave him a searching look.

Nick shrugged. "He is an acquaintance with whom I am on good terms, as is Richard. Only a fool would make an enemy of Buckingham. Is it not so, Richard?"

"Most certainly," De Winter agreed, blandly smiling. "When you meet him in different circumstances, Polly, you will see him in a different light."

"But he will surely remember the manner in which I addressed his coachman, and the fact that I treated his introduction with less than courtesy." Polly nibbled her thumbnail worriedly. "And if he is so important a figure, it is surely a disadvantage to stand in his bad graces."

"If that were so, it would be a disadvantage. But I think you may safely assume that you have merely piqued Buckingham's interest." Nick put his goblet on the table and smiled reassuringly. "Fetch your cloak now. If we are to go shopping before sunset, we had best make a move."

The prospect diverted her, as he had hoped. She ran downstairs to retrieve her cloak from the kitchen, where Goodwife Benson had taken it for brushing.

"An unfortunate meeting," De Winter observed.

"Damnably! If she has taken him in so much dislike, I fail to see how we are to achieve her cooperation." Nick paced restlessly.

"Wait until she has embraced her ambition, my friend, and has become a member of those circles where Buckingham is so courted and adored. She will see him in a different light then. She will, I am certain, respond to his flattering advances, as all the other fair frailties have done, and continue to do so. He is too grand a prize to reject."

Nicholas winced at this cynicism, but could not find it in his heart to disagree. There was no reason to suppose that Polly, once her enchanting ingenuousness had been superseded by the sophistication of the courtier, would prove to be any less worldly than any other lady of the stage with her sights set on an assured and comfortable future in the hands of a wealthy and influential protector. It was to this end, after all, that he was instructing her in the devious tricks of the world she would enter.

"And once she is safely ensconced in Buckingham's bed," De Winter continued with a calm that Nick found supremely irritating, "you will hold fast the chains of gratitude and pleasure, so that she is never far from *your* bed, where you may glean what you will. 'Tis not unusual, after all, for a lady to spread her favors."

"Such a neat and pleasing plan," Nick said. Richard did not miss the sardonic undertone, but he refrained from the obvious comment that the plan had been Nick's originally.

"I am ready!" Polly bounced into the room. "Where did I put my drawings? Oh, there they are." She scooped up the sheets from the sideboard. "You should know, sir, that Lord De Winter has been most helpful with the designs. Our morning was not spent entirely in idle pleasure."

"I am glad to hear it." Nick laughed, pushing away the sour taste of the last half hour. "D'ye care to accompany us, Richard?"

"If you think I might be useful, I should be glad to."

As the afternoon wore on, Nick found himself immensely grateful for Richard's support. Polly flitted from shop to shop in an ecstasy of indecision. One minute she would be fingering a bolt of white damask, the next had abandoned the eager mercer in favor of one of his competitors who had a flame satin on show. She stood ankle-deep in a river of unrolled bolts, exclaiming over the flowered sarcenet or the mulberry wool, before a tall black beaver hat with white plumes caught her eye in the milliner's across the court and she was off again.

"Think you 'tis perhaps time to take charge?" De Winter asked Nick gently, after Polly, having discarded countless hats, had succeeded in reducing the milliner to a state of gibbering anxiety.

"I suppose so," Nick replied with a regretful smile. "But seldom have I enjoyed another's pleasure so. It is a shame to bring the play to an end."

"But take pity on the poor mercers and milliners," chuckled Richard. "They have given of their best, and so far not a single purchase has been made."

Nick nodded, squared his shoulders, and entered the fray. "The felt copintank and the beaver," he said with brisk decision. "The muslin headpiece with the satin ribbons, and the lace mantilla."

"Yes, sir. A pleasure, sir." The relieved milliner smiled radiantly. "If I may say so, an admirable choice."

"Oh, do you think so?" Polly said doubtfully. "I had thought to purchase the gauze scarf rather than the mantilla."

"Another time you shall do so," Nick said. "Let us return to the mercer's where you saw the damask." After giving instructions for the delivery of the hats, he ushered the reluctant Polly out of the shop.

"Oh, only see those boots!" Polly exclaimed, just as they had reached his goal. "They are of the softest leather." She turned toward the shoemaker.

"Later," said Nicholas, holding on to her arm with vise-like fingers. "First we are going in here." De Winter, shoulders shaking, followed them inside, where the mercer greeted them in some trepidation, having only just managed to roll up all the bolts that had been previously inspected and found wanting.

On this occasion, however, he had no need to worry. The indecisive young lady was put in a chair, and the two gentlemen, on the basis of her earlier preferences and their own knowledge of prevailing fashion, proceeded to choose white damask and green taffeta to be made up into kirtles, and scarlet velvet and amber satin for the daygowns to be worn over them. Mulberry wool would make a warm nightgown to be worn within doors. Warm twilled saye was chosen for two of the three petticoats that would give fullness to the kirtles, silk sarcenet for the third petticoat, which would be displayed when she lifted her kirtle for walking.

Polly sat, listening as these matters were discussed and dispositions made. In truth, she was not sorry to be excused the final decision making, since the wealth of choice had set her

head to reeling, and Nick and De Winter appeared remarkably well informed about the necessities of female attire, not
excluding lace edgings for the sleeves of her smocks, which
would be displayed beneath the loose, elbow-length sleeves
of the gowns.

"That should suffice for the moment," Nicholas said finally. "It is hardly a complete wardrobe, but we can decide
on your further needs at leisure."

Polly's jaw dropped. It seemed impossible that one could
possibly need more. The materials were packaged, handed to
the coachman, and a visit was paid to the shoemaker, where
she got, in addition to her boots of Spanish leather, a pair of
the most elegant shoes she had ever seen. They had heels that
were all of an inch and a half high, and real silver buckles.

"Is it possible to walk in such things?" Polly regarded
them with some disfavor. Elegant they may be; practical they
were not.

"You will learn," Nick told her. "All that remains now is
the corset."

"Nay!" Polly exclaimed, stung at the last into mutiny. "I
have no need of such a garment. They pinch most dreadfully, and one cannot breathe! The lady where Prue was in
service was always swooning away, and the bones cut her
skin to ribbons, Prue said."

De Winter and Nicholas exchanged looks. While a lady
might manage without a corset in private, she could not
appear at any fashionable scene without them, and most definitely not on the stage. "I do not know how reliable an
informant Prue may be on such matters," Nick said dryly.

Polly's eyes flashed defiance. "I will not wear it even if you
buy it, so you will be wasting your money!"

"I see." Nicholas shrugged. He would leave that battle to
the combined forces of Thomas Killigrew and ambition.
"There seems little more to say on the subject."

Polly regarded him suspiciously. It had been a ready capit-
ulation, but his expression was bland, and when she glanced
at De Winter, she saw the expression mirrored there.

"Come, let us to the sempstress to put this work in hand,"

Nick declared as if the preceding moment of potential awkwardness had not taken place.

It was as well to be as gracious in victory as Nick was in defeat, Polly decided, offering her bewitching smile. "I am quite overcome by your generosity, sir. I do not know what I have done to merit it."

Nicholas looked down at her, his own smile a trifle twisted. "Do you not, Polly? That seems remarkably unperspicacious in you."

Polly was accustomed now to the manifestations of desire, both Nick's and her own, just as she was accustomed to the light tenor of their converse; but this that she saw in his face, and could feel reflected in her own, was quite different. She was aware of the familiar direct physical responses—the tightening in her belly, the sudden jarring in her loins—but much more powerful was the feeling that she was losing herself in his eyes, and his smile; that there was a secret he held that he would have her share, that he knew she did share but had not yet acknowledged. Her heart speeded. She took an involuntary step toward him as if the hustle and bustle of the Royal Exchange had vanished under a magician's wand.

Richard De Winter silently cursed the vagaries of the human heart. It was as he had suspected. They were both bewitched, at this moment both inhabiting some charmed circle, rapt in the wondrous discovery of shared love's benediction. "When beauty fires the blood, how love exalts the mind." Master John Dryden's lines came to mind, troublingly apposite.

"It grows late," he said. "If the sempstress is to be visited and instructed before the day is done—"

"Aye." Nick shook his head as if to dispel confusion and took Polly's hand. "A timely reminder, Richard. Come, moppet. You must test your drawings on an expert." He bundled her up the carriage steps, into the dim interior, his voice briskly cheerful as if that moment had never occurred. But she knew that it had, just as she knew what it meant.

This was a relationship that had had its roots in expediency. She had intended to use Nicholas, Lord Kincaid, for her own ends—use without deception, certainly, since she had never been less than honest about what she wanted from him. He had brought her to the acknowledgment of desire, the understanding of the power of passion and the delight of its fulfillment. But she had still thought of him as fulfilling also the necessary role of the protector/patron without whom she could not achieve her ambition. The sensual joys of their love nest were a bonus.

Now, it seemed that the priorities were reversed. Any help he might offer her in the achievement of her ambition was the bonus—one that had nothing to do with this overwhelming surge of joyous love she felt when they had exchanged that look.

What she did not know was that Lord Kincaid had reached exactly the same conclusion, but from the different standpoint of his own planned deception.

Chapter 10

Thomas Killigrew received Lord Kincaid's message while he was at his breakfast, some three days after the shopping expedition at the Royal Exchange. It was a message not unlike many the manager of the king's company had received in the past: A nobleman had under his protection a girl desirous of gracing the stage. Would Master Killigrew do him the kindness of seeing the aspirant and judging for himself whether she could be so employed? Lord Kincaid himself ventured to suggest that once Killigrew laid eyes upon her, he would be captivated. This message offered a choice of meeting place—either at the young lady's lodgings, or at the playhouse, where Lord Kincaid would bring Mistress Wyat at a time convenient for Master Killigrew.

Master Killigrew drank deep of his ale. He was on friendly terms with Kincaid, who had a lively wit and, while he eschewed the ultimate extravagancies of the court, could never be labeled a dull dog. The king held him in esteem, although he was by no means one of the favorites—did not put himself out to be so, Killigrew reflected. Not one for the groveling and simpering that marked the truly obsequious courtier. He took pleasure in the play, also; was fast friends with John Dryden, and was presumably well aware of what qualities were indispensable in a female actor. They were not qualities possessed by all mistresses, although they were the qualities that made a woman a superlative mistress, Tom thought on a sardonic chuckle. Those qualities had led their owners into many a noble bedchamber; in more than a few instances, to the altar and a countess's coronet.

He pondered his response before deciding that he would see the girl on her own ground first. The stage could terrify a novice initially. If he saw any promise in her, then he would try her out on the boards. A message to the effect that Master Killigrew would do himself the honor of waiting upon Lord Kincaid and his protégée at three in that afternoon was dispatched to the address at Drury Lane.

Nicholas had not told Polly that he had at last taken the long-awaited step. It seemed to him that the less time she had for nervous anticipation, the calmer she would be when the moment came. For reasons based, as he was reluctantly obliged to accept, upon a mixture of pride and love, he would have her appear at her very best. The white damask kirtle and scarlet velvet gown had been delivered with a speed that said much for the skill and application of the sempstress and her apprentices. It was no great work, that afternoon, to persuade Polly into her new finery, although she offered halfhearted protest that, since there was no one to see and admire, it seemed rather a waste.

"And am I no one?" queried Nick, leaning his shoulders against the mantel, watching her preening antics with both amusement and satisfaction.

"Do not be foolish," Polly chided, frowning into the crystal mirror on the tiring table. "Is the collar pinned aright? It is not easy to do for oneself."

"I shall have to hire a maid for you," Nick commented, standing back to give proper attention to the matter of the collar. "If I just move this pin . . . like so . . . There, perfect."

"You are a more than accomplished maid, my lord," Polly said easily, assuming that he had spoken in jest. She adjusted the lace frills at the wrists of her smock and smoothed down the fluted pleats of the damask kirtle revealed by the velvet gown, which hung open at the front, the two halves caught up at the sides.

"I will not always be here to assist at your toilet," he pointed out. "I am certain the goodwife will offer what help she may, but she has other duties. Nay, you have need of a tiring woman."

Polly looked at him, aghast. "I could not possibly! I would not know what to say or how to go on or—"

"Nonsense," he interrupted. "Of course you will. It is simply another part that you will learn to play."

"I learn to play those parts that please me," Polly said. "And it does not please me to play the mistress of servants." She spoke with firm purpose. "I do not mean to be disobliging, Nicholas, and I am sure you intend only to be kind, but it would not suit me at all."

Nick drew his snuffbox out of the deep pocket of his coat and flicked it open with a deft thumbnail. He took a pinch, thoughtful and deliberate. This was obviously one of those issues on which Polly was like to prove intractable; nothing would be gained by pushing the point to animosity.

"Why do you not try the shoes?" he suggested affably.

Polly had noticed that when Nick dropped a potentially contentious subject as abruptly as he had just done this one, it usually meant that he had decided to choose different ground on some other occasion. The subject was certainly not closed. It was a tactic that left the opposition in an uneasy position, since one could not continue to press a point when no argument was offered, yet dropping the issue, under even such passive compulsion, smacked uncomfortably of concession. But there was nothing to be done. She turned her attention to the high-heeled shoes.

"They require practice," Nicholas comforted as she teetered precariously around the room. "In ten minutes I guarantee that you will be quite at ease."

Polly muttered doubtfully, but found to her surprise that Nick was right. Practice did make, if not perfect, then a fair approximation of that happy state.

She was demonstrating a very creditable turn in the parlor,

managing to control the volume of her skirts as they swung around her, when the knocker sounded from below. Nick glanced surreptitiously at the watch at his waist. Thomas Killigrew was punctual to the minute. Goodman Benson's voice came from the hall, adjuring the visitor to mind the turn at the corner of the stairs.

"Is it a visitor?" Without thinking, Polly moved into the light from the window. The knowledge that the shaft of afternoon sun would catch the golden tints hidden in the honeyed curls clustering on her shoulders was a subliminal one, yet she possessed it nevertheless.

Kincaid smiled to himself. She was standing very erect, the elegance of her attire set off by the natural grace of her posture. The exciting prospect of an audience other than himself had deepened the glow of her complexion, made, if such a thing were possible, the forest pools of her eyes even more lustrous. Her lips were slightly parted over those even white teeth, and she radiated her own special inner energy that defied all resistance.

It was this latter quality that Killigrew noticed the minute he walked into the parlor. No damsel with die-away airs here, but a young woman with her eyes set upon a prize; every inch of her absorbing her surroundings; intent on ensuring that no opportunity evaded her watchfulness, on ensuring that her responses were those to make the most of every eventuality. It was only after he had assimilated this that the full impact of that extraordinary beauty struck him.

He looked at Lord Kincaid, who had been watching the visitor's reactions with a tiny smile beneath arched eyebrows. "It would be too much to hope that she might have some aptitude, also," Thomas murmured. "God is too sparing of his gifts—and those he has already bestowed . . . !" He raised his hands in a gesture of one rendered speechless.

Polly had been listening to this exchange in some puzzlement. Now she cast an imperative glance at Nick, and one foot tapped with unconscious impatience.

"Your pardon, Polly." He bowed slightly. "Pray permit me to introduce Master Thomas Killigrew. Thomas, Mistress

Polly Wyat." Then he stood back and prepared to enjoy the play.

Polly was thrown off balance for no more than a second. Then she was sinking into a curtsy, murmuring how delighted she was to make Master Killigrew's acquaintance. Her salutation was answered in kind; then the manager of the Theatre Royal said, "Make your curtsy again, but this time you are making it to one whom you would have as lover if your husband can be successfully deceived."

Polly thought for a minute. This was not how she had imagined her first meeting with this man. Somehow she had thought there would be ceremony, that it would all take place in the hushed glory of the theatre, which she had never yet entered, investing the meeting with all the magic of fantasy. But if this was the way it was to be, then she must adapt.

She imagined herself in a crowded drawing room, her husband standing to one side, Nick, as the prospective lover, bowing before her. Master Killigrew was clearly the audience, so she must ensure that he had the full benefit of her décolletage, the curve of hip when she pointed one delicate toe, and allowed her rear to sink onto her bent back leg. It was a very slow descent, her eyes lowered modestly as she dipped. But once in position, she raised her eyes and looked directly at Lord Kincaid. It was no more than the merest whisper of a glance, since to hold his gaze would bespeak an effrontery that would draw unwelcome notice from those around her. She had no fan, but it was not difficult to mime the unfurling as she fixed melting yet mischievous, inviting eyes upon the chosen one, while she held the position of subjection just long enough to underscore the invitation, and to allow both men full appreciation of her bare shoulders, artlessly tumbled curls, the rise and fall of her semiexposed bosom. Then she was swimming upward, turning her eyes discreetly to one side as if to deny that the exchange had taken place, gliding sideways as if she were moving on to another guest.

"Superlative!" breathed Killigrew. "You have had no experience of the stage?"

"To quote the bard, as far as Polly is concerned: All the world's a stage," laughed Nick. "She rarely loses an opportunity to perform."

Polly colored, imagining a note of reproof beneath the laughter. He had made it clear often enough that it was one of her habits which tended to displease him. "I have not served you such a trick for this age, my lord," she said with frigid dignity. "It is ungallant to refer to matters that I had thought were past."

"You misunderstand, moppet. I was but paying you a compliment on this occasion."

The flush of annoyance faded, the stiffness left her shoulders. "I beg your pardon, sir. I did not mean to jump to conclusions."

Killigrew listened, fascinated. She had the prettiest voice, light and musical, and was giving rein to her emotions quite without artifice, as if there were no one but herself and Kincaid in the chamber. A lack of selfconsciousness was a great gift for an actor as long as it could be channeled. If she was impatient of counsel and direction, however, it would not matter how beautiful her face and form, how natural her talent—and meek and submissive she most definitely was not.

Where had Kincaid found her? he wondered. There was a naïveté about her, a curious innocence that belied her position as a kept woman. She was very young, of course, and her speech and manners were not those of one who had been bred in Covent Garden or its equivalent. But the name was unknown to him, so presumably she was not the scion of some impoverished noble family, either. A merchant's daughter, maybe, willing to exchange her virtue for social and financial advancement. Impoverished nobility, genteel tradesmen's daughters, Covent Garden whores, had all found their way to the stage in the last few years, all in search of material or social advancement. Both were available for such a beauty as this one along the path she had chosen, and indeed, it would be a crying shame to leave such a paragon to the mediocre destiny of a merchant's wife.

"Do you care to accompany me to the playhouse, Mistress Wyat?" Killigrew said now. "I'd like you to read something for me, if you would be so kind."

Polly was about to say that she would be more than willing so long as the words were not too difficult when she caught Nick's eye, reminding her that she must give no indication of her true background. "I am at your service, sir," she said instead, the carefully formal response concealing both the quickening of excitement at the prospect of entering a playhouse at long last, and an apprehensive sinking at the knowledge that the moment had come to put to the test all that she believed she possessed. What if she was wrong, if she had no aptitude, if Master Killigrew rejected her? It was a prospect that afforded a most dreadful void of hopelessness— the void that she had fought so long and so hard to escape. "I will fetch my cloak." She went into the other chamber.

Nicholas picked up his own cloak from the chair in the parlor, slinging it around his shoulders. "You do not object if I accompany you, Thomas?"

"If you think she will not be distracted by your presence," spoke the manager of the king's company, no longer concerned with formal courtesies that were irrelevant to the making of a business decision.

"On the contrary, she will be less apprehensive," responded Kincaid, with a dry smile that encompassed his understanding both of Polly's feelings and of Killigrew's position. "The situation will be quite strange for her, and I would not have her ill at ease if I can prevent it."

Killigrew looked a little surprised. Such gentle concern was unusual in a court where the softer emotions were derided as lack of sophistication, as lack of understanding of the realities of a world where no man could be truly called friend, and only fools put their trust in another's word. The women were as hard-bitten as their menfolk, as quick to take advantage of another's disadvantage, as eager to bring about another's downfall if it would mean their own advancement, and as unscrupulous as to the methods they used in such work. If Lord Kincaid was going to cast a protective umbrella over his protégée, it would give rise to much comment, and not a little contemptuous amusement.

Nick had little difficulty in guessing the other man's thought processes. He shared them, indeed, and his rational self found his present obsession with the well-being of a seventeen-year-old miss a matter for considerable incredulity. But since he seemed to have little control over his feelings at the moment, he was obliged to accept love's shaft and follow where it led him.

It led him now into the bedchamber, where Polly had been closeted in search of her cloak for an inordinate length of time. He found her sitting on the bed looking like a paralyzed rabbit, hands clasped tightly in her damask lap, eyes gazing sightlessly into the middle distance.

"Perhaps I cannot do it," she said without preamble as he came in, closing the door. "Perhaps I have been mistaken all these years, and I cannot act at all. What will I do then, Nicholas?"

Nicholas reviewed his options rapidly. He could imagine the pit of desolation into which she was staring as the moment of trial loomed. For so long she had seen only one way out of the vicious and complete impoverishment of the destiny she had been dealt. If this way failed, she could at this moment see only a return to that destiny. He could offer her reassurance that he would not permit that, whatever happened in the playhouse; he could be hurt and accusatory at her failure to trust him; or he could put the steel back into her spine by stinging her into a resurgence of her old confidence.

"Are you telling me you mean to cry off?" he demanded, no sympathy in his voice. "For weeks you have made my life wretched with your constant importuning that I arrange a meeting for you with Master Killigrew. You have lost no opportunity to demonstrate this talent you insist that you have. Am I now to believe that the whole was a sham?"

Polly had stood up in the middle of this speech. The color

ebbed in her cheeks, but her eyes had focused again, her lips were set. She picked up her cloak. "You will see that it was not a sham!" With that, she brushed past him and marched into the parlor. "I am ready to accompany you, Master Killigrew." Without waiting for either of them, she continued her march out of the parlor and down the stairs.

"Mistress Wyat appears to be of a somewhat tempestuous temperament," observed Killigrew, drawing on his gloves.

"Only when provoked," Nicholas responded with a smile. "In general, she is of a most sunny disposition."

They were obliged to follow her impetuous progress along Drury Lane, since she showed no inclination to slow for either of them, and to catch her up would require a hastening of their own speed that was hardly consonant with the dignified lassitude of the courtier.

Polly waited for them when she reached the steps of the playhouse. The march in the cold air had served to clear her head, enabling her to view Nick's intervention in a new light. "That was done deliberately, was it not?" she asked when he reached her. There was a slight smile in her eyes, and when he nodded she laughed. "I beg leave to tell you, my lord, that your tactics are most underhand."

"But most effective," he countered, grinning.

"Aye." She sobered, saying, "I am most grateful . . . for that, and all else."

"I am amply recompensed," he said softly. That same intensity caught them again, held them in breathless acknowledgement of its force.

Master Killigrew, who had gone up the steps to unlock the great door, turned to see what was delaying them. He saw the naked emotion flickering between them, an almost palpable current. He drew in his breath sharply, then the force receded, freeing the lovers from its grip. Nick gestured courteously to the steps, and Polly came up ahead of him.

The door swung open, and Polly found herself in the king's playhouse. They had entered from Drury Lane by what she would soon call the stage entrance, and stood now in a dark passageway. "The tiring rooms are there." Killigrew pointed to the left as he pushed through a door ahead. Polly, following him, stood for the first of what would be countless times upon the stage of the Theatre Royal.

She stood and stared. A glazed cupola covered the pit that stretched below in front of the stage; there were boxes, ranged in galleries, to the side and the back of the theatre. She tried to imagine those seats filled. Why, there must be seating for at least four hundred souls. How lonely and exposed one would feel on this tiny, bare wooden platform. She shivered as cold despair threatened again.

Killigrew had gone to one side of the stage, where he picked up a sheaf of papers and began rifling through them. "This scene, I think."

"What play have you in mind?" Nick, with considerable interest, came to peer over Tom's shoulder. "Oh, *Flora's Vagaries*." He chuckled. "I could not have chosen better myself."

"Why do you not read Alberto?" Killigrew offered the suggestion casually, as if he had not drawn the conclusions that he had about Lord Kincaid and Mistress Polly Wyat. "You will perhaps find it less uncomfortable, Mistress Wyat, if Kincaid plays opposite you."

"I am no actor," Nick demurred.

"You have no need to be. Just read the lines. We will leave the acting to the lady." Killigrew, smiling, crossed the stage to where Polly still stood, taking in her surroundings, seemingly unaware of this exchange. "I will tell you a little about Flora," he said, and she shook herself free of her reverie. "She is a most sprightly young lady, not one to be dominated by circumstances or individuals, and most particularly not by men." He watched her as he drew the word picture of one of the stage's most engaging and daring heroines. "She is the ward of a foolish boor, a lout, who would keep both her and his daughter incarcerated to prevent their falling under the eye of love or lust."

Polly smiled, giving him a look of complete comprehension. Killigrew nodded and continued. "In this early scene, Flora's suitor, Alberto, commits the grave error of telling a

story about the lady that is not entirely to her credit. Flora
overhears and treats her would-be lover to a tongue-lashing
of some considerable eloquence." He handed her the pages.
"Read it through for yourself first."

"May I ask how Alberto reacts to this upbraiding?" Polly
flicked through the pages, praying that the words would be
easily made out.

"He decides that this is a lady worthy of serious respect."
It was Nicholas who answered her. "It is for you to convince
the audience that a railing female is not simply a scold in
need of bridling, but one who is entitled to object to mockery, and to speak her mind." He took her elbow. "Come,
let us go into a corner and read it through together. I have
never ventured to try myself in such a matter, and have need
of a few moments reflection."

Polly felt such a surge of gratitude that threatened to overcome her already frail equilibrium. But she said only, "By all
means, sir. I would welcome the opportunity to familiarize
myself with the text."

"I will sit in the pit." Killigrew stepped off the stage into
the auditorium, lit by the gray afternoon light filtering
through the cupola. "Begin whenever you are both ready."

"Read it for yourself first," Nick instructed in an undertone. "If there is a word you cannot make out, just point to
it."

Polly concentrated with frowning intensity on the
scrawled pages, her anxiety that she might stumble over the
text superseding the fear that she would be unable to act
the part. But as she read, she could hear in her head how the
lines should sound, could picture Flora—pretty, witty Flora
with a sharp tongue and a firm belief that she was second to
none. She looked up at Nick with a grin. "I find myself in
some sympathy with this lady."

He nodded. "If you are ready, then, let us engage in this
duel for Master Killigrew's benefit."

Thomas Killigrew sat forward on the bench as the two
came to the front of the stage. One hand rested lightly on
the lacquered knob of his cane, firmly planted upon the

floor; his other lay upon the hilt of his sword. He was quite motionless. After three lines he knew he had been offered a female actor who would make the most of the spirited love game that so entranced his audiences. With every vivacious toss of her head, every ringing accusation directed at the hapless Alberto, every provocative movement, she spun a web of excitement and titillation that could not fail to entertain even the most abysmally ill-behaved audiences—and there were plenty of those. Add to that the peerless beauty of face and form, contemplate her in the deliciously provocative breeches parts, and Mistress Polly Wyat was destined for greatness.

"I thank you both," he said at the end of the scene. "I do not think that Nicholas will ever make an actor, I fear." He sauntered across to the stage. "Mistress Wyat, on the other hand . . ." Pausing, he smiled up at her. She returned the smile with a somewhat vague and distracted air. It was an air with which he was familiar, and of which he approved. It denoted complete involvement in the part she had just been playing. "Do you wish to join the king's company, mistress?"

"Of all things," she replied, with a fierce intensity. "May I?"

"I see no reason why not. You will have to gain His Majesty's approval, of course, but we will not seek that just yet."

"What do you have in mind?" Nicholas, accepting with considerable relief that his brief venture into the thespian arena was over, took snuff.

Killigrew came up onto the stage. "A short spell in my Nursery at Moorfields first. There are skills and practices to be learned, and even a natural talent is the better for honing. Then I will put on *The Rival Ladies* here. It is one of the king's favorites and provides ample scope for an actor to show to advantage all that she may have to show." He and Nicholas exchanged a comprehensive glance at this. Polly looked between them in some bemusement.

"I do not quite understand. What is your Nursery, Master Killigrew?"

"A training school," he replied. "I put on plays for the people in a theatre at Moorfields. It is not the most appreciative audience, but one that provides valuable experience for a novice. You will learn much—not least how to win distracted and possibly hostile playgoers."

"I would rather start here," Polly said, indicating the theatre around her. "Why can I not learn here the skills and practices of which you speak?"

"Because you would do so at the expense of the experienced actors. They do not care to perform with a tyro, my dear, however talented she may be, or however much she may feel she has nothing to learn."

Polly swallowed this unpalatable statement with a grimace. Nick, though he recognized the justice in the snub, and appreciated Killigrew's need to establish mastery at the outset, felt a stab of sympathy for her discomfiture. "You will have but one chance to win the king's approval, Polly. It is surely wiser to take that chance when you are properly prepared."

"Yes. I understand. I do beg your pardon, Master Killigrew, if I seemed of an overweening conceit." Those great eyes were raised to his face, a tremulous smile hovered on her lips, and Thomas felt an overpowering remorse for his harshness.

He smiled warmly. "No, no, my dear. I did not think that. It is quite natural for you to be impatient of delay. But you must trust me, you know."

"Oh, but I do!" she averred passionately, her hands clasped to her bosom. "I will do whatever you suggest. I am so grateful—"

"That will do, Polly," Nicholas put in hastily, sensing that Killigrew was about to slide into a hypnotized trance under the full force of that melting gaze and the impassioned plea of her penitence.

Killigrew blinked, startled by this interpolation. Polly turned on Nicholas reproachfully. "I meant it! I was not playing. I am truly regretful if I seemed vain and importunate—except that I do not think I was being."

Nick's lips twitched. "You are a most beguiling jade! You will become accustomed to her tricks, Killigrew. She is possessed of more wiles than a barrel-load of monkeys. You fall for them at your peril, I can promise you."

"I begin to see that," Thomas murmured, stroking his chin. "It clearly behooves me to be on my guard." He chuckled. "I am an old hand at this game, Mistress Wyat, so have a care before you lock swords with me."

"Why, sir, I would not be so impertinent as to hazard such a thing." Polly sank into a deep obeisance, twitching her skirts to one side, bending her head so that the slender column of her neck was presented, bared as the honeyed ringlets fell forward. It was a posture of perfect submission, yet every line of her body radiated a coquettish impudence.

Killigrew gave a shout of laughter. "Ah, Mistress Wyat, I foresee that in the stage curtsy you will excel. It is by far the most important pose for a female actor to master, and you appear greatly proficient already, even without the assistance of a corset. You have had an accomplished dancing master, I gather."

"Most accomplished," agreed Polly, rising gracefully. She cast a covert glance at Nicholas, struggling with his mirth at the idea of a dancing master in the Dog tavern. "My governess was monstrous strict in matters of deportment, sir," she continued blithely. "I shall always be grateful for her care."

Nicholas, having no idea how far Polly's inventiveness would take her if she were allowed free rein, decided that matters were drawing too close to the brink of danger for comfort. The one thing that was abundantly clear was that she was enjoying every wicked minute, and he could almost hear Killigrew's mental calculations as he tried to fit her into some recognizable social background.

"It grows late, Thomas," he said. "And we have taken up enough of your time for one day." He held out a hand. "I am most grateful."

"On the contrary." Killigrew took the proffered hand. "I should thank you."

And no one should thank Polly, Polly thought; but it was only a passing grievance; her elation ran too high for niggardly remonstrance, and if these two wished to congratulate themselves on whatever she had to offer, they had her permission. She would indulge in a little self-congratulation and the heady knowledge of success. She had leaped the void of hopelessness.

Once outside, Nicholas tucked her arm beneath his, remarking casually, "You are going to be well served, I fear, when required to execute the steps of a coranto. Your fictitious dancing master will appear to have been not so accomplished after all."

"Oh, indeed, I trust not, sir," Polly returned, her lips curved impishly as she looked up at him, her face framed in the fur hood of her cloak. "I had made sure you would be a most accomplished dancer! Do not tell me you are not. I had thought such skill necessary for all courtiers."

"So I am to teach you to dance now, is that it? I had never thought to be awarded the title 'dancing master' . . . or 'monstrous strict governess,' for that matter," mused Kincaid. "It has a most undignified ring. But I daresay I will undertake that task, as I have undertaken all the rest." He gazed at her upturned face, thinking of all that he had taught her, of the wondrous flair she possessed, in one field at least, for taking those lessons and making their execution her own specialty. It was no longer unusual, when it came to love-making, for him to yield the initiative to the creative impulses of this gay and zestful elf.

Polly's gaze sparkled under the darkening sky, where the evening star glimmered, and she skipped—a joyous involuntary expression—on her high heels as the winter wind probed with icy fingers. "I *am* going to be an actor. I am!"

"It would seem so," Nick agreed, as calmly as if he were not in a white heat for her, as if his blood were not pounding in his ears, his loins aching, as if the touch of her fingers on his sleeve, the knowledge of the shape of her beside him, had not set up a chain of impassioned responses that seemed as if they must find physical expression if he were not to ignite with the wanting.

The electric quality of sensual excitement scintillated, and Polly caught her breath, engulfed almost without warning. Her fingers curled around his arm, her body pressed closer to his, her face lifted, lips parted invitingly, eyes glowing, luminous with needy passion.

"God's grace!" Nick stopped abruptly in the frosty lane and stood looking down at her. "Never have I felt such a wanting. I am consumed with desire for you."

"Now," she whispered, insistent, through suddenly parched lips, moving against him, heedless of the darkening street, the ice-tipped wind, the roll of carriage wheels behind her.

Nick dragged himself back from the edge of a madness that would have had him, there and then, yield to the demand she made, to the impulses of his own body. "Make haste!" he said, curt with the effort necessary to manage both of them until they could attain privacy. " 'Tis but a few yards now." His fingers circled her wrist, his stride lengthened, and Polly tripped on her high heels as she stumbled to match his pace.

The door of the lodging was bolted against the encroaching night, and he hammered vigorously upon the knocker. Goodman Benson opened it, his face creased with anxiety. "Is summat, amiss, m'lord?"

"Not in the least, Benson," returned his lordship. "But 'tis cold as charity, and we've need of the fire." Striding past the landlord, still holding Polly tightly, he made for the stairs. "God be praised!" Sighing with relief, he kicked the parlor door shut behind them and swung Polly into his arms.

It was a kiss that seemed to devour her, an embrace that would swallow her. She strained against him, desperate to become one with him, her mouth opened beneath his, receiving eagerly the deep penetration of his tongue as the hard shaft of his arousal pressed through damask and velvet against her thigh. His gloved hands pushed beneath her cloak

to span her narrow back, holding her against him. With an
urgent movement, her mouth still locked with his, she unhooked her cloak, throwing it off with a shrug of her shoulders. Her breasts were crushed against the silken brocade of
his coat; with another impatient movement, she pulled the
neck of her gown lower so that her bosom was bared. Her
head fell back on a sigh of abandonment as he released her
mouth and bent instead to capture the hard, thrusting nipples, his hands forming a support against which she leant,
bent backward, her hair falling almost to the floor, her lower
body still pressed to his.

A soft moan escaped her as he nibbled and nuzzled her
breasts, bringing that strange tugging deep in her belly, that
liquid fullness in her loins so that she moved restlessly against
him. The hilt of his sword obtruded with bruising pressure,
but she barely noticed it as her flesh, heated under the living
flame of passion, yearned for union. Her fingers twined in
the auburn head glistening against the white skin of her
breast; she spoke his name in urgent plea.

He raised his head to look deep into her eyes, where
golden lights flickered in the green-brown depths, gazing up
at him in suspended wonder. He laid a hand on her breast,
against the jolting of her heart. Then the instant of patience
vanished under the spiral of need; with a fine disregard for
the delicate material of gown and kirtle, he pulled them
from her body, his hands, rough in their vehemence, rending
the thin cotton of her smock. Then she was naked, her
breath coming in little gasps as she writhed in the hands and
beneath the mouth that explored and possessed her, opened
her and probed her, bringing the most sweet and piercing
pleasure until she was lost in sensate rapture, trembling before him, held in thrall, body and soul, to him who possessed
as he worshiped her body with his own.

Nick thought he would drown in her softness, in the fragrance of her skin. Her body's unashamed acknowledgment
of the pleasure he was bringing her delighted him and
aroused him more powerfully than he would ever have believed possible. He could not take his lips from her as he

branded every inch of her with his kiss, tasted of the eternal richness of her womanhood, felt her shuddering release again, and yet again.

With fumbling impatience, he divested himself of his own clothes, maintaining contact with her body even as he did so, a stroking finger, a brush of his lips, the quick dart of his ambrosia-sipping tongue, while she stood as if robbed of the power of movement or of will until he, too, was naked. Then, with a whispering sigh, she dropped to her knees, offering her own gift as she caressed him with her mouth, enclosed him in her small hand, returned the homage he had paid to her.

When the need for total union became finally invincible, he lowered her to the rug before the fireplace, smoothing a hand over the indentation of her waist, the soft curve of hip, as she lay bathed in the fire glow reflected in the emerald luster of the eyes that consumed her. Then he drew her beneath him, her thighs parting eagerly at the nudge of his knee, the tender, sensitized entrance to her body closing with joy around the throbbing monolith. He pressed deep inside her, lost in his own joy, sinking, plunging into her core, and she rose to meet him with a cry both wanton and wild under the suffusion of excitement that burst upon her, ripped through her, tearing her soul from her body, banishing all sense of self, of place, of purpose. Her hands gripped the corded muscles of his upper arms as she felt his body jarring, shuddering, heard her name on his lips; then they were caught in the wondrous flood of surcease, tumbled, drowned, to be tossed upon the shore of satiation while the tide ebbed.

Nick looked down at her as she lay clasped in his arms, the golden lashes fanned upon the damask cheeks kissed pink with his loving. Of all the wild cards he could have been dealt in the game he had intended to play, the onslaught of love was a rogue he could never have guessed. And the devil of it was that he could not help but thank the dealer—for all that it bode fair to play havoc with the game.

Chapter 11

◦───∞───◦

The piercing wails rending the air as Nicholas sauntered into Thomas Killigrew's playhouse at Moorfields a week later sounded as anguished as if they were wrenched by the rack. However, experience having taught him that the vigor of Polly's protests tended to bear little relation to the severity of their cause, he made no effort to hasten his step as he strolled down a narrow passageway in the direction of the tiring room, from whence emanated the pitiable cries.

Sounds of hammering and laughing voices came from the stage to his right. A lad, clutching a piece of planking taller than himself, scurried past at an imperative bellow from the scene-setters on stage. Nicholas pushed open the door to the tiring room, where he stood, for the moment unnoticed by its three occupants, surveying the scene.

"Half an inch more, Lizzie." Thomas Killigrew, perched on the edge of a tiring table, instructed the flushed and flustered tirewoman, who was struggling to tighten the laces of a bone corset behind a furiously complaining Polly.

"It is impossible!" Polly yelped, gripping the back of a chair until her knuckles whitened. "I cannot breathe. You would suffocate me."

"Nonsense," retorted the impervious Master Killigrew.

"A little discomfort is inevitable until you become accustomed to it."

"I will *never* become accustomed!" She squirmed, twisting her head over her shoulder, peering at Lizzie's busy fingers. "Oh, Nicholas!" Her eye fell on the spectator in the door. "Tell Thomas that he cannot *do* this. My bones are breaking!" This last emerged on a long-drawn-out wail as Lizzie finally secured the laces.

"Ah, Nicholas, you are well come, indeed." Killigrew, pushing himself away from his perch, greeted the new arrival with visible relief. "Perhaps you can better explain the realities to Polly."

Nicholas regarded the fulminating figure of his mistress. Only the linen of her smock protected her skin from the bone stays, which prevented any curve of her spine, any slump of her shoulders, and lifted her breasts to swell invitingly over the smock's low-cut bodice edged with a teasing scrap of Venetian lace.

"You must wear it," he said. "What you wear beneath your gown is more important than anything you may put atop."

"As I have been saying," interpolated Killigrew. "The corset governs your form, controls the way you move. Without it, your gowns will not sit right, and you will not be able to perform any stage movements correctly. It is particularly vital with the curtsy. Surely you would not wish to spoil the effect of what you already do so well?"

"I will not be able to do anything at all if my ribs are broken and I have no breath," she said, still mutinous, holding her narrowed waist.

Nicholas crossed the room, turned her around, assessing the fit with an expert eye informed by intimate knowledge of the shape beneath smock and corset. "It is a little tight, Killigrew," he pronounced. "It could be loosened somewhat—at least for the first time." Without waiting for agreement, he released the laces himself, not by much, but sufficiently to afford the sufferer considerable relief in contrast.

"I find it hard to believe that you have not been obliged to wear such a garment before," observed Killigrew. "If you had a governess with strict notions of deportment."

"My aunt died of tight lacing—when she was with child," Polly embellished shamelessly. "So my mother would not countenance it. Besides, my parents were of a Puritan turn of mind and did not encourage vanity."

That disposed of that, reflected Lord Kincaid, with some admiration. However, when they were private, it would perhaps be wise to advise such a consummate inventor of the truth that there were dangers inherent in gilding the lily. For the moment he contented himself with a change of subject.

"Do you still intend presenting *Flora's Vagaries* today sennight, Thomas?"

"If Polly will be so good as to be accommodating," replied Thomas, with a caustic edge. "I do not ask for much."

"Nay, only that I should be squashed like a preserved quince," Polly retorted.

Killigrew raised his eyes heavenward. Nicholas said appeasingly, "Put on the gown, sweetheart. You will then see the point in the corset."

Polly could not resist his coaxing smile or the softness of his tone. Having already realized that she was going to be compelled to yield, it seemed niggardly to continue with her waspishness. She offered him a tiny smile, part apology, part complicity, before turning readily to Lizzie, who was shaking out the folds of an embroidered petticoat. The brocaded satin gown that followed it was richer and more voluminous by far than any she had yet worn, and was encumbered by a long train.

She stood for many minutes surveying her image in the glass, not with vanity but with the air of one looking for information. The first thing she realized was that the corset, while restricting in one way, paradoxically freed her in other ways. She had no need to think of her posture, of whether her décolletage was appropriately displayed, of whether her skirts fell in a graceful sweep. The undergarment ensured all of those things. She stepped over to a low chair, feeling the swish and weight of the train behind her. Sitting on the chair with any grace was not going to be easy, she decided. She must somehow bring the train to heel if it was not to knock over the chair as she swung round; somehow kick her voluminous skirts forward if she was not to tread on and tear them; more important, somehow ensure that she did not miss the chair altogether as it became lost beneath her gown. And all these maneuvers must take place simultaneously.

"Why do you not hazard it? The chair will not bite you." Thomas broke into her cogitations, and she turned to him with a laugh, her earlier contrariness forgotten.

"I was wondering if it would stay still."

"I will show you how to do it." Killigrew came across to her. "Take your skirt at the back in one hand . . . like so . . . Now swish the train to the side as you push your right foot forward, kicking away the skirt. That's it. Now lower yourself onto the seat. There." He smiled in satisfaction. "That was not so very difficult, was it?"

"It is not very restful," Polly observed, sitting at the very edge of the chair. "If I lean forward or backward, those dreadful bones poke into me."

"But then, it is not at all becoming to slouch," Killigrew told her. "Flora may be a high-spirited, sharp-tongued young lady, but she *is* a lady and would never sit slumped upon her chair, as you are aware."

Nick was frowning. "Are you sure that a sennight will be sufficient time for Polly to learn as much as she must?"

"Indeed it will!" Polly spoke up vigorously. "I will practice all night, if necessary, but I am determined that I shall not stay in this backwater for any length of time."

"I think there is little fear of that," Killigrew said with a wry smile. "Moorfields will not be able to contain you for very long."

It became abundantly clear to Nick during the next seven days that Polly was as good as her word. Killigrew was a hard taskmaster, but there was nothing he expected of her that she did not expect of herself, and more. She had no difficulty learning the part of Flora, pressing Nick into service to read with her during the evenings, when he could think of many more exciting occupations. And with grim fortitude she gritted her teeth and wore the detested corset constantly until it felt like a second skin.

"I am most deeply apprehensive," Killigrew said with surprising gloom to Nicholas on the sixth day, as they both watched the rehearsal from the pit.

Nick looked startled. "How so?"

"Beside her, the rest of the cast appear as inept and as unappealing as wooden dummies. This audience will not know how to react. I doubt they have been treated to such talent or such beauty before. If they do not recognize the quality, but only that she is different both from what they are accustomed to and from her fellows, they may well hiss her off the stage."

"If there is any danger of that happening, Thomas, I'll not permit her to perform tomorrow." Nick spoke with finality. Polly was not going to be hurt in any way while he had a say in the matter.

Thomas smiled lazily. "How would you prevent her, my friend? I should dearly love to see you try." Rising to his feet, he strolled to the foot of the stage. "Polly, you are playing that fan as if 'tis a wet fish! It is a part of you, to be used as expressively as you use your eyes or your voice. In this instance, you are expressing annoyance. Flick your wrist so that it falls open and then closed. Just so. Do it several times, each time sharper than the last."

How would he prevent her? Nick shook his head ruefully, watching her as she discovered rapidly what Killigrew wanted, beginning, with obvious enjoyment, to add her own little touches. Of course he could not, short of locking her in her chamber. No, the performance must take place on the morrow. There would be some members of the audience who would know what they were seeing. Richard De Winter, Sir Peter, and Major Conway would be there, all as anxious as he to see how their protégée performed. Only then would they be truly able to judge whether their plan could succeed.

Nicholas knew that it could. He also knew that he did not want it to. What he did not know was how to reconcile those two facts with the promise he had made to his friends—a promise he was in honor bound to fulfill.

However, he had little time to dwell on his dilemma over the next twenty-four hours. Polly's moods fluctuated wildly and without warning as the hour of her testing drew nearer. She progressed through snappish irritability to unbridled temper to complete withdrawal. Nick struggled for patience, even as he wondered how such an extraordinary change could have been wrought in his sunny-tempered, equable, mischievous mistress. She was as impervious to his caresses as she was to his annoyance. It was not until, in complete exasperation, his patience finally shredded, he strode to the door of the parlor saying that he would leave her to enjoy her bad temper in solitude that she returned to her senses.

"Nay, do not leave me alone, please, Nick!" She ran to him, seizing his arm. "I beg your pardon for being so horrid, but I am so dreadfully afeard! I am certain I will forget what to say, or trip over my skirt, or sit on the floor instead of the chair! And they will laugh and throw oranges at me!"

"No one will throw oranges at you," he said in perfect truth. In Moorfields they favored tomatoes, but he did not add that. "Besides, you will have friends in the audience. You know that De Winter is promised, and Sir Peter, and the major. And I will be there—" He stopped, frowning, as the street knocker sounded from belowstairs. "Lord of hell! Who could that be at this hour?"

Polly ran to the window, peering down at the dark, rainy street. A lad with a lantern held a horse, which she immediately recognized as Richard's. "Why, Lord De Winter is come."

"A late visitor, I know." Richard spoke from the doorway, shaking free his russet frieze riding cloak in a shower of raindrops. "But I have some news that I thought might be of sufficient interest to excuse my intrusion."

"Come to the fire, Richard, and take some wine. No visit

from you could be termed intrusion." Nicholas gestured hospitably as Polly took their guest's coat and hat.

Richard smiled his thanks, while casting an appraising look at his hostess. He raised an interrogative eyebrow at Nicholas, whose returning grimace explained all. "You are not in best looks, Polly," Richard said with customary directness. "You are perhaps apprehensive about the morrow?"

Polly turned from the table where she had been filling a goblet of Malaga for him. "Do you find it surprising, my lord, that I should be?" She was completely at her ease with De Winter, accepting him as Nick's closest friend with a natural warmth and confidence.

He took the glass from her and shook his head. "On the contrary. But what I have to tell you may well ease your trepidation." He paused. "Then again, it might worsen it. You shall be the judge." He sipped his wine. "This is a good Malaga, Nick. My compliments."

He reposed his long, elegant length in a carved oak chair and sipped his wine again. Polly clasped her hands in front of her, compressed her lips, and stood, a veritable monument of patience, until De Winter was quite overcome and could persist in his teasing no longer. "I was at court this evening. There was a dance in the queen's apartments. A somewhat insipid affair," he added, as if his audience would be interested in the judgment.

Nicholas smiled, throwing another log on the fire. "Polly, come here." He patted his lap in invitation. "You look as taut as if you have received the attentions of a clock winder!"

De Winter waited until she was settled upon Nick's knee, her head resting on his shoulder, his fingers twisting in the hair spilling over the warm mulberry wool of her nightgown. "The talk was mostly of some surprise that Master Killigrew is keeping up his sleeve. It is said that if one were to venture to the Nursery at Moorfields tomorrow afternoon—should one be prepared to mingle with such playgoers as one might find there—" Richard waved his cambric handkerchief through the air as if to dispel whatever noxious attributes might be found amongst such an audience "—one might discover the surprise a little earlier than Thomas had intended."

"Clever," murmured Nick, mindful of the discussion when Killigrew had been afraid that a Moorfields audience would find Polly too rare a flower for their taste. If the theatre was filled with intrigued courtiers, who would most certainly respond with approval, those in the pit would either follow the courtiers' lead, or their disapproval would be drowned. "And is there a move to discover this secret?"

"It appears so." Richard smiled over his glass. "Even Davenant is anxious to see what is making his rival so smug. Buckingham has sworn to attend, and where the duke goes—"

"The world follows," Nick concluded, swallowing his unease before it could raise more than a prickle on his spine. "The king also?"

"He cannot. The French ambassador has requested an audience, and Clarendon is being most persuasive that it should be granted. There is still hope for an alliance in the question of this damned Dutch war."

"Fool's paradise!" scoffed Nick. "There'll be no help from the Spanish or the French. France has no need for gratuitous enemies, and Spain is too weak."

The conversation seemed to have veered off course as far as Polly was concerned. She sat up urgently. "I do not understand how anyone could know about me . . . Oh." A thought seemed to strike her. "That is, if I am the surprise of which you speak?" Receiving a reassuring nod, she went on. "If Thomas did not intend that anyone at court should know about tomorrow's performance, how is it that they do?"

"I expect he told them," said Nick easily, stretching his legs beneath her. "In a roundabout fashion. He is a devious man, our Master Killigrew."

"But why would he?" Polly resisted the arm that made to draw her back against his shoulder.

Nick was not about to add to her anxieties by telling her Killigrew's reason, so he shrugged, saying lightly, "I expect you have made more improvement than he expected in such a short time, and he considers you ready to face the world informally."

"Think you that the Duke of Buckingham will recognize me?" She stood up, drawing her gown tightly around her as if a finger of cold had penetrated the coziness of candlelight and fire-glow.

"Why should it be a matter of concern if he does?" asked Richard, deceptively casual. "You cannot expect to win the king's favor if you do not also win Villiers's."

"I had as lief not meet him again," she said simply, staring into the fire, where wraiths of blue and green spun in the red glow, and that cold, dissolute countenance seemed to take form, then dissolve. She turned back to the room. "I am being fanciful. I expect it is because I am wearied."

Nick stood up. "Get you to bed, sweetheart. I will ask Goodwife Benson to prepare you a sack-posset. It will help you sleep." Cupping her face, he stroked the high cheek-bones with his thumbs.

"You will stay tonight?" The question was whispered, not out of deference to Richard, who was gazing into his wine as if nothing else could interest him, but because speaking out loud seemed to require more energy than she possessed.

"Aye, flower, I'll stay. Bid Richard good night now. I will bring you the posset in a little while." He kissed the tip of her nose, then turned her with a little pat in the direction of the bedchamber.

"Rest easy," Richard said, taking her hand as she came over to him, raising it to his lips. "You will be the cynosure of the play, I can safely promise you. You are about to storm the theatre, carrying all before you." Polly shook her head, blushing in sudden embarrassment, more at the caressing tone and the elegant salute from one who habitually used her with a brisk, almost avuncular friendliness than at his words. "Well, perhaps you will not, if you do not sleep away the rings under your eyes," he said, reverting to the norm with instant comprehension. "Do as you are bid and get you gone. You look positively hagged."

The door closed behind her. Nick pulled the bell rope,

throwing a mocking smile at Richard. "Such softness, friend! Have a care lest you lose sight of the goal."

"That is a piece of advice I would give you," Richard replied soberly. "Having reached this point, it were foolish to throw away the prize for scruple."

The arrival of the goodwife in answer to the bell put an end to this conversation, but once she had left, Nick strode over to the hearth, kicking a fallen log, sending a shower of sparks up the chimney. " 'Tis a damnable dilemma."

"I do understand that the situation has changed somewhat," Richard observed, shrugging. "It would take a blind man to miss what has happened between you. But it need not make too much difference, I think. I understand that you would not now be comfortable using Polly as a spy without her knowledge—even supposing that, feeling as she does about you, she would be open to offers from Buckingham. So why do you not draw her in with the truth, involve her openly in our conspiracy? Ask for her help. She will not deny you." This last was said with complete confidence, and a considering silence fell between them.

Goodwife Benson reappeared with a steaming pewter tankard of spiced hot milk liberally laced with sack. "The posset, sir. 'Twill put the young lady to sleep in no time."

"In which case it will have served its purpose. I thank you." Nick took the tankard and smiled the goodwife from the room. "I will take this to Polly. If you are not anxious to be gone, I would have further speech with you." Richard bowing his assent, Nick took the drink next door.

Polly was propped upon the pillows, looking wan and fragile and much in need of nursery comfortings. Nick sat beside her on the bed as she sipped the fragrant, steaming milk. "If I am going to feel so frightened every time I must perform, I do not think I will make at all a satisfactory actor," she confided eventually into the undemanding silence.

"Why do you not wait and see how you feel the next time before you judge yourself?" Nick advised calmly. "This first performance is, after all, an unknown experience. Familiarity with it may well bring you ease."

"It is to be hoped so," she said fervently, "else I will die of the anxiety. Can one die of anxiety?"

"I doubt it." He took her empty tankard and bent to kiss her. "Sleep now, moppet."

"I wish you will tell Richard to go to his own bed," she grumbled, reaching her arms around his neck. "I would be held in your arms until I sleep, love, not put to bed like an overtired babe." She buried her nose in his neck, inhaling the warm, earthy scent of his skin, the rosewater freshness of his linen, running her fingers through the luxuriant auburn curls.

He caught her hands at the wrists behind his neck. "Sweet love, I must have speech with Richard. I will come to you as soon as may be. In the meantime, you will sleep like the overtired babe that you say you are not." He laughed as a monstrous yawn swallowed her attempt at indignant protest, and her eyelids drooped.

Polly felt the brush of his lips against her mouth, thought: What is so important that you must discuss it with Richard at this hour? Thought but could not articulate, as she dipped into the sleep of emotional exhaustion.

Nick picked up the bedside candle, shielding its flame with a cupped hand, carrying it over to the hearth, where its light would not fall upon the sleeper. Then he went back to the parlor to examine Richard's proposition.

"How can I ask her to become intimate with a man whom she appears to loathe?" He closed the door behind him, speaking in a low voice.

"She does not know him yet beyond an unfortunate encounter when he alarmed her with the scope and intensity of his power. You know as well as anyone, Nick, the extent of his charm when he chooses to exert it. If she catches his eye—and it appears that she has already done so—he will exert it. She will lose her loathing, and if you ask for her assistance, I am convinced she will not deny you." De Winter spoke also in an undertone. "Your relationship with her need not be altered fundamentally if she amuses Buckingham at your request and for a definite purpose. She has wit enough to understand and fulfill that purpose, to see her task for the practical solution to the problem that it is." He shrugged easily.

Nick walked over to the window, looking out into the night. Two short months ago he had been as cynical as Richard, would have believed such a thing as readily as his friend did. Why should lovemaking with one's mistress lose anything by the knowledge that she shared other beds? To suggest such a thing would bring ridicule upon one's head. Women at all levels of society used their bodies for their advancement—it was, after all, the only currency they possessed. No sophisticate would be troubled by such an unfashionable notion as infidelity, in many cases not even when applied to the marriage bed.

Roger Palmer, Earl of Castlemaine, showed no constraint with his wife; indeed, they lived in perfect amity together. Nick could think of half a dozen other men who accepted a cuckold's horns quite cheerfully, while going about their own adventures, and they were certainly not made the butt of society's malice or mirth by this graceful discretion. In fact, the reverse was in general true. A wife's fidelity was no longer necessarily a matter of honor, although duels were occasionally fought, and the seducer of a man's wife was honor-bound to meet the challenge of a wronged husband. But in the present climate, there was more scandal attached to the duel than to its cause.

So why should the idea of his Polly—a Newgate-born, tavern-bred bastard with few fanciful delusions—subjecting herself to the sexual attentions of George Villiers, or indeed, anyone else, fill him with such overpowering revulsion?

"I pledged myself to this matter, and I will not fail you," he said, the only thing it was possible to say. "But I must repeat: I will not expect her to do anything she finds repugnant."

"But you *will* encourage her to find Buckingham less repugnant?" De Winter watched him over the lip of his glass. "You have all the influence of the trusted mentor—as well as

of the lover. You may easily persuade her out of her dislike
before asking for her help."

Such calculating cynicism! To use the influence of love for
such a purpose. And yet, what choice did he have? At least
he would not be guilty of deception. But it was hollow
comfort for one who would be guilty of the blatant manipulation of a trusting innocent.

"I will do what is necessary," he said.

De Winter took his leave soon after. Nick snuffed the
candles in the parlor before going into the bedchamber.
Polly was sleeping the restorative sleep of youth and health,
her hair spread across the pillow, her hands curled open
above her head, lips slightly parted, presenting a picture as
guileless and ingenuous as the flower of which she so often
reminded him. That she was not as guileless and ingenuous
as she looked, Nick was all too well aware, but the awareness
did little to rid him of the sour taste in his mouth, the acrid
roiling in his gut, as he thought of what he must persuade
her to do.

He slipped into bed beside her, and she cuddled instantly
into his arms, warm and pliant. "Nick?" Her mumble was
sleepily questioning.

"Who else would it be?" A teasing response that rang in
his ears as hollow as a beggar's bowl.

Polly giggled, wriggling closer before sliding back into
sleep.

When she awoke, last night's rain had vanished. Early
morning sun was pouring through the window. A blackbird
trilled in insistent joy from the gnarled gray branch of an old
apple tree in the garden. It was the first intimation of the
closeness of spring, and she lay, snug in the deep feather bed,
under the heavy quilt, feeling Nick's warmth and strength
beside her. Contentment washed through her, bringing in its
wake such a resurgence of confidence that she could barely
believe her miserable panic of the preceding day. Remorse
prickled as she remembered how sorely she had tried Nick's
patience.

Propping herself on one elbow, Polly leant over Nick's

recumbent form, beginning with great deliberation to kiss him into awareness. His eyes stayed shut, but his skin rippled as her lips pressed into the hollow of his throat and she stroked him with her body, moving sinuously against him.

Nick yielded to the glorious languour as sleep gave way to wakefulness and his body stirred beneath the sensuous caress of her skin. Indulging a wicked impulse, he kept himself as immobile as control over his voluntary reactions would allow, his eyes tight shut as if sleep still claimed him. Polly's tongue fluttered against his nipples; still he did not move. She raised her head to look at him, puzzlement clear on her face. If this was a game, it was not one they had played before. Then, with a little smile, she twisted, burrowing headfirst under the quilt.

It was too much. Nick groaned with pleasure, running his hands down her back beneath the quilt, his thumbs pressing into her spine, which arched and curved in catlike response. "Stop now," he whispered huskily as the edge of bliss drew inexorably closer. Polly, indulging her own devilish impulse, ignored the request, merely increasing her attentions. Nick groaned again. He smacked her bottom imperatively. "Wicked one!" Catching her around the waist, he hauled her up. "Don't you know what you are doing to me?"

She emerged laughing from the warm darkness of the covers, tossing her hair back. "Of course I know. Would I do it, else? I had to find some way to waken you." She leaned down to kiss his mouth, swinging one leg astride the narrow waist. He ran his hands over the curve of her hips, along the smooth planes of her thighs as she knelt astride him, stroked the softness of her belly, reached up to cup her breasts, holding them in the palms of his hands.

"I want you," she said with fierce and unashamed candor, leaning backward against his updrawn knees, offering the essence of herself to his touch. He slipped one hand beneath her to hold her buttocks, lifting her for the touch of his free hand; she exhaled on a soft whisper of pleasure. With a leisurely twist of his hips he drove upward, and Polly gasped at the pulsing fire of his penetration.

"And now you have me," he said, gently taunting, catching her hair to draw her head down to his. "What will you do with your possession, my flower?"

"There seems but one thing I can do," she murmured against the corner of his mouth, answering his teasing with her own brand.

"Then let us make the earth move," he said, taking a firm grip of her hips, liquid fire alive in the jewels of his eyes.

"Yes, let us," Polly agreed, her own gaze drowning in his, her body seeming to become one with his, consumed by the same fire. The blackbird's invitation became almost frantic as he called for his own mate on this first springlike day of the year; and withindoors the earth moved.

It moved again that afternoon in a different way, and for more than just lovers. Polly had one moment of near-paralyzing panic, standing in the wings waiting for her cue; her ears buzzed, sweat dripped between her breasts, black spots danced before her eyes. She looked around frantically.

"I am here." It was Thomas, quiet, calm, at her shoulder. " 'Tis all right to be afeard now. It will go as soon as you walk onto the stage."

"How do you know?" Her voice rasped through a throat as stiff as dried leather. Her eyes held the desperate need to believe him.

"Because for all natural actors it does," he responded evenly. "I am not going to move from this spot. If you become afraid, look at me." Then the relevant words came from the stage, she gave him one last panic-stricken glance, and he pushed her forward with a ruthless hand.

Polly did not hear the buzz that greeted her arrival on-stage, was unaware of the gasps as the flambeaux so carefully placed by Killigrew illuminated her for the audience. She did not notice the extraordinary silence that fell as she began to speak; a silence that continued, rapt and spellbound, for long minutes, drawing a slow smile of satisfaction from Thomas Killigrew.

It was a smile that broadened at the first gust of laughter when the house, recovering from its stunned amazement at the sight of Killigrew's surprise, responded to the provocative wit, the vivacious, flirtatious manner in which she engaged in the duel of the sexes. Her own enjoyment was transparent, communicating itself to her fellow actors as well as to the playgoers. The former found themselves responding with greater effort; the latter kept their seats—not one rising, as was usual, to wander the pit and the galleries, to engage in idle conversation while keeping but half an eye on the stage.

Nicholas sat dazed by the welter of emotions that assailed him. There was pride, certainly; satisfaction at his own part in bringing this about; a lover's pleasure in the other's achievement; but there was a most unexpected jealousy, also. This afternoon Polly did not belong to him. She belonged to every member of the audience; that amazing beauty, the gliding sensuality of her body, the wicked invitations of voice and eye, were offered to all. And he could hear all around him the way the offer was received, with lustful murmurs and speculative eyes.

He had expected nothing else, yet forewarned had not been forearmed. Until the moment she had walked onto the stage, he had thought of her as his creation: snatched, bruised and violated, from a brutalizing existence; made whole under his care, the potential of beauty and personality nurtured until it could blossom into adult maturity under the knowledge of love. But that ravishing, magical creature on the stage was not his creation. She was her own, fulfilling her own promises made to herself, and reveling in that fulfillment. She was giving herself, freely and with all her heart, to every man and woman in the playhouse, and he must somehow learn to live with it because, after this day, there would be no dousing of that star.

George Villiers sat in the upper gallery. His eyes, narrowed and hooded, never deviated from the stage, and he remained as motionless as a graven image. He had been trying to find the girl for days, using every means at his disposal, and she had been here all that time, tucked away under Kil-

ligrew's umbrella, now presented in this spectacular fashion
without even a name to identify her. Of course, Killigrew
was a showman at heart. Knowing what a gift he had in the
wench, he would milk every last drop out of the advantage.
It was a brilliant strategy—to introduce her in this dingy
hole, amongst the unseeing and unfeeling populace of
Moorfields, to a curious court, dragged from their habitual
boredom by the possibility of something out of the ordinary.
And there was nothing ordinary about this Flora.

But who and what was she? He could hear her voice
castigating his coachman with all the eloquence of the gut-
tersnipe; then, almost in the same breath, greeting himself in
the soft tones of the gently reared lady. She was an actor,
which would perhaps explain some part of it. It would not
explain why she had run from him, though. In general, the
young women who graced her chosen profession tended to
be in search of a passport and were only too pleased to attract
the notice of the rich and wellborn. So why was this one
different?

Well, it should not be too difficult to discover. She had
broken cover and therefore tacitly agreed to the chase.

Chapter 12

"Now, before we leave for court this evening, I wish for your solemn word that you will not indulge in displays of the kind to which you treated us on Wednesday."

Nicholas adopted a severe mien as he regarded Polly, who was sitting before the mirror in the bedchamber threading a pearl-encrusted ribbon through her ringlets.

"If you do not engage in games of dalliance with painted ladies, I will not need to indulge in displays of any kind," she retorted. The defiant gleam in the hazel eyes sparked at him, reflected in the mirror.

Nicholas sighed. "Games of dalliance, Polly, are accepted sport at Whitehall. Indeed, they are de rigueur, and you must learn to play them, too. The one thing you may *not* do is descend upon me like one of the Furies, demanding that I take you home on the instant."

"But it was the only way I could think to stop your . . . your game with that . . . Oh, I cannot think of a suitable word for her," Polly said disgustedly. "All that paint and powder. Anyway, you did not take me home," she added, remembered resentment ringing in her voice.

"No, of course I did not. To have obeyed such an ill-considered and importunate summons would have brought ridicule on both our heads."

"Well, you did not have to tell me, in that bored voice, to find another escort because you were rather pleasantly occupied!" Polly scowled at him in the mirror. "Very pleasantly occupied, my lord, with your nose in her bosom!" Her hands fluttered in a gesture of denial. Her voice took on tone and accents that were not her own. "Fie on you, my dear sir, but 'tis an outrageous flirt y'are." The long lashes batted vigorously; her hands were clasped at her breast. "Indeed, and I can think of many a pleasant occupation, can ye not, my lord Kincaid."

In the next breath, before Nick could keep up with the transformation, she was speaking in a voice uncomfortably like his own, her eyes bent most sedulously upon an imaginary figure. "Sweet madame, *many* a pleasant occupation when such peerless charms are before me."

"Little shrew!" Nick exclaimed appreciatively. "Did I really sound like that?"

" 'Twas how I heard it," she said loftily, adjusting the lace at her neckline. "And monstrous ridiculous it sounded."

"In that case, I cannot imagine why it should have caused you to throw such a jealous tantrum."

"I did not. I merely requested that we return home."

"Well, we will not argue about it further," Nick said firmly. "But it is not to happen again. Is it understood? At Whitehall we go our separate ways. I will not be observing your every move, and you will not be seen to be observing mine. Because Wednesday was your first appearance at court since the king accepted you into his company, you will have been excused that indiscretion. But it will not be excused another time. Is it clear, moppet?"

Polly nibbled her bottom lip. "I do not wish to talk about it anymore. Richard was quite horrid afterward and took me into this dreadful room full of old ladies, who were just prosing on and on, and introduced me to his aunt, and I could not get away for *hours*! I thought I would expire with boredom. And you have not stopped scolding ever since."

"I want your word that you will behave in the manner Richard and I have explained is necessary."

"Cool indifference." Polly stood up, smoothing down her skirt. "You may dally with whomsoever you please, my lord. I will take my revenge in private." Her head tilted and she smiled up at him, her expression suddenly soft, resentment and defiance vanished. "Indeed, if 'tis important for you, Nick, I will do my utmost. But it is difficult for me to conceal these things."

"Aye, love, I know that." He touched her nose with a gloved fingertip. "But you have a good head on your shoulders, and all an actor's expertise. You can dissemble in this."

She could, Polly thought, as they left the house for the carriage that waited at the door. But it still seemed a ridiculous convention. However, she was enjoying her new life far too much to jeopardize its continuation for an obligation that Nick considered both necessary and simple enough to perform.

It had been four weeks since her debut at Moorfields. Thomas had put on *Rival Ladies* at the Theatre Royal two weeks later, and she had performed before the king, who, together with his courtiers, had come backstage at the end of the performance wreathed in smiles, brimming with compliments, and the invitation to attend at Whitehall whenever Master Killigrew had no need of her services; thus had Polly become a member of the king's company.

One could not attend Whitehall Palace without court dress, and the acquisition of this had taken some time, but two days ago Nick had escorted her to the palace for her first appearance in the thronged galleries and salons. And she had very nearly disgraced them both by giving rein to an indignant impulse that had no place in these circles . . .

"We are arrived," Nick said, breaking into her musings. "I will escort you into the Long Gallery; after that you must manage alone. You will not be short of admirers."

"Always assuming I might wish for them," she retorted, but without the earlier snap; this time as a shared jest.

Nick smiled and handed her down from the carriage, which had come to a halt in the Great Court. They progressed in stately fashion along the corridors of the palace.

The rank odors from the chamber pots situated at strategic points behind tapestry screens and in dark corners were so much a part of the atmosphere that they were noticed by none of the habitués of the palace, be they guests, servants, or inhabitants. Dogs snapped and tumbled, snarling over a disputed bone, diving under skirts and between legs, an ever present trap for the unwary.

Polly sidestepped a spaniel pup, lifted her skirts to avoid a patch of something she did not care to identify, and entered the Long Gallery.

"Why, Mistress Wyat, you have come to bring starlight to those of us who live in darkness." The greeting came instantly from a bewigged, beribboned, beringed gentleman of massive girth and raddled complexion.

"La, Sir John, I am come merely to bask in your moon-glow." Fan unfurled, eyes inviting, the rising star of the king's company curtsied, laid her hand upon the proffered arm, and glided off, leaving Lord Kincaid to his own devices.

From the far end of the gallery she was under a scrutiny of the most august nature.

"Quite extraordinary beauty." King Charles looked across to where Mistress Polly Wyat stood, surrounded by an admiring court. A ray of March sunlight danced playfully in the honey-hued river cascading over her shoulders, which rose in creamy perfection from the froth of lace at her bodice. "She remains under Kincaid's protection, d'ye say, George?"

"So I understand, sir," returned the Duke of Buckingham, thoughtfully taking snuff. "But he does not appear overly protective." A smile twisted the duke's lips.

The king glanced sideways at his interlocutor and chuckled. "Ye've designs there yourself, have you, George? I can't say I blame you. I'd have a play myself if I weren't so encumbered by the ladies already." He sighed, dabbing his lips with a lace-edged handkerchief. "I swear, George, that if Mrs. Stewart is not after my Lady Castlemaine's blood, it is the other way around. 'Tis enough to destroy a man's interest in the fair sex."

"Not yours, sir," said Villiers with a bow and a salacious smile. "It would take a much greater force than that possessed by those two charmers."

The king laughed in great good humor. "Aye, I daresay I may count myself their match. In truth, though, they can neither of them hold a candle to Mistress Wyat."

"I wonder where Kincaid found her," mused the duke, a hungry light in his eyes. "No one seems to know, and neither he nor the lady are telling."

"Did not Killigrew say that she was the daughter of a merchant—some respectable bourgeois?"

The duke frowned. "There's no taint of the Grand Seraglio about her, certainly," he said. "She has none of the obvious tricks of one born and bred to whoredom. But it is also hard to imagine such a rare flower springing from the seed of some staid and plebian bourgeois. I cannot believe such antecedents could produce that delicacy of face and form, or that lively wit. There's nothing of the Flemish mare about her." He chuckled involuntarily at the absurdity of the comparison. "I would guess she's some nobleman's by-blow, brought up in obscure respectability, a mediocrity from which she's anxious to depart."

The king shrugged. "It seems of little moment where she came from, George. She is here to grace our stage and, mayhap, your bed." A quizzical eyebrow lifted. "Will ye unseat Kincaid, think you?"

"If he will be so churlish as to refuse to share her, then I shall have to." Buckingham smiled pleasantly. "But Nick is not one to keep good things to himself. He has a generous streak."

"And the lady . . . ?" queried the king, tapping his fingers on the arm of his chair.

It was an indication that His Majesty was growing bored with the conversation, so Buckingham contented himself with a light laugh, a shrug that expressed the opinion that the lady's feelings in the matter could only be of a certain nature. In truth, that was exactly what the duke did think.

It seemed entirely reasonable to him that, Kincaid having

served his purpose by introducing her to the stage, she should now be looking around for a more powerful protector, one who could perhaps offer her greater prospects of advancement. Such a beauty could do much better for herself than a Yorkshire baron of moderate wealth and influence. Perhaps it was time for one who could offer her almost anything she might desire to press his suit.

Polly felt the duke's approach as he came up behind her. The hairs on the back of her neck seemed to lift, her skin crawled, and she could barely repress a shudder. Why did the man continue to have this effect upon her? Nick had introduced her to him when he had come backstage after her debut at Moorfields, but he had been one of many and it had been easy enough to keep him at a distance. Since then, he had appeared at the Theatre Royal, watching rehearsals and attending every performance. But then, so had many others. On Wednesday, here at court, he had been the soul of politeness and consideration, showing her a smilingly attentive countenance; yet she could not bear his proximity.

For some reason, Nick did not like to hear her talk of her aberrational reaction to a man universally known for his charm; indeed, when she had done so, he had accused her sharply of being fanciful. So now she kept her thoughts to herself, struggling for a neutral courtesy whenever she was in the duke's ken. But it was some considerable struggle.

"Your performance last night, Mistress Wyat, transcended anything I have seen upon the stage." His Grace bowed low before her.

"You do me too much honor, my lord duke." Polly sank into her curtsy, eyes demurely lowered. "With such a character as Isabella, it would be a poor actor, indeed, who failed to do justice to the part."

"Mr. Dryden must be honored," murmured the duke, taking her hand, raising her from the curtsy. "I can only hope you will grace my own poor efforts as dramatist. It must now be the ambition of all playwrights to produce a vehicle for your brilliance."

Polly tried to withdraw her hand, but his grip tightened.

A smile played over the thin lips as he said softly, "Why would you run from me, bud? Do my compliments offend you?"

Polly managed to produce a light laugh, a tiny shrug of her slender shoulders. "How should they, sir? An actor must needs have applause for survival. It is the very staff of life for us!" She let her hand lie, limp and unresponsive, in his, but her eyes sought escape. They met the steady regard of Richard De Winter, standing some ten paces away. Her gaze signaled him frantically; with a word of excuse to those around him, he sauntered casually across to her.

"Why, Lord De Winter," Polly said, as if surprised at his arrival. "I had not seen you here earlier." She could not make her curtsy with her hand held fast in Buckingham's grip, and this time her tug was rewarded.

"I have but just arrived," Richard said calmly, carrying her fingers to his lips in an elaborate salute. "I would congratulate you on your performance as Isabella. Never has the part been played with more wit and life."

"The credit is Mr. Killigrew's," Polly demurred, drawing imperceptibly closer to Richard, as if he would shield her from the duke. "I merely follow instruction."

"A man could only be gratified by such obedience," murmured the duke, taking snuff. "I can find it in my heart to envy Thomas. Are you as submissive with your protector, Mistress Wyat? Lord Kincaid is, indeed, a fortunate man. I trust your compliance is amply rewarded? There are those who would be most eager to rectify any omissions."

Her skin crept, as if slugs trailed stickily down her spine, under his mocking gaze, the delicately taunting tone that nonetheless made no attempt to disguise the naked hunger of voice and expression. The offer was as clearly made as it was possible to be, without overt crudity, and her eyes flew to Richard, desperately seeking rescue.

"I would add my own assurance of that fact, Buckingham," he said affably, thus making of the particular a general pleasantry. "Mistress Wyat must grow fatigued with all the

hearts laid before her feet. It becomes tedious, does it not?"
He smiled blandly at Polly.

"Ah, never tedious, sir," she responded, once more in
charge of herself. Her eyes sparkled roguishly as she dropped
them both another curtsy. "I would have a carpet of hearts,
had I my way."

"Cruel maiden!" De Winter threw his hands up in mock
horror. "Will you offer no quarter, then?"

"None, sir," she replied promptly. "I feed upon adulation, and without it will shrivel and die."

"Definitely a fate to be avoided." The light tones were
Kincaid's. Polly controlled the impulse to whirl 'round, to
greet his arrival with the warmth and relief that she felt.
Instead, she merely looked over her shoulder at him with a
cool smile. "We must all ensure that you have an ample
diet," he said, bowing gracefully.

Polly's mouth opened on a mischievous retort, but before
it could be uttered, a footman appeared with the statement
that His Majesty wished for the pleasure of Mistress Wyat's
company in his Presence chamber. It was not an unusual
request. The king frequently withdrew from these large
gatherings and had the company he chose brought to him.
But Mistress Wyat had not quite managed to forget the Dog
tavern, or her time as kitchen miad in the Kincaid household. Private audiences with the king were not consonant
with those memories. Her eyes flew in momentary panic to
Nicholas.

He smiled lazily, as if he had not read her message. "It
would seem that you are to receive adulation from the highest quarter in the land. Do not let the more humble of your
admirers keep you, my dear Polly."

The panic faded. Beneath the level tones, the easy words,
lay instruction, grounding her again. All feelings—including
fear and unease—must be kept hidden beneath a light mockery, and she must expect no open assistance from Nick in
public. Sincerity was a vice, overt expression of feelings the
mark of the unsophisticated, trust the folly of the naive. The

lesson had been drummed into her often enough, and she had promised to follow it.

"Permit me to offer you my escort, Mistress Wyat." Buckingham, who had been about to withdraw from the arena once Kincaid had appeared on the scene, now seized the opportunity afforded by his position as king's favorite. He could accompany the lady without invitation—a privilege that neither Kincaid nor De Winter could assume.

Polly put up her chin, smiled faintly, and laid her hand upon the duke's brocaded sleeve. "How kind in you, my lord duke. I shall be eternally grateful. I am as yet unaccustomed to these august surroundings, so must depend upon the support and guidance of those who are."

Buckingham felt a disquieting stab. Could she possibly be making game of him? It was inconceivable; yet she was radiating something that did not sit easy with him. His eyes skimmed Kincaid's expression; it was quite neutral. He looked down at Polly's face, turned up to meet his scrutiny with a blandly inquiring smile. The huge forest pools of her eyes offered no clue as to the thoughts behind that wide, alabaster brow. But he was overwhelmed again by her beauty, catching his breath under the assault of a lusting desire greater than any he had yet experienced.

Polly read the look in his eyes. Only with the greatest effort was she able to control her instinctive recoil, as revulsion crystallized into fear at the certainty that this was a man who took what he wanted—and he wanted her. Her fingers trembled slightly as they rested on his arm, her cheeks lost a little of their color, but her voice was clear and strong as she bade a polite farewell to Kincaid and De Winter, and went off on the duke's arm.

"Buckingham is hooked," De Winter observed in quiet satisfaction. " 'Tis time to play the line, my friend."

Nick fiddled with the lace at his sleeve, a somber look in his eye, his mouth set in a hard line. "She loathes him, Richard. Can ye not feel it?"

De Winter said nothing for a minute. He could certainly feel Polly's loathing of the duke; but he had also felt her fear.

It was an irrational fear, surely. Buckingham would not harm her; he would have not the least reason to do so. "You have not encouraged this dislike?"

"Nay, I have been at pains to do the opposite."

"Matters worsen, Nick," De Winter persisted softly. "We have been officially at war with the Dutch since the fourth of this month, yet nothing is done in preparation. The king does not attend council meetings, but leaves the management and direction of the affair to those whose main interest is in personal gain from this conflict."

"Aye." Nick nodded, sighed heavily. "The king spends more care and pains making friends between Lady Castlemaine and Mrs. Stewart when they fall out than he ever does on matters of government. Such loveplay gives Buckingham a free hand—a hand he does not scruple to use for his own advancement and that of his friends and family." Nick smiled bitterly. "There are lucrative government posts aplenty for those with the influence to acquire them. Buckingham has that influence with the king, and can put whomsoever he pleases into posts for which they are ill fitted. In exchange for his patronage, he can be certain that they will dance to his tune."

"A tune that does not have His Majesty's interests at heart," De Winter agreed. "Everyone but the king knows that his favorite has no interest in the affairs of the country, or the attitude of the people. Buckingham is ungovernable, drunk with power, but he cannot be satiated." He sighed. "It is, of course, partly the fault of a system that encourages such corruption. When patronage is the chief method of advancement, and without advancement a man's pockets remain thin, those with the patronage are those with the power."

Richard paused to acknowledge a greeting from a passing lady resplendent in puce satin over crimson. Both men had been talking in low voices, their expressions carefully schooled to ones suited to a light conversation of no particular moment.

"We need to know what the duke intends, Nick. If Clarendon falls, then the king will have no wise counselor. If the Duke of York takes command of the navy in this war, then who is to take over the vital post of Lord High Admiral of the Kingdom? If Buckingham and his cohorts persuade the king to leave the position and its responsibilities to be executed by them as a group, nothing will be done. They have too many other agendas to deal in timely fashion with the material needs of the navy that must fight this war. 'Tis said that Buckingham wished for such a division, however. If we have a friend in his most intimate circle, then we may hear the truth." Richard waited patiently, respecting his friend's struggle, even as he knew what the outcome would be.

"And his mistress could have access to the secret conclaves . . ." Nick kept his voice muted with immense difficulty. "D'ye think I do not know that? 'Twas my idea, was it not? But hell and the devil, Richard! I will not ask it of her myself. Do you put it to her. You will be more objective than I. You may tell her that the scheme has my approval, but do not, if you can help it, tell her that the plan was originally my own. I'd not have her believe that this has lain behind—" He smiled with wry bitterness. "You understand me, Richard?"

"Aye, I understand, and will put it to Polly tonight." De Winter spoke now with brisk decision. "Your scruples may do you honor, my friend, but this is not the time for them. They are a luxury we cannot afford. She'll not come to harm, and indeed, may do herself some good. The patronage of the Duke of Buckingham can only be to her advantage."

"More so than mine, I take it," replied Nick with that same wry smile.

"She is your mistress, not your wife, Nicholas," De Winter reminded him.

"I am aware of that," Nick said in a tone that caused his friend to look at him sharply.

"Is that your intention, Nick?"

"Not even this court would accept with credulity a man's lack of interest in his *bride's* infidelity, my dear Richard. There are some elementary courtesies, after all. A delay of a few months, surely, would be needed before a bride and groom could openly look around for fresh adventures?" Sarcasm lay heavy in his voice. "If she's to find her way to Buckingham's bed soon, she must do so unencumbered."

"It is a necessary sacrifice you make, Nick," Richard said quietly.

"How right you are, Richard." Self-mockery laced Kincaid's voice. "I am in no danger of forgetting the realities for a moment." He glanced around the room. "Perhaps I will go and amuse myself with Lady Fanshawe. She is always willing to play a little. I will leave you to take Polly back to her lodgings when the king dismisses her. You may tell her that I will come to her later." He offered De Winter a small mock bow before sauntering across the room in the direction of the egregious Lady Fanshawe, who turned her powdered and painted countenance upon him with undisguised eagerness; the ostrich plumes in her headdress bobbed wildly as she curtsied; her breasts, lifted almost clear of her neckline, showed rouged nipples.

"La, my Lord Kincaid! You have been neglecting us sorely, I swear it! You have barely shown your face at court since you found your pretty little actor." Full, vermilion lips pouted; eyebrows, arched and lengthened with a black pencil, assumed an impossible quirk over the top of her vigorously fluttering fan.

Nicholas smiled, allowing his gaze to travel with lascivious admiration over the charms thus displayed as he picked up his cards in the old, familiar game. At least while he was playing it, he could distance the inconvenient emotions that went with loving Polly.

It was a full hour before Polly was released from the king's Presence chamber. When she reentered the Long Gallery her eyes instantly and automatically went in search of Nicholas in her eagerness to show him that she had survived the ordeal. In fact, it had not been that much of an ordeal. The king had been all condescension, and she had really quite enjoyed herself. But there was no sign of Nicholas.

She scanned the brilliant, chattering throng. Dusk was

falling beyond the long windows, and servants moved to light the flambeaux and many-branched candlesticks so that the room, already heated with so many bodies, grew rapidly stuffy, sweat and the ripe overlay of perfumes mingling, heavy in the air. Coiffures grew limp, and many a lady surreptitiously dabbed at her face, examining her handkerchief for signs that her paint was running.

"You look weary, Polly. I will escort you home." Richard De Winter spoke at her shoulder. She looked up at him with a start.

"That is kind in you, Richard. But I will wait for Nick."

"Nicholas is somewhat occupied." De Winter took snuff. "He has commissioned me to see you safe home, with the message that he will come to you later tonight."

"I suppose he is occupied with another of his painted dolls," declared Polly, looking mischievously at Richard. "Perhaps I had better find him."

Richard gazed into the middle distance, observing casually, "My aunt did enjoy your company on Wednesday. She has expressed the desire to introduce you to others of her friends. You would find their discourse most edifying, I assure you."

"It is not friendly in you to fail to see the jest," Polly told him, somewhat aggrieved at this thinly veiled threat. "*Why* must you take me home, and not Nick?"

De Winter sighed. "Let us achieve a degree of privacy and I will explain. This is not the place for argument. If you have no objection, we will go by water. 'Tis a pleasant evening, and I have need of the air."

For all that they had become fast friends, and she had been using his first name for several weeks now, Richard could on occasion be irritatingly dictatorial, Polly reflected with a grimace. She much preferred Nick's methods of ensuring her compliance! However, she yielded to necessity without further objection, allowing De Winter to tuck her hand beneath his arm as he escorted her from the palace.

"Well?" she requested, once they had attained Whitehall Stairs. "Where is Nick?"

"Have a little patience, child," her companion advised, gesturing to a wherryman on the lookout for passengers to bring his small riverboat up to the steps. "Let us enjoy the evening on the water."

Polly compressed her lips, stepping into the wherry, managing her skirts with considerable dexterity as she sat down. De Winter took his place opposite her and instructed the wherryman to row to the Somerset Stairs. He smiled at Polly's indignant expression but said nothing, gazing about him instead with every sign of pleasure in the fine spring evening, as he hummed a little tune.

In fact, Richard was nowhere near as easy in his mind as he appeared. How best to broach the upcoming subject to Polly was exercising him considerably. He must somehow ensure that she did not feel betrayed by Kincaid; must somehow convince her of the vital political purpose that lay behind their request; must somehow couch the imperative in terms of a request, he amended to himself.

The wherry scraped against the steps at Somerset Stairs. Richard paid the oarsman his sixpence before assisting Polly onto dry land. It was a short walk from the river to the Strand, and from thence to Drury Lane. Polly kept silence as they walked. She had the conviction that something of moment was about to take place, yet she did not know why she should have this belief, since there was nothing overt in Richard's demeanor to encourage it. But intuition was a powerful persuader; and intuition was also telling her that she was not going to enjoy whatever this momentous happening would turn out to be. Why was Nicholas not here?

The answer to that question was revealed in short order once they had reached her lodging. Politely, Polly offered her guest a glass of sherry before she sat upon the window seat beneath the diamond-paned casement, and waited. De Winter walked around the parlor with a restlessness most unusual in this generally suave and impassive aristocrat.

"Why do you not make a clean breast, sir?" Polly prompted quietly. "I find myself growing apprehensive and would dearly like to make an end of this."

"Very well." He placed his sherry glass upon the side table. "You have heard talk both here and in Nick's house about the way matters of government are conducted—"

"Are *not* conducted," Polly corrected with raised eyebrow.

"Exactly so." He permitted himself a small smile. "You understand, then, where Nick and I stand in this?"

"That you consider the king ill advised," Polly said. "That the Cabal under Buckingham's leadership is to a large extent responsible for this, and you would bolster the position of the chancellor at this time, because he is a more reliable minister than the Earl of Arlington, for instance."

"I will tell you now, Polly, that myself, Nick, Sir Peter, and Major Conway have pledged ourselves to circumvent Buckingham's destructive influence." He picked up his sherry glass again, sipping slowly, gathering his thoughts.

"To set yourselves up in opposition to Buckingham can only be dangerous." Polly frowned uneasily. "You and Nick both said that only a fool would make an enemy of the duke."

Richard nodded. "We do not make our opposition obvious, Polly."

"So how would you do this thing?" she asked as the flicker of unease blossomed into flame, and she still did not know why.

"We need someone who has access to Buckingham's intimate circle," De Winter said, deciding that directness was his best policy. "Someone whose presence would be so accepted that conversation would go on around her without thought. Someone who could be in privy places where documents might be left lying around—"

"Her?" Polly managed to get the one word out, the word that penetrated her confusion with the blinding speed of a rapier thrust.

"You," affirmed Richard quietly.

"But . . . but how should I gain access to—" Then she saw Buckingham's cynical, dissolute countenance bent upon her, the eyes afire with that lusting hunger; and she knew.

She sprang to her feet in a swish of satin petticoats and lace-edged gown. "You say Nick would have me do this? He knows that I cannot abide Buckingham."

"Which is why I am deputed to present the case, Polly," Richard said quietly. "Nick would not ask this of you himself. It is not a lover's request, you must understand, but the request of a political faction of which Nick is a leading member. We have need of your services. England has need of your services, Mistress Wyat. Will you deny them?"

"I have little interest in politics," Polly muttered, pacing the chamber. "Why should I sacrifice myself in this way? If it were necessary for Nick himself, then . . . then, maybe, I could— No, not maybe," she added with a flash of impatience. "Of course I would . . . but—"

"This *is* for Nick," De Winter interrupted. "He has pledged himself to this cause. The specter of civil war still hangs over the land, Polly. If the king sets himself up against the people, as his father did before him, then the specter will take substance. Buckingham does not see this danger. He cares only for the acquisition of power—power he will hold by ruling the king. You say you have no interest in politics. But surely you cannot view such a prospect with equanimity."

"Nay." Polly crossed her arms, hugging her breasts as if she were cold. "Of course I cannot. But is there no other way, Richard?"

"Villiers wants you," Richard said bluntly. "That fact gives you the passport into his intimate circle. He will not suspect you of spying because he will see only what he thinks is there—a female actor with her bread to earn and one way in which to earn it. Such liaisons are common enough, and he is not known for his lack of generosity in these matters."

Polly shuddered. "I do not see myself as a member of the duke's harem, my Lord De Winter."

Richard chewed his lip thoughtfully. It was not as if he had not expected resistance. "Why must you be a member of his harem?" he asked, apparently casual. "Are you not special

enough to hold your own place? And in the holding, you
will provide us with the eyes and ears we must have."

Polly poured herself a glass of sherry, belatedly offering
the decanter to Richard. He accepted with a slight inclination of his head, refilled his glass, and waited for the result of
her cogitations.

"Special," she murmured after a few minutes, seeming to
savor the word with the idea that had dropped suddenly into
her head. There was one way to become special for George
Villiers—the rich, ungovernable, never-thwarted duke.

"Think you that perhaps His Grace might be piqued to
good purpose, Richard?" Her eyes glowed suddenly, lit with
a speculation based on relief as she saw a way around this
untenable dilemma.

"Pray continue," he invited, unable to resist that infectious smile. "I am open to any modification."

"Well . . ." She tapped pearly teeth with a slender forefinger. "His Grace is accustomed to his own way, is he not?"
A nod answered her. "Suppose he should find me elusive?
Sometimes offering, sometimes withdrawing, but always
willing for the pursuit?"

"If he wants you badly enough, you will snare him with
such tactics," De Winter declared.

"And he wants me badly enough," Polly stated quietly,
quite without vanity or artifice. It was hardly a fact that gave
her satisfaction, but in this instance, it could be put to good
use. "I can play that part, Richard. I will spin a web that will
intrigue him, that will ensure that he is constantly desirous of
my company, always waiting for the moment of surrender—
a moment that he is convinced is not far away. If I can
achieve entry into his intimate circles with such tactics, that
will suffice, will it not? I have only to be accepted as a
presence."

"I see no reason why it should not work," Richard said
thoughtfully, recognizing with relief that he was no longer
engaged in the recruitment of an unwilling accomplice, but
in shared planning with a partner. "We are interested only in

whatever impressions, whispers, plans, you can bring us, not in the methods you use to garner them."

"And Nick?" Polly asked, her enthusiasm fading abruptly. When had the idea first come to him and his friends? she wondered dully. *Since* it had become clear that Buckingham had his eye upon her? And whose idea had it been? "Will it be important to him, do you think, that I can manage to extract the information without surrendering to the duke? Or does he view such a matter with indifference?"

"I do not think you need me to supply you with the answer to that," Richard said gently. "He will be here soon. Why do you not ask him yourself? If you really need to know his answer."

Polly sat down under a wash of fatigue. She did not think she needed to ask Nick the question, but she still wished he had had the courage to involve her in this conspiracy himself. In her naïveté, she thought that it would have come easier from him.

Richard looked at her, compassion in his eyes. Maturity was a painful process, and the school in which Polly must grow was harder than many. Somehow she had managed to scramble unsullied through a life that should have destroyed all illusions. Then she had met Nicholas Kincaid—a man who, loving her, would foster her illusions rather than destroy them. Now she must face a harsh reality where even love failed as shield, where love asked more of her than she could easily give.

"You need your bed," he said after a while. "It has been an evening to try the strength of Atlas. Get you gone, now. I will remain until Nick returns."

She smiled wearily, rising to her feet. " 'Tis kind in you, Richard, but I'll not trespass further on your time. I am not uncomfortable with my own company."

"Maybe not, but I'll stay nevertheless." He spoke now with familiar briskness. "You've had no supper. I'll ask Goodwife Benson to prepare ye a caudle. Get you to bed."

"I do not need a nursemaid, Richard," she protested. He merely smiled and pulled the bell rope. With a defeated shrug, Polly went into the bedchamber to struggle alone with the ribbons, buttons, and laces of her complicated attire. The days of smock, petticoat, and kirtle were long gone, and she swore with Dog tavern vigor as she wrestled with the recalcitrant knots of her corset.

"I told you you have need of a lady's maid."

Polly whirled, pink-cheeked with her exertions, to the suddenly opened door of the bedchamber. "Nick! I did not hear you come in."

"You were cursing like a Billingsgate fishwife," he observed, shrugging out of his coat, crossing the room in his shirt sleeves toward her. "You could not possibly have heard anything but the sounds of your own voice." Setting his hands upon her shoulders, he spun her around and tackled the laces with experienced fingers.

"Ahh! My thanks." Polly breathed a sigh of relief, rubbing the life back into the constricted flesh beneath her smock. "I do not know why I ever consented to wear that instrument of torture!" She kicked the offending garment across the room.

"I think you do know why," he said with quiet gravity. "Do you also know exactly why you have consented to this other matter—one considerably more distasteful than the wearing of a corset? I would have you certain sure of your own mind."

"What did Richard tell you?" She walked over to the window and stood gazing out into the evening gloom, for the moment unwilling to look at him.

"Only that you had consented to participate in our plan; that you were fatigued and he had sent you to bed; and that since you had had no supper, he had bidden the goodwife prepare you a peppermint caudle."

Polly could not help smiling at what she knew had to be a faithful rendition of Richard's farewell speech to Nicholas. She could almost hear his voice delivering it.

There was a knock at the door. The goodwife bustled in with the bowl of spiced gruel mixed with wine. "This'll put the heart in you," she announced cheerfully, setting the bowl on the tiring table. She examined Polly shrewdly. "Ye look as if ye need it, too, m'dear. They're workin' ye too hard, I'll be bound." An accusatory glance at Kincaid accompanied this statement. "Every afternoon on that stage. It's not right, m'lord. Indeed, 'tis not. Barely a child, she is."

Nicholas scratched his head, murmuring something vaguely conciliatory that seemed to satisfy the landlady, who gathered up Polly's discarded clothes, taking them away with her. "If you had a maid, the goodwife would not be obliged to care for your wardrobe," Nicholas observed, turning back the cover on the bed. "Get between the sheets, now. I do not think I can face further accusations of neglect and exploitation."

"You do not neglect me, love. Or exploit me," she said softly, clambering into bed. "I do only what I choose to do."

"Is that truly so?" He handed her the peppermint caudle, then sat upon the bed beside her.

"Yes. But I could wish you had asked me yourself to engage in this spying." Polly kept her eyes on the gently steaming mixture on her knees, stirring it thoughtfully with a pewter spoon. "It was cowardly to ask Richard to do it."

Nick winced. "It was not through cowardice, moppet. I did not wish you to feel pressured. Perhaps it was conceit on my part, but I had thought you might find it harder to refuse me than Richard."

"But you wish me to do this thing?" She looked at him directly for the first time.

Nicholas shook his head. "No, I do not. But on occasion there are greater purposes that have to be served, and one must make sacrifices. This is one of those occasions."

It is possible we may be of service to each other. Where had those words come from? They had been spoken when she had been sitting in another bed in another chamber in the company of Nicholas, Lord Kincaid. Did this go back to that time, then?

"I am only a Newgate-born, tavern-bred whore, after all," Polly heard herself say, casually taking a mouthful of gruel. "It is hardly a great matter to sacrifice such a one to another's bed." Why must she test him? Did she want to know the answer? There was a sudden, devastating silence.

Nick was for an instant bewildered by the words. She could not possibly believe he saw the matter in that light. But once upon a time he had done so. He had seen in a hard-schooled, ambitious wench the possibility of mutual benefit. He would put the means of achieving her ambition in her hands; she would be encouraged to do no more than accept an offer that any woman in search of material benefit would seize eagerly.

But it had been a long time since he had thought in those terms. Polly was not in search of benefit of any kind. She had all she wanted now that she had proved herself capable of fulfilling the talent she had harbored with such dedication. And she loved, and was loved in return.

The thought that she might doubt him brought a surge of wrath, fueled by a guilty knowledge that her implicit accusation had its roots in a sad past truth, one that he would now deny to his last breath.

Polly looked up at him, and the spoon in her hand clattered into the bowl. Such stark anger stood out on his features, ignited the emerald eyes so that they flamed in his whitened face.

"Give me the bowl!" His voice was a lash as he snatched the porringer from her. "Now, get out of bed!"

Polly's knees began to tremble. She had had no idea that the humorous, easygoing Nicholas could look like this, could evince such a towering height of black fury.

"I said, stand up!"

With a little moan of fear, she stumbled to obey, although a small voice told her that she would be safer in bed. But resistance at this moment was unimaginable.

His hands gripped her shoulders through the thin cotton of her shift. "Do you dare repeat that?"

Polly shook her head, struggling to persuade her vocal chords into working order again, since a verbal response was clearly demanded. "N-no . . . please," she stuttered. "I did not really mean it . . . 'Twas just . . . just—"

"Just what?" he rasped as her voice faded. "Answer me!"

"I wanted to see what you would say," Polly whimpered miserably, hearing how lame the half-truth sounded, yet quite unable, under the piercing glare of those livid eyes, to attack by making explicit that moment of lost trust. She had needed reassurance, and she was getting it; but she had never imagined it coming in this shape.

"Now you are going to hear what I would say," he said, bringing his face very close to hers, his hands on her shoulders jerking her against him. "If you *ever* so much as think such a thing again, let alone articulate it, I promise that you will wish your parents had never met! Do you hear me?" Polly nodded dumbly. "You had better," he said with no diminution in ferocity, still holding her close. "Because I mean it. You will look back on Josh and his belt with nostalgia! I swear it!"

Polly swallowed, attempting to lubricate her throat, to lick dry lips. Why on earth had she expected him to enfold her in his arms, to whisper loving reassurances and sorrow for having to ask this of her, to kiss away the hurt and whisper his gratitude and admiration for her courage? Why hadn't she expected to be bullied and threatened in this savage fashion for having had such stupid, childish doubts?

"Get back into bed," Nick directed in his normal voice. "And finish your supper."

Meekly, Polly did as she was told, although her appetite for the rapidly cooling contents of the porringer had rather diminished. She took a spoonful, watching Nick warily as he began to get out of his clothes. Had Richard told him of her own modification of their plan? Presumably not, or he would have mentioned it at the beginning. She cleared her throat and put the spoon back in the bowl, waiting for him to turn 'round in response to the signal.

"Do you have something to say?" Nick approached the bed, unbuttoning the lace cuffs of his shirt. His expression

was still distinctly forbidding. "I suggest you reflect well before you open your mouth."

Polly could bear it no longer. "I have said I am sorry. It is
most ungenerous of you to continue to be so unforgiving."

Nick regarded her gravely, then sighed. "Sweetheart, I am
torn asunder by this business. Only desperation would force
me to lend my countenance to it, but the situation *is* desperate. However, I will not oblige you to play this part. Do you
understand that?"

Polly nodded, and the candlelight caught the burnished
golden tones in the hair tumbling across her shoulders, deepened the green and topaz brilliance of her eyes. "Richard did
not tell you of my own suggestion, then?"

Nick looked startled. "What suggestion?" He took off his
shirt, tossing it onto a stool, the gesture setting the muscles
to ripple in his back.

Polly averted her eyes from the distracting sight. It didn't
seem reasonable that at such a moment of intensity, lust
should intrude with its insouciant, all-absorbing power.

Nick continued with his undressing while she told him of
her discussion with Richard. When she had finished, he said
nothing for a minute or two, but poured water from the
ewer into the basin and splashed his face vigorously. Then he
turned back to the bed. "There is more risk for you in such a
ploy than in simply answering the call to Buckingham's bed.
If he does not care for the game, he will do all in his power
to injure you. He is a powerful enemy, moppet. You would
do best to have him as your friend."

"As lover, you mean," she said, plucking at the coverlet
with restless fingers. "I prefer to hazard his enmity."

"I do not want you to take such a risk," he said bluntly.
"We will forget the matter in its entirety. I will tell De
Winter and the rest that we must come up with another
solution."

"Nay!" Polly pushed aside the covers and knelt on the
bed, urgent in her determination. "If it is important to you,
love, then it is important to me. I have said I will do it, and I

will. It is no longer a matter over which you have any say. I will partner you in this."

Nicholas looked at her, a frown between his brows, but a tiny smile in his eyes. "You grow out of hand, young Polly."

"I grow up, my lord," she replied, meeting his eye. "Responsible for myself."

"Aye," he agreed slowly. "It was inevitable, and I will learn to like it."

Kneeling up, she reached her arms around his neck. "I have been full grown for many a year, love." Her lips brushed his, her breath whispering sweet and warm. "In all essentials."

Nick laughed, running his fingers through her hair, pushing it back from her face. "Yes, indeed, a veritable crone y'are," he scoffed. "Wrinkled and bowed down by the weight of experience— Ouch! Don't you do that!" In mock indignation, he bore her backward onto the bed, but she moved against him with sinuous urgency, her mouth hungry against his, her hands sliding imperatively over his back, gripping his buttocks with harsh demand.

Nick pushed up her smock, responding to her need with his own abrupt, unceremonious craving. They came together, clung, suspeneded in a moment of rough-hewn passion that excluded all but the need to lose themselves in each other, in the ravaging torrent of pure sensation.

Afterward, spent and at peace, Polly slept in the crook of Nick's arm, while he lay looking into the darkness, trying to rationalize the deep foreboding that had rushed into the void left by the retreat of bodily bliss.

Chapter 13

"Where are your wits this morning, Polly?" demanded a puzzled Killigrew the following day as she stumbled for the tenth time over her lines. "You had the part word-perfect yesterday."

"I seem to have forgotten it," Polly said apologetically, stepping to the front of the stage. "Will ye grant me some time to con the lines anew?" She smiled at him, but the smile was really directed over his head to where the Duke of Buckingham sat in the dim light of the auditorium. His Grace was not the only courtier in the theatre this morning, although Nick was absent. Watching rehearsals was one of the favorite activities of those who enjoyed the play, and often enough dabbled in the art of the playwright themselves.

Thomas sighed. "I suppose I must, since we can achieve nothing while you stumble and stutter in this manner."

Polly gathered up her skirts and stepped lightly into the pit. "Mayhap Your Grace will assist me?" She gave Villiers the lodestone of her smile. "If you would read with me, sir, then the task will be all the easier."

Buckingham rose immediately to his feet. "I can imagine nothing that would give me greater pleasure, Mistress Wyat."

"Then let us repair to the tiring room, where we may

have a little privacy." She turned back to the stage, still smiling at him over her shoulder. It was not an unusual service she was requesting; indeed, it was one eagerly performed by those gentlemen fascinated by the theatre and its actors. But this was the first time that Mistress Wyat had requested the help of any but her protector.

Buckingham hid his satisfaction. It was as he had expected. The lady had decided it was time to move onward and upward, and was delicately indicating her willingness to accept the invitation that he had issued at court the previous evening.

He reposed his elegant frame on the scroll-ended couch in the tiring room. "I am honored to be singled out in this fashion, my dear."

Polly merely smiled again, an enigmatic smile that hinted at much. "If you would read the other lines, my lord duke, I will test my memory." She handed him the script before sitting upon the couch beside him, carefully arranging her skirts, using the movements to conceal the quick look she cast up at him. Had he grasped the message? He would have to be a fool not to; and George Villiers, in matters such as these, was no fool.

She had the part by heart, but she made sufficient errors to add credence to her ploy, and to give her companion the satisfaction of correcting her and receiving her blushing thanks in return. Members of the company wandered in and out of the tiring room while Polly played her game. The lack of complete privacy suited her purposes perfectly. At no point did she wish to find herself in the position of having to declare herself openly as interested in the duke's patronage. With hints and innuendo she would intrigue him, and it was much easier to offer these tantalizing clues on a public stage than in private, where he might reasonably expect more openness.

"I am so grateful to you, sir." At the end of an hour, she stood up. "I think I now have it to Thomas's satisfaction. You have been most helpful."

"May I, perhaps, ask a small favor in return?" He took snuff, the eyes beneath drooping lids searching her face.

Polly curtsied. "How may I serve you, my lord duke?"

"I am having a small card party this evening. Just a few of my friends. Dare I be so bold as to hope that you might join us?"

He did not waste any time, reflected Polly. But then, why should he? Once the game had been started, why delay its conclusion?

"I am desolated, sir, but I am pledged to a supper party given by Lord De Winter," she said smoothly.

"Not an arrangement you could break?" he asked, the heavy eyelids drooping even lower.

"I am afraid not. I could not be so discourteous, Your Grace." She showed him a face free of guile, an expression of genuine regret in her eyes, an apologetic smile upon her lips.

There was a moment's silence while the duke considered her with narrowed eyes, his displeasure undisguised. Her heart began to speed. Did she truly know what she was doing by deliberately risking so much more than his simple displeasure? Then he smiled, shrugged, dropping his snuff-box back into his pocket.

"I can see I must ensure in future that my invitation is received early enough to take precedence, Mistress Wyat."

"That would please me greatly, sir," she responded, putting a wealth of promise into the soft voice, the inviting curve of her lips.

That naked hunger leapt into Buckingham's eyes, was for a moment etched upon that dissolute countenance. He bowed, raising her hand to his lips. "Your servant, madame."

"Polly!" Thomas strode into the room, then paused. "Your pardon, Buckingham, but if this play is ever to be performed, I need Mistress Wyat's presence onstage straightway."

"I am quite ready," Polly said, moving past the duke toward the door. "His Grace has been infinitely patient with me, and most helpful."

"Then I am in his debt," Thomas said somewhat caustically. "I do not know what came over you, to forget the part in that fashion."

And I trust you never will, thought Polly, fervently hoping that she would not again have to incur Master Killigrew's annoyance with a display of professional ineptitude. He was not inclined to the long-suffering and had no scruples about fining any member of the company for failing to perform to standard, regardless of excuse.

The duke returned to the auditorium, settling down to watch the remainder of the rehearsal, not a flicker disturbing the smooth impassivity of his expression. But when Thomas at midday released the company, Buckingham appeared at Polly's side.

"You will permit me to escort you to your lodging, Mistress Wyat." There was no question mark, and Polly did not make the mistake of pretending that there had been one.

"You are too kind." She returned the formal platitude, allowing him to help her with her cloak. "Your company will be most welcome, sir, although 'tis but a step."

They went out into the fresh spring day. Drury Lane was busy and bustling, women crowding around the stalls selling fresh meat and fish, haggling vociferously with the baker over his price to bake their own dough. Doors and windows stood open to the street in honor of the sun. Children tumbled in the kennels. Scrawny dogs yapped. It was London town on an ordinary March Tuesday, and Polly could force herself to relax, to talk naturally to her companion as they strolled through this familiar scene.

At the door of her lodging, she turned smiling to her escort. "I must bid you farewell, sir." It was at this moment that Lord Kincaid stepped through that same door onto the street.

Nicholas stood for a bare second, making rapid assessment. He could detect nothing out of the ordinary in Polly's face, as radiant as ever, upturned toward the duke as she placed her hand in his. "I give you good day, Buckingham," he said casually, drawing on his gloves. "It is rare to see you on foot, but for such company, what would a man not sacrifice?"

"What, indeed?" replied Buckingham, brushing the fingers he held with his lips.

"Why, my lord," Polly said with a cool smile, turning her attention toward Nicholas. "You did not say you would visit this morning. Are you come to dine?"

"No, I cannot. I had a commission to execute, but now I must be on my way."

"Oh." Polly frowned. "What commission?"

"You will see," he said, moving out of the door. "If you go to the Strand, Buckingham, I will bear you company."

Both men bowed in farewell to Polly, who curtsied politely, then stood watching them stroll in the direction of the Strand, talking companionably. Nick, she knew, would be making sure that Buckingham realized he had a complacent lover on his hands, one who would be quite indifferent to whatever sidelines his mistress might contemplate. The game was begun.

Polly turned into the house, wondering what Nick had meant by a commission he had had to execute. In the parlor, she found the answer to the puzzle. A familiar figure from the days of Lady Margaret's rule was tending the fire.

"Sue!" Polly exclaimed. "Whatever d'ye do here?"

Susan turned, a shy smile on the plain, good-tempered countenance. She looked hesitantly at Polly, who was dressed in working attire, a simple print gown over a plain kirtle. There was nothing in the figure to alarm, and Sue beamed. " 'Is lordship brought me. 'Tis wonderful, Polly. I'm to live 'ere with you." Prancing delightedly across the room, she embraced Polly with her usual warmth.

Polly returned the hug with equal enthusiasm, but then drew back, surveying the other girl in utter bemusement. "I do not understand, Susan. What do you mean that his lordship says you are to live here with me?"

"I'm to look after ye," Susan explained, her smile broadening. " 'Is lordship says ye've need of someone to keep yer wardrobe in order and 'elp with yer dressin' and things . . ." Her voice faded as she saw the look on Polly's face. "D'ye not want me?" she said, a stricken look in the brown eyes. "Oh, pray don't say so! I'm to 'ave me own chamber in the attic—all to meself, Polly, just imagine! And jest to 'elp the goodwife when she needs, and go with you to the theatre and 'elp ye there." Her eyes were very round. "Is it true? Y'are a famous actor now?"

"I do not know about famous," Polly demurred. "But I am an actor." A rueful smile touched the corner of her mouth as she remembered the conversation between Bridget, the cook, and Susan in Lady Margaret's kitchen, after Big Rob's visit. "Do you truly wish to live with a brazen hussy of Covent Garden breeding, Sue? And his lordship's whore into the bargain?"

That was how Susan would see it, Polly knew. Once a girl of their class lost her maidenhead without benefit of clergy, she was branded by her own kind as whore regardless of the circumstances. However, the words were no sooner between her lips than she looked guiltily over her shoulder at the door, as if afraid to see an irate Lord Kincaid as audience to the forbidden description.

"Gawd!" murmured Susan. " 'Is lordship don't behave as if you'm a whore, Polly. Talked to me about you as if y'are a proper lady, 'e did."

"Aye. Well, his lordship is a proper gentleman," said Polly a little tartly. "And he will not understand that when one has been a servant, it is very uncomfortable to have someone to wait upon one."

Susan's face fell to her boots. "I'd not make ye uncomfortable, Polly. Don't tell 'im ye don't want me, please. You don't know what it's been like since ye left. Lady Margaret's been in a pucker, summat awful! What with 'is lordship 'ardly ever in the 'ouse, and 'er knowing it's something to do with you."

Polly had little difficulty imagining the situation. It was not one to which she would condemn her worst enemy, and Susan had stood her friend through her own trying times in that household.

"Tell me what has been happening since I left," she invited, moving to the fire that, despite the sunshine, was still necessary to keep at bay the March wind.

Sue seized on the invitation with gusto, chattering cheerfully, filling the room with her merry presence, making Polly laugh with her gossipy prattle.

Polly had no woman she could call friend. There were men like Killigrew and De Winter whom she thought of as particular friends, in whom she reposed absolute confidence. In Nick she had thought she had everything one could want in the way of friendship, companionship, love—for as long as she had his undivided attention, of course. That rider had wormed its way unbidden to undermine her complacent satisfaction on more than one occasion. Nick would have to take a wife at some point. However, on this occasion she squashed the unpalatable thought as resolutely as always, and returned her attention to Sue.

Until this moment, she had not had a moment's yearning for the easy companionship of one of her own age and sex. Now, as she slipped without thought into a delicious discussion of Bridget's courting by a local ostler, she realized how much she had missed this. And she realized with slow appreciation exactly what Nick had given her. No maidservant, but a companion who would benefit from the situation every bit as much as Polly.

She stretched her fingers to the fire and smiled. "I am famished, Sue. Let us dine."

Susan paused. "I cannot dine with you. I'm to take me dinner in the kitchen, with the goodwife and 'er folk."

"Nonsense," declared Polly, reaching up for the bell rope. "When my lord is here, then I daresay that will be best. But when he is not, I am damned if I'll dine alone when I can dine with you."

Susan giggled nervously, clearly shocked by this forthright speech, but not unwilling to hear the sentiment thus expressed. However, she retained sufficient presence of mind to forestall Polly with the bell rope, saying that she would go belowstairs herself to fetch up the fricassee of rabbit and chicken that the goodwife had prepared for her lodger's delectation.

Nicholas heard their laughter drifting down the stairs when he returned to the house some three hours later. He paused outside the parlor door, feeling strangely as if he should knock to alert them of the arrival of an intruder. Then, with a little shake of his head, he opened the door as noisily as he could.

Both girls were sitting on the floor before the fire, glasses of wine in hand, the remnants of dinner still laid upon the table. Polly turned as the door opened, her cheeks flushed with wine and the fire's glow. "I swear you are as full of surprises as a bran tub, my lord," she declared in mock reproach, rising to her feet. "Although the last time I put my hand in a bran tub, at the Martinmas Fair last year, I pulled out the most meager surprise—a tin whistle, as I recall. And I had had such hopes that my farthing would bring me something wonderful!" She laughed, her pleasure glowing in her eyes as she came across to him.

"It is the disposition of bran tubs," said Kincaid, slipping his arms around her waist. "There is always the hope that blind fingers digging into the bran will produce the grand prize, worth far more than one's farthing. But, of course, 'twould hardly be a commercial proposition for the fairman if that were the case." He chuckled. "It is part of human nature, this triumph of hope over experience."

"I seem to have found myself a bran tub where the prizes far exceed the outlay," she said softly, standing on tiptoe to kiss him. "But I should tell you, sir, that I think you very devious in achieving your own object."

"My object being your compliance in matters where you show an unfortunate intractability," he returned, kissing the corner of her mouth. "I see that I have achieved that in this instance." He looked over her head to where an embarrassed Susan stood, unsure where to put herself, or to direct her eyes in the face of this display of affection.

"Susan, are matters arranged to your satisfaction?" he asked affably, in an attempt to put the girl at her ease. Unfortunately, such condescension merely served to render her speechless with discomfort.

"Oh, of course, they are!" Polly exclaimed impatiently. "And we have been having the most comfortable time until you appeared."

"My apologies, madame." He bowed low. "I will remove myself forthwith."

"Idiot!" Laughter sparked in her eyes. "That is not at all what I meant, as well you know."

Nick took pity on Susan. "Why do you not clear the table, Susan. It seems that the dishes have lain overlong."

Her relief patent at having a customary function to perform, Susan mumbled apologies and set to, disappearing from the parlor with a laden tray.

"Does Susan please you?" Nick pinched Polly's chin, looking deep into her eyes. "You are at ease with her, and she will have no difficulty understanding what you require of a helper."

"Aye, she pleases me," she said, touching his lips with a delicate finger. "As no one else could." She drew back from him as the cold shadow of the morning obtruded into this love-lit warmth. "You had a pleasant walk with His Grace, I trust?"

"He was at some pains to indicate his interest in my mistress," Nick said evenly. "As I was at pains to appear totally indifferent."

"Aye, 'twas what I thought would be discussed." She turned back to the fire. "I made it clear this morning that I was available. But I refused an invitation for this evening. It seemed wise to appear not overeager."

"How did he react to such a refusal?" Nicholas went to the sideboard to pour wine. "Have you had sufficient, or shall I refill your glass?" He held the decanter, an eyebrow raised in question.

"There is no performance this afternoon, but I have to return to the theatre for another rehearsal," she said with a grimace. "I had best have no more, lest I make further errors. Thomas is like to prove uncommon difficult in such a case."

"*Further* errors?"

Polly shrugged and told him the story of her morning's ploy. "It worked well enough," she finished. "But to answer your question about the duke's reaction to my refusal: I do not think he was best pleased, at first. But then he seemed to take it in his stride." She poked the fire, sending sparks shooting up the chimney. "I do not think 'twill be long before I receive another invitation—one that I will accept."

The following morning, the household quiet was shattered by the hammering of the door knocker. Polly, in the absence of Nicholas and his strictures on correct deportment at mealtimes, was consuming a peripatetic breakfast while she roamed the parlor muttering lines between mouthfuls, and improvising gestures as they came to her.

"I'll see who 'tis," Sue said, putting down one of Polly's gowns she had been examining for tears and stains. "Ye'll get the indigestion if ye don't stop all this muttering an' movin' whilst yer eating." She went to the parlor door.

"Y'are as fussy as my lord," Polly said with a chuckle, going to the window to see if any clue as to the visitor would be found on the street. A lad in the Duke of Buckingham's livery stood in the lane. All humor left her, to be replaced by a quiet stillness, the same stillness that always followed the moment of panic before she went onstage, one that allowed her to assume a persona not her own.

" 'Tis a message and a parcel for ye." Sue came into the parlor, bearing a small package and a folded paper. "From His Grace of Buckingham, the boy says. He's waitin' on yer answer."

Polly opened the paper. The script was bold and black, the invitation couched in flowery language and hedged about with compliments. She opened the accompanying package, and Sue gasped. A delicate brooch, shaped like a daisy, made of silver filigree studded with diamonds and seed pearls, lay on Polly's palm.

" 'Tis exquisite," Polly murmured, half to herself. Her refusal of such a gift would certainly intrigue His Grace, particularly when the returned present was accompanied by acceptance of his invitation to a small gathering at his house in the Strand the following evening. He would not know what to make of such mixed messages.

"Sue, ye must give this back to the messenger." She wrapped up the brooch again. "But tell him that Mistress Wyat is very happy to accept the duke's invitation for tomorrow . . . Of course," she added, a touch disconsolately, " 'twould be better if I were to write the message, but I cannot be sure of spelling it correctly, and I cannot wait for my lord's help."

Sue looked uneasily at Polly. "Why's His Grace sendin' ye invitations and gifts, Polly? 'Tis not right when y'are livin' under my lord's protection."

" 'Tis something I must do for my lord and Lord De Winter," Polly told her. "Rest easy. My lord knows all about it."

"Doesn't seem right to me," muttered Sue, taking the package.

It wouldn't, of course, Polly reflected as the door closed on the departing Susan. Sue could not begin to comprehend the hypocrisies and contradictions of court life, where a married woman could bear another man's child and her husband would cheerfully claim the bastard as his own, where harlotry was practiced as openly as in the stews of Covent Garden, yet did not go by that name. Beauty, good manners, and the ability to play the game with discretion were the only virtues.

And Polly, who came from Sue's world where no distinction was drawn between mistress and whore, frequently found herself unsure of where she fitted in the scheme of things. As far as the court was concerned, she was the mistress, open and acknowledged, of Lord Kincaid. If Prue and the other inhabitants of the Dog tavern knew of it, they

would call her his lordship's whore. So which was she? And
did it really matter, anyway? It was how Nick regarded her
that mattered, and he had made that very clear . . . Yet he
had been ready to ask a whore's work of her . . .

When had they first thought to use her in this way? Who
had thought of it? *It is possible we may be of service to each other*
. . . Lord of hell! she thought in furious imitation of the
man in question. What did it matter? She was now involved
in this of her own free will.

She went to the window, looking down on the lane to see
how the duke's servant received her message. He did not
look very comfortable as Sue pressed the package upon him;
indeed, seemed to be putting up some kind of argument.
Perhaps it would be considered that he had failed in his
mission, Polly thought, and he would be judged culpable for
her refusal. Well, there was little she could do about that.

" 'E didn't want to take it back," Sue informed her, returning to the parlor. "Said as 'ow His Grace would be
angry."

"It is hardly the lad's fault." How angry would the duke
be with *her*? Polly shrugged, dismissing the question. It was a
bridge to be crossed when she reached it. "I must send a
message to my lord . . . The Bensons' lad can take it." She
pulled the bell rope, suddenly filled with a restless energy, as
if, now that the business was launched, she would have it in
full play without delay.

The Bensons' lad did not have far to go, as it happened, to
deliver his message. As he trotted down St. Martin's Lane, he
espied Lord Kincaid astride his raking chestnut gelding.

"M'lord . . . m'lord . . ." Breathlessly, the lad jumped
into the middle of the cobbled street.

Sulayman came to a well-trained halt, and his rider peered
down at the panting urchin, demanding sharply, "Is something amiss?"

"Don' think so, m'lord." The boy looked puzzled at the
question. "Mistress Wyat jest sent me to fetch ye as soon as
may be."

"Which you proceeded to do at all speed." Kincaid

laughed, reaching into his pocket for a coin. "For your speed and your trouble, lad." He left the boy in the middle of the street, examining this unexpected bounty with the speculative eyes of one who could not decide what amongst a plethora of delights to purchase with his sixpence.

Nicholas found Polly pacing restlessly between the parlor and the bedchamber in a state of half undress. Sue had given up attempting to get her to stand still long enough to lace up her corset and had returned placidly to her earlier task of examining the contents of Polly's wardrobe, exclaiming occasionally at its magnificence.

"Oh, Nick, you are come at last," Polly greeted him as he stepped through the door.

"I cannot have been so very long," he said with a smile, tossing his hat onto a chair and drawing off his gloves. "I was on the way here when your messenger came up with me in St. Martin's Lane. What is all the hurry? Why are you not dressed at this hour?"

"I did try, m'lord," Sue said hastily, as if Polly's dishabille were due to some dereliction of duty on her part.

"Oh, 'tis not your fault, Sue," Polly declared impatiently. "I am quite able to dress myself, you know. I have been doing so for almost the last seventeen years."

"Then why have you not done so this morning?" inquired Kincaid. "Are you excused attendance at the rehearsal? 'Tis near ten of the clock, you know."

"I have some news," Polly said, turning back to the bedchamber. "I thought it urgent."

"Then you shall tell me while you dress," Nick said in soothing tones. He followed her into the bedchamber, closing the door on Sue in the parlor. "What is it, sweetheart, that has so thrown you into such disarray?"

"Why, 'tis Buckingham, of course." Polly picked up her corset and gave him her back in mute request. He fastened the laces, listening as she told of the duke's gift and invitation, and of her response.

"Tomorrow night?" he mused. "I heard mention of the gathering at court last even. 'Tis to be one of Buckingham's revels—the entertainments he puts on for his intimates." He frowned. "You will not be the only woman there, moppet."

"Women are part of the entertainment at these revels, then?" Polly stepped into her gown, under no illusions as to what Nick meant.

"Aye," he said slowly. "But there are also always women guests."

Those who would not find the prospect of such entertainment a matter of disgust. Polly nodded thoughtfully. There were plenty such at court. "Will there be opportunity for me to glean impressions of some import, think you?"

"Undoubtedly," Nick said. "These are the gatherings that are closed to all but his most intimate friends and those he provides for their entertainment, of course," he added. "But since the entertainers are unlikely to have any understanding, let alone interest in, the political undercurrents, on such an occasion there will be no dissembling. If you know what to look for, you will see it."

"And you will tell me what to look for?" She sat before the mirror, beginning to comb her hair, the automatic movements serving to calm her, to still the restless energy.

Nick came up behind her, laying his hands on her shoulders. "You will be told exactly what to look for, Polly. But it is not too late to call a halt to this. You have but to say." She looked into the eyes fastened upon hers in the mirror. They were calm and matter-of-fact. How long had he contemplated this role for her? Since Buckingham had shown interest in her? Or before? The question would not lie down, yet she could not ask it for fear of the answer.

" 'Tis not unlike a part I played before," she said, dragging her eyes away from his. "I have played lure—"

"There is *no* similarity!" Nick exclaimed, anger chasing away his composure. "How can you talk such foolishness, draw such a stupid comparison?"

Polly shrugged, letting the question go by default. She could see the similarity, if Nick could not. She tucked her hair under a lace-trimmed cap and stood up. "I had best make haste if I am not to be late."

"I will accompany you to the theatre, then I must go and talk with Richard and the others." Nick spoke briskly. "And if you wish for there to be peace between us, you will not speak in that fashion again." He strode into the parlor, picking up his hat and gloves, waiting by the door for Polly, his lips set in an uncompromising line.

They walked in silence to the Theatre Royal. It was as if this shared conspiracy, this partnership that ought to have drawn them closer, had instead raised up a barrier between them, a prickly tension where before there had been laughter and love.

"Will you stay with me this night?" Polly asked as they reached their destination. She looked up at him, her face framed in the demure blue and white cap, and he was dazzled afresh by her beauty. Familiarity did not blunt its effect in the least.

"I would have this last night, before we begin in earnest, just for ourselves," she said softly.

Nick nodded. "After the performance we will go to supper at the French house that you are so fond of, and you shall have the finest Rhenish with lobsters and lamprey pie."

"And cheesecakes," added Polly, entering into the spirit of this effort to return matters between them to their customary humorous ease.

"And cheesecakes," he agreed with mock solemnity. "And afterward . . ."

"Having plied me shamelessly with all my favorite good things in my favorite eating house, you will have your way with me." Polly chuckled and gave an involuntary skip at the prospect.

"Exactly so."

"Shame on you, my lord!"

They stood for a moment enmeshed in the promise, with no need of words when their eyes were so articulate. Then Nick shook himself free of enchantment. "Be off," he said. "Thomas has a short way with the tardy."

"Aye." Polly turned to the door behind her. "Until this afternoon, my lord."

Nick saw her into the theatre, then went back to the lodging for his horse. Why would Polly say something like that? Surely only if she suspected that he had had an ulterior motive all along. But Richard had said there was no suggestion of such a thing in the discussion he had had with her. And surely he himself had put the possibility of such a suspicion to rest with his angry responses. He must not allow these shadows to fall between them, must not allow his own apprehension to spill over to her. She needed all the strength he could impart; and her greatest strength would come from the rigorous, matter-of-fact preparation he and the others could give her.

Chapter 14

"You understand what we want of you, Polly?" The
question was posed by one of the four men crowding
the parlor the following evening. Smoke from two
clay pipes curled, drifting on the breeze through the open
window.

Polly nodded at Sir Peter Appleby, resplendent in full periwig and scarlet satin—the veritable epitome of dandyism,
except that the foppish exterior concealed a needlesharp wit.
She had become familiar with these friends of Nick's since
taking up her abode in Drury Lane, but only now did she
know that beneath the friendship lay a stern commitment.
"It seems clear enough, Sir Peter."

"Then perhaps you would run through it for us, so that
we can be sure there are no misunderstandings," suggested
Charles Conway.

Nick, leaning against the mantel above the empty hearth,
puffing reflectively upon his pipe, was content to observe,
leaving Polly's briefing to his colleagues. She would receive
his instructions, of a more personal nature, before she left for
Buckingham's revels.

"I am to pay particular attention to any conversations between the duke and the Earl of Arlington, noting any references to the Earl of Clarendon," Polly said readily.

"You do understand why this is important, Polly?" asked De Winter.

"Well, as I understand it," said Polly, "Lord Clarendon wishes to strengthen the alliance with France—an alliance which the king favors—but the Earl of Arlington, who is secretary of state, wishes to draw closer to Spain. Arlington and Buckingham are working together to undermine the chancellor's influence with the king, and will impeach him if they can produce just cause. Since you consider it would be dangerous for England to be at odds with France at this time, with the Dutch war going on, it is particularly important to know what plans Buckingham and his friends have for Clarendon." She smiled cheerfully as she completed this exposition. "Do I have it right?"

"You do," said Richard, chuckling. "Word-perfect, my dear. One other thing you might be alert to—any talk of the Duke of Monmouth's legitimacy. If Buckingham is encouraging the king in this, there will be a civil uproar. Parliament will not stand for it, and if we know how far Buckingham is prepared to go in his support of the idea, we will be better able to decide on our own moves."

"You think they will talk of these things?" Polly asked, tapping her closed fan against her palm. "They seem uncommon serious matters for a private party."

"It is because it *is* a private party that they will be discussed." Major Conway spoke with customary vigor, both voice and expression resonant with intensity. "We are closely acquainted with no one but you who might have access to these occasions, Polly. For that reason you must ensure that you do nothing to jeopardize your acceptance."

"In what way would I do so?" asked Polly.

The major regarded her with the burning eye of the committed. "You must not allow Buckingham to suspect that you do not intend fulfilling your promise eventually. Indeed, if such fulfillment becomes necessary, you must—"

"Such imperatives, Conway, are not for you to declare." Lord Kincaid interrupted quietly, but with an unassailable authority. "Polly has agreed to lend us her assistance, but she

will do so in a manner that is comfortable for her. She will
not be asked to do anything repugnant to her." His gaze
drifted, seemingly casual, around the room. "That is understood, I trust."

Polly broke the silence that greeted this statement. "I understand what you want of me, gentlemen. I will do all I can
to ensure that you have it." She smiled with a mischievous
glee that chased the intensity from the room, and only she
knew how much effort had gone into its production. "I find
that I do not care for the duke, as I am sure you know. I shall
enjoy the game of deception, and enjoy furnishing you with
the information you require." She stood up, smoothing
down the pleated folds of her embroidered damask petticoat,
adjusting the Venetian lace at her décolletage. " 'Tis perhaps
time to begin this venture?" A delicate eyebrow arched.

"Aye," Nick said, " 'tis time. But I would speak with you
in private first . . . You will excuse us, gentlemen?"

It was command, couched as polite request, and achieved
the immediate departure of their guests. Richard paused in
the doorway. "You have simply to perform, Polly. Y'are an
actor of rare genius. Do not forget that." The door closed
behind him, and Polly smiled tremulously.

" 'Tis unlike Richard to pay me compliments."

"He speaks only the truth," Nick said, turning toward her
with quiet purpose. "Now, you are to listen to me. Your
acting ability is not in question; your ability to hear and
remember what is important is not in question; your ability
to deceive such a one as Buckingham is not yet proven. You
must remember that he and his friends are far from stupid,
and you must remember above all else that they are very
powerful." The emerald eyes held hers steadily, his voice was
level, but Polly was in no doubt as to the utter seriousness of
his words.

"I will not forget."

"And you will not forget this last thing I shall say. The
very minute that you become uneasy, that you sense someone . . . anyone . . . might be looking at you with suspi-

cion, you will leave. Instantly! Is that quite understood, Polly?"

"And if I decide that the goal will be better achieved by my staying and allaying those suspicions in whatever manner seems necessary . . . ?" She returned his look with her own, straight and candid.

"Nay, Polly, you will not. In such a circumstance, the goal will be sacrificed."

Polly shook her head. "That is a decision that I will make, Nicholas. You would have me involved in this, and I agreed to be so, of my own free will. How the game is played must now be up to me."

"And if I say that, if you take that stand, I will call a halt to the plan?"

"I would deny you the right to do so."

There was no anger in their words, no real sense of confrontation. It was simply the establishment of new ground.

"I will be careful, love," Polly said in soft reassurance, seeing his unease, feeling his discomfort as she took the reins into her own hands.

Nicholas looked at her for long minutes, then yielded. She was the chief player in the game. It was only reasonable that she should play by her own rules. "I will be waiting here for you," he said. "John Coachman will take you, and he will wait to bring you home."

The duke's mansion on the Strand was ablaze with light. Great flaming torches, set in metal sconces on either side of the imposing front door, threw illumination onto the flagway before the house. A linkboy ran to the carriage door as it drew up, holding up his torch as Polly descended, bending her head low as she stepped through the carriage door to avoid disturbing the high-piled artistry of her coiffure, carefully managing the weight of her skirts and train, which settled around her as she stood on the flagway, taking a moment to compose herself.

A liveried footman stood bowing in the opened door as

the linkboy lit the way. Polly passed through into a huge tiled hallway, where chandeliers swung from a domed ceiling and gilded moldings adorned the walls and doorways. A wide staircase curved upward, its steps shallow, its banisters elaborately carved. There was more grandeur here than in Whitehall Palace itself, Polly reflected. The immense wealth of the mansion's owner was declared from every corner.

The strains of lute and viol wafted down the stairs, a voice raised in laughter, the sound of hands clapping. Polly followed the footman up the staircase. At the head of the stairs, double doors stood open onto a salon, richly decorated and furnished. A group of musicians played at one end. Four men standing with their backs to the door were huddled over a long, low table, their laughter rising on a lubricious note. A cluster of women, painted and powdered, stood before the fire, fans fluttering, voices, light and artificial, drifting in the warm, scented air as they responded to the sallies of their male companions. Lady Castlemaine was one of their number, Polly noted, recognizing the others also as faces she had seen at court, but she could not put names to them all.

"Mistress Polly Wyat," intoned the footman, and the four men around the table straightened. The Duke of Buckingham, in peacock satin with gold lacing, his powdered periwig sweeping his shoulders, turned instantly to the door. The thin lips flickered in a smile as he came over.

"Why, Mistress Wyat, I had begun to despair of you." He made a magnificent leg, showing off his embroidered stockings and the high-heeled shoes where diamonds glinted, set into the heels and the gold buckles.

"Am I late, my lord duke?" Polly swept into her curtsy, a stage curtsy from which not a nuance was missing. "I am desolated to have offered such discourtesy. Your invitation did not specify a time."

"That was remiss of me," he murmured, kissing her hand. "In my eagerness to dispatch the invitation, I must have forgot such a trifling point." The heavy lids drooped even lower. "I am devastated at the thought that my poor gift did not find favor, madame."

"On the contrary, Your Grace, it was exquisite. But far too valuable a present for me to accept." She met his meager smile with one as blandly polite and unexpressive.

Buckingham inclined his head. " 'Twas but a trinket, madame. I had thought it pretty enough to please you."

"I am not in the habit of accepting . . . trinkets . . . of any value from those with whom I am but slightly acquainted," Polly said carefully, still smiling.

Buckingham pursed his lips. "Then I will keep the brooch until such time as we are become better acquainted, Mistress Wyat."

"A pleasing suggestion, sir." Polly could feel the sweat breaking out upon her body under the strain of this loaded exchange. How long could she keep it up? Her gaze shifted with apparent naturalness to look around the room, reminding the duke of the presence of other company and his duties as host.

"I am delighted you agreed to grace my little revels," Buckingham said, turning back to the room. "You will be acquainted with some of my guests . . . but not all," he added delicately, regarding her through his hooded eyes as she took in what had been occupying the gentlemen around the table. The girl spread upon it was quite naked.

"Is she not a little chilly?" Polly asked carelessly.

Villiers chuckled appreciatively. "A few guineas can be amazingly warming, my dear madame, for such a one as she."

A brazen hussy of Covent Garden breeding, thought Polly. If Nicholas, Lord Kincaid, had not entered her life, *she* could have been earning her bread in such a manner . . . She banished the distracting thought; it only led to that other question, the one she must not dwell upon.

"I see my Lord Arlington," she said now, as if the matter of whores displayed upon tables was of no further interest. "Talking with Lady Castlemaine. I would have speech with him, sir. He was so kind as to send me a letter of compliment after the performance this afternoon, and I must thank him."

Buckingham bowed his acquiescence and escorted her to her goal. She accepted a glass of canary from a footman and set out to play the coquette.

The duke rarely left her side, and it was clear to Polly, from the speculative looks sent her way from all and sundry, that the company had deduced the meaning of her presence at this private gathering. Carefully, she ensured that not just the duke was the object of her coquetry, even while her eyes, when they met those of His Grace, told him otherwise.

"George, a game of macao, dear fellow. You owe me my revenge!" The laughing invitation came from a newcomer, John Maitland, Earl of Lauderdale, one of the Cabal.

"Aye," agreed Arlington. " 'Tis the devil's own luck ye have with the cards, George. Ye took a thousand guineas off me last time."

Buckingham laughed, flicking open his snuffbox to take a leisurely pinch. " 'Tis like taking toffee from a babe, but if ye've a mind to be trounced again, then by all means let us repair to the card room." He turned to Polly beside him. "I'd have ye with me, bud, if y'are willing. Such beauty can only bring a man good fortune."

The public endearment sealed the matter for all, as did the proprietorial hand cupping her elbow. If Mistress Wyat was not already gracing Buckingham's bed, she soon would be, and her acceptance in this group was now assured.

Assured for as long as she made no slips, Polly thought, accompanying the men into the card room leading off the main salon.

"Nay, sir, I'll stand at your shoulder," she said, laughing, as he directed a footman to draw up a chair for her beside his own at the round table, gleaming mahogany under the candlelight. " 'Tis the place of luck, is it not?"

Buckingham raised her fingers to his lips, saying with soft meaning, "I trust my luck will hold beyond the cards."

Polly allowed an elusive smile to play across her lips, before raising her fan, concealing all but her eyes. Sweat trickled down her back under the strain of keeping her revulsion hidden.

"What think you of the king's hints about his marriage to Lucy Walter, George?" The question came from Arlington, and it brought Polly to prickly awareness. Lucy Walter was said to be the mother of the illegitimate Duke of Monmouth, the king's sixteen-year-old son.

Buckingham shrugged, gesturing to the boy who stood on his other side holding a heavy leather purse. He took out a hundred guineas and laid them upon the table. "I'll see you, Henry." He watched as Arlington laid his cards upon the table, then chuckled, exposing his own hand. "My twenty to your nineteen, Henry . . . No, I think the king is playing a lost cause here. If he claims marriage to the Walter woman, he must produce evidence, witnesses, documents. If he had them to produce, he would have done so by now."

"They could be found," observed Lauderdale, sipping his claret, frowning as he examined his cards.

Polly kept very still, praying that the sudden tension in her body would not be transmitted to the seated figure so close to her. This was what she was here to hear.

"But think what a trouble," drawled Villiers. "One can never be sure that a bought witness will stay bought, or that a document one happens to . . . to discover—" An elegant beringed hand passed through the air in graceful explanation "—will stand up to informed scrutiny."

"So ye'll not encourage His Majesty in this?" inquired Arlington.

Again Buckingham shrugged. "I've no objection to York's succeeding to the throne. Monmouth's a callow lad, overindulged and a trifle empty-headed."

"Vain and ambitious into the bargain," chuckled Lauderdale. " 'Twould not suit your purposes, George, I'll be bound, to have such a one on the throne."

Buckingham's lips moved in the semblance of a smile, and his eyelids drooped heavily. "I cannot imagine what you could mean, John. Why should it be a matter of moment to me who succeeds His Majesty?"

A laugh rippled around the table, and the conversation turned to gossip.

Polly drew her lace-edged handkerchief from her sleeve and surreptitiously wiped her clammy palms. She had done what she had come here to do, established her position in this circle, and heard something of importance to Nick and the others. Surely she could make her escape now, for this time at least. But how to extricate herself gracefully?

She yawned delicately behind her fan. "La, my lord duke, but 'tis monstrous fatigued I am grown. I must ask you to excuse me. 'Tis to be hoped I have brought you sufficient luck for one night." She smiled over her fan, yawned again.

The duke's expression was not encouraging. His eyes hardened. "Why, bud, 'tis early yet."

"But you forget, sir, I am a working woman and must be at the theatre at ten of the morning."

Buckingham pushed back his chair, rising fluidly. Polly, taking this to mean that he would escort her from the room, curtsied to the men at the table. "I bid you good night, sirs," she said, and moved away toward the salon.

"Come now, you would not be so unkind as to run away, madame," the duke protested softly as they entered the still-crowded salon.

"Run away from what, duke?" inquired Polly sweetly. "I have enjoyed myself most wonderfully, but, indeed, I must seek my bed if I am to satisfy Master Killigrew tomorrow."

His fingers circled her wrist, lightly, yet Polly felt her skin jump with alarm. "You would not have me disappoint my audience, would you, sir?"

"But you disappoint me," he said gently, still holding her wrist.

It was time for the withdrawal. "Then I am sorry for it, sir, but I was not aware I was under an obligation." She met his gaze directly and saw the flash of puzzlement cross that generally impassive countenance, a flicker of uncertainty lurking in the eyes. The duke had thought the game and its rules understood. Now he was not so sure.

Then he released her wrist, bowed deeply, and said, "I am desolated at your departure, madame, but I realize I have no claims, much as I would wish for them."

"They have to be earned, sir," she said. It could not be much plainer. If he went about it the right way, he could have what he wished for. It was up to him to discover the right way.

The duke bowed again. "Then I shall endeavor to do so, bud." He beckoned to a footman. "Summon a chair for Mistress Wyat."

"There is no need, sir. My coachman awaits."

If that surprised him, it did not show on his face. "Then permit me to escort you to your carriage."

He saw her into the elegant, well-kept interior of Kincaid's coach and stood upon the flagway, staring after the conveyance. This one was not going to be easily or cheaply bought. She had clearly a very firm idea of her own worth, and would not sell herself for less. Well, His Grace of Buckingham could respect that. He must set about wooing her. It was a novel game, and there was no reason why he should not take pleasure in it. With a little smile, he turned back to the house.

"Standing staring out of the window is not going to hasten her return, Nick," remarked De Winter.

"Aye, I am aware." Nick turned from the window, reaching for his wineglass on the sideboard. "But I cannot rest, Richard."

"She'll not come to harm," Richard reassured. " 'Tis a gathering; Buckingham cannot compel anything from her in such a situation. If she finds she cannot perform the part, then she may leave at any time she pleases. While nothing will be gained, by the same token, nothing is lost."

Nick's frown etched deep lines between his red-gold eyebrows. "I fear she has taken the bit between her teeth on this, Richard, and she will run with it." He paced restlessly for a minute, then stopped. "Did you hear a coach?"

Richard went to the window, flinging it wide, looking into the darkness. "You have sharp ears, my friend. A carriage has just rounded the corner."

Nick came to stand beside him, and Richard felt the tension run from his friend as the carriage, the unmistakable figure of John Coachman upon the box, came to a halt before the door below.

Nick resisted the urge to run down to her. He wanted to see how she was when she thought herself unobserved. She might play a part for him—the part she thought he would want to see—and he was not confident that he would be able to distinguish acting from reality without some clues, so skillful had she become.

The coachman opened the door, let down the footstep, and Polly descended into the strip of light shining down from the upstairs casement. "My thanks, John Coachman. I trust 'twas not too tedious a wait for ye." Her clear tones rose to the opened window. Then, as if magnetized, she looked up.

"Are ye still up, my lord?" There seemed to be a light, teasing note in her voice. "I made sure you would have been abed an hour since . . . and Lord De Winter, also."

A window was flung open next door, and a protesting bellow rent the air. Polly put a guilty finger to her lips, her eyes widening in mock horror.

"Come in," Nick instructed in a piercing whisper, wondering how she had made him want to laugh at such a moment. He went to the parlor door to wait for her.

She came up the stairs with swift step and tumbled instantly into his arms. She was shaking like a leaf, and all desire to laugh left him abruptly. He held her close, feeling the fragility beneath the elaborate dress, the armor of corset and layers of petticoats.

"What is it, sweetheart? Are you hurt?" The anguished questions whispered against her ear as he stroked her back and she shuddered against him.

"Nay . . . nay . . . not hurt," she managed at last. "It is going to succeed, I think, but . . . but I did not realize how hard the work 'twould be, Nick. 'Tis a thousand times worse than the theatre."

Nicholas drew her into the parlor, closing the door quietly. "Is that all that is the matter? That maintaining the part was hard work?"

"If it were just a matter of maintaining the part, 'twould not be so difficult," she said, her voice a little quavery, although she had stopped shaking. "Oh, my thanks, Richard." She took the glass of claret he handed her. "But I must also write the lines, Nick. I had not thought of that."

The two men looked at each other. Somehow, they had not grappled with that complexity, either. "But you managed to do so?" Richard prompted.

Polly nodded, drinking deeply of the wine as if it were the elixir of the gods. "I think it was convincing. Nothing of moment was said of Lord Clarendon. However, there *was* talk of the Duke of Monmouth." She told them what she had heard, moving around the room as she did so, pausing to refill her glass. Nick frowned at the speed with which that glass had been emptied, but for the moment held his peace.

"And how did you leave Villiers?" asked De Winter when the story seemed told.

"With an invitation to find my price," Polly said bluntly, reaching again for the decanter.

"Nay, moppet, you have had sufficient." Nick stayed her hand, and she turned on him with a flash of fury.

"By what right do you tell me that? I have barely touched a drop all evening for fear I would make an error. Surely now I may be permitted some relaxation!"

"As much as you need," he said evenly. "But you are drinking too quickly."

Polly glared at him. Richard got out of his chair, reaching for his cloak.

"I think 'tis time I left you." He drew on his gloves. "My compliments, Polly. Not that I doubted you," he added with a dry smile, bending to brush her forehead with his lips.

"But pay heed to Nick, now. He has more experience than you when it comes to the bottle."

"Aye," agreed Nick cheerfully. "A dreadful sot I was in my youth."

Polly looked between them, saw the way they had drawn together implicitly, knew that her well-being was the reason. "I give you good night, Richard," she said.

Nick saw Richard from the house, then came to the parlor, where Polly still stood as he had left her.

"I ask your pardon," she said softly. "I did not mean to snap in that manner."

"There is nothing to pardon." He took her in his arms. "Let us go to bed now. Let me ease you in ways infinitely more pleasurable than those to be found in wine."

"What in the world . . ." Nick stood staring around the parlor the following noon.

" 'Tis His Grace of Buckingham," Polly choked. She had returned from the theatre five minutes earlier to find the parlor turned into a veritable conservatory. Exotic blooms were massed in every corner, and Sue and the goodwife had been quite distracted by the shortage of containers in which to display this glory. "Where could he have procured them?" She gestured helplessly. " 'Tis enough to decorate Westminster Abbey."

"Buckingham's conservatories are famed," Nick told her. "Was there a message?"

"Aye." She took a paper from the table, holding it out to him. "He desires me to wear orchids at my breast this evening when we go to court, that he may know *this* gift is acceptable."

"And shall you?" Nick raised an eyebrow at her. She was looking her usual self, he thought, all traces of last night's tension vanished.

Polly shook her head. "Nay. But I shall wear the freesias in the lace of my sleeve, and he may make what he can of that."

Nick could not help chuckling. "Y'are a rogue, Polly. I begin to think you enjoy the prospect of this game."

Some of the mischief faded from her eyes. "In a way, perhaps, I do. Tonight we shall be at court, and you will be there. I may play the elusive wanton on ground that is not the duke's. 'Twill be less of a strain."

"I had thought not to attend this evening," Nick said. "Richard and I thought it sensible to reinforce my indifference to the duke's pursuit. But if you need me, then of course I shall accompany you."

Polly turned away abruptly, beginning to rearrange a bowl of tulips with apparent absorption. She had not expected the normal pattern of her life with Nick to be affected by this conspiracy, yet she should have done. He had his own part to play. So why did it feel as if, having prepared her and thrust her upon this stage of his choosing, he was now withdrawing, leaving her to play the part he considered of paramount importance? But if this spying was what he had intended for her all along, from the earliest moments of their meeting, then it was hardly surprising it should now take precedence over a loving companionship that had simply facilitated his original plan.

"No, of course I do not need you. I had just assumed that you would come, but I see that it will be best if you do not." She heard her voice, cool and even in the small room where the mingled scents of hothouse blooms hung heavy like a stifling, exotic blanket. Paradoxically, instead of imparting the light freshness of spring flowers, they seemed to carry an aura of corruption. An involuntary shudder fingered its way down her back.

Nicholas frowned at her averted back. There was a stiffness about her suddenly, an almost forced neutrality in that normally expressive voice. "What is it, sweetheart?" he said, coming up behind her, placing his hand between her shoulder blades. "Is it that you are frightened?"

"No . . . no, I am not frightened," she replied, moving away from the warm pressure of his hand. "There is nothing to be afeard of. I shall go to court and spin my web around the duke." She turned to face him, smiling brightly. "Mayhap you will be here when I return. Or must you stay at your house this night?"

"I have invited some friends for supper and a card party," he said carefully, watching her face. "But I will come here afterward."

"There is no need," she said with a shrug. "I expect 'twill be late when your friends leave."

"What is it?" he repeated. "When I first came in, you were in great good humor. Something has upset you."

"What could possibly have upset me?" Polly went to pull the bell rope. "The goodwife is waiting to bring up dinner. She has prepared a chine of beef especially for you, since she knows your fondness for it."

Throughout the meal, she chattered in her customary fashion, and Nick put his unease behind him, reflecting that it would not be extraordinary for her moods to fluctuate at this trying time. The greatest service he could offer would be to follow her lead and avoid exacerbating her perfectly natural tension.

The Duke of Buckingham, on the watch for her arrival, was conscious of a most unusual emotion as Mistress Wyat made her entrance into the Long Gallery at Whitehall that evening. He was aware of chagrin. The orchids he had confidently expected to see adorning that matchless bosom were nowhere to be seen.

He moved casually through the throng toward her. "Mistress Wyat. How fortunate we are that you are come to grace us with your presence." There was a sardonic undertone, and his bow was so deep that it could only be considered a mockery.

Polly remembered what Nick had once said about compliments being offered as insults. This was clearly an example. She smiled and curtsied with matching exaggerated depth. "My lord duke, how kind in you to say so." Her fan unfurled, fluttered, then closed with a snap.

The duke's eyes narrowed at these clear signs of her own annoyance. In general, people trembled when George Villiers was at odds with them; they did not return gestures of displeasure in kind. But then she smiled at him, that heart-stopping, radiant smile that made him catch his breath.

"Your Grace, I must thank you for such a pleasing gift." She raised one hand, showing him where a cluster of freesias had been threaded into the lace of her smock sleeve. "As you see, I have put it to good use."

"I am honored, madame," he said, taking her hand and turning it, raising it to inhale of the delicate scent of the flowers. "But I had hoped—"

"Why, sir, you could not expect me to wear orchids with this gown," she interrupted with a tinkling laugh. "Neither would show to advantage."

The duke was obliged to concede that scarlet satin and orchids would not do. She could have chosen to wear another gown, of course, but he was beginning to suspect that the lady was playing a devious game. Well, for as long as it amused him, he would play it with her.

"Lord Kincaid does not accompany you this evening?" He took snuff, his eyes resting casually on that exquisite countenance. Not a flicker passed across it.

"It does not appear so, Your Grace," she returned easily. "I understand he had another engagement."

"I cannot imagine an engagement that could take precedence over escorting such beauty," Buckingham murmured. Polly merely smiled. "D'ye care to listen to the music, madame?" The duke offered her his arm. "The king's musicians are most talented."

Polly acquiescing, they made their way into the music room, where were gathered Buckingham's cronies, the king, and my Lady Castlemaine. The king greeted Polly with flattering attention; his mistress, after a speculative, all-encompassing assessment of Polly's appearance, bade her a bored good evening and addressed Buckingham, pointedly excluding Polly from her conversation.

Polly, ingenuously, wondered what she could have done to offend this powerful lady. She moved closer to the musicians, seeming to give them her full attention while keeping her ears pricked for any useful morsels that might come her way, but it was not until the arrival of Lord Clarendon that anything of interest to the spy occurred.

"What is it, Clarendon?" the king inquired testily as the chancellor bowed before him. "We would not be troubled with business this night, and judging by your somber looks, 'tis business you have on your mind."

This remark was greeted with laughter from those around the king. "Indeed, sir," drawled Buckingham, "methinks you should instruct the musicians to play a dirge. 'Twould better suit the chancellor's mien than their present merriment." This unkind sally drew further amusement at the expense of the old man.

Clarendon bowed again stiffly. "I would ask for a moment's private talk, Your Majesty."

"We are in no mood for your pessimism and strictures, Chancellor. We had thought to have made that clear," snapped His Majesty, tapping his fingers on the arm of his chair. "This is a private gathering we would have in this room, with those disposed to listen to pleasant music and engage in agreeable conversation."

There was nothing for the discomfited Clarendon to do but accept this humiliating dismissal. No sooner had he left than Buckingham said with a contemptuous curl of his lip, "I do not know why Your Majesty continues to tolerate such a dullard. It says much for Your Majesty's generosity that you continue to honor him. But he has outgrown his usefulness."

The king sighed. "I know it, George, I know it. But short of impeachment, what's to be done? He has the support of Parliament."

"He is your minister, sir," reminded Buckingham softly. "Not Parliament's. He holds office at your behest."

The king shrugged. "We will talk no more of it." He

gestured toward the musicians. "Let them play a galliard and we will dance."

Polly spent the entire evening in this select company, and she was under no illusions but that she was invited at Buckingham's request. He danced with her, plied her with refreshment, made every effort to ensure her comfort. She, in turn, trod the razor's edge between coquetry and commitment, so that he could never be sure exactly what she was promising. At the end of the evening, she refused his escort home, and he accepted the refusal with apparent grace.

"You would have me dance to an intricate tune, bud," he said with a wry smile, kissing her hand. "But I'll endeavor to learn the steps."

"You talk in mysteries, sir," Polly said as he handed her into her carriage. "But I must thank you for making my evening so enjoyable."

The carriage lurched forward, and she sank back against the squabs under a wash of exhaustion. Perhaps it would be simpler just to yield, play the part as it had originally been written for her. The thought made her shudder with revulsion. She closed her eyes and imagined how wonderful it would be if she were already in bed, if she did not have to go through the tiresome business of leaving this soothing, swaying darkness, of climbing the stairs, of undressing herself . . .

"Mistress Wyat." The coachman's insistent voice parted the mists of sleep, and she struggled up, heavy-limbed, to climb out of the carriage, heedless in her fatigue of the correct management of skirts and train. She dragged herself up the stairs, thinking wishfully that maybe Sue had waited up for her and would help her with her clothes. But she had not asked her to do so. Wearily she pushed open the parlor door and was shocked by a stab of dismay at the sight of Nick drowsing by the fire. She wanted to be alone tonight, alone with her exhausted body and overstretched mind, alone to find oblivion for the both, out of which would come the strength necessary for the morrow.

Nick came awake the moment she stepped into the room. "Y'are late, sweetheart." Smiling, he stood up, stretched, and came toward her.

"I had thought you intended staying at home this night." She stepped away from him as he would have reached for her, and headed for the door to the bedchamber.

"I have had warmer welcomes," Nick mused, following.

"Your pardon, but I am awearied beyond thought," she said shortly, reaching to loosen her hair from its pins. "If I do not find my bed instantly, I will be asleep on my feet."

"Then let me aid you." He came up behind her, reaching over her shoulders for the creamy swell of her breasts, dropping a kiss on the top of her head.

She pushed his hands away with an impatient gesture that stunned them both. "I do not wish for that, Nick."

"Now, what the devil is this?" There was anger in his puzzlement, and he spun her round to face him, catching her chin, pushing her face up to meet his scrutiny.

"Oh, why will you not let me go to bed?" she cried, tears of frustration sparkling in her eyes. "I am just tired. I have been playing this wretched game all evening . . . I think you are right; it would be better if I surrendered to Buckingham—" Now, why had she said that? Why did words just say themselves sometimes?

"Nay," Nick said fiercely. "I'll not have that."

"Why not?" she demanded. "Until recently, you were quite prepared for it."

"That is true." Nick released her chin and ran his hands through his hair in an uncharacteristically distracted gesture. "But I made an error in assuming that I could tolerate it."

"An error in assuming that we could be of service to each other?" Dear God, she had said it. She looked at him, aghast, searching his face for denial. But it was not there. He had gone very still, the emerald eyes shaded with the truth. The angry words of contradiction that she wanted to hear more than anything, this time did not come.

She turned away from him, cold and empty. "So it does

go back to the beginning, then. I did wonder." She shrugged. " 'Tis not important, I daresay. But I could wish you had been honest with me." With careful concentration, she began to unthread the freesias from her sleeve lace.

Nicholas searched for words. Had he been less than honest with her? He had intended to be, certainly; had intended to use her as an unwitting tool; but so far back, it was surely no longer relevant. He had not wanted her to draw the correct conclusion, though, to remember that long-ago statement. Now he must somehow find the way to put all right, to repair the shattered trust.

"Look at me, Polly," he said quietly.

Reluctantly, she did so. "Nick, I am too weary for this tonight. 'Tis not important." But the bleak misery in those hazel eyes gave the lie to the words.

"I am sorry, but it *is* important, and we will resolve it before we sleep." He knew now what had to be said and spoke with quiet determination. "It is true that in the very beginning I had thought—"

"That you had rescued a would-be whore who could be put to a whore's work to your advantage," she broke in flatly.

"That is the last time you will say such a thing with impunity," Nicholas told her, his voice as quiet and determined as ever. "It was you, if you recall, who first propounded the plan to find your way to the theatre via *my* bed. After which, as I remember, you were kind enough to inform me that if I no longer wished to be your protector, you would find another one." He noted her sudden confusion with some satisfaction. "It struck me at the time that your plan could very well mesh with my own. So yes, your present work with Buckingham was planned at the beginning of our association."

"Why did you not tell me?" she asked in a low voice.

"Because I thought the truth would hurt you, as it has. I have been on the rack!" He spoke now fiercely. "I had promised you to my friends long before I came to love you. I had made a commitment, one I could not in honor renege upon. To ask for your cooperation seemed the only possible way of resolving such a dilemma. But I have never pressed you, have I?"

Polly shook her head in silence as she struggled to make sense of the confused tangle of thoughts and emotions twisting in her weary brain.

"Now, I want you to answer me honestly." Striding toward her, he took her chin again. "Loving you, I would never have asked this of you if I had not already, in another life, made the commitment. Is it not more unpleasant a thought that I might have decided you could serve our purpose *after* I came to love you? That, knowing your revulsion for Buckingham, I could callously demand of you that you share his bed?"

Polly swallowed. Why had she not thought of that? She had feared only manipulation from the beginning, had not questioned the kind of person who could cold-bloodedly conceive the use in such a fashion of one he purported to love.

"Answer me," he insisted, his fingers tightening on her chin.

"Aye, 'tis a much more repugnant thought," she murmured.

"Do you believe that I love you?"

She nodded.

"And have we done with this now?"

Again she nodded.

"And there's to be no more talk of whores and a whore's work."

Polly shook her head.

Nick smiled suddenly. "Lost your tongue, moppet?" he teased gently.

Polly returned the smile tremulously. The relief she felt could not be described. It was as if the weight of the world had rolled from her shoulders. She knew now that she could manage this business with Buckingham, if not with a carefree heart, at least in businesslike fashion. It was simply a task that she was supremely fitted to perform. That was all. It was perfectly simple.

She surrendered herself to the embrace that would provide shield and buckler against the hurts of the world, to the love that would render all arrows harmless, that would drain her of all but the promise of the morrow.

Chapter 15

"Ah, Buckingham, are you come to watch the thespians at work?" Lord Kincaid greeted the duke with a flourish of his plumed hat as the two men met at the front entrance of the Theatre Royal some two weeks later.

"In my humble capacity as playwright, I think to see how Master Killigrew will have my lines spoken," Buckingham responded with a politely self-deprecating smile. " 'Tis an irresistible curiosity, I fear. Or mayhap I mean an irresistible conceit."

Nick laughingly demurred, and the two entered the building, going directly into the auditorium—to be confronted with tumult. The small stage was packed with a milling crowd of actors, scene-setters, painters, and carpenters. Thomas was bellowing in an effort to restore order, but his words were drowned in the general cacophony. Everyone seemed to be shouting at once, and Mistress Polly Wyat's voice rose above them all. She was clutching something to her bosom; tears stood out in her eyes and trembled in the distraught tones.

"They have nearly drowned it, Thomas! How could you have let them do such a thing?"

"Polly, I did not give permission. It was never asked of

me," Killigrew said in exasperation. "Such incidents are not my concern."

"Oh, how can you say that? This is your theatre. Everything that happens in it is your concern. These . . . these brutes are in your employ. What they do *is* your responsibility!" Impassioned, she turned on the group of artisans. "You are murdering louts, every one of you!"

"Polly, please calm yourself. 'Tis only a puppy, and besides, 'tis not drowned." Edward Nestor, Polly's leading man and utterly devoted admirer, attempted to step into the breach. It was an error, since she swung on him, holding her burden beneath his nose in fervent accusation.

"Only a puppy! How could you say such a thing? You have been feeding it like the rest of us." Her voice became choked with angry tears, and Nick, unthinking, stepped quickly toward the stage.

"Nicholas! Thank God!" exclaimed Thomas, seeing him in the gloom of the pit. "Perhaps you can calm her."

Polly swung 'round, crying distressfully, "Oh, Nick . . . Nick, they were drowning the puppy in a bucket, and it was crying so piteously. 'Tis more than half-dead." She tumbled from the stage, still clutching her burden. She did not immediately see Buckingham standing in the shadows as she ran weeping to Nicholas. "See what they have done, love." She held out the sodden scrap in her arms, then fell against Nick's chest.

"What an extraordinary fuss about nothing," Nick said coolly, making no attempt to hold her.

Polly jumped back from him as if she had been burned, her eyes wide with shock and outrage. Then she saw Buckingham behind him, watching her from beneath those drooping lids. There was a moment when her face registered utter dismay as she realized what she might have revealed, then she was saying coldly to Nicholas, "You are as unfeeling as the rest."

"Come now, Mistress Wyat," the duke said, stepping out of the shadows. "I daresay they assumed that the animal would have suffered less by such a death than by being left to roam the streets, starving, a prey to every young bully with his sticks and stones."

It was calm good sense; the drowning of unwanted litters was an inescapable part of life. But it went with life in the Dog tavern, and somehow her sensibilities had become as refined as her present existence. Polly recognized this truth, and it helped her recover herself.

"You are quite right, sir. 'Tis just that I had developed a fondness for the creature." She went back to the stage. "Here, you may do what you can to revive him. I shall take him home with me." She handed the puppy to one of the guilty men, brushed her hands off, and turned back to Thomas. "Shall we continue?"

Buckingham sat in the pit, apparently watching the rehearsal, but in fact he took in little. Her voice: *See what they have done, love.* The way she had run to Kincaid: so naturally, as if this man who had gone to such pains to give the impression of studied indifference to his mistress were her only resource from pain; such confidence she had had until he had responded with that coldness. And the disbelieving shock with which she had jumped away from him . . . until she had seen Buckingham himself. There had been fear and dismay on her face then, just for a minute.

What the devil did it mean? Buckingham's expression took on a look that any who knew him would read with alarm. If Mistress Wyat was playing a deeper game than he had believed, then he would discover the truth without delay. Quietly, he rose and left the theatre.

Nick registered the duke's departure, but gave no sign. Instead he sat damning sexually incontinent dogs, Polly's soft heart, and the callous pragmatism of the artisan who saw in an unwanted animal merely another mouth to feed. The rehearsal was not going well. Polly was tense, Edward Nestor overanxious after her scathing response to his attempt to ease the situation, and Thomas was exasperated. Secure in the knowledge that there was now no one but himself as audience in the theatre, Nicholas got up and went forward to the stage.

"Your pardon, Thomas, but I think you'll all be better for a recess."

"I daresay y'are right, Nick." Thomas wiped his brow with a cambric handkerchief. "Everything is going awry. Take Polly and that damned puppy home. We must trust to luck and the gods this afternoon."

Polly came to the forefront of the stage. "The puppy could live in your stables, could he not, Nick?"

"I do not see why not," Nick said, then softly, "Say a kind word to Edward, moppet. He is looking most crestfallen, and it will not aid his performance this afternoon."

Polly glanced over to her hangdog colleague. She gave Nick a rueful smile and went over to Edward. "I do beg your pardon for being so sharp, Edward. 'Twas most unjust of me, but I was greatly distressed."

The young man's face cleared like the sky after a storm. "Oh, pray, do not mention it, Polly. I spoke hastily. Shall we see how the puppy is now?" The two went backstage in perfect amity, and Thomas sighed with relief.

"How was I to know she would take such a thing so much to heart?" he asked Nick, who still stood in the pit before the stage. "The wretched animal has been a complete nuisance, always underfoot. It could not possibly be allowed to stay here. Why would she react like that?" He shrugged at the unfathomable temperaments of actors, and female actors in particular.

"He seems all right." Polly reappeared, holding the dog. "A little subdued, but he is quite warm and breathing well." She held him out for Nick's inspection.

It was quite the most unprepossessing creature, Nick thought dispassionately, scrawny, with overlarge ears and feet. But then, ugliness was hardly sufficient reason to be condemned to a watery grave. He reached up and lifted Polly and the puppy to the floor of the auditorium. "Come, let us go home. We'll give the dog to John Coachman to take to the stables."

Outside the theatre, Polly said hesitantly, "Do you think Buckingham noticed anything strange, Nick?"

"I do not know," Nick replied honestly. "Let us hope that we both recovered quickly enough to allay suspicion."

For the next week, Buckingham played a waiting game. He issued no invitations, sent no little gifts, was agreeable when in Mistress Wyat's company but singled her out for no special attentions; and he watched her.

"I wonder if he thinks to pique me by this treatment," Polly suggested to Nicholas and Richard. "It would be a logical tactic. So far I have been the one offering, withdrawing, tantalizing. Mayhap he thinks to play me at my own game."

"If so, how do you think you should react?" asked Richard. They were walking in St. James's Park, in the company of the majority of the court enjoying the balmy April sunshine.

"I think I must approach him," Polly said. "If he's to believe that my eventual surrender is inevitable, that I am merely negotiating the price with my advances and retreats, then in this instance I must advance, humble and anxious as to what I could have done to offend."

Nick tried to identify the unease he felt at the turn matters had taken. If Buckingham had sensed things were not as they were presented, it would explain his withdrawal. Polly, by the tactics she proposed, would put his mind at rest. Yet Nick could not like it. However, he had no concrete reasons for objecting, so gave the scheme his agreement.

That evening His Grace of Buckingham found himself the object of the most flattering attentions from Mistress Polly Wyat. Those enormous soft eyes were fixed upon him, anxiously questioning. Her mouth quivered with unhappiness as she implored in a whisper to know her offense. A small hand rested upon his sleeve. Placing his own hand over hers, he assured her that there was no offense and begged that she would be his guest at a small supper party after the performance on the morrow. The invitation was accepted with alacrity and a show of pleasure that could not fail to gratify.

And both participants in the game went home well satisfied with the outcome of their tactics.

The following afternoon, however, Nicholas found a very thoughtful Polly preparing to go to the theatre for the afternoon's performance.

"I have received a note from Buckingham," she told him without preamble. "A confirmation of the invitation to supper, at the Half Moon tavern, and the most fervent request that I not delay in order to change my costume after the performance."

Kincaid said nothing for a minute. He stood very still behind her as she sat before her mirror, his hands playing absently with her hair. He stared over her head at the wall beyond as if it might reveal some secret. "It is a breeches part you play today, is it not?"

"Aye." Twisting her head, she looked up at him over her shoulder. "Buckingham is aware of that, I am sure."

"Doubtless," Nick agreed with a dry smile. "And like everyone else, finds the sight of your figure in such attire enough to inflame him to madness. I cannot fault his taste in wishing you to grace his party in such costume. But if you agree to do so, you are tacitly giving consent for whatever sport he may have in mind."

"I think, in this instance, I must do as he asks," Polly said. "To refuse would make nonsense of my approach last evening." Reaching behind her, she took his hands, smiling at him in the mirror. "I will pander to his taste in this matter, but will seem to fail to see an ulterior motive, and therefore will not respond. After all, have not some ladies of the court amused themselves on occasion by dressing as men?"

"That was different. It was a piece of indecorous mischief undertaken by a group of ladies who wished to shock. Buckingham is giving you a most definite message with this request. He is asking for an overt display of a kind that could only have one meaning. I cannot like it, Polly."

"But if I refuse, we might as well forget the plan," she pointed out. "For that would be giving him a most definite message in return. 'Tis a supper party in a tavern, Nicholas, hardly a bawdy house. What could happen?"

Nick frowned, chewing his lip. Then he sighed. "I suppose it is safe enough. You will enjoy your supper, at all events. The tavern is known for its cooking. I will send you, as usual, in my carriage, and John Coachman will wait for you. You will then be free to leave whenever you wish."

"That will do well," she agreed matter-of-factly, tucking her hair beneath a round velvet hat. "If I arrive in your coach, the duke will realize at the outset that I am still not prepared to take the sport further tonight, for all that I will provoke in my breeches." She turned away from the mirror, offering a placatory smile. "It is no great matter, love. Indeed, there is some pleasure in making game of Buckingham. I must use my wits, and that in itself gives some satisfaction."

"Aye." He picked up her cloak. "Put this on; it has begun to rain." He draped the garment around her shoulders, then said soberly, "Moppet, you must have a care. I am not saying that your wits are not as sharp as Buckingham's, but he's been using his a deal longer than you have yours. Do not become overconfident."

"I am not, am I?" She frowned at him.

"I do not know." Nick shook his head. "You are a deal more relaxed in the part than you were at the outset, and you might, therefore, underestimate the risks. You are crossing swords with a master duelist, and I would have you remember that at all times."

There was a wickedness to the performance Polly gave that afternoon that did little for Kincaid's peace of mind. She missed no opportunity to flaunt the curves of hip and thigh, the neat turn of her ankle, the soft roundness of her calves—womanly attributes only ever seen in public on the stage. Her asides were delivered to the audience with a pert mischief that brought gales of delighted laughter ringing to the glazed cupola. At the uproarious conclusion, when the pretty young man was discovered to be endowed with a bosom of definitely female contours, Polly offered her bared breasts to the audience with a gesture of invitation that brought King Charles and his court to their feet on a shout of approval.

"Something more than usual has bitten her this afternoon," Killigrew murmured to Nicholas as they stood in the wings, watching the play. "Not that I have any objections, you understand. It is a supreme performance. Even the king is on his feet."

And George Villiers, thought Nick, realizing that it was for Buckingham that Polly was acting this afternoon. She was issuing an invitation that would entrap any man. If Buckingham already believed that she was well on the way to fulfilling her promises, he would now be convinced of it. He would be slavering this evening, and would meet a light coolness for his pains, even as her costume taunted him.

Nick's unease blossomed into anxiety. Did she really understand how dangerous was this game she played? he thought with a sudden savage stab of anger. At the moment she was behaving as if she played with a harmless fool instead of one of the most powerful and deadly men in the land.

"Methinks they have enjoyed the spectacle!" Laughing, Polly came off the stage, dancing up to the two men, her hair, released from the peruke that had provided part of her masculine disguise, tumbling down her back, adding spice to the wanton provocation of her costume.

"They would need to be something less than men to fail to do so," Nick snapped, looking at her as she stood, bright-eyed with excitement, her shirt still open, revealing her breasts in all their creamy, rose-tipped beauty. She was still as unselfconscious as ever about her body. The thought did nothing to appease him.

"Are you displeased?" Polly asked, puzzled at this unwarranted annoyance.

"God's grace, why should I be?" he returned. "Do up your shirt. I realize such exposure was necessary onstage, but it is hardly necessary now."

Polly gulped, drawing her shirt together. "You are be-come uncommon prudish, my Lord Kincaid." Her chin went up, and she met the anger in his eyes with her own.

Thomas Killigrew stepped back into the shadows. It was a most interesting exchange, and he could feel some sympathy for Kincaid. It must be galling for a man to see his mistress become the common property of every man who cared to attend the king's theatre, particularly when the mistress in question took such obvious pleasure in the sensation.

"Pray excuse me, my lord. His Grace of Buckingham awaits," Polly was saying frigidly. "I must put up my hair." With a perfectly executed bow, her plumed hat passing through the air in the elegant gesture of an accomplished gallant, she took a mocking leave of her teeth-gnashing lover.

Polly greeted the stolid figure of John Coachman before stepping into the carriage emblazoned with the Kincaid arms. She sat in the darkness, gnawing her lip, trying to find the equilibrium she knew she would need for the hours that lay ahead. Why had Nick snapped at her like that? It was unreasonable that at such a time he should become this acid-tongued stranger. He knew what lay ahead of her. For all that she seemed more relaxed in the part, she still had to overcome the deadly loathing, to rid herself of the slimy tendrils of apprehension whenever she was in Buckingham's orbit. While she laughed and flirted, promised and withheld, she was queasy with fear as she recognized the power of the man with whom she played her reckless game.

George Villiers watched her arrival from the window of the upstairs parlor at the Half Moon tavern. Just what had her performance this afternoon meant? Well, he was about to find out. The time had come for Mistress Wyat to commit herself. He walked to the door, opening it, standing ready to greet his guest as she ascended the narrow staircase.

"My lord duke." Polly greeted him with a bow similar to that she had given Kincaid a short while before—except that this salute was carefully engineered to entice, displaying her figure to best advantage. "I am not late, I trust."

"By no means." Smiling, he invited her into the parlor. "I am honored that you did not stay to change your dress."

"My haste was too great, Your Grace," she responded. "You will forgive such anxiety."

"Rarely have I been more complimented." His gaze ran over her as she stood in the empty parlor, trying to conceal her surprised dismay at the absence of other guests. "A glass of wine? I am sure you are in need of refreshment after that stellar performance this afternoon. You won all hearts, bud."

Polly accepted the compliment with an inclination of her head, the touch of a smile, and took the glass of wine he proffered. "I need not have been anxious about being late, it would seem," she observed carefully. "Your other guests have not yet arrived."

"But did I not say that this was to be a private party?" The duke looked credibly discomposed. "I do beg your pardon if I led you to expect more amusing company than that my own poor wit can provide." He gestured to the supper table. "At least I can assure you that your palate will not go ungratified."

Polly's thoughts whirled as she felt the trap closing. If Buckingham was going to force the issue in this private room in a tavern where all ears would have been paid to be closed, then there was nothing she would be able to do to prevent him.

He came up behind her, and she felt his breath on the back of her neck. She started violently as his hand flattened against the curve of her hip outlined by the breeches. "My lord duke—"

"Such formality, bud," he interrupted, his voice low and caressing. "I have a name."

"And I, my lord duke, have no desire for a tête-à-tête," she said, finding that fear could be transmuted to anger with little difficulty under the prod of desperation. "I do not find trickery conducive to intimacy. You invited me to a small supper party, and it was that invitation I accepted. You will excuse me. My coachman is waiting."

"Just as I thought," he said softly. "Let us have done with

games. What do you want, Mistress Wyat? I am prepared to meet your price, if you will but declare it."

"So crude, Your Grace." She lifted a disdainful eyebrow, trying to stiffen her knees as rage flamed in his narrowed, hooded eyes. "Perhaps I am not to be bought."

"Everyone has a price," he said, softly menacing. "I will find yours, make no mistake."

Polly backed to the door. The duke watched her, knowing her fear. He made no attempt to stop her, but as she reached the door, he said gently, "I do not know what game you think to play, wench, but I am a poor sportsman unless it be a sport I enjoy. I do not appear to be enjoying this one, I should warn you."

"I do not know what you mean, sir." Her hand on the latch, escape now secured, Polly's courage returned. "But I accept only those invitations that mean what they say. I do not care to be deceived." On that note of hauteur, she beat a retreat, the flash of Dutch courage carrying her as far as the interior of the coach. Once there, in the swaying darkness, hearing the reassuring pounding of Kincaid's cattle taking her home, fear swamped her anew so that she shook as if in the grip of an ague. Buckingham had declared his intent. Who was she, a puny, insignificant, Newgate-born bastard with a modicum of talent and beauty, to withstand that intent?

Polly tumbled out of the carriage almost before John Coachman could let down the footstep. The street door was unlocked. She whisked inside, drawing breath with a wash of relief in the dim light of the tiny hall. Once safe behind her own door, the surge of panic ebbed, to be replaced by a bitter, self-directed anger. She marched upstairs, banging open the door of the parlor, expecting to see Nicholas and not sure whether she wished to or not. But the chamber contained only Susan, who turned from the table where she was arranging a dish of sturgeon and a bowl of figs, presumably for Nick's supper.

"Why, Polly." Sue's round eyes opened even wider as she

took in the other's astonishingly daring costume. "We wasn't expectin' ye 'till later."

"I did not expect to be back," Polly said shortly. "My lord is not here?"

"Said as 'ow he'd return for supper at ten," Susan informed her. " 'Ave ye been out dressed like that? I never seen nothin' like it."

"Then you should pay a visit to the theatre," Polly said between compressed lips. She threw her plumed hat into the corner of the room, dragged off the heavily embroidered coat, tossing it to follow the hat, and tore at the buttons of the satin waistcoat, her fingers as vicious as the furious thoughts roiling in her head. For some reason, her costume seemed to symbolize the humiliation of the evening's debacle. A wanton in a whore's costume, she had revealed her fear to Buckingham and had thus ruined everything. The plan lay in tatters because her courage had failed her. She had offered a harlot's tawdry provocation, then had turned and run like a child who found her challenge taken up and the consequences greater than she had bargained for.

The waistcoat flew across the room as Susan stood, stunned into immobility by this extraordinary divesting. The high-heeled pumps, under the influence of a vicious kick, arced through the air to crash against the far wall. Polly yanked off her satin breeches and the silk shirt, dropping both to the floor and stamping on them, before pulling off her stockings.

Polly was well aware that the violence she was doing to her clothes was sacrilege. Her richly elaborate costume represented a substantial financial investment for the king's company; technically it was the king's property, and it was a property to be treated with the greatest care. If an actor was required to lie upon the stage boards, sheeting was placed over the bare floor to protect the garments, and mock battles were always undertaken with the greatest caution. However, such considerations carried no weight under a flood tide of temper designed to wash from her the bitter taste of anger and disgust.

"God's good grace!" Nick stood in the doorway, staring at the sight of Polly, stripped to her skin, poised in a rich, vibrant sea of satin and embroidery. Heedless of this ejaculation, she kicked at the discarded breeches.

"Pick those clothes up!" Nicholas closed the door smartly behind him, trying to sort out this astonishing scene.

"I hate 'em!" Polly spat, catching the breeches on a toe, lifting her foot clear of the floor. "I'll not wear 'em again!" An agile high kick sent the garment soaring through the air.

"That is a matter you may discuss with Killigrew," Nicholas declared. "Pick them up at once! No, not you!" He spun round on Susan, who, with a frightened whimper, had run to the corner of the room, bending to gather up the fallen coat. "Leave it where it is and go downstairs."

The girl dropped the coat to the floor, scurrying from the room like a scared hedgehog.

Nicholas had no idea what could have caused this amazing tantrum, but decided that explanations would have to wait. For the moment, he would deal with the fact itself. "Pick up the clothes, Polly," he repeated quietly, walking over to the sideboard, pouring himself a glass of wine.

"No," said Polly, with another disdainful kick.

Nick turned to face her as she stood, sublimely indifferent to her nakedness, hands planted on hips, head thrown back, defiance and something else lurking in the topaz depths of her eyes. It was the something else that interested him, but he could not get at it until he had dealt with the defiance. "Pick them up, Polly."

It was at this moment that Richard De Winter stepped through the street door to come face-to-face with the panicked Sue at the foot of the stairs. "Good even, Susan," he greeted pleasantly, moving to set one foot on the stairs. "Lord Kincaid is above?"

"Yes . . . yes, please, m'lord," stammered Susan, the image of the stark naked Polly filling her internal vision. "But I don't think as 'ow 'es receivin'," she gasped, stepping on the bottom stair, barring his progress with her stubby body.

Richard surveyed this courageous stance with a quirked

eyebrow. "If that is so, he may tell me himself, may he not?" he observed equably.

Susan's jaw dropped as she struggled to find some unarguable reason to prevent his lordship's progress. But he was not to be prevented. Taking the girl by the shoulders, he calmly moved her out of his way, saying good-humoredly, "Be off, wench. I'll not intrude where I'm not welcomed, so ye need have no fears." Then he ascended the stairs. At the top, he knocked hard on the parlor door.

Within, impasse still held. Polly started at the knock, but other than that, made no move. Nicholas continued to look at her over the lip of his wineglass. "Who is it?" he called.

"Richard."

"Your pardon, but I crave a moment's indulgence, Richard," Kincaid answered, not taking his eyes off Polly. "Now," he said softly. "Whether you pick up those clothes and put on your nightgown *before* I bid Richard entrance is a matter for your choice. But pick them up, you will. Make no mistake."

Pride and common sense warred, every engagement played out visibly on the mobile countenance. Nicholas was obliged to school his features with the utmost severity as he watched the battle. The least indication of his inner amusement, and he would lose.

Common sense won. With a muttered "Lord of hell!" Polly bent to scoop up the abused garments, stalking to the bedchamber, her arms full. "You have missed a stocking," Nick pointed out affably. "In the far corner."

Polly flung a Billingsgate oath at him, grabbed up the stocking, and stormed into the bedchamber, the door shivering on its hinges under the ferocity of its closing.

"Pray come in, Richard." Nick went to open the parlor door. "My apologies for the discourtesy in keeping you without."

"Not at all, dear fellow." Richard raised an eyebrow. "Trouble?"

"It would appear so." Nick frowned. "Wine?"

"Thank you. I thought Polly was to be with Buckingham."

"She was. But something has occurred to put her in the devil of a temper."

"If it is anger rather than distress, my friend, it will be the more easily mended," observed Richard, sipping his wine.

"I have the feeling the two are intertwined," Nick said gravely. "But she was in no mood for any kind of reasonable converse. It was necessary to get her attention first."

Richard smiled, spreading the wide tails of his coat as he sat down. "I see. And now you have it . . . ?"

"We may endeavor to dig for the cause," Nick said briskly. He strode to the bedchamber door, calling with clipped authority, "Polly, come out here. I wish to talk to you."

She came out immediately, respectably clad in her nightgown, her hair braided demurely over one shoulder; it was very clear from both expression and posture that the tantrum was over. Indeed, she appeared subdued, if anything.

"Now, what lay behind that unseemly display?" Nick demanded, keeping his tone unconciliatory. "I would not be in your shoes if Killigrew finds that those garments have suffered from such treatment."

Two spots of color pricked on Polly's cheekbones. "Will you tell him?"

She looked very young and vulnerable suddenly, as if defeated by events. Nicholas dropped the pose. "What has happened, sweetheart?" Taking her in his arms, he stroked her back, holding her tightly against him.

"I am so angry with myself!" Polly exclaimed, her voice muffled against his shoulder. "I have ruined everything, and I do not know how to tell you how stupid I have been." Pushing herself away from him, she began to pace the room, rubbing her hands together in angry frustration as she poured out the tale of the evening's events to a silent and attentive audience.

"I ran away," she finished on a note of despair. "I could not carry the play through. Buckingham knew I was afraid.

He knew then I had never had any intention of willingly yielding him what he wanted. So now the plan is destroyed. I am sorry." She looked at the two men, twisting her hands into impossible knots. "I thought I was a better actor than I am, and now we must all pay the price of my conceit."

"There is no need for self-reproach, Polly." De Winter stood up, crossing to the sideboard to refill his glass. "You could not expect to best Buckingham in such a situation."

"But I was overconfident," Polly murmured, glancing at Nick, who still had said nothing. "I deliberately made the invitation irresistible." She bit her lip. "That was why you were so vexed this afternoon, wasn't it?"

"I suppose so," Nick said. "I became afeard suddenly that perhaps you did not fully realize what you were doing."

"And you were right," she said miserably.

"Your performance this afternoon could certainly have been construed as most definite invitation if one felt it were directed at oneself," Richard agreed with a smile. "But you have committed only the faults of youth and inexperience, child. There is nothing to be gained in bewailing."

"Aye," Kincaid agreed with reassuring firmness. "Wisdom is acquired with years, my love. And few mistakes are irretrievable. You must behave publicly with Buckingham as if the incident had never happened. You may rest assured that he will respond in kind."

Polly walked to the window. She had not told them of the duke's threat, and now decided that she would not. It would alarm Nicholas, and she had already caused him sufficient upset. "The game is over, is it not?" Slowly she turned back to the room, scanning their faces.

"I think so," Richard said. "But we have been able to win the support of the Duke of York as a result of your findings. He will not willingly see his father-in-law ousted as chancellor. He has also said that he will appoint the Duke of Albermarle to act alone as Lord High Admiral in his own absence with the navy. That will ensure that Buckingham and his friends do not divide the responsibilities and the spoils of the post." He smiled, coming to lay a hand on her shoulder. "You have done well, my dear. One cannot expect to achieve miracles. We advance slowly over rough terrain. But we *have* advanced . . . Besides—" He walked over to the table, selecting an apple from the copper fruit bowl, tossing it thoughtfully between his hands "—I do not think there will be inclination or opportunity for plotting on either side for a while. It was for that reason that I came this evening."

"Oh?" Nick looked at him inquiringly. "You have news?"

"Aye." Richard bit into the apple. "There is talk of the royal family's moving to Hampton Court within the month."

There was a long, considering silence. A candle spluttered under a breeze from the open window. "The plague?" Nick said eventually.

Richard nodded. "A dozen houses have been shut up in the city already. 'Tis to be hoped it will contain the outbreak, but there are those who advise greater caution. It is feared that this may be more than a few isolated incidents, as occurred in December."

Polly had heard the rumors in the last week or two, but had thought them no more than the tales of alarmists. True, the shutting up of afflicted households was a drastic move on the part of the city aldermans and justices, but she had thought little of it, so wrapped up was she in the excitements, strains, and joys of her present existence. But now, the thought that the king and court were planning to leave a city where the sickness lurked put a different complexion on the matter. Perhaps there was real cause for fear? She looked into the eyes of De Winter, then turned to Nick. The answer was clearly to be read as they both returned her gaze in grave silence.

She turned again to the window, looking down on the familiar bustle of Drury Lane, where links flickered, lighting a walker home, carriages rolled, lamps shone yellow behind casement windows, witness to the warmth and life within. It was an ordinary London street where the business of birthing

and dying went on in ageless fashion, according to social
ritual and at nature's pace. What would happen if a wrench
were thrown to alter that pace, to destroy the rituals?

A gray specter filled her vision, and her scalp contracted as
a graveyard shiver ran down her spine. She looked again at
her companions; and saw that the specter had touched them,
also.

Chapter 16

"I will *not* travel with Lady Margaret!" Polly repeated fiercely, for the tenth time in the last hour.

Nicholas struggled to hang on to the remaining threads of temper and patience. "You cannot expect me to make two journeys, Polly. Do you really imagine I should leave you here, escort Margaret and the household to her brother in Leicestershire, then come back to take you to Wilton House?"

"I do not expect you to do anything," Polly said, her mouth stubborn. "I have asked nothing of you, have I? I understand that you have a duty to your family, but I am not a member of your family. Look after Lady Margaret, and I will make my own way to Wiltshire. I can go on the public stage." Turning her back to him, she looked out of the tight-shut window onto Drury Lane, languishing under a May heat wave fiercer than any other in living memory.

There were few people about; those there were walked in the middle of the street, well away from doorways and side streets where they might find themselves suddenly in contact with a fellow human being—one who might be distempered, even without his knowing it. They carried handkerchiefs soaked in vinegar pressed to mouths and noses, for it was said that one drew in death when one breathed.

She noticed that two more houses across the street bore the red cross and the scrawled letters of the only prayer left for the inhabitants to pray: Lord have mercy upon us. The watchman leaned against one of the doors, absently picking his teeth. A window opened above him; a head appeared. The watchman stood away from the door, looking up. Then, with a short nod, he went off up the street. To fetch the physician, perhaps, Polly wondered, or the nurse; not the dead cart yet; that would not start its rounds until nightfall, when the city would resound to the melancholy tolling of the bell, and the cry to "Bring out your dead."

Nick stood looking at her averted back as he fought with an anger fueled by desperation and fear. The longer they remained in this city-become-lazar-house, the more inescapable their fate. The court, anxious to get as far from London as possible, had moved from Hampton Court to the seat of the Earl of Pembroke, Wilton House, near Salisbury. People were fleeing the city in droves; he had an absolute family duty to ensure the safety of his sister-in-law and the household dependent upon him. And Polly was telling him that that duty did not encompass her.

If she were his wife . . . No, now was hardly the appropriate moment to bring up that particular matter. He had intended, once the wretched affair with Buckingham was dealt with, to tackle the question at leisure. It was a subject of some considerable complexity, involving as it would the inevitable, boundless opposition of his sister-in-law; questions of residence, both Margaret's and theirs; and not least his own unresolved difficulties with the idea of sharing his wife with the theatregoing public. It was hard enough for him to share his mistress with an outward show of equanimity—but the mother of his children! In the last weeks, however, all issues had become subsumed under a brutal and undiscriminating scourge. Death, and its avoidance, were the only relevancies at present.

"I am not asking you to travel in the same coach as Margaret." There was a frayed edge to his voice that warned Polly she was pushing against his outer limits. "You may travel in your own vehicle, which, like Margaret's, will be under the protection of my outriders and postilions."

"And what about the stops we must make along the way?" demanded Polly, unable to understand how he could not see how impossible it would be for her. "Must I stay under the same roof, or will you scout the countryside each night for two suitable neighboring inns in which to house your—" She was about to say "whore" in imitation of Lady Margaret, but caught herself in time. "Your mistress and your sister?"

Nicholas gave up the attempt to reason with her. "I will make what arrangements I deem necessary," he said. "If you oblige me to use force to achieve your compliance, I will do so. But in such a situation you will find your position much more embarrassing than anything you fear at the moment, I can promise you."

"Dear me," came a quiet voice from the door. "I do beg your pardon for intruding, but matters must be serious if Nicholas is obliged to resort to threats." Richard stepped into the parlor, closing the door behind him. "I am come to bid you farewell. I leave for Wilton House this evening, and assume you will be gone yourselves without delay."

"I will *not* travel with Lady Margaret!" Polly cried in despair. "And Nicholas is going to make me! Can you imagine what it would be like, Richard?"

"Worse than being dead of the plague, I suppose," snapped Nick.

Richard frowned, stroking his chin thoughtfully. "As usual, I suffer from the dubious gift of seeing both sides. It would be wretchedly uncomfortable for you, Polly, but Nick cannot be in two places at once, and neither you nor Margaret can travel without his escort."

"I am quite willing to do so," muttered Polly, then her eyes lit up. She clapped her hands with inspiration. "Why cannot I travel with you, Richard? If you go to Wilton House, we may go together, and Nick can join us there once he has seen his sister-in-law safe with her brother."

There was a short silence, while Polly looked hopefully

between the two of them. "I would not be any trouble," she assured hesitantly.

Richard laughed. "My dear, I should enjoy your company. Will you entrust me with the charge, Nick?"

"If you are willing to take on such an intractable wench, then you have my blessing . . . and my condolences," replied Nicholas, his annoyance for the moment unabated. "If she has Susan with her, at least you will not be obliged to act as tiring woman!"

"Well, of all the things to say!" spluttered Polly, pink-cheeked. "As if I would ever—"

"You are capable of anything," Nick interrupted. "It was not so long ago you unilaterally decided I would make a suitable patron and proceeded to adopt me—quite without my say-so, as I recall."

"You are unjust," Polly accused, blushing furiously.

"My patience is not inexhaustible, and you have tried it sorely," Nick retorted in explanation. "If you are to leave with Richard, you had best call Susan and get on with your packing."

"I will leave you to make peace." Richard, ever the diplomat, went to the door. "I will delay my departure until tomorrow sunup, Polly. Can you be ready by then?"

Polly assured him that she could, and the door clicked shut in his wake. She turned to Nick with a tentative smile. "I did not mean to try your patience, love. I do not wish to part bad friends, and you will be all of three weeks upon your journey." The smile hovered on her lips, the anxiety of an innocent unjustly accused swam in the deep forest pools of her eyes, her chin trembled, and her shoulders sagged a little. Nick groaned in defeat, reaching for her with ungentle hands.

On a glorious morning at the end of June, thoughts and images of a plague-ridden metropolis no longer sharply etched in mind and memory, Lord Kincaid and Mistress Wyat were riding through the fields skirting the park of Wilton House. Polly was atop a broad-backed piebald of sluggish disposition. Her own disposition left much to be desired.

"I will not have my bridle held any longer!" Polly declared on a lamentably petulant note, plucking crossly at the leading rein, which her companion held loosely with his own. "You said you would teach me how to ride, not how to sit like a cabbage whilst you lead my horse."

"For as long as you sit like a cabbage, so shall I hold the leading rein," Kincaid said equably, waiting for the explosion. It came with predictable force.

"I do not sit like a cabbage—"

"Your pardon, Polly," he murmured. "I thought that was what I heard you say."

"You are detestable," she said with feeling. "I can make this stupid animal go forward and left and right and stop. When will you allow me to do it alone?"

"When I am satisfied that your seat is secure enough," he responded coolly. "You do not wish to fall off, do you?"

"I am not going to fall off," Polly muttered. "It is so mortifying! There is to be a hawking expedition on the morrow, and I would wish to go. But I cannot when you lead me like a baby."

" 'Tis your foolish pride that will prevent you," Nick said, with a touch of acerbity. "There is no reason to be abashed simply because you were not bred to horsemanship from childhood. You will be a good horsewoman, I promise you. But for the moment you are learning, and I am teaching you. So do as you are bid and cease this shrewish railing, else I abandon the task."

Polly glowered at him from beneath the wide brim of her black beaver hat. "I do not need this leading rein. I will prove it to you."

"Indeed you shall," Nick said soothingly. "By the end of the week, if we ride every day, you shall then show me exactly what you can do on your own."

Polly compressed her lips. She had no intention of waiting until the end of the week, and she had every intention of joining the hawking expedition on the morrow—without another hand on her bridle.

They turned onto a broad ride running among majestic oaks, chestnuts, and copper beeches; the sun filtered through the leaves, dappling the mossy ground beneath the horses' hooves with dancing will-o'-the-wisps. The sound of voices drifted through the sultry air along the path ahead.

Polly pulled back on the piebald's reins; the stolid animal came to a puzzled halt, tensing his neck against the contrary tug of the leading rein.

"Now what is the matter?" Nick drew rein.

"Can you not hear the voices? 'Tis Lady Castlemaine and Buckingham," Polly whispered, trying to turn her mount, who became thoroughly confused by the conflicting instructions he was receiving from leading rein and bridle. "They are coming this way, and I will not be seen by them like this." She tugged again at the rein Kincaid held. "Lady Castlemaine never loses an opportunity to say something belittling, and I'll not put the weapon in her hand . . . Move, you stubborn, stupid animal!" Frantically, she urged the piebald to turn. Nick, grinning, provided the necessary encouragement with his own rein.

"Perhaps we had better try a canter," he said, still grinning, "If you've a mind to outdistance them." He set his own mount to a trot, and Polly's piebald reluctantly increased its speed. Nick did not ride his powerful chestnut during these hours of instruction, since Sulayman would have difficulty keeping his pace to the plodding of the animal his lordship had chosen for Polly, but even the calm mare he was riding today, once she got into her stride, threatened to outstrip the piebald lumbering into a reluctant canter on the mare's flank.

They broke through the trees into the open fields again. "Can we stop now?" Nick called over his shoulder, throwing her a teasing, glinting smile. "Have we removed ourselves far enough from the danger of mockery, or should we attempt a gallop?"

" 'Tis not funny," Polly expostulated, bouncing in the

saddle as her horse slowed abruptly, throwing up his head with a disgusted snort. "She would regale everyone this evening with the story, and I cannot abide the snickers." Her voice automatically took on the exact inflections of Lady Castlemaine's. "Why, my dear Mistress Wyat, how I admire your courage to take up horsemanship in this way." A trill, in perfect imitation of the countess, accompanied the statement, as she continued in the same voice, "I am too full of conceit, I fear, to expose myself by attempting to learn something in the company of those who cannot imagine what it would be like to be a novice. One is so inelegant, initially—"

"That'll do, Polly," Nick interrupted, although he was laughing. "Why should you imagine that people will mock you?"

"Have you not noticed, sir, how the female court follows where the countess leads in such matters?" Polly asked with asperity. "For some reason, ever since I arrived here, it has pleased my lady to make game of me when she can. I do not understand what I could have done to offend her."

Nick looked curiously at his companion. Had she really no understanding of the nature and workings of feminine jealousy? Surely she had to realize that a woman who commanded the admiration, bordering in some cases on besottedness, of practically every man who crossed her path was going to fall foul of her own sex. The Countess of Castlemaine was not alone in fearing that in these close quarters the beautiful young actor would attract the more than friendly eye of the king. At the moment, King Charles treated this young female member of his theatre company with an easy familiarity, akin to that shown her by Killigrew and De Winter. She responded with the natural unselfconsciousness that she exhibited to those others, and it was not hard to see that the king, accustomed to the flatterers and the overawed, was pleased with her, and found her company amusing. But Nicholas had the shrewd suspicion that it would go no further than that. King Charles was far too busy juggling the competing claims of Frances Stewart and Lady

Castlemaine to add to his seraglio one who would infuriate them both.

"The men do not make game of you," Nicholas said now, watching her. "Perhaps therein lies your answer."

Polly frowned. "Lady Castlemaine could not possibly be jealous of me. She is the wife of an earl and the king's mistress, while I am nothing. True, she does not know exactly how much of nothing I am, but unless she wished to be your mistress also, I cannot imagine why she should be envious." She offered him that mischievous, heart-stopping smile, and chuckled. "Of course, I could hardly blame her for wishing such a thing. You are a great deal more handsome than either the king or the Earl of Castlemaine. But I should tell you that I will not permit it. Should you succumb to blandishment, sir, you will take damaged goods to another's bed."

"Why, you ferocious shrew!" exclaimed Nicholas. "I had not thought you bloodthirsty!"

"Merely careful of mine own, my lord," she said sweetly. Then the laughter died from her eyes. "Methinks His Grace of Buckingham follows my Lady Castlemaine's lead. Since he arrived from his country estate two days ago, he has had barely a word for me, civil or otherwise. I have done as you said and behaved as if that last meeting had not occurred, but he has not forgotten it. I know it." She shivered in the warm summer air. "Have you marked the way he looks at me sometimes?"

Nicholas had, indeed, noticed the covert and still covetous gaze of His Grace resting upon Mistress Wyat, and it had certainly occurred to him that Buckingham had possibly not left the field. However, he could see no immediate cause for alarm. "I cannot imagine what he could do to harm you here," he said. "There are too many eyes upon him. Nay, he will have forgotten his annoyance by the autumn, I'll lay odds, if you continue to treat him with a purely social courtesy. He will find other fish to fry."

Polly shrugged in apparent acceptance of this reassurance. But she could not feel completely easy. Nick had arrived just over a week ago, and until Buckingham's appearance, this country sojourn had proved delightful, apart from the needling of the king's mistress and her ilk, and Nick's infuriating intransigence over the matter of the leading rein. There was a constant round of entertainments—masques and dances, tennis matches, hunting and hawking—and she found herself taking inordinate pleasure in them all. Master Killigrew would occasionally put on an impromptu play for His Majesty's entertainment; then Polly was required to earn her place at court, but she did not find the earning at all arduous; much less so than on the stage at Drury Lane. And Nick, for all that he treated her with fashionable casualness when they were in public, never forwent an opportunity to be alone with her, as now.

While at night . . . Well, Polly smiled to herself. What went on behind the closed door of his bedchamber in the west wing of the house was no one's concern but theirs. If his lordship's man found Mistress Wyat tucked up in his lordship's bed of a morning, he was too discreet and well trained to betray a flicker of surprise. Polly secretly thought it ridiculous that she was obliged to keep pretense of using her own apartment, keeping her clothes in there, performing her toilet in absurd privacy. It seemed a most profligate waste of space, she felt, to have two rooms when only one was necessary. But such thrifty and practical considerations were bred in the crowded city slums, not in the lofty mansions of the rich.

Kincaid, although he accepted the Earl of Pembroke's hospitality at Wilton House, stabled his horses at an inn in the village, seeing no reason why they should be a charge upon his host, who was already put to great expense by the king's gracing him with his presence.

Polly was glad of this arrangement, since it ensured that the mortification of her riding instruction was kept between themselves and the stable lads at the inn. At her insistence, they rode off the beaten track, where encounters like the one they had just narrowly avoided would be unlikely. However, as they clattered into the stable yard at the inn and she accepted Kincaid's hand to dismount, she was firmly resolved that she had had her last ride in that manner. The piebald seemed as happy to be rid of her as she was to be of him, clopping off to his stable with the relieved air of one who had performed a tedious duty and could now look forward to his reward.

Polly strolled casually over to the stable block, her long, extravagantly pleated riding skirt caught up over one arm. Outside one box, she stopped, peering into the gloomy interior, where a fly buzzed monotonously, and the rich aroma of horseflesh, hay, and manure filled her nostrils. The inhabitant of the box came over to the door at an inviting click. "Good morrow, Tiny," Polly murmured, stroking the dainty creature's velvety nose, reaching 'round to run her hand over the sinewy neck, which arched in pleasure as the mare whickered and nuzzled into her palm. "I did not bring anything this day," Polly apologized. "But tomorrow I will."

"You commune with that animal as if she were possessed of tongues," Nick said, a laugh in his voice as he came up behind her.

"So she is, of her own kind," Polly returned serenely. "We understand each other, do we not, Tiny?"

The mare rolled thick, pink lips against her hand in answer and pawed her stable floor, liquid brown eyes glowing. "See?" said Polly. "How could she be clearer?"

"With difficulty." Nick smiled, reaching in to stroke the horse. "Next to Sulayman, she is my favorite."

"May I ride her?" Polly asked directly, shooting him a sideways glance.

Nicholas nodded immediately. "She will suit you very well when you are able to handle her. But she is a spirited filly. It will take an experienced pair of light hands to achieve mastery. Her mouth is too delicate for a curb, and her spirit will not take kindly to the whip."

"And you think my hands are sufficiently light?"

"If you will but listen to your instructor, and do as you are bid, they will be so," he teased, twining around his finger a stray curl that had escaped her hat.

"I think you are overcautious, my lord," Polly declared.

"Impossible, when you consider what it is over which I exercise such caution," he answered solemnly, although his eyes glinted with humor. "I would not have a bruise mar that ivory skin."

"I am not unaccustomed to bruises," Polly pointed out.

"But not with me," he said, the gravity now genuine.

Polly inclined her head in smiling acceptance. "Nay, not with you. But I meant only that I am not so delicate that a tumble will spell disaster. If I am prepared to risk it, why are you not?"

"Because I am not." The pronouncement effectively closing the discussion, Nicholas turned to leave. "Do you return to the house with me, or will you stay and commune further with Tiny?"

"There is no need to be vexed." Polly walked beside him across the yard, out into the main street of the little village clustering at the gate of Wilton park.

"I have told you before that my patience is not inexhaustible. You are persistent as a wasp at the honeycomb."

"Then I will cease my buzzing," Polly declared cheerfully. "Shall you dress up for the masquerade tonight? I have it in mind to play a May Day milkmaid, with petticoats all tucked up and curls atumble. Think you t'will be pretty?"

Nicholas felt a flash of suspicion at this instant docility. He looked down at her, saw only the wide hazel eyes full of ingenuous question, her lips parted in a soft smile. He dismissed the suspicion as unworthy. Polly always capitulated with grace. "I can think of few costumes more delightful, moppet; particularly on you. But then, it matters little what you wear, as well you know. You enchant, regardless; hence my Lady Castlemaine's distemper."

"Well, I am determined not to allow her to trouble me anymore," Polly said, reaching up to adjust the starched folds of her cravat. "If the ladies will not talk with me, then I shall devote my attention to the gentlemen with good conscience.

Mayhap His Grace of Buckingham will accord me more than a cold nod." Brave words, she thought, but she must try to overcome these surely fanciful fears that every time she felt the duke's eyes upon her, he was contemplating the price that he had promised to find.

She was as good as her word that evening. Sue had entered with enthusiasm into the idea of a May Day milkmaid, and the two girls spent the afternoon adapting a daintily flowered cambric petticoat that Polly would wear over her smock, without gown or kirtle. The gardens yielded pinks, marigolds, and daisies, which Susan's nimble fingers entwined in the loose ringlets tumbling about the milkmaid's shoulders.

" 'Tis not a costume one would wear gladly in winter," Polly said with a chuckle, surveying herself in the glass. "I must go barefoot if I'm to play the part with accuracy."

"You would go barefoot before the king?" Sue, in the process of pinning up the skirt of the petticoat to reveal the shapely curve of calf and the neat turn of ankle, looked up, stunned at the idea of such brazen immodesty.

"I hardly think it is any the more indecent than appearing before the king in smock and petticoat," Polly said tranquilly, adjusting the neck of her smock with a critical frown. "Besides, His Majesty is hardly unfamiliar with the female form in various states of undress."

Sue giggled, in spite of her shocked disapproval at this irreverence. "Lor', Polly, ye shouldn't say such things."

" 'Tis but the truth," her companion returned unarguably. "I am going to my lord's apartments to show myself before appearing below. If there is anything amiss, he will tell me so."

Her chamber, while it was smaller and less luxuriously appointed than Kincaid's, as befitted the anomalous position in the court hierarchy of an accredited mistress with no husband's status to define her own, adjoined his lordship's. Polly had exclaimed at this convenience, until Kincaid had pointed out dryly that the Earl of Pembroke's steward would be apprised of all relevant facts appertaining to his master's guests, and would make disposition accordingly. Such tactful disposition had converted a dressing room to Polly's bedchamber, enabling her to enter Kincaid's apartments through the connecting door. She did so now, with no more than a light tap to herald her arrival.

"Oh, I beg your pardon, sir. I did not realize you had a visitor. Shall I come back later?" She smiled at De Winter, resplendent in crimson satin embroidered with turquoise peacocks, sitting by the window sipping a glass of canary.

Nicholas, engaged in inserting a diamond pin in the heavy fall of lace at his throat, said easily, "Not a bit of it, sweetheart. We talk no secrets." He turned to examine her, and a smile spread slowly across his face. "What a bewitching jade you are. What think you, Richard?"

"That the knives will be sharpened to a fine keenness," De Winter said with open amusement. "You have courage, I will say that for you, Polly. There will be much wailing and gnashing of teeth amongst your fair rivals when you appear in such fashion."

"Well, I do not care for that," Polly declared stoutly. "If I were to put ashes in my hair and clothe myself in sackcloth, it would not alter Lady Castlemaine's disposition toward me, so why should I care?"

"Why indeed," Richard agreed easily. " 'Tis such an ingeniously simple costume." He laughed in rich enjoyment. "I'll lay odds 'tis that that'll cause the most grief. Imagine how galling to have spent hours and fortunes and positive buckets of paint and mountains of powder, only to be outdone by a milkmaid in petticoat, smock, and a few flowers."

"If you are not to wear shoes, you had best have a care where you put your feet," Nick said, rising and smoothing down his coat. "And what have you to say about mine own dress, mistress?" He cocked an eyebrow at her, turning slowly for her inspection.

"Magnificent!" Polly breathed, taking in the rich black satin with gold arabesques, the glint of diamond, the wink of silver on his shoes, the deep burnished auburn hair falling in heavy luxuriance to his shoulders, to lie in rich contrast against the dark cloth. The emerald eyes danced, seeming

even brighter against the somber black and gold of his suit.
"You are a very prince." She stepped across the room, metal
to his magnet, quite forgetting Richard's presence. Placing
her palms against Nick's chest, she stroked the silky cloth
with its raised golden decorations, then stood on tiptoe to
place her smiling lips against his.

"A prince should have a princess as consort, not a milkmaid." Just as Baron Kincaid should have his baroness. The
old, unbidden apprehension nibbled again at the edges of her
present contentment. Again she quelled it, and fluttered her
eyelashes against his cheek in a wicked little caress that
brought his nerve endings to prickly arousal.

"That would depend upon the milkmaid." De Winter
interrupted the play, rising to his feet with a deceptive lazi-
ness. "However, you shall descend upon my arm, Polly, not
that of your prince."

"One must not wear one's heart upon one's sleeve," Polly
said with an ironic smile. "But Buckingham knows where
mine does *not* lie."

Richard's eyes met Nick's across the flower-strewn honeyed head. "Are you uneasy, Polly?" he asked quietly.

Everyone has a price. I will find yours. Oh, 'twas nonsense to
be concerned about a remark made in the anger of chagrin.
It had no place in this self-enclosed world, far removed from
life's realities, from the monstrous terrors of a plague-
stricken metropolis. In this world where the pursuit of pleasure and the fulfillment of desires of whatever kind were the
only object, why would Buckingham concern himself with
an old and private thwarting? Nick was right. The coldness
would soon dissipate as other interests took over, and she
would not have these two concerned about her sinister fan-
cies.

"Indeed not, Richard." Polly spoke firmly. "What is
there to be uneasy about? In truth, I prefer the duke's coldness to his attentions. I do not find that familiarity has less-
ened the repugnance I feel for him."

With a smile of sweet innocence, she dropped De Winter
a curtsy. "Are you sure, my lord, that *you* are not paying me

too much attention? After all, I arrived here under your escort, and I am as often upon your arm as upon Nick's."

"Jackanapes! You are going to make a very bad end," Richard declared with feeling, taking her hand and laying it upon his arm. "Strive for a modicum of conduct, if you please."

Polly gave him a smile glinting with mischief before glancing over her shoulder at Nicholas, dropping one eyelid in a conspiratorial wink that brought a shout of laughter from him.

"Be off," he said. "We will dance the coranto later, if you can remember the steps."

"If *you,* my lord, will promise not to tread upon my toes," she said, wriggling one bare foot pointedly; on which Parthian shot, she left him still searching for rejoinder, herself well satisfied that she had dissipated that moment of tension.

Her entrance, as had been predicted, caused no small stir. "What a rustic simplicity, mistress!" trilled Lady Castlemaine. "But one must have the simplicity of mind to accompany such a costume."

"Indeed, the least sophistication and one would look perfectly ridiculous," concurred Lady Frobisher, fanning herself vigorously.

"You are too kind, my ladies." Polly sank into a deep obeisance, each movement in the sequence radiating insolence. "I am most complimented that my poor performance should be so convincing."

Richard De Winter, shoulders shaking, left her in the vixens' den, confident that she could hold her own. However, she was not to be left there for long. A liveried footman appeared at her shoulder, bearing the king's summons.

Polly, smiling around the circle of ladies, excused herself. King Charles was sitting in a carved chair at the far end of the state drawing room. "I'faith, but 'tis a deuced pretty child y'are," he declared, radiating bonhomie. "I'll have a kiss, God save me." Seizing her hands, he pulled her down upon the royal lap, embracing her with hearty enthusiasm.

Polly, emerging somewhat breathless from her sovereign's

lusty salute, forced herself to laugh and flutter as if quite
overset. In truth, she was a trifle overcome, never having
conceived of the moment when she would receive attentions
of this intimate nature from England's monarch. But knowing how easily bored the king could become, she recovered
rapidly. Plucking a marigold from her hair, she placed it in
his buttonhole with a delicate blush and a pretty smile.

"A gift in return, sire."

The sally earned her another kiss, and when she made a
move to rise from his knee, King Charles circled her waist
with a restraining arm. "Nay, my bud, I'll have your company a while longer. Such a sweet weight as it is." Laughing
in great good humor, he took a perfumed comfit from the
bowl on the table beside him and popped it between her lips.

For half an hour Polly sat upon his knee as he plied them
both with sweetmeats, and his hands strayed just a little, and
he engaged her in a risqué exchange that required all her
wits. A circle of admiring courtiers surrounded them, laughing heartily at each sally, complimenting Polly on her wit,
her dress, her beauty, in faithful recitation of their king. All
the while, Polly was conscious of the darting venom directed
at her from Barbara Palmer, Lady Castlemaine, who stood
just outside the circle.

"A consummate performer, is she not, Barbara?" George
Villiers took snuff, smiling with a hint of malice at his
cousin. "Think you she is enjoying her present position?"

"How could she not be?" snapped the king's mistress,
betrayed into a display of genuine emotion.

"You, madame, are a fool if you believe that," Villiers said
lazily. "She cannot wait to be released."

"She is a conniving whore!" spat Barbara. "But if she
thinks to worm her way into the king's bed, she must think
again."

"Fear not, my dear. The king has no intention of any such
thing. He has mistresses enough to plague him," laughed
Villiers. "Or so he says to me. A quick and careless tumble,
maybe, but only if the jade were eager." He paused, looking
thoughtfully at the scene. "I do not believe she is."

Lady Castlemaine regarded him with interest. "What of your pursuit of the milkmaid, George? You were mighty hot upon it, as I recall."

Villiers shrugged easily. "I have yet to find the right price in the right currency." A smile flickered on his lips, a smile that did nothing to lighten his countenance. "But the little trollop shall pay the cost of arrogance in full measure; be assured of that, Barbara. You shall yet enjoy her downfall."

Lady Castlemaine shivered slightly at the clear menace in the soft tones. "What has she done to you, George, that you would promise me such a thing?"

The duke placed his palms together, hinged his thumbs beneath his chin, and reflectively tapped his forefingers against his mouth, his narrowed eyes fixed on the king and the figure upon his knee, swinging her bare feet with apparent insouciance. "With Kincaid's connivance, the silly child thought to make game of me. For that I shall rub her exquisite little nose in the dirt," he responded, for once revealing his true colors without adornment. "And I shall ensure that Kincaid knows every detail of his mistress's degradation. Thus, quite simply, shall I be revenged upon them both." Then he laughed. "Pray excuse me, cousin." He bowed and sauntered over to the group around the king.

"Do you join the hawking on the morrow, Mistress Wyat?" He addressed Polly, who, having just earned her release from the royal embrace, was standing beside the king's chair, waiting for the nod that would give her permission to leave his presence.

It was a pleasant enough question; the tone had even a hint of warmth, Polly noticed. But for the moment she had thought only for the fact that the question suited her own purposes. She glanced surreptitiously at Nicholas, who had appeared, it seemed, from nowhere. "I think no, Your Grace," she said. "I am not overly fond of leaving my bed at such an early hour."

The duke turned to Nicholas. "And you, Kincaid. Do you leave your bed early enough to join us?"

Without a flicker, Nick inclined his head. "I cannot imagine what could provide competing pleasure, Buckingham. I shall certainly attend. I've a new gerfalcon to fly."

The conversation turned rapidly onto matters of falconry, and Polly made her escape, well satisfied with Nick's response to Buckingham's goading. Of course, she had provided them with the cues, and with complete intention. She had hoped to discover without the question direct whether Nick would go ahawking in the morning, and she had also hoped to encourage him to do so, since she had every intention of surprising him with her own presence. Buckingham's question had left him with little option but to respond as he had. The rest was up to her. A little ingenuity and careful timing were all that was required.

Chapter 17

Nick woke just before dawn and lay for a minute returning himself to the shape and sense of the daytime world. Polly lay sprawled on her stomach beside him, one arm flung across his chest, her legs tangled up with his. A strand of honey hair tickled his nose. He brushed it aside and ran his hand in a dreamy caress down her back, lingering on the silken curve of her bottom.

Polly stirred in sleepy arousal beneath the touch, the gently questing finger slipping between her thighs. Her body lifted, moved in an invitation that she was too deliciously languid to articulate. She burrowed deeper into the pillow, stretching her arms above her head as Nick rose above her, swinging himself over her prone body. Catching up the tumbled ringlets from her neck, he bent to kiss her nape, nuzzling softly, moving his mouth to her ear so that she squirmed in sensual enchantment, lifting her hips as invitation became demand.

He slipped his hands beneath her, holding her on the shelf of his palms, gliding into her with slow sweetness. He exhaled in deep pleasure to find himself where he belonged, feasting his eyes on the narrow ivory perfection of her back, the sharp points of her shoulder blades that begged for the teasing caress of his darting tongue.

Polly whispered and moved beneath him, lost in the magical realm where reality and dream were intertwined as the tender benediction of this loving flowed through her, anointing muscle and sinew, thinning her blood, bringing profound peace and languour to every cell in her body.

Dawn, pink and gray, was filling the easterly casement when Nick reluctantly left his bed. This proposed hawking expedition had somehow lost its appeal beside the competing charms of the still somnolent Mistress Wyat. A smile quirked his lips as he thought of his response to Buckingham's taunting question the previous evening. Lying in his teeth, he had been!

He drew the curtains securely around the bed, ensuring the sleeping figure privacy, before pulling the bell rope for his man, who would be awaiting the summons. An hour later, astride Sulayman, a gerfalcon, hooded and jessed, perched on his wrist, he joined the other hunters, milling around on the driveway, awaiting the king's arrival.

Polly had lain in the darkened tent of the bed curtains, waiting impatiently for the manservant to cease his bustling as he tidied the chamber, laying out my lord's clothes against his return from the hunt. At last the door clicked shut on his departure; she flew out of bed, into her own chamber. Susan was asleep on the truckle bed, but she struggled up in sleepy bemusement at the sound of the door.

"Lor', what time is it?" She straightened her nightcap, blinking at the naked Polly.

"Oh, 'tis past dawn," Polly said hurriedly, opening the armoire. "I need my riding habit." Pulling out the skirt and doublet of tawny velvet, she tossed them onto the bed, and turned to the ewer and basin. "Damnation, I do not have the time to wash the sleep from my eyes!"

"What're ye up to?" demanded Susan, now on her feet, assembling smock and petticoats, stockings and boots for the clearly distracted Polly.

"I go riding!" Polly said with an exultant laugh. " 'Tis time my lord realized that I have learned more in the last week than he gives me credit for . . . My thanks." She took the proffered smock, dropping it over her head. "Pass me my stockings, will ye, Sue?"

"There, that must serve." It was barely five minutes later when Polly tucked her hair beneath her black beaver hat, adjusted the plume so that it fell in fetching fashion over her shoulder, and drew on her leather gloves. " 'Tis to be hoped I do not arrive at the stables in a muck-sweat, for I must run."

"Is it mischief ye brew?" asked Susan uneasily.

Polly threw her a smile as she hastened to the door. "Of a kind; but fret not, I have the matter well in hand."

The door closed. Susan shook her head in bewilderment. Life never grew tedious these days, that was for sure.

Polly hastened to the village. All was quiet at this early hour, and there were few to see and remark upon her impetuous progress as she half ran, skirt gathered over one arm, hat plume bobbing, to the stable yard at the rear of the inn. Nick's groom would have accompanied his master, she knew, so there was only a stable lad employed by the inn to convince that it was at my lord's instructions that Tiny was to be saddled, and Mistress Wyat assisted to mount.

The lad was morose, sleep still in his eyes, and if he thought it strange that one he had seen riding only at the end of a leading rein should now be mounted on his lordship's spirited mare, he did not consider it his business to question. It was easier and quicker simply to do the job; he was sore in need of the breakfast that even now cooled while he labored.

Polly had a moment of panic as she urged Tiny out of the yard. Nothing about her position atop this dainty, sweet-stepping creature bore the least resemblance to being mounted upon the piebald. Tiny moved eagerly, sniffing the wind, reacting instantly to the slightest touch on the rein, the least pressure of her rider's knee, even when these signals were accidental. Polly took a deep breath, forcing herself to relax. As she did so, she felt the change in Tiny, the instant response to her rider's attitude. The mare lengthened her stride as if settling into a comfortable enjoyment of the exer-

cise. Polly settled down to enjoy herself. There was nothing
in the least alarming. How could there be when she and the
animal were so much in tune, could communicate with each
other so readily?

She directed the mare into the park, knowing that she
would come up with the hunt in the fields beyond the ha-
ha, the deep ditch boundary that separated the park from the
fields. The quarry that hawks and huntsmen sought was to
be found on the flat land bordering the river. Falcons could
not be flown in the woods. They must be given uninter-
rupted view of their prey, and an unhindered flight path.

She heard voices, clear in the still morning air, as, greatly
daring, she set Tiny to jump the ha-ha. The mare gathered
herself, sailed over, landing gently on the other side, the
whole movement so smoothly accomplished that Polly was
barely conscious of the change in motion.

"You beauty," she whispered exultantly, leaning forward
to pat the long, arched neck. "How could Nick have made
me ride that insensate, mindless hulk? No one could learn to
ride with such a mount."

The hunt came into view when she crested a rise and
could look down to the broad stretch of the river, flanked by
wide green banks and open fields. Rooks circled above a
spinney off to the right, and the sun, mist-wreathed, set the
dew on the grass to winking so that each blade appeared
jewel-tipped. The richly dressed riders and their elegant
mounts made a colorful scene on this misty morning, when
the promised heat of the day was for the moment in abeyance, and the land looked new-washed in its fresh greenery.

Tiny whinnied softly, becoming aware of her own kind
and a sport in which she might take part. She increased her
speed, but tentatively as if to be certain that her rider was
content to have it so. When no restraining tug came on the
bit, she broke into a full canter. Polly, after a second of fright
because this canter was twice as fast as any the piebald had
managed, fell in with the rhythm, found that she was in no
danger of falling off, and began to relish the dashing picture
she was going to present, cantering up to the hunt on her

splendid mount, in her elegant habit, insouciant and utterly confident at this equestrian business.

Thus it was that Nicholas, Lord Kincaid, looking up from securing the jesses of his newly returned gerfalcon, beheld a sight to entrance the most hardened cynic: dainty, silver-gray Tiny cantering across the meadow in the morning mist; upon her back, as firmly seated as if affixed with cement, the ravishing figure of his lordship's mistress, all smiles and sparkling eyes, her complexion rosy with the fresh air, exercise and excitement.

"I give you good day, sir," she greeted him, drawing rein with the lightest touch. Tiny came to a walk, obeying the direction to turn and range herself alongside Sulayman. Polly beamed up at Nicholas, who was staring at her, stunned. "I have decided to join you after all," she declared to the company at large. "It is such a beautiful morning, is it not? Far too beautiful for lying abed."

"Indeed, it is," the Earl of Pembroke agreed, cheerfully. "Made more so by your presence, madame." He doffed his hat graciously as he offered the compliment, before turning an experienced eye to her mount. " 'Odd's bones! But that is the prettiest filly! Beautiful lines; Arabian, I'll lay odds."

"Aye," Kincaid said, finding his voice at last.

"Ah, my lord, I must thank you for permitting me to ride her," Polly said swiftly, turning back to Nick with another smile, but this one contained more than a hint of placation and appeal. "I was overjoyed yesterday when you said I might."

Nick's lips thinned as he recalled the conversation in the stable yard. He met her anxious regard in stony silence. There was not a damn thing he could do, not here in the middle of a hunt—a fact on which Mistress Wyat had presumably gambled.

When it appeared that Nicholas either would not or could not respond, Polly dropped her gaze, turning back to Pembroke. "Pray, my lord, will you show me something of this falconry? I have yet to witness a flight."

The earl agreed with alacrity and invited her to ride with

him to the outskirts of the group, where he would loose his bird.

"My congratulations, Nick," De Winter said, watching them go off. " 'Twas pure inspiration to mount her on that gray. They make the most enchanting pair, do they not?"

Nick grunted, looking a little sick. Richard glanced at him sharply, then whistled as comprehension dawned. "Did you not give her leave?"

"No, dammit, I did not!" Nick said savagely. "At least, not for the moment. I did not consider her sufficiently skilled."

Richard continued to watch Polly. "I think you may have been mistaken," he observed. "She has a good seat, and the mare is clearly responsive. They appear made for each other."

The hunt moved off along the riverbank, and Polly kept herself out of Kincaid's vicinity. The covert glances she directed at him were not encouraging. There appeared to be no softening of his countenance. However, she was receiving her usual quantity of admiring attention elsewhere, so put up her chin and set out to play the coquette-on-horseback.

All went well for about an hour, during which falcons hovered and swooped, returning to the master's arm with their catch, yielding it up against all nature's instinct, accepting the hood and jesses again until given permission for another foray. Nick had just tossed his gerfalcon into freedom when disaster struck.

Polly, on Tiny, had fallen back a little to watch the elegance of the Earl of Pembroke's merlin as it swooped upon an unwary sparrow. The sparrow, suddenly alerted to the danger, twisted in the air to fly in blind panic toward the hunters. The merlin, hot in pursuit, swooped low over Tiny's head, clawed feet poised for the kill, the vicious beak curved in deadly intent, the small black eye gleaming malevolence. The mare reared up in fright and took off across the field in the direction of the spinney.

Polly had no time to feel fear. Her first instinct was to yank back on the reins, but she remembered Nick's warning that the mare had a delicate mouth, which would be ruined by a heavy hand. So she concentrated on keeping her seat, leaning instinctively forward over the horse's neck, making her body follow the lines of the bolting mare, offering no unbalanced resistance, trusting that Tiny would run herself to a standstill eventually.

Nick, seeing the merlin's swoop, tensed in anticipation of Tiny's reaction. "Sweet Jesus!" The color ebbed from his face as the mare bolted. Why in hell was Polly not using the rein? But it would not help, he knew that; Tiny had gone beyond mastery. There had been but a moment when an experienced rider could have forestalled the bolt. Forgetting the public arena, he cursed Polly's obstinacy, offered a prayer to the heavens in the same breath as threatening most fearful reprisals, and put Sulayman to the gallop after the runaway.

George Villiers, newly joining the hunt, witnessed this extraordinary display of emotion, the violence of Kincaid's alarm. Kincaid had not reacted with ordinary consternation. He had gone as white as whey, had spoken in unbridled passion, and was now hurtling in pursuit as if it were a matter of life and death; yet the wench was still in the saddle and looked little likely to be unseated.

An unpleasant smile played over the meager lips as the duke was reminded of another moment when a dropped guard had hinted at a new perspective on the affairs of Lord Kincaid and Mistress Wyat. If what he suspected was, indeed, the case, then maybe he could make use of it. The Duke of Buckingham turned his own horse to follow the flying hooves of Sulayman.

Nick's heart was in his throat as he saw Tiny veer toward the spinney. Would Polly have the sense to imagine what could happen if the mare left the paths, plunging into the trees, heedless of low-hanging branches? At that speed, Polly would lose her head . . . break her neck . . . God's death! "Keep your head down!" he bellowed, with little hope that she would hear him. Sulayman was closing on the mare, but Tiny was still galloping *ventre à terre,* and he would not catch them before they entered the spinney.

Polly heard the shout but not the words. All her energies were concentrated now on keeping in the saddle. She maintained a nonstop flow of soothing words as she clung to Tiny's neck, hoping that her reassurance would communicate itself to the petrified animal, locked in its own world of pure instinctual response. Polly saw the danger from the tree branches just in time. She ducked her head below the level of Tiny's neck as the branch snapped overhead. A nut of nausea lodged in her throat at the thought of what could have happened; she clung grimly to the mare's mane, deciding that the fun had gone out of this adventure. But she could sense that the horse was beginning to lose the spurt. Her neck was lathered, her breath coming in great tortured sobs.

They broke out of the spinney into the meadow beyond. Sulayman drew level with the mare; Nicholas swung sideways, catching the bolter's rein above the bit. Hauled thus unceremoniously to a stop, Tiny reared up; Polly, her precarious balance finally overset, flew from the mare's back to land with an agonizing, jarring thud on the base of her spine.

"Why did you *do* that?" she demanded on an angry sob, tears of pain and frustration welling in her hazel eyes. "Everything was all right until you did that!" Her hat had shot from her head under the force of her fall. Her skirts were heaped about her as she sat upon the hard ground, every bone in her body groaning in complaint under the jarring that made her head ache and her behind throb with the bruising. She glared up at him, tears running down her face, weeping with pure anger that Nick should have caused this fall, and so proved her incapable of managing anything more lively than the sluggish piebald.

"She was going to stop in a minute, anyway," she wailed, dashing the tears from her eyes with the back of her hand. "I knew exactly what I was doing—"

But Nicholas had swung himself from Sulayman in the midst of this impassioned tirade and put a stop to it by seizing her upper arms, yanking her to her feet. "How *dare* you frighten me like that!" he raged. "Those trees would have broken your neck!" He shook her with all the frenzy of a terrier with a rat, giving vent to the pent-up anguish of the last minutes. "You are my life, Goddamn it! Never have I been so afeard!"

"P-please stop!" Polly begged, when it seemed as if her head would leave her shoulders, and her body, already shaken to its core by the fall, screamed its protest at this further assault.

Nick pulled her against him, wrapping her in his arms in a convulsive hug that was as violently expressive of fear and relief as the shaking. "God's grace, Polly. How could you do that to me?" he whispered into the fragrance of her hair.

"But it was all right, love," Polly cried against his shirt-front. "There was nothing to be afeard of. It would have been perfectly all right if you had left well alone. Tiny was tiring; she would have stopped soon enough. I did not want to draw back roughly on the rein in case I hurt her mouth."

Nicholas paused as the world settled again on its axis. The sun still shone, the river still flowed, hawks flew, and the earth continued on its accustomed circuit. Tiny was wind-blown, catching her breath in sobbing gasps, but she would recover. Polly was whole, pliant, and warm beneath his hands. She had given him the fright of his life, but he, too, would recover.

He drew back to look at her, her hair tousled, eyes wide, glistening, tears streaked on that flawless complexion, mouth opened to continue her indignant defense and accusations. "Are you hurt?" he asked in his customary calm tones. "That was quite a tumble."

"My arse," Polly muttered with a sniff, rubbing her aching rear. "It is all your fault."

"It seems that there is natural justice in this world, after all," Nick said, a tremor of laughter in his voice. "You'll not be up to sitting a horse again for a while, in that case." He turned from her to remount Sulayman. Reaching over, he took Tiny's bridle, drawing it over her head to hold it loosely with his own. " 'Tis to be hoped your injuries do not preclude your walking," he observed. "It cannot be above four miles to the house."

Polly stared, for the moment speechless, as he turned both horses and set off homeward. "You bastard!" she yelled, then followed the insult with the more colorful examples of the vocabulary that had informed her growing. Nick's only response was to doff his hat, waving it in cheerful salute as he rode way. She picked up her own hat from its resting place on a spiky thornbush, dusting it off vigorously against her skirt, before cramming it back on her head. Then she limped after the fast-disappearing rider and horses, muttering curses and imprecations with all the vituperative malice of an entire coven of witches.

George Villiers, motionless within earshot, hidden by the screen of trees at the edge of the spinney, remained in seclusion for a good five minutes after the close of that fascinating and enlightening confrontation. It was always pleasing to have one's suspicions confirmed. It was with a most satisfied smile that he rode back to join the hunt.

The morning was far advanced by the time Polly arrived back at Wilton House. She was hot, and the walk had done nothing to improve her bruised muscles and spine, and even less for her temper. Unwilling to be seen in her bedraggled, dusty state by any guests, she used the back stairs to reach the peace and privacy of her chamber.

"Lor', Polly! Whatever's amiss?" exclaimed Susan. "Ye looks as if ye've been dragged through a hedge backward."

"Just as I feel," Polly groaned, sitting gingerly on the bed to pull off her boots. "If you love me, Sue, contrive some hot water and a tub. I am one enormous bruise."

"Whatever've you gone and done?" Susan, consternation wrinkling her round, placid countenance, bent to help with the boots.

"Oh, everything has gone awry!" Polly sighed. "And what is so infuriating is that it was not my fault." Thoughts of Nicholas brought an alarmingly ferocious glint to her eye. "I need a bath, Sue. Can ye contrive it?"

"Aye." Susan bustled to the door. "There's a footman who's monstrous willing to oblige." A flush deepened the already healthy coloring, and Polly forgot her own ills for a minute.

"Willing to oblige *you,* is it, Sue?"

"Well, I dunno about that," the other girl mumbled, and whisked herself out of the room.

Polly took off her habit; mindful of the imminent arrival of Sue's swain with hot water and a tub, she put on a wrapper. She went to the door connecting her chamber with Kincaid's, pressing her ear to the keyhole. No sound came from within. He had probably returned to the hunt, sending his groom back to the stable with Tiny, thus advertising to all and sundry that the filly's rider had been unhorsed. She blinked away angry tears at the injustice.

Susan and the footman appeared, laboring under the weight of a round wooden tub and steaming brass kettles. Polly observed the two with interest, looking for the signs of an understanding between them. Nick, she knew, would be more than generous with his wedding gift, if such an understanding existed and could be brought to fruition. Sue's heightened color and a certain complacent air of the footman's seemed to lend credence to the idea. She would sound out Nick, Polly decided, before remembering that she had no intention of ever again exchanging as much as two words with the odious man!

"Thank 'ee, Oliver," Susan said with another fiery blush, holding the door for him. The footman grinned and chucked her beneath the chin as he went out.

"So that's the way the land lies," Polly commented with a teasing chuckle.

"Oh, give over," Sue said, still blushing. She hefted one of the jugs, pouring its contents into the tub. "Are ye gettin' in 'ere or not?"

"I am." Polly tossed aside her wrapper and stepped into the tub.

"Lawks!" squeaked Susan. "Ow d'ye get that bruise? 'Tis bigger than a saucer!"

"It feels as big as a serving platter." Polly groaned, sinking into the hot water, arranging herself delicately on the bottom of the tub. "I fell off a horse with some considerable force onto very hard ground. Actually, I did not exactly fall; I was practically pushed," she amended with a resurgence of indignation, hugging her drawn-up knees, resting her chin upon them. "And if I had my way—"

"You would see me drawn and quartered!" Nick's voice came laughing from the connecting door behind the occupant of the tub and her attendant. He lounged against the jamb, arms folded.

"How long have you been there?" demanded Polly crossly, without turning her head.

"Oh, long enough," he said cheerfully. "You were both far too busy complaining and exclaiming to notice me. However, Susan has the right of it. That is an enormous bruise."

"And whose fault is that?"

"Susan, I think you had better find something to do elsewhere. See if you cannot procure some witch hazel from the stillroom," suggested his lordship, pushing himself away from the door.

Susan bobbed a curtsy, disappearing in short order. Nick crossed to the window seat, where he sat facing Polly in her bath. "And whose fault is it?" A red-gold eyebrow lifted in punctuation.

"I would never have fallen if you had not pulled on the rein in that manner. It was quite unnecessary; I had matters well in hand. And then, to ride off and leave me . . . !" She glared at him over her knees, shifting slightly to take the weight off her bruise. "It was unkind and unjust—"

"Now, there I take issue with you," Nick interrupted, raising a forefinger to halt the tirade that was bidding fair to assume majestic proportions. "You took my horse—a blood Arabian. You took her not only without my permission, but also in direct contravention of my wishes, intending to force me into a corner; and, I might add, succeeding. It was for that, that you had your walk."

Polly was silent for a minute, gazing beyond Nick, out of the window. Then she sighed, yielding with customary grace. "Indeed, it was wrong of me to take your property without leave, and I ask your pardon. But I could think of no other way to prove my point." The slender shoulders shrugged, the gesture accentuating their bare, rounded perfection. "However, you need have no further qualms. I'll not be riding again."

"That bruise will not last forever," Nick pointed out, rising to his feet, tossing his coat onto the bed.

"I was not referring to that," Polly said, attempting a dignified note, but Nick was rolling up the sleeves of his shirt, and it was hard to sound stiff and distant when images of what his action might presage ran rampant in her head.

"To what were you referring?" He knelt beside the tub, reaching a lazy hand over the edge to flick playfully at the water before delving beneath. " 'Tis to be assumed there's soap in here—"

"Here!" Polly picked up the soap from the floor beside the tub, grabbed his questing hand, and slapped the precious cake into it. "I would not leave it in the water; t'would melt."

"Such habits of thrift as you have," he said in wonderment. "Kneel up and let me wash your back."

"I am not ready to wash my back yet," Polly objected. "I am still enjoying the hot water. It is beneficial for aches and bruises."

"On which subject, if those aches and bruises are not going to prevent your riding, what is?" Finding one warm wet breast beneath the water, he lifted it clear, soaping the ivory mound with an air of great concentration.

"I refuse to ride that sluggard ever again, with or without a leading rein," she told him. "So I will not ride."

"I had not envisaged your riding the piebald again," Nick said, transferring his attention to the other breast. "I, too, was in error."

"Oh." Polly could find nothing more to say for a moment, particularly when Nick had taken her nipple between thumb and forefinger, and was rolling it in the way that set butterflies of delight aflutter in her belly.

"Tiny is yours," Nick said softly, tipping her chin with his unoccupied hand. "I gift you each to the other."

"Oh," Polly said again, at the mercy of such a welter of emotions that she was quite unable to express herself.

Nick kissed her, and there she could find expression, her lips melting against his, her tongue flirting with his in sensual promise. Drawing back, he smiled down at her face, flushed with the warmth of the bathwater and his kissing. "Am I forgiven for causing your fall, moppet?"

"You would buy your pardon, sir?" Her eyes glowed; she reached up with wet hands to clasp his face, pulling it down to hers for renewed thanks. "In the face of such a birthday gift, who could be so mean-spirited as to deny pardon for any offense that stopped short of murder?"

Nick frowned. "Birthday gift, Polly? What mean you?"

She shrugged casually. "Why, 'twas my birthday on Wednesday."

Nick sat back on his heels, regarding her gravely. "Why would you say nothing of it earlier?"

She shrugged again. "It has never been a day of note. I do not regard it." A tiny smile touched her lips as she remembered. "Well, one year it was. It was my fifth birthday, as I recall. Prue had made me a rag doll." She laughed, quite unaware of the effect this revelation was having on Nicholas. "I kept that doll until it fell apart, then I had a scrap of the material that I talked to as if 'twere still Annie. But Prue threw it away eventually, when it became so dirty that she would not give it houseroom. It must have been very dirty," Polly reflected. "Prue was not overly scrupulous about such things."

"That was the only birthday present you have received?" He spoke slowly, as if to be sure that he was understood.

"Why, yes, I think so," she responded. "I would have remembered, I expect, if there had been others."

"Yes, I imagine you would," Nick said, swallowing the lump in his throat. There was no point in expressing his feelings at this gulf of deprivation. It would hardly benefit Polly to be made aware of a loss that she did not consider in the least. However, he was resolved that never again would her birthday pass unremarked. "So you have attained the great age of eighteen." A finger ran over her lips, gently teasing. "I must learn to treat you with the respect due such maturity; or, at least, endeavor to do so."

"I do not think I should care for that at all." Polly caught the teasing finger between her teeth, nipping with a degree of seriousness. "Respect sounds very dull. Except that I could wish you had shown me a little before pulling Tiny up short like that. I would not else have fallen."

"Stop worrying that bone. I had thought it buried."

"Indeed, it is."

"Then kneel up and let me wash your back. I have a certain cure for bruises of both pride and flesh . . ."

Chapter 18

〰️

"You have recovered from this morning's mishap, I trust, Mistress Wyat." Buckingham took snuff, smiling blandly at Polly. They were in one of the small drawing rooms that evening where card tables had been set up; voices rose around them in laughter and occasional exclamation.

Polly looked at her interlocuter, and for a moment was deprived of the power of speech. The duke was regarding her with a look of contemptuous amusement, radiating menace. The cheerful buzz around her seemed to fade under the inescapable conviction that this man was going to hurt her. Without thought, her eyes darted in a desperate search for Nicholas, needing the certainty of his presence as shield.

The duke's smile grew blander as he absorbed her confusion. "I appear to have said something to upset you," he murmured. " 'Twas but a polite inquiry."

Polly licked her lips and found her voice. "I do beg your pardon, my lord duke. My mind was elsewhere. I am quite recovered, thank you. It was a most minor mishap."

"Your . . . uh . . . protector seemed not to consider it minor."

"I do not know what you mean, sir." Why did she feel as if she were dancing at the end of a string being manipulated by those long, beringed fingers? Her gaze raked the room again, wildly searching for Nicholas.

"Why, I mean simply that Kincaid appeared monstrous disturbed," replied the duke casually. "Most flatteringly concerned for your safety."

"I cannot imagine why that should surprise you, Duke." From somewhere came the strength to resist the creeping paralysis produced by those drooping, hooded eyes and the soft tones where some as yet undefined threat lurked, barely masked.

He gave a little laugh. "Oh, it did not surprise me in the least, bud. Not in the least." He watched her as she struggled to make sense of this. "Love is a most demanding master," he murmured.

Involuntarily, she gasped, her eyes widening in shock. "It is, of course, not at all a fashionable emotion," continued the soft voice dripping its honey-coated menace. "But we shall keep it as our little secret, shall we?" Seeing Polly for the moment incapable of response, he offered a mocking bow and sauntered over to a table where an intense game of three-handed Gleeke was in progress.

Polly stood for a minute trying to shake herself free of the enveloping dread. What was going on? What had he seen? What did he mean? She must find Nicholas.

Gathering up her skirts, she hastened from the room, then stopped. What was the point in describing that exchange to Nicholas? It could not possibly mean anything. Why should it matter that Buckingham now knew that Polly and Nick were not simply two individuals involved to their mutual benefit in a perfectly ordinary liaison? Her own association with the duke was over, so nothing was lost by his knowledge. What did matter was that she had betrayed her fear even as she had confirmed his words with her shocked silence.

With determination, she returned to the card room, taking her place with a laughing group around the shuffleboard.

• • •

"Something appears to have pleased you mightily, duke," observed Lady Castlemaine, her eyes gleaming through the slits in her black silk mask.

"Perhaps I, also, should adopt the fashion of the vizard," drawled His Grace. "I'd not have my every thought broadcast upon my countenance."

"Only broadcast to those who have the code and can therefore read," responded her ladyship. "You are uncommon satisfied by something. Confess it."

The duke smiled and reposed himself elegantly upon the scroll-ended chaise longue beside her. He straightened an imaginary wrinkle in his aquamarine hose, turning his calf for further inspection, thus offering his companion the opportunity to admire the fine shape of his leg.

"Has Lord Kincaid's little actor at last come to appreciate your manifold attractions?" hazarded Lady Castlemaine, her baleful gaze wandering to where the subject under discussion sat at the shuffleboard. Polly wore no vizard, her own having been removed by the king himself, on the grounds that beauty such as hers had no right to be concealed beneath a mask. Such a statement had done little to improve Lady Castlemaine's disposition, and her mouth thinned spitefully.

Buckingham read her expression correctly, despite the mask. He chuckled. "Do not let your ill will show, my dear. Malice is not a pretty emotion. Its manifestation wreaks havoc with the complexion; such hard lines as it produces."

Lady Castlemaine managed a wan smile. "I am indebted to you, my lord duke, for your advice. I will make certain to heed it. But, pray, will you not answer me? Does your present complacence have aught to do with the actor?"

"Well," the duke murmured, "I think you could say that I have justification for feeling satisfaction." His eyes rested on Polly, and he nodded pleasantly to himself. "I have found both the currency and the price, my lady."

The countess closed her fan, tapping the ivory sticks against the palm of her hand. "Will you say no more, sir?"

"If I may count upon your assistance," the duke replied, "you shall be a party to the entire plan."

"Gladly," the lady agreed. "I will render whatever assistance I may."

"I shall need you to plant a few seeds in the king's ear," Buckingham explained, his voice low, a smile on his lips, his eyes still upon Mistress Wyat. "Easily done in the privacy of the bed curtains."

"On what subject?"

"Why, treason, my dear, and my Lord Kincaid."

"You talk in riddles." Barbara momentarily forgot the need for caution, and her voice rose above an undertone. "What has Kincaid to do with treason?"

Buckingham shrugged, smiled. "I am sure I can find a connection if I look hard enough, madame; sufficient to impeach him and lodge him in the Tower."

"But how would such a manufacture assist your cause with the actor? She does not appear to hold him in ill will, for all that they do not live in each other's pockets."

"Ahhh, now there is the nub," the duke said, his smile broadening. "The facade they present for public consumption is precisely that—a facade presenting the complacent protector and the kept woman with an eye to the main chance. In fact, matters run much deeper." He shook his head in mock wonder. "So beautifully they play it, too. But I tell you, Barbara, if aught were to be amiss with my Lord Kincaid, I'll lay any odds you choose to name that his mistress will make whatever sacrifice demanded of her to buy his safety."

"And you will name the price," said Lady Castlemaine, her eyes brightening as comprehension dawned. " 'Twill be a high one, I imagine."

"By the time I have finished with the little whore, she will never want to show that glorious countenance at court again." The vicious words, spoken in a soft, pleasant tone, fell from smiling lips. Barbara Palmer shivered in sudden chill. "She will know herself for what she is—a slut whose place is on her back in Mother Wilkinson's brothel."

Indeed, reflected Barbara with a renewed shiver, one did not refuse the patronage of the Duke of Buckingham with impunity. The wench would suffer well for such presumption; for imagining that a creature coming from nowhere, with a little talent and a moderately pretty face, could dare to play fast and loose with the most powerful man in the land.

"When do you begin?" she asked, taking a cheese tartlet from a tray presented by a bowing page.

"There is no time like the present." Buckingham waved the tray away and took snuff. "You will begin to make little murmurs about Kincaid, which I will follow up with graver doubts. By the time we are returned to Whitehall, the crop should be ripe for harvesting."

It was not until after Christmas, however, that the metropolis was considered sufficiently plague-free for the court's return. Polly did what she could to overcome her fear of Buckingham, to regain her pleasure in the sojourn in Wiltshire. Her efforts were assisted by the duke, who seemed to lose interest in her altogether, and eventually she was lulled into a sense of security, able to believe that he had enjoyed tormenting her in revenge for her rejection of his advances, but had now found other interests.

He had, indeed, found other, related interests, and the quiet work of discrediting Nicholas, Lord Kincaid, went on behind the scenes, and in the privacy of the king's bed.

The twelve days of Christmas at the court of King Charles II surpassed Polly's wildest dreams of that pleasure-oriented celebration.

Christmas at the Dog tavern had, in latter years, been celebrated with less than Puritan severity, certainly, but Polly had been kept far too hard at work to glean much amusement from the mummers and the musicians; the mistletoe hung upon the rafters had merely served to add to her burdens. There had been Christmas fare, and she had eaten her fill of goose and mince pies, but nothing in that experience had led her to expect the magnificence of this Christmas.

Day after day, the junketings continued to the music of viol and drum; tables groaned beneath the boar's head, the pheasants, the sturgeons and carps, the venison pasties, cheesecakes and sugar plums, nuts and fruit. Faces remained flushed with the canary and sack, the punch and best October ale that flowed from earliest morning until the last reveler had sought his sodden slumber. And each night, the festivities were directed by the man who meant Christmas—the Lord of Misrule.

Polly had thought it the most famous jest that Richard De Winter, elegant, aloof Richard, should have been chosen for this role, but she realized rapidly how clever a move it had been. It was the Lord's task to keep the wildness from becoming out of hand, and De Winter enforced his discipline by fixing sconces, or penalties, of wickedly witty appropriateness, so that the miscreant, in paying his forfeit, would provide lavish entertainment for the assembled company. A sullen look, an unkind remark, the bringing of dissension, were punished instantly, as was horseplay that crossed the boundary of play. To be accused as a spoilsport of either kind meant the ordeal of firecrackers and squibs, and while the company might split its sides laughing at the antics of the offender, leaping and dancing as the fiery things tied to his heels and hems exploded, the delinquent was unlikely to repeat his offense.

Polly, who had the misfortune to hiccup with laughter in the midst of some exaggeratedly dignified speech of the Lord of Misrule, was required for her insolence to walk upon her hands for the length of the state room. Fortunately, her costume for that evening permitted her to perform the gymnastic feat without loss of modesty. She was dressed as a grimy street urchin, in tattered breeches and torn shirt, soot smudges on her cheeks, her hair hidden beneath a ragged cap. Not a costume that detracted from her beauty in the least, Kincaid reflected, watching her progress between the lines of cheering revelers. The cap fell off, and her hair tumbled loose over her face, but she completed the walk nevertheless, flipping her legs over her head at the end to land neatly on her feet, brushing her hair away from her face, flushed with the upside-down exertion, as unselfconscious as if she had performed for them upon the stage at Drury Lane.

"How did you know she could accomplish such an exercise?" Nick asked Richard, standing beside him.

"An accurate surmise," said the other, laughing. He glanced at his companion, who was looking in soft amusement at the antics of his mistress. "What d'ye intend, Nick? Now that the business with Buckingham is over."

"About Polly?" Nick's smile broadened. "There's no hurry, Richard. She is happy with matters as they are. I'll not lay the burdens of wife and motherhood upon her just yet. I'd have her enjoy some playtime first. She's had little enough in her life . . . not even a birthday present, Richard—" He broke off abruptly as the subject under discussion came prancing over to them.

"Am I granted absolution, my Lord of Misrule?" Polly bowed before Richard, cap in hand.

"You have done your penance," he said solemnly, tapping her shoulder lightly with his black rod of office. "But have a care, lest you offend again."

The musicians, who had played a march tune during Polly's gymnastics, struck up a galliard. Polly, despite her incongruous costume, was whisked away into the stately line. Taking advantage of this peaceful interlude in the generally riotous proceedings, the two men turned their backs on the room.

All softness and amusement had gone from Kincaid's expression now. "D'ye mark it, Richard?" he said quietly. "There is a most noticeable coolness. It has been building these last weeks, and now he barely accords me a nod in return for a bow."

"Aye," Richard replied in the same low voice. "I mark it well. Can you think of a reason for it?"

"I have racked my brains, man, but can come up with nothing. I wondered if, perhaps, 'twas Polly. His Majesty would have her in his bed and chooses this manner to tell me to withdraw. But that is not his way. All his mistresses have husbands or keepers; 'tis useful, is it not, to have someone available to acknowledge as his own any royal bastards?" This last was said with a cynical twist of his lips, and received a simple nod of agreement from his friend.

"Our sovereign is a man of moods," Richard said. "Mayhap this will pass as quickly as it came."

"It's to be hoped so," Nick said somberly. "Else I fear to receive my congé without ceremony. Say nothing of this to Polly. I'd not spoil her present pleasure for the world."

"No indeed," Richard agreed, turning back to the room. " 'Twould be the act of a rogue to do so. Such unaffected delight is a gift to all."

Polly's own gifts this Christmas numbered twelve as her true love followed the old carol. Each morning she found upon her pillow some new delight. There was a saddle of tooled Spanish leather, then boots to match; a little locket of mother-of-pearl; inlaid combs and lace ruffles; and one morning, a tortoiseshell kitten with a blue satin ribbon around its neck.

"She is called Annie," Nick said, propping himself on one elbow beside her, enjoying every nuance of expression on the mobile face. "With care, she should not become so dirty that she will have to be thrown away."

"Oh, I love you!" Polly declared, hugging him fiercely.

"And I you." He stroked the rich honeyed mass tumbling over his chest, looking beyond her head into the middle distance. From somewhere the storm clouds were gathering, and for the life of him, he could not grasp a thread of explanation.

"What is it?" Polly felt his sudden tension in the stroking hand on her head, in the broad chest against her cheek. She sat up.

Nick smiled and put aside his foreboding; there was nothing he could do until he knew what he was facing. "What could possibly be the matter? Let us go riding."

By the end of January, Polly was once more ensconced with the Bensons in Drury Lane, the court was back at Whitehall,

Parliament at Westminster, and the decimated capital began to pull itself back together. There were still cases of the plague, but the recovery rate was now much higher than that of the fatalities, and the populace ceased to fear; and ceased to observe even the most minimal precautions. As a result, the scourge retained the sting in its tail.

The Theatre Royal opened again. Thomas Killigrew assembled his scattered company, setting to with a will to entrance the playgoing public.

Polly was once more absorbed in the magic of the theatre. The Duke of Buckingham became as he had once been, just a member of the audience and a courtier she would avoid when at Whitehall. So busy and involved was she that she had little time for Susan's gloominess, and quite failed to notice Nick's increasing distraction. Until both were brought forcibly to her notice.

"Just what is the matter with Susan?" Nick demanded with unusual irritability as the parlor door banged on the departure of a red-eyed Sue. "She has had a permanent cold in the head since we returned from Wilton."

"Oh, I meant to talk to you about that!" Guiltily, Polly clapped her hand to her mouth. "It is just that Thomas is being so pernickety, and Edward wants to play a scene differently, and Thomas says he can go and play for Sir William Davenant in that case, and—"

"Yes, I do not need a recitation of all the trials and tribulations at the playhouse," Nick interrupted, rubbing his eyes tiredly. "What is amiss with Susan?"

Polly, swallowing an indignant retort at this impatient response, looked at Nick carefully. His face was drawn and haggard, the emerald eyes somehow dulled, sunken in the hollows of his face. It occurred to her, with a wash of remorse, that she had been so full of her own activities in the last two weeks that she had asked him nothing about his own concerns. He was frequently in conference with Richard, and sometimes she would come into the room and have the unmistakable impression that they had abruptly switched the subject on her arrival. But she had simply dismissed the vague puzzle, assuming they would share the confidence when they chose.

"Are you ailing, love?" she asked now, coming over to him, stroking his face with a fingertip. A note of fear tinged her voice as she thought of the plague, but Nick shook his head.

"I am quite well; just fatigued. What is it with Susan?"

She bit her lip, not willing to be so easily dismissed. But perhaps Nick did not want to be pressed, and to do so would simply increase his weariness. She turned to the sideboard, pouring him a glass of wine, wishing that she had thought to mix him a bowl of the punch which she knew well he enjoyed on these cold, inhospitable nights.

"Come feel the fire," she said softly, taking his hand, encouraging him to the hearth warmth. She pushed him into an elbow chair, then sat at his feet, resting her head against his knees. "Sue is sore afflicted, my lord."

The amusement in her voice told him that he need not react to this as to tragedy. He ran his hands through the bright locks pouring like molten honey over his knees. "Enlighten me, pray."

"Why, 'tis Cupid's dart," Polly said solemnly. "Did you not mark Oliver at Wilton?"

Nick thought. "I do not think that I did," he said.

"He is a footman, and most comely," Polly went on. "And Sue is smitten with Oliver and Oliver is smitten with Sue. So you see, 'tis not at all convenient for the one to be here and t'other in Wiltshire."

"No, I can see that it is not at all convenient," Nick agreed. "It could well cause a permanent cold in the head. Well, what's to be done?"

"It seems that Oliver is only an underfootman at present and cannot begin to think of marrying; but what he really would like is to be a gamekeeper in a little cottage, and Sue could have a tribe of babies, which would suit her very well—"

"Just a minute." Nick tugged on a strand of hair to bring

this vision of domestic bliss to a conclusion. "How is this ambition to be achieved?"

"Well, I do not see how it can be if you do not take a hand." Polly turned 'round, kneeling up to rest her elbows on his lap. "I have been meaning to bring it up this age, but—"

"You have been somewhat occupied," Nick finished for her.

"And you have been somewhat distracted," Polly said quietly, examining his face with grave attention. "What is troubling you, Nick?"

"Nothing of any moment." He shrugged. "To return to Sue and her headcold; in what fashion am I to take a hand?"

"It is obvious, is it not? You must employ Oliver as a gamekeeper on your estate in Yorkshire. Then they may marry and live happy ever after."

Nick scratched his nose thoughtfully. "Yorkshire is a very long and arduous journey away. 'Tis a very different life from the one to which they are accustomed. Would you really be doing them a favor? Mayhap Oliver can find such work in Wiltshire. It is a softer life, and not so far removed from London for Susan."

"You will not help, then?" Polly sounded as disappointed as she looked, and more than a little surprised.

"I did not say that. I suggest that you think about it, and consult further with Sue before we make any decisions."

"But if she thinks it a good idea, you will agree?"

"I will write to my steward to see what work and accommodation are available," he promised. "But do not be in such a hurry, moppet. You are not so anxious to lose Susan, are you?"

"No, of course not. I shall miss her most dreadfully. But I cannot be so selfish as to hinder her happiness for such a reason."

Nick smiled at her very clear indignation at such an implication. He pinched her nose. "Your pardon, madame; I did not mean to cast aspersions on your character."

Polly's chuckle was swallowed in a yawn. Nicholas stood

up, drawing her up with him. " 'Tis past your bedtime, sweetheart. And I must away."

"You will not stay?" She looked at him in that same searching way, but could see nothing more than weariness. "Where must you go at this time of the night?"

"To Sir Peter's. There are some matters we must discuss." He reached for his cloak. "But if it is not too late, I will come here afterward. Although I'd not wish to wake you."

"Then I cannot imagine what point there would be." Polly pouted in mock vexation, receiving an ungentlemanly swat for her pains. She skipped to the door and opened it for him. "Begone, sir. The sooner you are about your business, the sooner will it be done, and you may return."

Nick pulled on his gloves, picked up his rapier stick, and turned up the fur collar of his cloak against the January winds. "I had better find you asleep on my return." Tilting her chin with a gloved finger, he kissed her closed mouth, lingering on its soft, pliant sweetness for long minutes before reluctantly releasing her.

Polly stood at the head of the stairs, shivering at the cold blast of icy air as he opened the street door. Then it had closed behind him, and the draft set the fire in the parlor spurting orange. She went over to the warmth, hugging her arms across her breast, a small frown buckling her forehead. Whatever Nick might say, something was causing him powerful worry. Yet if he would not confide in her, how could she help him?

She sighed, staring down into the fire as if, within its constantly shifting pattern, she would see answers. But the pictures formed and dissolved, offering no enlightenment. Turning her attention to a matter in which she could be helpful, she strode to the door.

"Sue! Sue, are ye busy?"

The girl appeared from the kitchen quarters, coming to the foot of the stairs. "D'ye need summat?" she asked apathetically.

"Only some company," Polly coaxed. "I have some news that might cheer you. And there's chestnuts we can roast."

Susan, looking as if she could not imagine being cheered by such offerings, came up to the parlor. " 'Is lordship gone out, then?"

"Aye, some business he had to attend to. But pray listen, Sue. I have talked to him about you and Oliver, and guess what he has said." Eagerly, Polly expounded her plan and the positive part of Nick's reaction. She could see no reason to depress Sue further by explicating possible drawbacks to the scheme.

"D'ye think he really means it?" Susan breathed, all evidence of tears vanished. "Why, t'would be the most wonderful thing." Reaching into the coals, she hitched out a glowing, ashy chestnut, dropping it abruptly onto the hearth, licking her singed fingers.

"But Yorkshire's a mighty long way." Polly decided that in good conscience she should perhaps point out this fact, at least. Picking up the chestnut, she tossed it from hand to hand, in the hopes that the movement would cool it.

Susan, however, disregarded this disadvantage completely. "I've no family 'ere," she said. "An' Oliver's folk're in Cornwall, so 'e don't pay them no mind as 'tis."

"Well, perhaps you should write and ask him what he thinks," suggested Polly, peeling the steaming nut. "Before my lord writes to his steward. Just in case Oliver does not care for the idea."

"Oh, 'e will," Sue said with confidence. She looked dreamily into the fire. "Just think on't, Polly. To be married, with my own 'ouse, and babes, and a cow, and a chicken . . ." The thought of such plenty rendered her speechless for a minute, then she said curiously, "D'ye think of marrying, Polly?"

The question triggered the old unease, the uncertainty that she usually managed to suppress by refusing to think beyond the loving glories of the present. Now she lied. "I've never thought on it, Sue. I'm an actor, and there's Nick. Why would I want to marry?" She smiled slightly, reaching into the fire for another chestnut so that Sue could not see her face. "There are wives and there are whores in the world you and I come from, Susan. You are made to be wife, and I to be whore." She shrugged and made the lie complete. "I am content with my lot. Cottages and chickens and cows and babes would not please me half so much."

"But what about when 'is lordship takes a wife?" Susan asked diffidently. "Will 'e keep you, d'ye think?"

That was the nub—the aspect of the future that Polly dared not dwell upon. Nicholas, Lord Kincaid, would need a wife—and it could not be a Newgate-born, tavern-bred bastard. Society might not frown too heavily on an actor's becoming a baroness, but Polly Wyat had more than just the stage in her background, as she and Nick knew. Women with her dubious origins did not make the wives of noblemen and the mothers of their heirs, however much they were loved. So what would happen when Nick did take a wife? Would a wife look complacently upon an established mistress? Or would she demand he throw up his whore and devote his full attention to the marriage bed? In the shoes of this putative wife, Polly felt that *she* would most certainly insist. It was a desolate thought. "One day I must ask him," she said with a light laugh, another shrug. She was not an actor for nothing.

"Now, do you not think ye should discover Oliver's views on this?" She returned briskly to the original subject, and Sue, fortunately, found it sufficiently absorbing to put the other matter out of her head.

"But 'ow am I to ask 'im?" Susan frowned, then her face cleared. "Ye'll write the letter for me, won't ye, Polly? Now y'are so book-learned."

Polly looked a little doubtful. "I can read all right, anything at all now; but I've not a fair hand." She grimaced. It was a subject on which Nick was inclined to be testy, maintaining quite correctly that if she bothered to apply herself to the task, she could manage to produce something that did not look as if it had been written by a rampant rabble of centipedes. "But I'll try."

Getting up from the floor, she went to the press for paper, sharpened a goose quill, and sat down at the table to compose the missive. Sue came to stand behind her, exclaiming in admiration as Polly demonstrated this amazing art of writing. "Who's to read it for him?" Polly asked, shaking the sand caster over the script.

"Oh, there'll be someone." Susan peered closely. "What's that squiggle there?"

" 'Tis just a squiggle," Polly said regretfully. "I told you I have not a fair hand. But there's fewer blots than usual. Shall I read it to you? Then you can say what else you want written."

The task took them well into the night, as the fire died and the candles guttered, but so absorbed were they, they noticed nothing until Polly shivered suddenly. "Put more coals on the fire, Sue. We're like to freeze to death."

The sound of the front door made them both start. " 'Tis Nick," Polly said, relaxing at the familiar tread.

"What the deuce goes on here?" demanded Nick, coming into the parlor. " 'Tis near two in the morning."

"Oh, we have been writing a letter to Oliver," Polly told him cheerfully, reaching up to kiss him in greeting. "At least, I have been writing."

"Then heaven send Oliver uncommon powers." Nick tossed his cloak onto the settle. "He'll never be able to decipher it, else. You might just as well leave him in ignorance."

"Oh, that is unjust," Polly exclaimed. "I have made it fair. Only see." She held out her handiwork.

Nick scrutinized the communication, returning it with a head shake of mock exasperation. "You spell most vilely, Polly. I swear I should have used the rod to teach you with."

"Oh, I do not care a jot for your opinion," Polly declared. "It says what Sue wished it to say."

"Then it had best go to the carrier without delay." Nick took his long clay pipe from the mantel. "Be off with you to your bed, Susan."

He lit the pipe and stood, shoulders to the hearth, squinting through the fragrant blue smoke as if trying to decide on something.

Polly stood immobile, afraid that a movement would distract him, and she did not want him distracted because just possibly he was deciding to confide in her. A dreadful thought reared an ugly head, nurtured by her conversation with Sue. Perhaps he had resolved to take a wife, and was even now trying to think how best to break it to her.

Nicholas was thinking of the conversation he had just had with his friends. It was clear to them all that for some cause, Kincaid was regarded with deep disfavor by the king. While he had not been denied admittance to Whitehall since their return from Wilton, he was made to feel like a leper, ostracized by all but his special friends. It was a pattern familiar to all habitués of Whitehall in these days of favoritism and conspiracies, both real and imagined. In a society defined by a complete absence of trust, no one was really safe. A certain coolness would be noticed, an absence of attention if one approached the king; then came the frown, the turned shoulder that denied audience; then came the whispers that fed more whispers; and a man was on his way to outer darkness.

Matters had now reached this last stage for Nicholas, and he was no nearer to understanding the cause than he had been at Christmas. None of his friends could throw light on the matter, either. They knew only that Kincaid was persona non grata, that the king mistrusted him, and it was best not to be seen in his company if one was not to be tarred with the same brush.

His present dilemma was a difficult and a dangerous one. He had two choices: to brave it out, taking the risk that no more than mood and whim lay behind his present disfavor; or he could flee London, rusticate in Yorkshire until some other matter took the king's attention, to put Kincaid out of sight, out of mind. The latter course would be the sensible one if he thought there was a concrete reason for King Charles's anger and mistrust. Concrete reasons led to the Tower and the executioner's block. But he could come up with nothing. And if he fled, what was to be done with Polly? As his mistress, she might also be endangered if he left her behind. Yet to take her away would take her from her beloved theatre at a high point in a career that depended upon being in the public eye. He did not think he had the right to do that—not without absolute certainty of danger. She was not his wife yet, when all was said and done. Fortunately for her, he thought mirthlessly. In his present anomalous position, the greater the perceived distance between them, the better.

"Are you going to leave me?" Polly heard herself whisper, quite without volition. The bleak look on his face frightened her more than anything she could have imagined, and the need to know what caused it had become invincible, regardless of what misery the knowledge might spell for her.

Nick started at this uncanny reading of his thoughts. What could she know of this? "Why would you think such a thing?" he demanded, his voice harsh without intention.

Polly bit her lip, her fire-warmed cheeks cooling with the chill that seemed to enwrap her. "I do not know why; but you appear so distracted, and you will not tell me of the cause. I . . . I was thinking of marriage." This last came out in a rush, and she dropped her eyes lest he read her panic.

"Marriage!" What sort of a mind reader was she? But now was not the moment for such a subject in all its complexities; not now when he was enmeshed in a web of an unknown's spinning, and he must make immediate decisions that could well have far-reaching consequences for both their lives. "Do you know what o'clock it is?" he demanded irritably. "When I decide 'tis time to talk of marriage, I will apprise you of the fact in good order."

"And I suppose that then I must find another protector," Polly said, unable to help herself. Once the monster had risen, it would not return peaceably to its lair.

Nicholas closed his eyes on a weary sigh. Why on earth was she playing this silly game now? Had she no more understanding of his bone-deep exhaustion, his dreadful apprehension than to make ridiculous jests? He heard truculence in her voice, rather than the anxiety this was designed to mask. He saw her pallor and interpreted it as fatigue; the gaze that would not meet his, he interpreted as the petulance of an overtired child.

"Do not talk such arrant nonsense," he said shortly. "It seems to me that you lack even common sense. You were exhausted four hours ago, but instead of seeking your bed like the rational grown woman you are supposed to be, you waste the night in idle chatter with the maid."

"I had thought that was why Susan lived here," Polly fired back, confused resentment overcoming anxiety. "So that I should have someone with whom to engage in idle chatter!"

"I do not always make the right decisions, particularly where you are concerned," snapped his lordship. "Get you to bed straightway."

"I will not on your say-so," she declared, furious at this apparently unprovoked attack.

Nicholas sighed. "Polly, I am awearied, too much so to join battle. Go to bed or not, as you please."

"I do please!" Polly banged into the bed chamber, there to crawl beneath the quilt, falling asleep with sticky lashes and tear-wet cheeks and salt upon her lips.

Nicholas remained beside the fire, tobacco and wine providing a measure of spurious ease. Eventually he went to bed, slipping an arm beneath the sleeping figure, rolling her into his embrace before finding his own uneasy oblivion.

Chapter 19

They came for Lord Kincaid that same night, in the hour before dawn when the spirit is at its lowest ebb and the night's chill at its most pervasive.

The hammering at the street door, the bellowed "Open in the name of the king!" brought casements flung wide the length of Drury Lane, and Goodman Benson, in nightcap and gown, hurrying from his bed, shivering with fear and cold, to draw back the bolts.

The lieutenant pushed past him, a troop of six soldiers at his back. "We are come for Lord Kincaid. Where is he to be found?"

Benson, quivering like an aspen leaf, pointed abovestairs, unable to find his voice in the face of this terrifying visitation.

The lieutenant, hand on sword, mounted two steps at a time, flinging open the door to the darkened parlor. He crossed the empty room, threw wide the door to the bedchamber. "My Lord Kincaid?" he demanded into the darkness, his soldiers crowding at his back.

Nick had heard the banging, had had time to recognize what was about to happen, but not to prepare himself. Now he reached for flint and tinder, lighting the candle beside the bed. Polly had sat up, her eyes wide in incomprehension, her

tumbled hair doing little to conceal her breasts as the quilt
fell to her waist.

The intruders' eyes, as one pair, became riveted upon that
creamy, rose-tipped perfection. Nicholas took hold of the
cover and drew it up. "You have need of this," he said quietly. "To what do I owe this pleasure, gentlemen?" An eyebrow quirked in sardonic question.

"You are Lord Kincaid?" The lieutenant approached the
bed, one hand still on his sword hilt, although the man in the
bed was both naked and unarmed.

"The very same," Nicholas said with an ironic bow of his
head.

"What is happening?" Polly found her voice at last,
clutching the sheet to her neck as she stared at a scene that
smacked of a Bedlamite's lunacy.

"Hush, sweetheart," Nick commanded, gently but with
authority. "You are to say nothing at all."

"I bear a warrant for your arrest, my lord," intoned the
lieutenant. "You are to be committed to the Tower, there to
await impeachment."

"On whose authority?" asked Nick, still quiet.

"His Grace the Duke of Buckingham signs the warrant in
the king's name," came the answer, promptly.

"And the charge?"

"Treason, my lord."

Polly gasped. "But that is—"

"Hold your tongue!" Nicholas snapped. "May I see the
warrant, Lieutenant?"

Polly subsided, realizing that she must sit still, and watch
and listen. Only thus could she perhaps find a clue to this
mystery. Surely it was a mistake; Nick would read the warrant and laugh, because it was meant for some other Lord
Kincaid. But she knew that there was no mistake, and when
Nick, having perused the document, handed it back without
a word, the little cold space in her heart began to expand
until she felt a great, terrifying emptiness.

"Will you grant me privacy to dress, Lieutenant?" Nicholas asked politely. "If you await me in the parlor, I will join you in a few moments."

The soldier's eyes went to the casement. "You have my word," Nicholas said.

One could not refuse to take the word of a gentleman. "Very well, my lord." The lieutenant clicked his spurs together, spun on his heel, and left the bedchamber, his cohorts following.

"I do not understand what is happening," Polly whispered. "What is this of treason?"

"If I knew, I would be better able to form a defense," Nicholas said, swinging out of bed. "But 'tis my own fault."

"How so?" Polly sat watching him dress, in thrall to a confused terror that numbed her like the poisonous bite of a spider. The world she thought she knew was disintegrating, and she could not seem to do anything to hold it together.

"I had foreseen this, but dallied overlong," Nick said bitterly, buckling his sword belt. "Because I did not understand it, I did not believe in the urgency. I should have left London last week."

"But why?" Desperately, she still sought for a kernel of understanding. "What will they do to you, love?" Kneeling on the bed, she stretched out her hands toward him. "They will realize it is a mistake, and then you will come back. That is how it will be, isn't it?"

Nicholas looked at the huge eyes in the pale face, beseeching him with the dark, haunted terror of a small animal in a trap. He took the outstretched hands, folding them in his own, holding them to his breast. "You must go to De Winter and tell him of this. He will know how best to protect you. Tell him that the warrant bears Buckingham's signature. I know not how I have fallen foul of the duke, but it is certain sure that therein lies my offense."

Polly listened to the calm instructions, felt the warm strength of his hold, and heard again in memory Buckingham's voice: "Everyone has a price. I will find yours, make no mistake." How naive she had been to imagine that, having played with her a little at Wilton House, he considered his revenge well taken. He had told her as plainly as he could that he had found her price—the incalculable value of love.

Premonition took on a dread shape; what had been only specter solidified. Nick's voice, softly urgent, continued to reach her across the gray wasteland of knowledge, telling her that she must not lose courage, that he had friends aplenty who would work in his cause, that in these friends they must both trust, because, once lodged in the Tower, Nick could not act on his own behalf; until the charges were made clear when he was impeached, he could formulate no defense.

An imperative knock came at the bedchamber door. Nick kissed her—a short, hard farewell—and released her hands, pulling the quilt around her shoulders. "Do not lose courage, sweetheart. In that you must not fail me," he said, the deep green eyes holding hers. "And you must trust Richard. He will look after you."

"My lord?" The door opened, and Nick turned to face the lieutenant.

"I am ready." He reached for his cloak.

"I must ask you to surrender your sword, my lord," the lieutenant said in wooden accents.

Nick's hesitation was barely perceptible; then, an enigmatic smile playing over his lips, he drew forth his sword, presenting it with a bow, hilt first, to his guard. At the door, he looked over his shoulder to where Polly still knelt, wrapped in the quilt. He could feel the coldness of her hands in his, the stark terror that rendered her motionless, and he could not bear to abandon her in such a plight. He took a step back to the bed. The lieutenant laid a restraining hand on his shoulder. Nick, with a violent curse, flung the hand away. The lieutenant drew his sword, and Polly in that instant returned to her senses.

She tumbled off the bed, clutching the quilt, the life again glowing in her eyes as her blood began to flow hot and fast. "I will not lose courage, love," she said, her voice strong. Tripping over the quilt in her haste, she ran toward him. "You must not think of me. You require all your thoughts and energies for yourself." She turned to the lieutenant, her chin lifting as she looked him in the eye, her voice icily scornful. "Put up your sword, sir. It is not meet to draw it against an unarmed man and a woman."

Nicholas relaxed. "Bravo, sweetheart," he approved softly. "You will do as I bid you?"

"Aye," she said strongly. "Fear naught for me." Ignoring the guard, who, having sheathed his sword, was now shifting his booted feet impatiently, she reached up to kiss Nick. "I will see you back soon, my love."

He left then; it was not a farewell to be prolonged, for all that in the bleak recesses of his soul he knew that it could be the last.

Polly flew to the parlor window, looking down into the dark street, where a closed, unmarked carriage awaited. The escort and his prisoner climbed in, the troop mounted their horses, and the sinister procession set of in the direction of the Tower, from whence so many never returned. For one dreadful minute she saw the scaffold on Tower Hill, the executioner with his ax, heard the crowds laughing and jeering, come to see the sport; Nick, his hair tied back, shirt collar loosened, laying his bared neck upon the block. That paralyzing terror threatened again. This was not a world where one could rely on justice. Justice was an instrument of putty to be bent and shaped by those who possessed the power. George Villiers, Duke of Buckingham, possessed that power.

The terror receded, a cold, clear purpose taking its place. She would consult with Richard first, because that was what Nick had bidden her do. But if De Winter would not agree to support her when she did what she knew had to be done, then would she play the game alone.

She dressed rapidly, then hastened down the stairs. The Bensons appeared from the back of the house as she laid her hand upon the latch. "Where've they taken my lord?" quavered Goodman Benson, his face waxen in the light of the candle that wavered in his shaking hand.

"To the Tower," Polly said shortly. "Ye've no need for fear. 'Tis no great matter, and will be soon sorted."

"But he was ta'en in our house," moaned the goodwife, dabbing her lips with her handkerchief, her nightcap askew on the thin gray curls. " 'Tis us they'll come fer next."

"You talk foolery," Polly snapped, understanding their fear but having little time for it. "Ye'll not be traduced. Why should the Duke of Buckingham concern himself with the likes of you?"

Indeed, neither of the Bensons could think of a single reason, and some of the anxiety faded from the faces still raised, half in appeal, half in anger, toward their lodger without whom this dread happening would not have occurred.

Polly could not stay for further discussion. She left them by the stairs, going out herself into the cold and the gray gloom of a winter dawn. Richard lived in a fine house in St. Martin's Lane. It took her no more than ten minutes before she was hammering on the great knocker, caring not if she woke the dead.

The bolts scraped back, and a sleepy footboy stood, indignant, in the doorway, rubbing his hands in the icy air. "What business d'ye have at this hour?"

"Business with my Lord De Winter," Polly announced briskly, pushing past him into the hall. "Pray tell him at once that Mistress Wyat desires speech with him."

The footboy looked as if he was about to take issue with this peremptory and outrageous demand, but Richard, alerted by Polly's vigorous knocking, appeared on the stairs, a warm furred nightgown drawn close about him against the early morning chill.

"Why, Polly! What's amiss, child?" Quickly, he came down to the hall. "No, you shall tell me in my parlor. Lad, kindle the fire, then bring hot milk to the parlor!" He snapped his fingers at the bemused boy, who scampered off in obedience. "You are chilled to the bone. Have you walked from Drury Lane?"

"Aye," Polly said, a hint of impatience in her voice. "There is not time for fires and hot milk, sir—"

"There is ample time for both, child," Richard interrupted calmly. "You will learn as you grow older that very little cannot wait upon hot milk and a fire."

"But they have taken Nick!" Polly cried.

"Yes, it was to be expected. But wait until we are private to tell me the manner of it."

Polly yielded. She had not the strength to batter against the wall of De Winter's calm impassivity. "You expected it?" She allowed him to lead her into the small, booklined parlor at the back of the house, where a fire now blazed in the hearth.

"Aye, but we miscalculated. We had thought to discover what lay behind Nick's fall into disfavor, and thus hoped to circumvent it." Richard tapped his fingers on the carved wooden mantel, staring down into the fire. "He is imprisoned in the Tower?"

"Yes." Polly sat wearily on a leather-covered stool beside the fire. "They took him but a half hour since. He said—" She broke off as the door opened to admit the lad with a steaming pitcher and two mugs, which he set on the table.

"That be all, m'lord?"

"For the moment," Richard said, strolling over to the table. He poured hot milk into one of the mugs, then added brandy from the decanter. "Drink this, Polly. 'Twill put the heart back in you."

She took the drink, warming her chilled hands on the mug, then, between grateful sips, told the tale, carefully repeating Nick's words.

"So we must lay this at Buckingham's door," Richard mused when she had finished. "Why?"

He looked shrewdly at Polly, sitting upon the stool, hands still clasped around the mug, a strange expression on her set face. "Ye've some light to shed on this, Polly?"

"I think so," she said.

"How so?" He waited, curious to hear what this exquisite creature could have to say. She had shown herself quick-witted in the past, possessed of an eye and an ear for the important, the ability to select from a mass of information and impressions that which was salient.

"The Duke of Buckingham promised . . . nay, threatened that he would find my price," Polly told him, staring fixedly into her mug. "It would appear that he has done so."

De Winter whistled softly. "You think he would have Nick accused for such a reason?"

Polly shrugged. "I am certain of it. Let me tell you what transpired between us at Wilton House."

Richard heard her out in attentive silence, then spoke firmly. "Buckingham is a cunning bastard, my dear. A great deal more cunning than you." He leaned forward to poke the fire. "I would have you do nothing until I have had a chance to smell the wind. It may be that you are mistaken, that this is nothing, that the king will lose interest and will be persuaded to rescind the order—"

"And while we wait for such an illusion to take shape, Nick languishes in the Tower, in God knows what conditions!" Polly interrupted, impassioned, leaping to her feet. "Tread softly, lest ye rouse the devil! Is that it, my lord?"

"It seems to me that the devil is already roused," Richard said dryly. "Moderate your tongue. Nick may allow you uncommon license in your badgering, but I will not."

Polly flushed and resumed her seat. The rebuke, as had been intended, served to bring under control the sudden surge of panic that had led to her outburst.

Richard permitted himself a smile, lifting her chin. "I understand your fear. Indeed, I share it. But nothing will be gained without due thought and care. Trust me."

"I do." Polly offered a wry smile. "But I should warn you that I will act on my own if you will not assist me."

"That were foolish in you. I will not deny you assistance, but I ask that you let me do what I can first."

Polly looked into the calm, strong face. Richard would have no chivalrous scruples about permitting her to make whatever sacrifice she chose, if that was the only path open to them. Had he not already asked such a thing of her? But beside his deep and abiding friendship for Nicholas, he also had a fondness for her. She could count on him to behave with pragmatic realism, but he would take no unnecessary risks.

"Very well," she agreed. "But you will not ask me to wait overlong?"

He shook his head. "How should I? But Nick would prefer that you not make this sacrifice, so let us see if we can obviate the necessity."

"He must not know," Polly said. "If it is necessary, he must never know of it."

Oh, the naïveté of the young, thought Richard. But he would not enter that murky arena—not yet, at least. "Now, listen carefully, Polly. You must, for the moment, behave as if you are quite unaffected by this. Puzzled, certainly, but not unduly disturbed. You can always find another protector, can you not? That is what the world must think."

"Yes." She nodded. "The play must go on, must it not?"

"Good girl." He released her chin. "Go to the theatre and give the performance of your life. Can you do that?"

"Of course," she said simply, getting to her feet. " 'Tis to be *Rule a Wife and Have a Wife*. I shall be the most wicked, defiant Margarita imaginable, and hint to the entire playhouse that, like Margarita, I conduct my love affairs where I choose, accepting no man's authority—be he husband or keeper; and the absence of my keeper at the king's pleasure makes little difference to my roving eye. We will see what my lord duke makes of that." Then the spark faded from her eye, the challenge from her voice. "Can you discover if Nick wants for anything, Richard?"

"He'll be lodged as a lord, child. He will not suffer discomfort."

"But 'tis a dark and gloomy place, the Tower." Polly shuddered. "Damp with the river slime, and lonely, with only the ravens for company."

"He'll have the governor for company," Richard reassured. "And they'll not put him to the torture without cause; which cause must be declared for all to hear."

Polly's pallor increased, and Richard realized with annoyance that he had planted a thought hitherto not conceived.

"Be not afeard," he said swiftly. "We will not permit such a thing."

"I wonder how you would prevent it," she said in dull truth. "I would sell my soul to Buckingham first."

Richard, for once, had no answer, but he bade her wait beside the fire while he dressed; then he would escort her home, where she should try to repair the broken night.

That afternoon Buckingham sat in his box at the king's house and watched her performance with cold admiration. He had been given a detailed account of the dawn events at the lodging in Drury Lane; he knew that Kincaid's mistress had not reacted to his arrest with equanimity. Yet here she was, investing the part of the amorous, designing Spanish heiress, intent on cuckolding a foolish husband, with such flagrant provocation as to make it a challenge to every man in the audience. It was almost as if she herself were saying, you may have me if I choose to be had, but let no man think to rule me. It was a clear statement that the abrupt removal of her present protector—a piece of gossip on everyone's lips—was not causing her any grave unease.

Thomas Killigrew, better attuned to the actor's skills, sensed the brittle edge to the performance. It was an edge that sharpened her act, but increased its fragility. It would take little to fragment the coherence of the part she played, and he found himself biting his lip in anxiety, for once feeling the play drag as he wished it to a speedy conclusion before disaster struck. It was not a wish shared by the audience, who were responding with gusts of laughter and shouts of encouragement when Leon revealed himself as far from the fool Margarita had believed him, and set about the task of bringing his errant wife to heel.

Polly alternately appealed to and challenged the spectators until they did not know what outcome they wanted in this particular duel of the sexes. Edward Nestor, as Leon, had no doubts at all and played better than he had ever done, a fact duly noted by Killigrew. One of Polly's great attributes was her ability to bring out the best in her fellow players. However, it was with a deep sigh of relief that Thomas heard the epilogue spoken.

As Polly came off the stage, the strain of the act she had just put on showed clear in her eyes, in the tautness of her mouth, the tension in her body. Thomas called her, and she came over to him, expecting his usual words of approval and the inevitable constructive criticism. "How often do you think you can do that?" he demanded bluntly.

"I do not know what you mean." She found herself avoiding his eye. "Was there something wrong? *They* did not think so, at all events."

"You know well what I mean. It is because of Nick, is it not?" He laid a compassionate hand on her arm.

"I will not let you down, Thomas," she said, ignoring the question. "If that is your concern, you may rest easy."

"My concern is for you. You will not be able to continue at such a pitch of desperation for very long. You will break, and you will take everyone down with you."

"I will not fail you," she reiterated. "I have matters well in hand, Thomas."

It was a statement that Thomas had some difficulty accepting, but before he could say anything, a noisy, laughing, chattering throng of courtiers, the Duke of Buckingham at their head, came into the tiring room, exclaiming and congratulating, waving perfumed handkerchiefs in emphasis, quizzing Polly through monocles as they called her a wicked jade, a sorceress who knew too well how to enslave the poor male with her charms and her wit.

Polly smiled, disclaimed prettily, flirted with accomplished ease, and gave them exactly what they wanted, except that she singled out no one for a special smile or unspoken promise. Suggestions were made, some overt invitations, but she deflected them all, conscious all the while of the unwinking scrutiny of Buckingham, who did not add his own voice to the chatter, but seemed to be watching her for something. It required every last effort to keep her voice from faltering, her smile from vanishing as if it had never been. It was as if he were deliberately trying to disconcert her, and when, involuntarily, her eyes met his, she saw there a cold satisfaction, a quiet calculation that pierced her facade as if it were gossamer, revealing the naked vulnerability of her love.

He smiled lazily, drawing out an enameled snuffbox from the deep pocket of his gold-embroidered coat. "You will sup with me this evening, Mistress Wyat." It was the first time he had spoken, and there was no question mark. He took a pinch of snuff on his wrist, not taking his eyes off Polly.

Polly felt a great stillness fill her, a cool space surround her, as if she stood alone on the edge of an uncharted, horizonless sea. Richard had said she was to do nothing until he had had time to do what he could. But then, they had not expected the duke to move so quickly. She looked into the cold eyes, saw again the power of his lust and now the knowledge of its imminent satisfaction. Somehow she forced a smile as if she had not seen those things. "Nothing will give me greater pleasure, my lord duke."

He bowed. "I will send my carriage for you at nine o'clock." Then he walked away, leaving Polly's admiring court to exclaim at his good fortune and to complain at the lady's hard heart that would not unbend for them.

Polly walked alone back to her lodging. Richard had said he would spend the evening at court, where he would learn what he could. He would not wait upon her until the following day, by which time her assignation with Buckingham would be a thing of the past, and recriminations pointless. Richard never engaged in pointless exercises.

Her apartments carried a desolate air, a bleak loneliness in the two rooms once so cozy, so redolent with love's warmth and laughter. Susan appeared stunned, unable to comprehend the extent of the disaster that had come from the blue to shatter the orderly world to which she was accustomed. She could think only of how this would affect the plan to establish herself and Oliver in Yorkshire, and Polly was hard-pressed to bite her tongue. But she knew that Susan had to focus upon something in order to make some sense of things, and the matter that concerned her most nearly was the obvious choice. So she let the girl moan and bewail and speculate while she helped Polly with an elaborate toilet designed both to indicate to Buckingham that she was unbowed by events, and to convince herself of that fact.

She wore a gown of ivory satin, looped up at the sides to reveal a rose damask petticoat edged with lace, stiffly encrusted with seed pearls. The long train of the gown swept behind her; her hair was piled artfully on top of her head, the knot contained by a delicate filigree coronet; this headdress and a pair of high-heeled satin pumps added to her stature—a prop sorely needed by the actor this night. The string of perfect pearls that Nicholas had given her as a belated eighteenth birthday present were clasped around her neck, and she drew strength from them as if from a talisman. They bore his spirit, and nothing that Buckingham could do or say would defile that.

Yet when the carriage arrived at the door on the stroke of nine o'clock, the sweat of fear broke out on her brow, and nausea tugged at her belly, loosened her gut. She drew on lace-edged gloves over her clammy, shaking hands, and Sue draped her velvet-lined cloak about her shoulders.

It was simply an attack of stage fright, she told herself, descending the stairs. She was accustomed to such attacks, knew just how to deal with them. She was about to go onstage; once there, all fear would disappear, because she would no longer be Polly Wyat, who could be afraid, but someone else for whom fear was a stranger and an irrelevancy. But while she sat in the carriage with the Buckingham arms emblazoned upon the panels, she was still Polly Wyat, miserably afraid, and there was no Master Killigrew waiting in the wings, sending out his support and encouragement.

The carriage came to a stop all too soon; the door opened, the footstep was lowered, and Polly stepped out. Only then did she realize where they were. This was not the Duke of Buckingham's mansion in the Strand. It was Covent Garden, and she was standing at the door of one of the most notorious bawdy houses in the Piazza. That door was opened, and a servant stood there, clearly bidding her entrance. She could refuse, turn and walk away from here in her elegant gown of a lady of the court, behaving as if her costume were an accurate reflection of the person it clothed; or she could go inside to perform her whoring with the rest of the house's occupants. She had come here to sell her body. How and where the buyer chose to conduct the purchase was up to him.

Well, at least her role had been defined for her from the outset. There were to be no polite pretenses. She could play the harlot as well as any other character—probably better, since she had been bred to play it from puberty. With a cold detachment, Polly gathered up her skirt and entered the house.

The servant closed the door. Polly stood for a minute as the sounds of the house enveloped her. There were giggles, and squeals, loud male laughter, the smack of flesh upon flesh, scurrying feet, slamming doors.

The servant leered, looking in open speculation at her dress and bearing. Polly returned the look with one of haughty derision. "Is it too much to ask that ye cease your gaping and take me to my host?"

The man's jaw dropped, but he gestured toward a narrow flight of stairs at the rear of the hall. "This-a-way."

Polly followed him to an upper landing. A man, wig askew above a face glistening and scarlet with drink, his clothing in a state of considerable disarray, emerged from a chamber, laughing as he fumbled with the buttons of his breeches. He, too, gawped at Polly as if he could not quite believe his eyes. Polly allowed her gaze to roam insolently down his body before she looked up in scorn, as if finding him wanting. His color heightened; he took a step toward her, whether in menace or interest, Polly did not stay to discover.

Her escort led her down a narrow corridor to pause outside a door at the far end. It was quieter in this part of the house, the floor no longer bare but covered with a canvas carpet, the candles in the sconces wax, not tallow. The man tapped on the door, then opened it, standing aside for Polly to enter.

"My lord duke, what novel surroundings," she said, sweeping past the servant, allowing her train to swirl around her in a pool of ivory satin.

Buckingham was standing beside the hearth, a glass of ruby claret in his hand, an expression of anticipated amusement on his face. At her crisp greeting, the amusement faded somewhat. "Brothels and whoring partner each other remarkably well," he said, softly insulting. "I had thought you would find such surroundings more comfortable."

"Indeed?" Her eyebrows lifted. "How considerate of you, my lord duke." She looked around the chamber with every appearance of interest. It reminded her of the room at the Dog tavern where she had taken the gulls and undressed for them. It was cleaner, certainly, more comfortable, but it reeked of its purpose, as had the other chamber. If it had not been for Nicholas, she would have been whoring for pennies in that room, when Josh was not taking payment in kind for her keep. And no doubt she would have died of the plague, and any misbegotten bastards with her.

Life came full circle sometimes. She would do now what would have been forced from her, if fate had not intervened. The Polly of the Dog tavern had many strengths, and knew how to overcome the degradation, how to distance herself from assaults. All she had to do was to rediscover that Polly— the one Buckingham did not know had ever existed, the one Nicholas had spent so much loving care on obliterating.

"Shall we discuss terms, Your Grace?" Her hands went to the clasp of her cloak, but Buckingham forstalled her.

"Allow me." He eased the manteau from her shoulders, laying it with great care over a chair back. "A glass of wine, perhaps?"

"Thank you." Her hand was perfectly steady as she took the glass, and she was aware of a distance between herself and this man who was going to torment her if he could. But he would not be able to, because he did not know that Nick's Polly was not in this room. Here was a street-hardened tavern wench, accustomed to blows and curses, well able to hold her own in a world informed by brutality and degradation—a world in which such a place as this was utterly familiar. If he did but know it, His Grace had done her some considerable favor by this initial humiliation. It made the role much easier to carry.

"Why should you imagine, Mistress Wyat, that you are in a position to discuss terms?" the duke now said, returning to the fire, leaning one arm negligently along the mantel, regarding her with that same air of amused interest, as one who waited for the entertaining antics of a creature in a circus, obliged to perform to his piping.

Polly sipped her claret. "Indeed, Your Grace, should you choose to take from me whatever you wish without my consent, there is none to say you nay." She looked around the room. "The door is not locked, but I am sure that if I chose to run from you, there would be those to stop me." She walked over to the window, drawing aside the curtain to look down onto the bustling Piazza, where the full gamut of fleshly pleasures and perversions was for sale. "I did not have to enter this house. But you knew that I would, since you appear to have discovered my price." She turned and smiled at him over her glass. "Rape might appeal to you in some instances, my lord duke, but I'd hazard that you want more than that from me."

Buckingham pulled at his chin, regarding her now thoughtfully, quite without amusement. He had expected abject fear, pleading for her lover, and finally the desperate acceptance of the terms he would dictate. Instead, she was standing there telling him that she understood the game and was prepared to play it.

"No," he said, pushing himself away from the mantel. "Rape has limited appeal, although I might choose to fabricate it at some point in our acquaintanceship."

"Your terms, duke."

"Can you not guess, mistress? You seem remarkably perspicacious." He strolled over to the long deal table against the far wall and tore off a chicken leg from the bird resting on a humble pewter platter. "Will you not sup?"

"I find I have no appetite." She took his vacated place at the fire. "Perhaps I should tell you my own terms." She waited for a response, but Buckingham gnawed on his chicken leg, offering neither invitation nor denial. "You may have me, Duke. In exchange, I will have, now, the order for Lord Kincaid's release from the Tower, and the dismissal of all charges, either stated or predicated, against him; the document to be written by you, signed and sealed, and given to me before we commence whatever play you have in mind."

Buckingham smiled. "The play I have in mind, bud, will be of seven nights duration, here in this chamber. I will have from you your willing—nay, eager—participation." The smile broadened, and the banked fires of lust flared for a second in the eyes resting upon her face. "Any hesitancy to comply with my wishes, the hint of a refusal to accede to my demands, will nullify the bargain. You will come at this time every evening for seven days, returning to your lodgings in the morning."

So there it was. Polly forced herself to meet his searching gaze without flinching. She must lend herself to whatever quirks this man's notoriously dark lust might produce. A whore's work—no more than that. "What guarantee do I have that you will keep your side of the bargain?"

For some strange reason such an aspersion seemed to catch him on the raw. "You have the word of a Villiers!" he snapped, losing his equilibrium for a second.

Polly raised an ironic eyebrow. "Your pardon, my lord duke, I meant no slur upon your honor. How should I, indeed?" She paused for a minute, but the duke had himself well in hand again, so she continued calmly. "I would have your word, also, that you will do me no serious hurt, and that you will not spill your seed within." She was negotiating like a whore, Polly thought distantly. A whore's terms, for one must keep intact the goods with which one had to bargain in the future.

Buckingham suddenly laughed. "By God, but y'are more

than I reckoned on! As consummate a courtesan as my Lady Castlemaine or any. Know your value and keep it! Well, the sport will be the better for it, I swear." He strode to the door, flung it wide, and bellowed for the servant. "Bring me paper, quill, and sand caster."

They were produced, the order written, the charges declared dismissed. Buckingham dropped hot wax from the candle, sealing the document with the impress of his signet ring. "This will be delivered to the governor of the Tower in seven days time, on condition that you have fulfilled your side of the agreement."

"You'll not find me wanting," Polly said.

George Villiers refilled his wineglass, selected two walnuts with some deliberation from a bowl, then leaned against the table, looking at her. He held the walnuts against each other between his hands and squeezed slowly. The shells cracked in the sudden stillness. Smiling, he turned his attention to peeling away the husks cupped in his hands before looking up at her as she stood, immobile by the fire. His eyes narrowed as he said softly, "I'd have you show me what I've bought."

No different in essence, Polly thought, than the little chamber in the Dog tavern. She began to unhook her gown.

Chapter 20

⌒⌒⌒

The seventh morning after the seventh night dawned, its cold gray light filling the square casement. Polly lay wide-awake, stiff and chilled, as she had done since her bedfellow had finally fallen asleep. Her wrists were bound beneath her, and Buckingham had neglected to share the quilt before he had slept, so she could do nothing about her exposure to the ice-tipped air.

There was an eerie silence. She had noticed in the last seven nights that this silence fell for no more than a couple of hours, just before profound night yielded to the dawn. It fell very suddenly, as if the wildness of the Piazza had run its course, its inhabitants stopped dead in the tracks of debauchery. The house slept in the same way, screams, giggles, footsteps, cries, all ceased as if at a signal, and it was as if Polly were the only person awake in this squalid corner of the universe.

She shivered convulsively, but nothing would persuade her to edge closer to the warmth of her companion's body—not when it was not required of her, and her revulsion could not be detected.

"Are you cold?" Buckingham spoke into the gray light, sleepily matter-of-fact.

"You neglected to untie my hands," she said, as matter-of-fact as he. "And I have no quilt."

"Careless of me," he said, his voice arid as the desert. "D'ye find no pleasure in the sensation of helplessness, bud?"

"Had I done so, my lord duke, I venture to suggest that *your* pleasure would have been diminished," she responded with acid-tongued truth.

Buckingham chuckled. He had no objection to her tartness so long as she entered his sport without physical reservation; and she had certainly done that. Indeed, it had been a most rewarding seven nights; he was sorry that they were over. But he would have tired of her eventually, and there was a certain sweetness in an ending that came before one was truly ready. Rolling her onto her belly, he unfastened the silk scarf that bound her wrists.

"My thanks, sir," Polly said formally, sitting up and shaking the life back into her numbed arms, chafing her wrists. "Our bargain is completed, I believe."

"Aye." Villiers sighed regretfully. "But I'd as lief continue it for a while longer. If I'd known what a joy you would be, I'd have fixed upon a month." He got out of bed, stretched and yawned, then went to throw coals upon the fire's embers.

Polly made no response, merely huddled beneath the quilt, which still retained his body warmth, trying to stop her teeth from chattering. She watched him dress, thinking dispassionately that it was for the last time. She would go home, and Susan would have the tub of hot water waiting before the blazing fire, and she would scrub the night's violations from her body, and the memory from her mind for the last time. And Nicholas would return, and would replace those grimy memories with his own fresh, present reality.

Dressed, the duke went to the mantel, where he took up the sealed document that had lain there for the last seven nights. He tapped it thoughtfully against the palm of his hand, regarding the figure on the bed. "Extraordinary!" he murmured, shaking his head. "That one would voluntarily expose oneself to such a fatiguing emotion as love." He crossed to the bed, thrusting the document into the deep pocket of his coat. "A farewell kiss, sweet bud. 'Tis the last demand."

Eventually, the door closed on his departure. Polly flew from the bed, scrambling into her clothes, drawing her hooded cloak tight about her. The house reeked of stale liquor and tobacco smoke, and many other less savory remnants. A ragged, skinny girl, her chapped hands blue with cold, her nose dripping, was sloshing cold water over a pool of vomit in the corner of the landing. Polly drew her skirts aside and stepped quickly past. The doorkeeper, grumbling and mumbling, spat phlegm onto the sawdust-covered floor as he pulled back the bolts on the street door.

"It'd 'elp a body if'n ye'd come down t'gether!"

It had been the same complaint for the last six mornings. Buckingham always left before Polly—just another client leaving his whore in the brothel, where she belonged—and the doorkeeper always bolted the door after him, then grumbled mightily at having to open up again five minutes later. Polly ignored him today, as she had done every previous day. Out in the street, where the night's debris still littered, she took a deep breath of freedom. She would cleanse both mind and body of the soil of those nights. She was no delicately nurtured flower, no piece of porcelain to be cracked and broken by such doings. She had seen worse, had known as bad. For many, such sordid degradations informed their lives from birth until death. For her it was over.

She ran, gulping the air in great drafts, enjoying the icy scalding as it pierced her lungs. Susan, who as usual had been watching for her from the parlor window, had the door open before she could knock. Polly thanked her and leaned gasping against the newel post until she could get her breath.

"Bath's all ready," Sue said. "My Lord De Winter's abovestairs, waitin' on ye."

Still somewhat breathless, Polly went upstairs. Richard was standing beside the fire, waiting for her return as he had done for the last five mornings, ever since she had told him

of Buckingham's bargain. He looked at her searchingly.
" 'Tis done?"

"Aye." She nodded and came to the fire, stretching her
hands to its warmth. " 'Tis done, Richard. He'll not renege?"

"God's grace, no!" Richard caught her chin, tipping it
up. "And you, child?"

"Am no child," she said with a tiny smile. "But I am
whole. The scars will not run deep."

His frowning examination continued. She returned the
look with candor. After a while he nodded slowly. "It's well.
But I could wish you had stayed for advice before taking the
bit between your teeth. Mayhap I could have spared you
these last nights."

Polly shrugged. "Even had you been able to, Richard,
'twould have taken a tedious long time. This way was speed-
ier, and Nick will be free within the day. Indeed—" An
exciting, yet somehow terrifying, thought struck her
"—maybe within the hour, and I must bathe. I cannot greet
him with . . . with . . ." Her hands passed down her
body in a gesture expressive of disgust. "And he must not
find you here, Richard, at this hour. It will puzzle him
mightily." She began to push him toward the door. "Nothing must arouse his suspicions."

Richard resisted the inhospitable pressure of the small
hands in his back. "You have Buckingham's pledge of se-
crecy?"

All the light died from the hazel eyes. She shook her head
in sudden defeated weariness. "I thought not to ask for it."

"Then, if you will heed the advice of a friend who knows
Nick of old, you will lay the whole before him without
delay," Richard said briskly. "It is no great tragedy. He is a
man of the world, Polly."

"I do not wish him to know," she said fiercely. "I would
not have him share my own hells with the feeling that he was
responsible for them. Can you not understand that?"

Richard sighed. "And suppose he should hear it from
Buckingham, or from court whispers? Why do you imagine

Buckingham will keep it a close secret? He can have no reasons for doing so."

"But by the same token, he can have no reason for not doing so," Polly pointed out. "I cannot bring myself to tell him, Richard." She shuddered slightly. "Mayhap when it has faded a little, but not now."

She looked wan, fragile, seven sleepless nights etched upon her face, giving that usually vibrant beauty an ethereal appearance. Three afternoons, during this dreadful week, she had performed at the Theatre Royal, and only three members of the audience knew what superhuman effort it had cost her: Thomas Killigrew knew because he alone could read the professional actor; Buckingham and Richard knew. She had come close to breaking, and was still perilously close to the edge.

Richard decided that he would be unwise to push the issue at present. Her exhaustion, Nick would put down to worry, and maybe, for a few days, they would keep close to this house. Nick would not feel inclined to venture into society immediately, and when he was ready, Polly would perhaps be strong enough to tell him the truth of her ordeal.

"I will leave you to your bath, then," he said, picking up his cloak. "An hour or two of sleep would not come amiss, either."

Polly helped him with his cloak. "I could not have managed without your strength, Richard," she said softly.

He smiled. "You underestimate yourself, my dear. You would have done what you felt you had to, with or without my support." He bent to kiss her cheek. "Nicholas is a most fortunate man."

Nicholas, at that moment, was standing on the parapeted walk outside his prison. He drew his cloak tight against the wind gusting from the Thames. The river ran, gray-brown, below the parapet, a major highway on which the townsfolk went about their business, sparing little attention as they passed beneath Tower bridge for those within the massive gray walls of the Tower itself. Perhaps they looked at Traitor's Gate, where the green river slime clung to the step, and the water slopped against the portcullis. And if they did so, perhaps they spared a thought for all those who had made the melancholy river journey, to enter this great and gloomy prison through that gate, to leave it only for the scaffold on Tower Hill.

It was a gloomy thought, but Nick could see little reason for cheer. True, he had not entered the Tower through Traitor's Gate, but he was as securely held as any, and he still had no concrete charges to defend.

He turned to look over the other side of the parapet, down into the great court of the Tower, where the distinctive black ravens squabbled amongst themselves, circling and strutting with the self-importance of those who had inhabited this place for longer than any human soul. Even at this early hour, the scene was lively, guards and servants hastening about their business, troops of soldiers responding with well-trained obedience to bellowed orders, heralds and liveried messengers on horseback passing back and forth through the gates. The governor appeared, striding briskly across the quadrangle. He looked up to see his prisoner, and raised a hand in salute.

Nicholas returned the salute. The governor was a civilized man, one who enjoyed civilized and intelligent company over a fine port, and Kincaid had rarely spent a lonely evening during this sojourn in the Tower.

"Breakfast's 'ere, m'lord." A guard appeared in the narrow entrance to the tower where Nick was housed.

"I'd have more stomach for it with a deal more exercise," Nicholas said, but he turned within. A fire burned in the round stone chamber of his jail, a thick quilt and feather mattress furnished the narrow bed, a pile of books stood upon the plank table beneath the small, barred window. There was little discomfort in his conditions, if one did not count the loss of freedom. He met no insult, not even a hint of discourtesy, from his jailers, but they were still his jailers.

He turned desultory attention to ale and sirloin. Was Polly

still abed? It was past seven, but if she had not sought her bed before midnight, then she could well be asleep, preparing herself for the morning's work with Killigrew, and the afternoon performance. But what could she have been doing in his absence that would have kept her out of her bed into the small hours? Mayhap Richard was squiring her to court, encouraging her to maintain the casual, mercenary front that they had perfected over the months. Whatever happened, she must not be tarred with this unknown brush that painted her protector. Richard would understand that, and act accordingly.

Nick had received no communication from the outside world, the governor apologizing for orders that prevented this. Neither had he been permitted to send any—even instructions to Margaret as to domestic financial arrangements. De Winter would see that Polly lacked for nothing, of that he was certain, but nothing could assuage the aching fear for her, the desolation of his utter helplessness. He could feel her, smell her, see her, hear her. He could remember, as if he were still living them, the times when she had angered him, exasperated him, then disarmed him; the times when she had entranced him, had transported him to the outermost limits of joy, had brought him laughter and delight such as he had never known. And he wanted to weep with a loss that his prison walls seemed to insist was final.

"Lord Kincaid?" The ponderous tones of the governor tore him from his reverie.

"Governor, your pardon. I find myself somewhat distracted." He turned from the leaping flames and the dancing memories, putting his back to the fire as he greeted courteously the man who held dominion over his immediate circumstances. "Ye've some news of the impeachment, mayhap?"

"On the contrary, my lord." The governor was beaming. "A messenger has just come from Whitehall with this." A parchment was extended, the smile broadened. "I'll be sorry to lose your company, sir, but I can rejoice for ye."

Kincaid read the order under Buckingham's seal for his

release, and the dismissal of all charges, stated or yet to be so. "Why?" he asked softly. "It defies comprehension."

The governor had no light to shed and, indeed, could not understand why his noble erstwhile prisoner should tarry in questioning. He gestured to an accompanying guard. "Your sword, Lord Kincaid. The carriage awaits you in the court."

"Then I'll thank you for your courtesy and your many kindnesses, Governor." Nick sheathed his sword, feeling himself whole again, belonging to his own world again; the two men exchanged bows. The governor accompanied Nick to the court, where he entered the same unmarked carriage that, this time, bore him beyond the walls of the Tower, into the familiar streets of freedom.

Polly's wrists stung under the kiss of hot water as she sank into the tub before the bedchamber fire. The sensation brought the most unwelcome thought. "Sue, can ye see any marks on my skin?" She stood up in the tub, dripping, peering down at her body. Buckingham's sport had caused her no worse than occasional discomfort, but she had not had the foresight to worry about a telltale finger bruise, or a scratch of haste and passion—signs that a chaste and lonely seven days should not have put upon her body.

Sue had been given no details of the nights' events; she knew only that they had something to do with Lord Kincaid's disappearance, and it was a secret to be kept guarded with her soul; but she was worldly enough to make a guess at the nature of Polly's nightly experiences—experiences that sent her, each morning, into hot water, scouring every inch of skin, before she fell into an exhausted sleep for an hour or two. So the request did not cause any exclamations.

Sue examined the slender figure carefully. "Ye've a little bruise on your arm, a scratch here." She touched beneath a pointed shoulder blade. "Naught else that I can see."

"Apart from my wrists." Polly sat down in the water again, examining the slightly reddened skin. "Mayhap witch hazel will help. 'Tis not too bad, but my lord must not notice."

"My lord!" Sue dropped the soap that she was about to hand the bather. "Is he released, then?"

"I expect him at any moment," Polly said with perfect confidence. Even Richard had said that a Villiers would not break his word, and somehow, she knew that she had lost her fascination for Buckingham now. He had wanted her, and he had taken what he wanted, proving to himself and to her the extent of the power that she had scorned. He had used her and could now discard her, a cast-off whore of no further interest. He would find fresh challenges, and leave Kincaid and his little actor-harlot to their own devices.

It was a prognosis with which Polly could find no fault. She was perfectly content to leave Buckingham in possession of the field, if that was what he chose to believe. He had thought to debase her, but he had not succeeded. She knew that, and it was her own knowledge that was all-important. It mattered not a jot what the duke thought.

But it might matter what Nicholas thought. Polly sank deeper into the tub. She could not imagine how Nick would react. Would he, as Richard said, treat it as pragmatically as he had their plan that she should spy for them from the duke's bed? Or would he see her as debased? A plaything of that notorious debauched wencher? Used and discarded, and therefore unlovely and unlovable?

A loud banging at the street door resounded through the house. She heard his voice, his quick tread on the stair, and all such anxieties fled for the present. He was safe, and that was all that mattered.

She sprang from the tub, running into the parlor, to fling herself, naked and dripping, into his arms as he pushed open the door. "Nick! Oh, Nick!" she sobbed repetitively against his chest, holding him with all her strength, clasping her hands at his back, squeezing tightly. "I have missed you so!"

For a few moments he just held her, saying nothing as he allowed the feel, the shape, the scent of her to become a part of him again; then, gently, he prized apart her hands at his back and stood away from her, holding her arms wide at her sides. "Let me look at you."

"But I am all wet," she hiccuped on a half laugh, half sob.

"Why should that prevent my looking at you?" he teased, the emerald eyes devouring her with the hot flame of need, until she thought she would dissolve into his gaze.

"I said it would be a mistake and you would come back," Polly whispered, realizing that she must make some comment about this return that was supposed to be a surprise.

"Aye, so you did." He pulled her back against him, running his hands down her back, cupping her buttocks, pressing her against him. "I do not know what the devil has been going on, but I intend to discover."

Polly arched backward to look up at him, although her lower body remained cemented to his. "But you might stir the waters again," she objected on a ring of anxiety.

"If I do not know what lay behind it, love, I'll never be sure it will not happen again," he pointed out, kneading the firm, rounded flesh beneath his hands. "Nay, some game is being played, and I must discover it. 'Tis possible Richard will have some inkling. Have you seen him?"

"Yes, every day," she said, sliding her hands beneath his coat again, feeling the warmth of his skin against her fingertips. "Must we talk of this now? I have been so afeard for you." She pressed her lips against his chest as her fingers deftly unfastened the buttons of his shirt.

"I have not been entirely sanguine, I'll confess," he said, his fingers raking through her wet hair. "Why do you bathe at this early hour, moppet? You are not accustomed to doing so."

"I have been unable to sleep, and I thought it might refresh me," she extemporized, reflecting that it was not entirely an untruth. "But what of you? Have you breakfasted? Will you bathe, sleep—"

"There is but one thing I wish to do," he interrupted, a changed note in his voice, a purposeful smile playing over his lips. "And I shall not be able to do it, foolish jade, if you catch an ague, standing around in your wet skin on a bitter winter's morn."

"My joy at the sound of your voice would not admit of such mundane considerations," Polly returned, with a haughty sniff. "And I take it mighty ill in you, my lord, that you should find fault when . . . Ouch!"

"Cease your railing, shrew!" Nick swept her up into his arms, the gem-bright eyes laughing down at her mock indignation. "I had thought, after such an absence, to woo you with soft words and tender kisses, but it seems you'd liefer have a tumbling match!" So saying, he strode with her into the bedchamber, tossing her unceremoniously onto the bed.

Picking up the towel that Susan had left beside the bath, he set to work on Polly's wriggling body, rubbing her dry until her skin glowed and the blood ran swift in her veins. Laughing and squirming helplessly beneath the hands that lost no opportunity to explore, tickle, probe, that tossed her and turned her as if she had no more resistance than a straw doll, Polly thought of those other hands that had rendered her as helpless as these were doing. But here she was helpless with pleasure, in thrall to the magic of one who knew and cared how to pleasure her. There was no comparison, even if the fundamental act had been the same. She let the thoughts and images slide away from her, sloughed like an outworn snake's skin.

"Have I missed anywhere?" Nick mused, hovering over her, towel still in hand.

"I think you forgot my toes," Polly responded, wriggling them invitingly. "They are all damp 'twixt and 'tween."

Nick grinned. He knew well how sensitive were Polly's feet. "How remiss," he murmured, slipping an arm beneath her knees and sweeping up her legs, circling the narrow ankles between thumb and forefinger.

"No!" Polly squealed as his tongue licked along the sole of each foot, stroking into the high-arched instep. "Oh, you know I cannot bear it!" She thrashed wildly on the bed as the delicious torment continued, and he took her toes into his mouth, suckling on each one, his thumb massaging her heels and soles, setting up a chain of sympathetic reaction all over her body. It was as if every nerve in her feet was connected to some other part of her. Finally exhausted, she ceased her struggles and protests, abandoning herself to the wickedly skilled arousal, the slow sensitizing of each nerve and pleasure center.

"Monster!" she whispered, defeated by delight.

"You asked for it, my love," he replied in perfect truth, smiling, still holding her legs as he looked down on her flushed face and heavy eyes, the rise and fall of her breasts in response to the thudding of her heart and her swift breath. He moved his hands to the insides of her legs and slipped slowly down their length, spreading them wide as he caressed the tender satin of her inner thighs, approaching with tantalizing delicacy the throbbing cleft, while Polly lay, breathless in expectancy, poised for the touch that she knew would send her surging over the edge to which he had brought her with such demonic knowingness.

Her eyes implored him, her tongue ran over her lips, her body became as molten wax, a formless puddle on the featherbed, centered only on that nerve-stretched apex. Hot tears of near unbearable delight scalded her cheeks. The muscles in her belly tightened, sending little flutters across the surface of her skin; and then, when there seemed nothing in the world but the tension of expectancy, he touched her.

Her body leapt as if beneath a burning brand, and she thrummed like a string of a plucked lute. It was as if, after an eternity of denial, she had been given back what she had lost. The loving touch of bodily joy, the turbulent plane of ravishing bliss were hers again.

"Come to me, love," she whispered, "inside me," desperate in her urgency for the fusion that would make them both whole again.

Nick stripped, careless of buttons and hooks in his haste, then he gathered her against him and, as she lifted her hips, pressed deep within her. Her body closed around him, holding him within her silken toils; he exhaled slowly, smiling in soft satisfaction. "Such honeyed delight, love," he whispered, bending to kiss her eyes. "Velvet and honey, you are."

"No spice?" she murmured. "Such a concoction sounds a trifle sickly."

"There's salt enough upon your tongue to add savor to marchpane," he said. "Shall I punish you for that?" Slowly, he withdrew to the edge of her body.

"Quarter, my lord," she begged. "Indeed, 'twas a thoughtless impertinence." Her legs curled around his hips, pulling him toward her again.

"To respond to compliments in such fashion is, indeed, impertinence," he said gravely, tightening his buttocks in resistance against the pressure of her heels.

"I crave pardon, and will accept any penance except this." Her hips arced as her heels increased their pressure, and Nick chuckled, yielding with a show of reluctance.

Then the laughter died from his face, and his eyes burned into hers. "As you love me, sweetheart, do not move. I would have you with me, but one wriggle and I shall be lost."

She smiled. "And I would have you lost. I shall be with you, never fear." Slowly, she tightened her inner muscles around him, saw his face dissolve with joy, tried to keep at bay her own tempest the longer to enjoy his pleasure; and then was engulfed herself.

"God's grace, but I have missed you." Nick opened his eyes, his heart slowing against the still rapid beat of the one below. "I have missed being angered by you, as I have missed being entranced." He kissed the corner of her mouth, the cleft of her chin. "Tell me what you have been doing this sennight."

"Apart from worrying?" Polly asked, feeling her heart race again, a light sweat misting her palms. Stage fright, she told herself sternly.

Nick frowned. "You look worn to a frazzle, love,"

" 'Tis nothing, now that you are back. I could not sleep, and there has been the playhouse . . . Oh, what is the time?" She sat up in a panic not entirely feigned. "We are to rehearse this morning." She sprang to her feet.

"Is there a play this afternoon?" Nick rolled off the bed, since clearly the moment for softnesses and cuddling was past.

"Nay, but tomorrow we are to perform Master Dryden's new play, *Secret Love*. 'Tis monstrous funny in parts. Melissa becomes Master Florimell." She struck a pose, beginning to mime the combing of a full peruke. " 'Save you, Monsieur Florimell! Faith, methinks you are a very jaunty fellow.' "

Nick laughed at the absurdity of her naked femininity and the very masculine swagger she produced. "Does Edward play opposite you?"

"Aye, as Celadon, my lover. 'Tis very awkward, as he challenges me to fight at one point." She twinkled mischievously.

"And how does the fair Florimell avoid such a happenstance?" he asked, much amused, and no longer aware of the signs of strain that he had noticed a minute ago.

She struck another pose, haughty, one make-believe handkerchief passing through the air. " 'Out upon fighting: 'tis grown so common a fashion, that a modish man condemns it.' "

Nick roared with laughter. "I will see no more, lest it spoil me for the performance." He stepped into Polly's neglected bathwater. " 'Tis cold, but I daresay will serve to refresh me. Had you better not dress?"

"Aye." Polly went to the armoire. "Will you not come to the rehearsal this morning?" She turned, offering him an apologetic smile. " 'Tis just that I fear to lose sight of you again."

"I must visit Richard, sweetheart," he said seriously, splashing water on the back of his neck. "There are matters that bear investigation—"

"But not today, surely," she broke in. "And mayhap Richard will come to dine if we send him a message to say that you are released."

Nick frowned, saying slowly, "I had thought to go to court this morning. I've a need to judge my reception."

Polly bit her lip, wondering whether continued pleading would arouse his suspicions. She allowed her shoulders to sag, her head to droop; her lip quivered, but she said nothing, continuing with her dressing.

Nick's frown deepened. He had no reason to suspect that this display of unhappiness bravely borne was less than genuine and, as usual, found her impossible to resist. "Very well. We will keep close today, except for Richard. Why do you not send to his house with an invitation to dinner?"

"And you will come to the theatre?" She turned eagerly to face him, hands clasped, eyes huge and glowing.

Radiant as a violet after the storm, Nick thought with customary resignation. "Aye, if you wish it. But I think it unkind in you to spoil my first view of the play by obliging me to witness the blunders and the promptings, and Master Killigrew's irritations and castigations."

She danced over to the tub, bending to kiss him. "I will find a way to recompense you, I promise."

Nick shook his head in familiar defeat. "Send the message to Richard. But for the love of God, do not write it! A verbal invitation will do."

Polly stuck her tongue out. "How do you expect me to improve when I receive so little encouragement?"

Master Killigrew greeted Nicholas with heartfelt relief. "God's bones, but 'tis good to see you safe, man. I have been in more than half a mind to cancel tomorrow's performance."

"Why so?" Nick took snuff, hiding his amusement that Killigrew's relief at seeing him appeared to have more to do with his theatre than congratulation on Nick's happy release from imprisonment.

"Why, 'tis Polly! Such an edge of desperation as she has been walking. I have been afeard that she would slip at any moment, and with the first performance of a new play—"

He shrugged expressively, confident that his interlocutor would fully comprehend the gravity.

"She has been greatly anxious," Nick said, watching the stage.

"Aye, but 'tis more than that," Thomas declared. "There has been something else amiss, but she'd not confide in me." He watched the action critically, then nodded. "But all's well now, it would seem." He strode forward. "Polly, we all know what Master Dryden wrote the part of Florimell for you, but you must not let it go to your head! It is still necessary to perform, unless you wish to be bombarded from the pit."

"You are unjust!" Polly declared, swinging 'round on her mentor. "What would you have me do?"

Nicholas smiled, listening to the lively exchange. It was as if the last week had never happened. Except that it had.

"Well met, my friend." Richard De Winter spoke softly from the gloom of the pit, and Nick turned, hand outstretched in welcome.

"Ah, Richard, it does me good to see you again." They clasped hands in a moment that said more than words could. "Did you receive Polly's message?"

"Aye." Richard laughed. "Much garbled with joy, but the meaning was clear." He turned his attention to the stage, then nodded, much as Killigrew had done. "I see that she is herself again."

"Did you notice aught else but uncommon anxiety about her these last days, Richard?" asked Nick.

Tread softly, Richard reminded himself. "Uncommon anxiety is all-pervasive, Nick. D'ye have a reason for asking?"

Nick shrugged. "Not really. I daresay Killigrew in his own uncommon anxiety saw more than there was to be seen." Linking arms with his friend, he drew him into the shadows of the pit, where their whispers would not disturb the rehearsal. "Have you any light to shed, Richard?"

De Winter shook his head. "Nay, but I am charged with a message—a most kindly message." He paused, and Nick raised an eyebrow in silent question. "His Majesty bids you attend the levee on the morrow. A small matter of misunderstanding to be resolved."

"Lord of hell!" Nick raised his eyes to the cupola. "A misunderstanding had me arrested at dawn with great sound and fury! A misunderstanding kept me lodged in the Tower for a sennight!"

"Softly, now," Richard advised, laying a hand on his arm. "Let be, Nick. Let the hound snore, and do you smile at the king. No great harm's done, when all's computed."

Nick seemed irresolute, but slowly he relaxed, accepting the sense of his friend's words. He looked toward the stage. Polly had suffered no lasting hurt, and neither had he. Better to leave the hound snoring, as Richard said.

Chapter 21

"Why such a long face, moppet?" Nick bent to kiss his favorite spot on her neck as Polly sat before her mirror the next morning. "You have been staring into the glass as if 'twas a green-haired fright that you saw. You are quite in looks, I assure you." He laughed, moving his mouth to her ear, trying to coax her out of the dismal mood that had accompanied her waking.

"Why must we go to court?" Polly demanded, reaching her hands up to close over those on her shoulders, her gaze imploring him in the mirror. "I would have further time alone with you, instead of listening to the chatter and the nonsense and—"

"You know that I am bidden by the king's majesty," Nick said, mastering his irritation at this unreasonable request. "I must reestablish my position at court, Polly, and I'll not do that by skulking behind doors as if I had aught to hide."

"I do not see why you should want a position at court, anyway," she said with more than a hint of petulance. "It is all such a sham."

"A sham in which I have a part to play," Nick told her brusquely. "Now, make haste. We must leave within the half hour."

Polly bit her lip. She could refuse to go with him, of

course, and he would not really be able to object. *She* had not been bidden by the king's majesty. But it would be insufferable to cower at home, imagining the malicious whisper dropped into his ear, dreading his return lest he should come with the knowledge of her dealings with Buckingham. At least if she was there, she would not live on the razor's edge needlessly.

They walked to the palace, the day being crisp and clean, the streets dry, and Nick in much need of exercise in his regained freedom. He left Polly in the Long Gallery, with the chattering throng, and went to the king's private apartments, as he had been bidden, to wait upon His Majesty during the levee—the elaborate ceremony of his morning toilet.

King Charles, submitting to the attentions of his barber, greeted Nicholas warmly, calling him through the press of favored courtiers. "Kincaid, dear fellow." The royal hand was extended for the subject's kiss. "Devil's in it, but ye know what rumors can do. Particularly these days. Can't trust anyone. Can't think where they came from now, can ye, George?"

"A word here, a word there, sir," drawled the Duke of Buckingham, his heavy-lidded eyes resting with seeming casualness on Lord Kincaid's face. "Sorry as I can be, Kincaid. 'Tis to be hoped you passed not too uncomfortable a sennight."

"I have been more comfortable," returned Nick with a dry, tight smile.

"And the incomparable Polly?" Buckingham smiled benignly. "I trust she made you welcome."

The king chuckled. "Aye, incomparable, indeed. Y'are a lucky dog, Kincaid, if you can keep her."

"I shall do my best, sir." Nick bowed, waited for a few moments until it became clear that His Majesty had said all he deemed necessary about the unfortunate misunderstanding, then faded into the background. He was angry, and he was puzzled. A word here, a word there. It was no convincing explanation; and what the devil had Buckingham to do with it?

He found out soon enough.

Polly stood amid the laughter and the chatter, a smile fixed upon her face, her eyes glazed. Lady Castlemaine knew. Nausea rose, urgent in her belly; she swallowed desperately, hearing again that spiteful little trill, feeling the malevolent eyes, stripping her bare.

"I trust you found ducal attentions as pleasing and as rewarding as those of a baron, my dear Mistress Wyat?" had been the question, uttered with blatant crudity and in no undertone. It had brought titters from those around; Polly had managed to produce a stare of total incomprehension before turning away. But there was no refuge anywhere, and she dared not leave before Nick reappeared.

"God's grace, but you have the mien of a sick cat!" Richard's fierce whisper came from behind her. "If you ignore it, there will be no sport, and they will let the matter drop. It will be put down as Barbara's malice. Everyone knows she holds you in enmity. But if you appear guilty as accused, the story will take hold."

"But Nick—"

"He has just come into the gallery. Pull yourself together."

Polly put up her chin, smiling a greeting as Nicholas pushed through the crowd toward them. "Was His Majesty pleased to favor you, my lord?"

Nick gave an acid laugh, although his expression remained blandly smiling. "He was pleased to bid me welcome, and trust that I did not suffer too much discomfort as a result of this misunderstanding whose genesis he cannot even remember."

"Then 'tis over," Richard said swiftly. "Nothing will be gained by angry brooding."

"Ah, my Lord Kincaid. Pray accept my congratulations on your happy deliverance." Barbara Palmer's tinsel voice shimmered in the air, and Polly felt herself again in the grip of that numbing, poisonous spider's bite. Nick made some careless response that made light of the incident, and the countess's laugh trilled. "How stoic you are, my lord." Her eyes turned to the frozen Polly. "Not so your mistress, I fear. She appeared to lose faith in your eventual release. But then, a wise woman always looks to her future, does she not, Mistress Wyat? It is always necessary to make provision. One cannot place one's trust in luck and fortune in this harsh world. And even actors must needs grow old—as must harlots." She smiled. " 'Tis wise to garner the fruit while it is on the tree, is it not? And the Duke of Buckingham's tree is rich and heavy. I am certain you were well paid for your services. He assures me that they were worth the payment."

A swish of satin, a wafting of musk, and the Lady Castlemaine had gone, leaving devastation in her wake. Nick looked at Polly's white face, then at Richard. Both told him all that he needed to know at this point.

"Put your hand on my arm, Polly," he instructed in an expressionless tone. "We are going to promenade the length of the gallery."

"Take me home," she whispered.

"Not yet. There are some friends I must greet, and we shall greet them together. Should we happen to meet Buckingham, you will make your curtsy."

Polly looked in desperate appeal at Richard, but he merely nodded at his friend's good sense and fell into step beside them.

It was the longest half hour that Polly would ever spend. Somehow she managed to keep the smile on her face, even to speak when spoken to, but it was for Nicholas and Richard to maintain the urbane flow of carefree wit that marked the courtier. At the end of the gallery, George Villiers stood, Lady Castlemaine beside him.

Nick felt Polly stiffen; her fingers on his arm quivered. He tightened the muscle of his arm beneath her hand in encouragement. She found herself curtsying to the duke, felt his eyes linger on her bosom as if in insolent reminiscence. There was a moment under that look when she felt what he would have her feel—soiled by use. Then she remembered that, whatever he might think, Buckingham had not been the victor. She was, in essence, untouched by his violations. Her eyes met his; she smiled in bland friendliness.

"Good morrow, my lord duke. Lord Kincaid is returned to us, as you see."

"My congratulations to you both," he replied, a hint of admiration lurking in his eyes. "I am most eager to see your performance this afternoon, mistress. 'Tis said John Dryden's new play is monstrous amusing."

"I trust you will not be disappointed, Duke." Another curtsy, and she turned away, her escorts with her.

They left the palace, having demonstrated to all that any dealings with Buckingham that Kincaid's mistress may or may not have had during her protector's absence were accounted of no importance by any of the protagonists. The walk back to Drury Lane was undertaken in silence. At the door of Polly's lodging, Nick, his face chiseled in stone, turned to Richard. "My thanks for your support. You will understand if I do not ask you within."

"I have no desire to be importunate, my friend, but I think you have need of me," replied Richard easily. "If matters grow heated, clarity may be lost. I believe that I may provide the latter."

"Richard is right." Polly spoke for the first time. "He has been my supporter in all this, and 'tis only right he should bear a part in the explanation."

"Very well." Nick opened the door, gesturing politely that they should precede him. In the parlor, he dismissed Susan, who was setting out the platters for dinner, before saying, "Let me have the truth, Polly."

Polly looked helplessly at Richard. "I do not know how to begin."

"Then I will tell it," Richard said. "Pour us wine, child. You may interrupt me if I do not tell it correctly."

Nicholas listened to the bald narrative told in De Winter's unemotional tones. Since Richard did not know of the brothel, or any details of the seven nights, Nick did not hear of them, but what he heard brought an icy, fearsome rage to fill and enfold him. There was no overt sign of it, however. When Richard finally fell silent, turning his attention to the Rhenish in his wine cup, Nick looked at Polly. She was standing by the table, as she had been throughout, her eyes fixed upon him with a painful intensity.

"Why did you not stop her, Richard?" Nick asked, still looking at Polly.

"The matter was in full flood before I knew of it," Richard answered quietly. "But, in any case, I would not have considered I had the right to stop her. To advise, yes, but not to direct."

"I would not have admitted anyone's right to prevent me." Polly spoke at last. "The matter was between myself and the duke. And it rests there."

"Ah . . . no," Nick said with finality. "It rests with me." He turned his cup between his hands, frowning. "Let us dine. You've to be at the theatre at four o'clock."

"I do not understand what you mean," Polly said, feeling distressfully for the right words. "I . . . I understand if you should feel I . . . I have betrayed you, but, in truth, I have not. It was not me he touched, Nick—"

"Enough!" Nick cracked. "How can you talk such foolishness? Do you imagine I do not know what hell you endured? You will put the matter out of your head, in as far as you are able. It now rests with me, and when I have dealt with it, I will do what I may to heal you." He went to the table, pulling out a chair for her. "Come, take your place. Richard." He gestured to the chair opposite Polly, then pulled the bell rope.

Polly looked uneasily at Richard, but he was his customary impassive self, turning the conversation to trivialities as Susan and the goodwife put the venison pasty upon the table.

"What do you mean, the matter rests with you?" Polly asked when the door had closed on the two women. "It is finished, love. I am quite whole, and you are safe. Lady Castlemaine may whisper, but I shall not mind that now that you know. I was only afeard this morning because I wished to keep it from you."

"To spare my feelings, I daresay," Nick said with heavy irony. "And I am to be grateful for such consideration, I suppose." He sliced the pasty, placing a piece on Polly's platter. "Eat your dinner."

"I ask your pardon," Polly whispered, staring down at her platter, where the food blurred in a haze of tears. "I could not think of anything else to do."

"You are harsh, Nick," Richard remonstrated quietly.

"Harsh!" Nick exploded. "I am to understand with a grateful smile that a woman living under my protection, having undergone an ordeal of God alone knows what degrading torment to buy my freedom, feels it in her province to keep such information from me! What manner of man do you think me?"

There was an uncomfortable silence, while Polly's tears continued to plash upon her uneaten dinner. "It was not Richard's doing. He said I should tell you," she managed finally.

"Then I could wish you had heeded him." His tone softened. "Eat your dinner, now. You cannot perform on an empty belly." He turned to Richard. "I will visit Buckingham after dinner. I may count on you in this?"

"You would demand satisfaction?" De Winter asked, for once startled out of his calm assurance.

Polly's knowledge of court rules and etiquette had still occasional gaps, but there were some things she did know. "You cannot possibly!" she exclaimed, aghast. "The duke would not meet you over such a matter. It is a question of a whore—bought and paid for. Wherein lies the insulted honor? He would laugh in your face." Then she sprang to her feet, as Nick's chair clattered to the floor under the force of his own rising.

"By God, I told you what I would do if you ever spoke like that again!" His fury now blazing, open on his face, he strode round the table.

Polly, choosing the better part of valor, fled for the door.

"Why will you not understand?" she cried, no longer tear-ful, simply angry and frustrated at his blindness. "In this case, it is merely the truth—an insignificant truth. If I do not mind it, why should you?"

Wrenching open the door, she jumped through it. The door banged shut in Nick's face. With a wrathful oath, he reached for the latch.

"Nay, Nick, stay!" Richard spoke, sharply imperative. "Have you not lashed her sufficiently?"

Nicholas turned slowly. "I did not mean to do so."

"But you did, nevertheless. She has endured enough; and if she wished to spare you pain, then you should honor her for it."

"Richard!" Nick's face was contorted with anguish. "Do you think I do not know what she has suffered? I cannot bear to think of it. It is as if vultures tear at my gut. But I will have that debaucher's blood for it!" The promise was spoken softly, but the ferocity chilled Richard.

"Talk sense, man! Polly is quite right. Villiers would laugh in your face, and the story would keep the court in mirth for months to come. You would be a laughingstock, and so would she. She is your mistress, Nick. You hold no umbrella of honor over her. Would you commit murder? For 'tis your only option."

Nicholas stood very still, feeling the warmth of a ray of sun on the back of his head. The chamber was bright with winter sun and the fire's glow; the air was redolent with the good smells of Goodwife Benson's cooking; the dinner table was laden with plenty, the wine rich in the cup. A scene of perfect domestic tranquility, except that the lady of the house was missing. He shook his head in annoyance. "I should be pilloried for a fool! I have been procrastinating for no sufficient reason—" He shrugged. "Well, that is done with now. Come, Richard. You must forgo the rest of your dinner, I fear. I need your help, for there is much to arrange in a short time."

•   •   •

Polly had reached the theatre without fully realizing that that was her destination. But once there, she knew that it was the only place where she would be able to compose herself for the task ahead. Whatever had happened, whatever lunacy Nick might yet decide upon, she had to go onstage. Too many people would be depending upon her this afternoon— John Dryden, Thomas, her fellow actors. And even more, herself. She had relied on pride and determination to carry her through the last sennight. Those resources were not exhausted—they could not be. This afternoon she would demonstrate to Buckingham, and to Lady Castlemaine, and to anyone else who was interested, that, bloodied though she may be, she was unbowed. They could not touch her with the slimy coils of their own sordid souls.

She went into the tiring room. Her costumes were laid out: the gown and petticoats for Melissa in the first act, then the breeches, wig, and waistcoat when Melissa became Florimell. Melissa/Florimell was a character she enjoyed, a triumphant character, who carried the duel of wit and words to victory, for all that she suffered a degree of tousling at Celadon's hands in the unmasking. Amazingly, Polly chuckled to herself. The role had been created for her, and she would do justice to the creation.

Thomas Killigrew found his leading female actor early at her dressing. She responded cheerfully to his greeting, and he was relieved to see that the light in her eyes contained none of the fevered piquancy of the last days. Thanking God and the fates for Kincaid's safe and timely return, he turned his attention to the pressing matter of a recalcitrant box hedge that was disinclined to remain upright on the stage.

Nicholas and Richard arrived halfway through the performance. Polly was not aware of their arrival, any more than she had been aware of their absence. The audience was, as always, a featureless mass below her. She was attuned to their reactions, but as a whole, not as individuals, and she knew that they were enjoying every luscious, wickedly provocative second of Master Dryden's *Secret Love*.

Nicholas experienced again the emotions of that first per-

formance of *Flora's Vagaries,* at Moorfields. He knew he had
to come to terms with the knowledge that that ravishing,
magical creature created her own world into which she invited every lusting, eager member of the audience. But frequently, as now, he failed lamentably. She belonged to
everyone, by her own choice, understanding the hungers
and needs, gratifying them with grace and pleasure. And he
must learn to live in peace and harmony with such creative
generosity. There was no alternative, and there never had
been.

He glanced sideways at De Winter. Richard smiled in
complete comprehension. "Faith, but you'll be the most un-
popular man in London, Nick, if you take her away from
this."

"Think you I could?" Nick asked, with a wry grimace.

"Not and keep her happy," Richard agreed. "By God,
listen to her purr. I fear poor Celadon is about to lose this
encounter."

"And count the world well lost for love," said his companion softly.

The play reached its conclusion: Florimell, after much delicious tousling and mousling, was revealed as Melissa; the
lovers were reconciled; and the audience came to their feet,
those who were close enough crowding upon the stage, expressing their pleasure as vigorously as they would have done
their displeasure. Polly emerged, laughing and breathless
from the throng, tumbled and disheveled in her breeches and
boots, her ruff torn by Celadon's unmasking, peruke lost in
the fray.

Nicholas stepped onto the stage from the wings. "Come."
He took her hand. "We have no more time to waste."

"Come where?" Polly protested, following willy-nilly,
tripping over her feet. "I must change and—"

"No, you need not."

"But I do need." She pulled back on his hand, trying to
orientate herself in the real world. For three hours she had
lived in another universe, and now Nick was behaving in a

most extraordinary fashion. There was a grim purpose about him that set butterflies dancing in her stomach.

"Nick, if you are still vexed about what I said—" she began tentatively.

"I have decided to overlook it on this occasion," Nicholas interrupted, marching her toward the rear door of the theatre. "You'll not say it again."

"Oh." She skipped to keep pace with his long stride. "But, please, where are we going, and why may I not change?"

"We do not have the time," came the succinct reply. They emerged through the stage door onto Drury Lane, where Kincaid's coach stood waiting, Richard De Winter and Sir Peter Appleby beside it.

"Good even, Polly," Richard greeted cheerfully, opening the carriage door.

"Good even; and you, Sir Peter." Bewildered, Polly returned the courtesies in an automatic mumble.

"Seldom have I enjoyed such an afternoon at the theatre," Sir Peter said. "You surpassed yourself, Polly."

"Th-thank you. I am glad you enjoyed it," Polly said as she was hustled into the dark interior of the coach. The three men climbed in after her; Nick slammed the door. "What is happening?" Polly asked in some desperation. "I am all tumbled and disheveled, and my hair is fallen down." To her indignant consternation, her three companions began to laugh.

" 'Tis hardly fair, Nick, to do such a thing to a maid," chuckled Sir Peter. "Ye might have granted her time to tidy herself."

"For what?" cried Polly, receiving renewed chuckles in answer. She put her hand on the door latch. "I am getting out. I do not like people laughing at me when I do not know the cause."

"Keep still, sweetheart." Nick, laughter still bubbling in his voice, caught her against him with an arm at her waist. "You will share the jest in a moment."

Polly subsided, grumbling under her breath, until the carriage came to a halt. She stepped out to find herself on the broad thoroughfare of Holborn. She stood looking around her for some clue to this mysterious journey. The Fleet River flowed nearby; Hatton Garden and Leather Lane were across the street. St. Andrew's Church, showing lamplight, stood behind her.

"Come," Nick said, taking her elbow, turning her toward the church.

"Why must we go to church? 'Tis not Sunday. I am hungry, and I want my supper." Protesting vociferously, Polly found herself jostled into the church. Whatever this jest was, it was not one she wished to share, she decided furiously. The day had been one of unremitting strain from the moment she had woken, and she could feel tears of weariness and hunger pricking behind her eyes. It was so unlike Nicholas to be inconsiderate, even when he was angry. He did not seem to be vexed at the moment, however. Indeed, there was an air of elation about him, and the emerald eyes bent upon her face contained only warmth and gentle amusement.

"You should have eaten your dinner, moppet," he said, propelling her up the nave to where a cassocked clergyman stood before the altar.

"Ah, my lord, I was about to give you up," the clergyman said ponderously. Then his eye fell upon the resistant, disheveled, breeched Polly. "This is the young lady?" His eyebrows disappeared into his scalp.

"Aye," Nick agreed briskly. "Shall we proceed?"

"I will not play this game anymore!" Polly cried, finally pushed beyond bearing. She stamped one booted foot on the cold stone of the nave. "I do not know what is happening—"

"If the lady is unwilling, my lord," broke in the clergyman, "I could not in conscience perform the ceremony."

Polly's jaw dropped. She looked up at the smiling Nick, 'round at Richard and Sir Peter, who were both beaming. She shook her head in bemusement. This was some fantastical joke.

"You are not unwilling, are you?" Nick asked softly, catching her face between his hands.

"But . . . but you cannot possibly wed a—"

"You *dare*!" A hard finger pressed against her lips. "Will you marry me, Mistress Wyat?"

Polly seized his hand, pulling him urgently into the shadows of the Lady Chapel. "I was going to say a Newgate-born, tavern-bred bastard," she whispered, a little resentfully. "That is not a truth you have ever denied."

"It is a truth known only to Richard and ourselves," Nick said softly. "As far as the world knows, you are either some nobleman's by-blow or the stagestruck daughter of a respectable bourgeois. Noble bastards abound at court, and no one will turn a hair at bourgeois gentility. Now," he repeated patiently. "Will you marry me?"

"You are run mad, my lord."

"Then will you take a madman to husband?"

Polly stood, for the moment silent, in the chill shadows of the chapel. What he had said was the perfect truth. And if no one knew her antecedents, and Nick was not concerned by them, then why should she not accept the conquering hand of love? The unquestionable, undeniable love that had fallen upon them with such unbidden force when they had first come together in the ways of passion. Slowly she nodded, returning his smile. "Aye, if that is truly what you wish, love."

Nick sighed with relief, drawing her back into the dim light of the nave. "It seems we may begin, Master Parson."

It was a short ceremony in the dank, winter-night cold of the drafty church. But Polly was quite unaware of her surroundings, or of any lack of magic in such a wedding—never having expected to have one at all. Her hand remained in Nick's throughout; she said what was required at the required moments, and wondered when she would wake up. At the end, the witnesses duly signed the Parish register, the parson was paid his fee, and the four went into the night.

"John Coachman will take you home now," Nick said, opening the carriage door for her.

Polly peered up at him, studying his expression in the faint starlight. "Take me home? But what of you?"

"I have some business to transact," Nick said evenly. "I will be with you as soon as may be. You are in sore need of your supper, as you have been saying so vociferously." He smiled, gently teasing, but Polly was not to be cajoled.

"Then I will come with you. I am not so hungry that my supper cannot wait."

"No," he said. "You may not accompany me." The laughter had left his mouth and eyes, a certain grimness in its place. "Go home. I will come to you soon."

Polly shook her head. "You would wed me in one breath and banish me in another. It makes no sense, my lord."

Nick sighed. "I seem to recall that not so many minutes past you made some solemn vows. Would you break them so soon?"

"I was not aware, sir, that I promised obedience to commands I do not understand," she said tartly.

"Rule a wife and have a wife," Richard murmured in the darkness. "Have done with this, Nick. 'Tis cold as charity, and the night grows no younger."

"A timely reminder," Nick said grimly. He scooped up his wife, bundling her unceremoniously into the coach, closing the door firmly on her protests. "Drury Lane, John." The coachman whipped up his horses and bore Lady Kincaid, cursing like any tavern-bred wench, back to her lodgings.

" 'Tis no way to start a marriage," sighed Nick.

" 'Tis not a marriage you can start in good earnest till this business be done with," Richard reminded him. "Let's to it."

The three men walked to Temple Stairs and took the water to Somerset Stairs. From there they walked in silence to the Duke of Buckingham's mansion in the Strand.

Villiers was in his library when he was brought the information that Lord Kincaid, Lord De Winter, and Sir Peter Appleby were desirous of waiting upon him.

"At this hour?" Villiers frowned. "Bid them enter." He

awaited their arrival in thoughtful silence. If this was a social call, it was a damned unsociable hour for it. And if it was not . . .

"Gentlemen." Smiling, he greeted them. "This is a most unexpected pleasure, but nonetheless welcome. Ye'll take wine?"

"I think not," Nicholas said. " 'Tis a matter of honor that brings us, Buckingham."

All superficial bonhomie was wiped from the duke's face. "You pleasant, Kincaid, surely."

"Nay, 'tis no pleasantry." Nick threw his gauntlet upon the table before the duke. "There's an insult to be avenged."

The duke's lip curled in derision. "Y'are mad, man. There's been no insult to honor that I know of. Don't let passion go to your head. 'Twill only make you a jesting-stock."

"Pick up the glove, Duke, else you'll be the butt of more than jest," Nick said quietly. "There's witnesses to coward-ice."

Buckingham went white about the lips, but scorn laced his voice as he said, "Pray tell me, just whose honor has been insulted?"

"My wife's," Nicholas replied. "And, therefore, my own."

Shock leapt into the heavy-lidded eyes, then Buckingham recovered himself. "I see." A twisted smile touched his lips. "Why did I not expect it? That were foolish in me." He picked up the gauntlet. "Where and when, gentlemen?"

"Barn Elms, at dawn." It was Richard who spoke. "As seconds, Sir Peter and I claim the right to fight beside our principal. You will choose your own seconds accordingly, Duke." A polite smile accompanied the statement.

Buckingham merely bowed and pulled the bell rope be-side the hearth. "You will excuse me, gentlemen. It appears I have much to accomplish in a few hours."

Outside, the three men went their separate ways after a brief word about arrangements for the morning. Nicholas walked back to Drury Lane through the frosty night, preparing himself for a most unenviable task. How the devil did a man break to his wife of a few hours that she had an even chance of being widowed on the morrow?

He found her curled up, asleep on the floor by the parlor fire. It took but the most cursory observation to realize that she slept the sleep of complete exhaustion, so far gone in unconsciousness that she barely breathed. Her face was deathly pale, the golden lashes forming dark crescents against her pallor, and Nick knew he must not wake her, even if he could.

She did not stir when he lifted her and put her into bed. Nick undressed and climbed in beside her; thus he passed his wedding night in wakeful reflection, holding the fragile figure against him as the memories crowded in.

Chapter 22

Polly first heard the voices as part of her dream, then, as she crossed over into wakefulness, became aware of them as reality. She lay still, her head turned toward the crack of yellow light edging the doorway to the parlor. Richard's voice came through the partly open door, low but clear.

" 'Tis seven miles to Barn Elms, Nick; less than an hour's ride."

"The surgeon?"

"Will meet us there. As will Peter. What of Polly?"

"I have written a letter. I can think of no other way, Richard. She was dead to the world last night, and I could not bring myself to waken her with such news."

"Be of good cheer." Richard's voice was bracing. "Ye'll be back here, the business done, before she awakes, I'll lay odds."

"And you not a gambling man," declared Nick dryly.

"Let us away."

"Aye. Go you on; I'll be but a minute."

The edge of light broadened. Polly closed her eyes, breathing with deep regularity. She felt him come to the bed, standing over her. Then his lips brushed lightly across hers, and he whispered, "Fare you well, sweetheart."

Polly held herself still while confused turmoil roiled in her head, then the light was extinguished as the door closed gently. She sat up, blinking in the dark, listening intently. There was no sound from the other room, only the silence of emptiness. Springing from the bed, she ran to the parlor door, opening it carefully. The chamber was in darkness except for the fire that had been newly kindled. She padded to the window, peering down into the dark street. The shadowy figures of two horsemen were disappearing rapidly in the gray-dark.

A letter. Nick had said he had left a letter. She lit the lamp with shaking fingers and saw the paper, folded on the table. It was explanation, and a farewell of searing sweetness; in postscript, sealed with his ring, the deeding of his entire estate to his wife.

Polly swallowed the threatening tears. This was no time for female maudling. Nicholas, having married her in order to avenge her, was now going to fight Buckingham, and there was not a damn thing she could do to stop it. Dueling had been outlawed by proclamation repeatedly, but in reality no one would deny a gentleman the right to answer insult with the sword, to execute the laws of honor for himself.

Could she not prevent it? Had she not also the right to execute the laws of honor? The thought grew, dazzling in its daring and simplicity. It fathered instant action, and in the action was found surcease from dread anxiety.

She dressed in Florimell's breeches and shirt, her own riding boots and riding cloak, slipped down the stairs, out into the street, and 'round to the stables. Tiny greeted her with a friendly whicker, holding still for the bridle, nostrils flaring at the prospect of exercise.

"I have only a sidesaddle, so we must go bareback," Polly whispered, nuzzling the mare's neck before swinging nimbly astride. It felt rather strange at first, but then wonderfully easy, and somehow much more natural. Men were the most fortunate of creatures, Polly decided, turning Tiny in the direction of Piccadilly.

Barn Elms was across the river, way the other side of

Knightsbridge and Chelsea, close to Putney. She knew the
way because she and Nick had passed it when they had rid-
den to Richmond just after their return from Wilton.

Her head was as clear as the morning air. She knew only
this crystalline dread that the man who had once done all he
could to harm her would now succeed in destroying that
which she loved more dearly than life itself. Nick's love for
her was without question, but if their precipitate marriage
had been for the wrong reasons, he must not die for those
reasons. She urged Tiny to increase her speed. She could be
no more than fifteen minutes behind them, and there would
surely be formalities that would take time; but to arrive too
late would be the final irony.

The sun came up just as she crossed the river at Parson's
Green. She had but a mile to go, and now encouraged Tiny
to give of her best. The common and coppice of Barn Elms
glistened under the feeble light of the newly risen sun. Seven
horses stood beneath the trees; the clash of steel upon steel
carried on the frosty air. Tiny's hooves pounded the mud-
ridged frozen sod. The thin ice of puddles crackled, their
exquisite patterns destroyed beneath the heedless hooves.
Polly's heart beat with a nauseating speed; the sweat started
on her brow, ran down her back, dampening her shirt, despite the whistling cold air that numbed the tip of her nose
and made her eyes water.

As they reached the group of horses, Polly drew back on
the rein, careful as always, despite the spur of fear, to avoid
the tug that would damage the sensitive mouth. She flung
herself from the mare's back, knotting the reins on Tiny's
neck so that she would not catch her foot if she dropped her
head to graze.

Sulayman turned his head in recognition when she laid an
alerting hand on his rump as she came up behind him. He,
like his six fellows, was tethered to a tree branch. Nick's
cloak was slung across the saddle, and in the deep pocket, as
she had known it would be, was the bulge of his pistol.

Polly drew it forth. It was ready primed, since Nick maintained that there was little point in carrying a firearm that

could not be used without preparation when one might need urgent protection against footpads, highwaymen, and any other of the rogues plaguing the highways and byways.

Holding the pistol gingerly, Polly moved forward, for the moment hidden by the horses, until she had a clear view of the field. Six men, in riding breeches and shirt sleeves, were moving over the ground like dancers, paired in an elaborate deadly ballet with no score. The seventh man stood to one side, his breath steaming in the air, cloak drawn tightly about him, the leather bag at his feet proclaiming his profession.

Buckingham and Kincaid were closest to Polly. They wore their hair tied back, revealing emotionless faces, eyes fixed on the dancing blades, mouths set in grim concentration. The swords joined, parted, each ring of steel setting Polly's heart to beating even faster until she could barely hear over the drumming in her ears. Slowly she raised the pistol, squinting along the barrel, which would not keep still in her shaking hands. She had never handled a pistol before, but surely it could not be so very difficult. One had but to pull the trigger, and the target was hardly small.

She did not think she should kill Buckingham. The fate of the murderer of the king's favorite and one of the foremost peers of the realm was bound to be unpleasant. It would also effectively curtail her loving with Nick, which would be a rather pointless conclusion in the circumstances. But where should one aim in order to disable? Always supposing that one could aim.

There was a moment when Buckingham was half-turned toward her, his sword arm parrying his opponent's lunge. Polly fixed her eye on the angle of his shoulder opened toward her, then, before she could think further, squeezed the trigger.

The explosion, the flash of fire, shattered the eerie, concentrated silence. Buckingham's sword dropped; he sank slowly on one knee, his hand clapped to his shoulder, where the bright blood welled shockingly between his fingers, startling against the white of his shirt.

For a long moment the scene was a still life, then the

picture dissolved; the surgeon was running over to the fallen man, the others following, voices rising in the clear air. Polly stepped out from behind the horses, walking as if in a trance toward the circle of men, the still-smoking pistol dangling from her hand.

"I hope I did not kill him," she said in a flat voice. "I did not think it would be a good idea, although I should have liked to have done so." She looked down at the wounded man with a curious dispassion.

"Odd's bones!" Amazingly, it was Buckingham who broke the stunned silence, the words faltering through blue-tinged lips. "What a blood lust ye have, bud." A painful chuckle escaped him. " 'Tis a powerful enmity you bear me."

"Did you expect amity?" Polly asked coldly, with the same dispassion.

"Nay! But to be felled by a slip of a wench! My plans do not in general miscarry to such a degree." His eyes closed as the surgeon laid bare the wound.

Nicholas seemed to come out of the hypnotic trance that had gripped him from the moment of the shot. "Do you have any idea what you have done?" he demanded of Polly, snatching the pistol from her. "To interfere in an affair of honor—"

"But I could not allow him to kill you!" Polly exclaimed.

"Your faith is touching!" Nick rasped. "I suppose it did not occur to you that the reverse could have been the outcome?"

"Well, yes, it did. But I could not be certain of it, could I?" She looked down at Buckingham again. "Is he sore wounded, Master Surgeon?"

The doctor glanced up at her. "This is the most irregular affair. But I do not hold with dueling. 'Tis a barbarous practice, and it would appear, young lady, that you have spilled less blood than might otherwise have been let. The ball has passed through the shoulder. The exit is clean. I see no reason why he should not recover completely, once I have staunched the flow."

Nicholas looked around at the four seconds. "What's to be done, gentlemen? I will abide by whatever decision you make."

It was Buckingham who answered him. "Let it be said that I earned my wound at your hands, Kincaid, and honor is avenged." He coughed painfully. "I'd as lief not have it known that a wench was responsible for such a mortifying mishap."

"And I'd as lief not have it known that my wife felt it necessary to protect me in such fashion," Nick declared. "If there's any who feels dishonor, I will make what reparations are required."

"If you continue in this fashion," Polly broke in, "you will find yourself offering to fight them all again."

"Hold your tongue!" Nick rounded on her. "Have you not disgraced me sufficiently? Never, ever have I suffered such humiliation! That my wife should—"

"I do not have to be your wife," Polly interrupted recklessly. "I understand that you only married me in order to challenge the duke—" She stopped abruptly, her breath suspended, as he strode toward her.

"Oh, Polly! Polly!" murmured De Winter, shaking his head in disbelief.

Nicholas caught the thick braid hanging over her shoulder, twisting it around his wrist until he held her on a short leash. "Let us go apart into the trees," he said pleasantly. "Pray excuse us, gentlemen."

"God's grace, but 'tis a stout arm Kincaid'll need if he's to keep such a wife in a decent order," observed one of Buckingham's seconds in an awed tone. "I take it we're all resolved to keep this matter scotched? 'Twill be the scandal of the year, else."

In the privacy of the coppice, Nick leaned his back against the trunk of an elm, regarding his captive with a gimlet eye. "Pray explain yourself," he invited.

It was not an invitation that Polly thought it safe to accept. "It will only make you angry," she demurred.

"Doubtless. But since I cannot be more so than I am

already, you have nothing to lose, and just possibly something to gain. I can assure you we are not leaving here until you have satisfied me."

Polly shrugged. "I only meant to say that I realize you would not have married me if you had not wanted to challenge the duke, so . . . ." As his expression did not alter, but maintained its air of polite interest, she continued. "So I thought that now it is all over, we could be annulled."

"We could be *what*?" Nick had not expected that she could have any more surprises in wait for him, but this one transcended all others.

Polly frowned. "Is that not the right word? I thought it was what happened when a marriage was not a marriage." She turned her hands, palm up, in a gesture of emptiness. "I was asleep last night when you came back, and . . . and, well unless something happened when I was asleep, we are not yet properly married, so we can be annulled."

Nicholas wondered absently how long it would take before she drove him to Bedlam. Perhaps he would wring her neck first, in which case he would meet his own end on Tyburn Hill. "Would you wish to be . . . uh . . . annulled?" he asked in a tone of mild inquiry.

Polly searched his face for clues, but it was quite unreadable. She opted for candor. "Not really. But I do not need to be married to love you. We have managed quite nicely for more than a year, and I would be content for matters to continue in that manner. I understand that you could not avenge yourself upon Buckingham without marrying me—"

"That is certainly true," Nick interrupted calmly. "But I have had every intention of marrying you for months. It did not occur to me that you did not know that." He chuckled at her startled expression. "Sweetheart, would it be wise of me to ask what other outcome to our liaison you had imagined?"

"No, I don't think it would be," Polly said frankly. "But you might have given some indication. Did you truly wish to wed me, then?" She sought the final clarification. "For all time?"

"For all time," he affirmed softly. "I will have no other wife but you, and I fear you must learn to like it." His wrist took another turn of the braid, so that her face was brought up against his shoulder. "Is the matter now clear?"

"Quite clear," she whispered. "But it will be clearer still when my husband kisses me for the first time since we were wed."

"Lord of hell!" muttered Nick. "Is it true that I have not done so?"

She nodded, her eyes gleaming mischief. "You were so busy delivering challenges and fighting duels, my lord—"

He silenced her mischief in the simplest fashion, releasing her mouth only when her breath came in sobs and her body drooped against him, all resistance gone from her, so that she was pliable, malleable as wax, molten with the desire that he knew so well how to kindle.

"If it were not so cold, and I did not have your outrageous interference to sort out, we would put this marriage beyond annulment here and now," Nick said, his own hunger throbbing in his voice. But he stood her upright, releasing his grip on her hair. "You owe an apology, and I would have you make it."

"You would not have me beg Buckingham's pardon?" she exclaimed. "I would hang, rather."

"Nay, I will excuse you that. But for the others, so rudely interrupted in a matter of honor—"

"Honor! Pah!" Polly interjected, and stalked out of the coppice. The scene in the field was much as she had left it, except that swords were sheathed and Buckingham was sitting up, propped against a saddle, his wound tightly bandaged, a brandy flask in his hand.

Polly walked over to them, turned her back pointedly on her victim, and addressed herself to the four seconds. "I am told that I disrupted an affair of honor, gentlemen. I ask your pardon for any inconvenience I may have caused you. I am sure you would have much preferred to have left the field on a hurdle."

A sardonic crack of laughter came from behind her.

"God's body, my lady, but ye'd dare the devil himself, I swear it!"

Richard spoke thoughtfully. "Nick, ye'd best remove yourself and Polly from London for a spell. The king will not pardon either you or Buckingham in short order; he's but this month declared another out against dueling, and will not take kindly to being so soon disobeyed."

"Aye, you have the right of it," agreed Buckingham, morosely. "The king will find it easier to pardon us in our absence. I'm for France, once Master Sawbones here says I'll not bleed like a stuck pig if I move."

Nick nodded. "Then we'll to Yorkshire for a few months."

"But I cannot leave Thomas," Polly objected.

"To the devil with Killigrew," Nick declared savagely. "He must do without you for a spell, as must your slavering admirers. I would have you perform for once before a limited audience. We are going into Yorkshire straightway."

Polly thought that perhaps Thomas *would* have to manage without her for a bit, then she was struck by a most happy notion. "Why, then Sue may accompany us, and we may stop at Wilton on the way for Oliver. In that manner, they could be wed and settled in a gamekeeper's cottage without any difficulty." A sunny smile of satisfaction fell in benediction upon them all.

Nicholas contemplated a three-week journey on horseback in the close company of Susan and the unknown Oliver. He looked across at De Winter in appeal.

"Aye, leave it with me," Richard said, struggling for a straight face. "I'll have 'em conveyed somehow."

"But will not that be a great trouble for you, Richard?" asked Polly, concerned.

"It is not a trouble that Richard will regard in the least," replied Nick firmly. "Gentlemen, are we in accord on this unfortunate matter?"

"Aye," Richard said briskly. " 'Tis a scandal to be scotched, and there's none here that'll breathe a word of it."

"In that case, I beg leave to leave you." Nicholas bowed

formally to his erstwhile opponents. The salutation was returned with equal gravity.

Buckingham regarded the scene with a twisted smile. It was clearly a case of honors even, and he would do well to accept the situation with a good grace. If the full story got out, he would be a laughingstock. He was unaccustomed to defeat, and his present downfall had been achieved in the most unorthodox fashion. But then, there was little of the orthodox about Lady Kincaid. He had been guilty of a gross underestimation—one that did not take account of the power of love. One must pay the price for such foolishness. It was not a mistake he would make again.

"You leave for Yorkshire immediately?" Richard asked, accompanying them to the horses.

"As soon as may be," Nick agreed with a grin, cupping his palm to receive Polly's booted foot, tossing her up onto Tiny. "But first I am obliged to ensure that this marriage cannot be threatened with annulment."

"You talk in riddles," Richard said, unable to resist Nick's infectious grin.

"Not at all. Polly will explain the matter in full."

Polly blushed rosily as Richard looked to her for enlightenment. "My lord is being most ungentlemanly," she said.

"And since when was a Newgate-born, tavern-bred bastard deserving of gentlemanly consideration?" demanded Nick, swinging onto Sulayman.

"Since she became Lady Kincaid," retorted Polly smartly, pressing her heels into Tiny's flanks. The mare took off at a gallop across the common.

"Now, just when did she learn to ride bareback?" Nick wondered.

"Probably at the time she became Lady Kincaid," Richard answered, chuckling. "You'd best be after her before she has any more bright ideas. I'll send word when 'tis safe for you to return."

"With Buckingham exiled for a spell, you may be able to work some good with the king," Nick said thoughtfully.

"We'll do what we can, though I doubt that Villiers will

be easily unhorsed," Richard said. "But we'll keep trying."
He held up his hand to the mounted man. "Ye've a honey-
moon waiting, my friend. Get to it. I'll explain matters to
Killigrew, in as far as they are explainable."

Nick nodded, pressed his friend's hand in thanks and farewell, and put Sulayman to the gallop in pursuit of his fast-
disappearing wife.

"I think," Polly declared, stretching with languid pleasure,
"that I am well and truly wed, my lord." She reached a hand
to stroke the rich auburn head pillowed on her breast. "You
will not be rid of me now."

Nick raised his head, bracing himself on his elbows to
regard her quizzically. "Instead, I must endure afternoon
upon afternoon watching as my wife becomes the property
of half London."

A tiny frown creased her brow. "Would you have me leave
the king's company, love?"

Nick shook his head. "Nay. I will assuage my husbandly
grudging with the knowledge that I am the envy of all, and I
have a most faithful wife, despite the promises she makes
upon stage." He smiled lazily. "I think, madame, so that
there shall be no doubt of that, I shall insist upon the most
proper modesty, the most decorous dress, whenever you are
not performing. We will have Margaret choose you a wardrobe of a Puritan severity—"

He fell back, laughing, under the vigorous assault with
which this provocation was received. "Nay . . . nay, peace,
my shrew!" Still laughing, he pulled her on top of him,
holding her hands at her sides, pinned to the mattress. "Will
you cry peace, or must I compel it?"

The hazel eyes glowed with laughter, the residue of loving, and a sparking anticipation at the feel of him, again hard
and throbbing against her belly. "And how would you compel it, my lord?"

"Why, quite easily," he said, parting her thighs with a
hard knee. With a slow twist of his hips, he entered her

again, and Polly gasped with the delight that was as familiar as it was always different.

"So this is the manner in which you will enforce your husbandly authority," she mused, moving with his rhythm in a dreamy circle.

"Rule a wife and have a wife," he mocked gently. "And I intend to have this wife, madame, for all time."

"And I this husband," Polly replied with a contented smile.

"And we shall count the world well lost for love," Nick promised, sliding his hands beneath the fragrant curtain of her hair to cup her face, drawing it down to his. "For all time, sweet Polly."

"They say, 'Love, 'tis a noble madness,' " Polly whispered, "and I did wed a madman, did I not?"

"For all time," he averred.

"Aye, for all time."

About the Author

Jane Feather is the nationally bestselling, award-winning author of *Vanity, Vice, Violet* and many more historical romances. She was born in Cairo, Egypt, and grew up in the New Forest, in the south of England. She began her writing career after she and her family moved to Washington, D.C., in 1981. She now has over a million books in print.

"An author to treasure." —*Romantic Times*

Jane Feather

Vanity

A seductive thief with a deceptive air of innocence picks
the wrong pocket. ___57248-2 $5.99/$7.99 in Canada

Valentine

An arrogant nobleman must marry one of four sisters if he
is to inherit his fortune. ___56470-6 $5.99/$7.99

Velvet

A daring beauty sets out to seduce England's cleverest spy . . . only
to find that seduction works both ways. ___56469-2 $5.50/$6.99

Vixen

When a reclusive lord finds himself saddled with a beautiful ward, life
takes a dangerous and seductive turn. . . . ___56055-7 $5.99/$7.99

Virtue

She was a reckless beauty who played for the highest stakes: one
man's ruin and another man's heart. ___56054-9 $5.50/$6.99

Violet

A dazzling tale of espionage in which a beautiful bandit accepts a
mission more dangerous than she knows. ___56471-4 $5.50/$6.99

- -

Ask for these books at your local bookstore or use this page to order.

Please send me the books I have checked above. I am enclosing $___ (add $2.50 to
cover postage and handling). Send check or money order, no cash or C.O.D.'s, please.

Name _____

Address _____

City/State/Zip _____

Send order to: Bantam Books, Dept. FN131, 2451 S. Wolf Rd., Des Plaines, IL 60018
Allow four to six weeks for delivery.
Prices and availability subject to change without notice.   FN 131 6/96

DON'T MISS THESE FABULOUS
BANTAM WOMEN'S FICTION TITLES

On Sale in May

From Jane Feather, nationally bestselling author of
Violet *and* Vanity, *comes a sinful new romance*

VICE

Juliana drew the line at becoming a harlot. After all, she had already begun the week as a bride, and ended it as a murderess. But now she's at the mercy of a powerful, handsome Duke . . . and in no position to bargain. ___57249-0 $5.99/$7.99 in Canada

THE ENGAGEMENT
by beguiling bestseller Suzanne Robinson

An enticing Victorian tale of passion and intrigue that pits the daughter of a duke against a handsome stranger—a man who's part cowboy, part hero, and part thief . . . but altogether irresistible. ___56346-7 $5.50/$7.50

NIGHT MOVES
by award-winning Sandra Canfield

"A master storyteller of stunning intensity." —Romantic Times

With a spellbinding mixture of passion and suspense, past lovers struggle to find a daughter who has been kidnapped . . . and the courage to reclaim love. ___57433-7 $5.99/$7.99

SWEET LOVE, SURVIVE
by Susan Johnson

"A queen of erotic romance." —Romantic Times

In this powerful finale to the bestselling Kuzan Dynasty series begun in *Seized by Love* and *Love Storm*, a man and a woman find themselves in a desperate and passionate liaison, while the fires of a nation in revolution burn around them. ___56329-7 $5.99/$7.99

Ask for these books at your local bookstore or use this page to order.

Please send me the books I have checked above. I am enclosing $____ (add $2.50 to cover postage and handling). Send check or money order, no cash or C.O.D.'s, please.

Name _____

Address _____

City/State/Zip _____

Send order to: Bantam Books, Dept. FN159, 2451 S. Wolf Rd., Des Plaines, IL 60018
Allow four to six weeks for delivery.

Prices and availability subject to change without notice.   FN 159 5/96

DON'T MISS THESE FABULOUS
BANTAM WOMEN'S FICTION TITLES

On Sale in June

MISCHIEF

AMANDA QUICK, blockbuster author of ten consecutive
New York Times bestsellers, dazzles with her newest hardcover.
Only one man can help Imogen Waterstone foil a ruthless
fortune hunter—and that's the intrepid explorer
known as "Coldblooded Colchester."

____ 09355-X $22.95/$25.95 in Canada

RAVEN AND THE COWBOY

SANDRA CHASTAIN, praised by *Affaire de Coeur* as
"sinfully funny and emotionally riveting," serves up another
western delight when mismatched lovers Raven Alexander and
Tucker Farrell embark on a perilous quest for treasure.

____ 56864-7 $5.99/$7.99 in Canada

THE MAGIC

A deposed heiress with the "Sight" enlists a returning Crusader's
help on Beltane Eve to regain her lost kingdom, in this spellbinding tale from dazzling new talent JULIANA GARNETT.

____ 56862-0 $5.99/$7.99 in Canada

Ask for these books at your local bookstore or use this page to order.

Please send me the books I have checked above. I am enclosing $____ (add $2.50 to
cover postage and handling). Send check or money order, no cash or C.O.D.'s, please.

Name _____

Address _____

City/State/Zip _____

Send order to: Bantam Books, Dept. FN158, 2451 S. Wolf Rd., Des Plaines, IL 60018
Allow four to six weeks for delivery.
Prices and availability subject to change without notice.   FN 158 6/96

Bestselling Historical Women's Fiction

AMANDA QUICK

____28354-5 SEDUCTION .....$6.50/$8.99 in Canada
____28932-2 SCANDAL ....$6.50/$8.99
____28594-7 SURRENDER ....$6.50/$8.99
____29325-7 RENDEZVOUS ....$6.50/$8.99
____29315-X RECKLESS ....$6.50/$8.99
____29316-8 RAVISHED ....$6.50/$8.99
____29317-6 DANGEROUS ....$6.50/$8.99
____56506-0 DECEPTION ....$6.50/$8.99
____56153-7 DESIRE ....$6.50/$8.99
____56940-6 MISTRESS ....$6.50/$8.99
____57159-1 MYSTIQUE ....$6.50/$7.99

IRIS JOHANSEN

____29871-2 LAST BRIDGE HOME ......$4.50/$5.50
____29604-3 THE GOLDEN BARBARIAN ..$4.99/$5.99
____29244-7 REAP THE WIND ....$5.99/$7.50
____29032-0 STORM WINDS ....$4.99/$5.99
____28855-5 THE WIND DANCER ......$5.99/$6.99
____29968-9 THE TIGER PRINCE .....$5.99/$6.99
____29944-1 THE MAGNIFICENT ROGUE .$5.99/$6.99
____29945-X BELOVED SCOUNDREL ....$5.99/$6.99
____29946-8 MIDNIGHT WARRIOR .....$5.99/$6.99
____29947-6 DARK RIDER ....$5.99/$7.99
____56990-2 LION'S BRIDE ....$5.99/$7.99

TERESA MEDEIROS

____29407-5 HEATHER AND VELVET ....$5.99/$7.50
____29409-1 ONCE AN ANGEL ....$5.99/$6.50
____29408-3 A WHISPER OF ROSES .....$5.50/$6.50
____56332-7 THIEF OF HEARTS ....$5.50/$6.99
____56333-5 FAIREST OF THEM ALL ....$5.99/$7.50
____56334-3 BREATH OF MAGIC ....$5.99/$7.99

Ask for these books at your local bookstore or use this page to order.

Please send me the books I have checked above. I am enclosing $_____ (add $2.50 to cover postage and handling). Send check or money order, no cash or C.O.D.'s, please.

Name _____

Address _____

City/State/Zip _____

Send order to: Bantam Books, Dept. FN 16, 2451 S. Wolf Rd., Des Plaines, IL 60018
Allow four to six weeks for delivery.
Prices and availability subject to change without notice.   FN 16 8 /96